"Laurelin Paige writes an _____ kind of romance and sexy that draws the reader in and doesn't let go until long after the last page is read."

—K. Bromberg, *New York Times*
bestselling author of the Driven series

"Edgy sex and pulsating mystery make this fast-paced and sensual story impossible to put down."

—Jay Crownover,
New York Times bestselling
author of the Marked Men series

"Laurelin creates a romance that comes in many touches. Romance from her best friend, their bond, their past. Romance from her lover, their connection, their future. Each chapter leads you deeper into mystery, twisting what you knew, making you love who you're meant to hate. A fascinating read!"

—Pepper Winters, *New York Times* bestselling
author of the Pure Corruption series

"*First Touch* is a heart-chilling page-turner from a master storyteller—and the hottest thing I've read this year, hands down." —M. Pierce, bestselling author of
the Night Owl trilogy

"Dark, intense, and incredibly sexy, *First Touch* kept me on the edge of my seat from page one up to the very last word." —*Shameless Book Club*

"Gritty, edgy, dark, and compelling. *First Touch* pulls no punches and just might leave you reeling."

—Megan Hart, *New York Times* and *USA
Today* bestselling author of *Tear You Apart*

FIRST

TOUCH

LAURELIN PAIGE

St. Martin's Paperbacks

FIRST TOUCH

For information address St. Martin's Press, 175 Fifth Avenue, New York, NY 10010.

ISBN: 978-1-250-13620-6

Our books may be purchased in bulk for promotional, educational, or business use. Please contact your local bookseller or the Macmillan Corporate and Premium Sales Department at 1-800-221-7945, extension 5442, or by e-mail at MacmillanSpecialMarkets@macmillan.com.

Printed in the United States of America

St. Martin's Griffin edition / December 2015
St. Martin's Paperbacks edition / November 2017

St. Martin's Paperbacks are published by St. Martin's Press, 175 Fifth Avenue, New York, NY 10010.

10 9 8 7 6 5 4 3 2 1

TO CANCUN

ACKNOWLEDGMENTS

Of everything I've written, this was the hardest book for me to birth. It's also the one I'm most proud of for that reason, and I'm so grateful for the many people who got me through the labor.

To my family—I'm blessed and lucky in many ways, but most of all to have you. Tom, especially, thanks for letting me live my dreams, even when it seems they're killing me.

To my editor, Eileen Rothschild—You fought for me, and that means everything. Thank you for not freaking out about the extra 25k and for so much more.

To the team at St. Martin's Press—I always thought I liked to do things better alone until I met all of you. Now I wish I could convince you to help me with everything else in my life.

To my agent, Rebecca Friedman—You knew it was a good story from day one. Thank you for seeing what it could be with me.

To Bethany—The first eyes, the first critic, the first lover.

Your touch is everywhere in this book. You're my doula and my distraction and I couldn't have done it without you.

To Kayti—You kept me sane! Many days I only made it through because of you. Thanks for "keeping" me. I'm sorry in advance for what I'll be like on the next one.

To Melanie—Thank you for always believing in me. Your turn to believe that hard in you. I do.

To Shanyn—You're so patient to put up with me. There's nothing I can say or do to thank you enough.

To the many authors and bloggers who read early—I'm afraid I'll miss someone if I try to name you, so I won't. Your time and enthusiasm have made all of this worth it. Thank you for all of the support and praise. How lucky am I to know you? I should probably apologize for making you wait the longest for book two, but I'm not really sorry.

The women who guide me—Fab Four, Domination, Wrahm, Naturals, FYW, and others (you know who you are), I'd be lost in the woods without you.

To my God—Any gift I have comes from you. Please help me to always remember that.

PROLOGUE

When I heard the message she'd left, it had been more than six years since I'd spoken to Amber. Hearing her voice on my mother's old answering machine shocked me. It wasn't that we'd parted on *bad* terms, necessarily, but they were *final* terms. We were on different sides for the first time in our friendship. The only way past it was to separate.

The last words she'd spoken to me in person played in my mind so frequently it was as though they'd been scratched into the audio portion of my brain with professional recording equipment. They reverberated clear and crisp: *"I'm sure someday's gotta happen for us all one day. But it doesn't mean mine's happening at the same time as yours."*

So I left her to live my *someday* while she took off for Mexico on the yacht of the latest sugar daddy to buy her a designer bikini stuffed with hundreds that she'd later let him stuff with his pathetic excuse of a cock.

In our time apart, I'd grown up completely, reinvented myself, put the past behind me, yet her voice on the machine sounded as bright and young as it had when we were twenty three. It instantly triggered a longing and regret that I hadn't let myself feel since we'd said goodbye.

"Emily." Her bubbly tone spilled into my ear. "It's been ages, I know. But I've been thinking about you. God, I'm not even sure if this is still your number." She paused for only half a second, the space of a sigh or maybe taking a moment to reconsider. "Anyway, I wanted to ask—do you still have that blue raincoat? Miss you. Bye."

She'd said nothing really. Her voice hadn't cracked or stumbled or betrayed emotion of any kind. But I knew one thing with clear-cut certainty: Amber was in trouble and she needed my help.

CHAPTER

1

Even with my head below the surface of the water, I felt his arrival. My arms continued moving in fluid strokes, my legs kicking out behind me, but as drops of water trickled down my exposed skin, it itched with the awareness of no longer being alone.

I kept swimming—kept heading toward the end of the pool. The words I used to push me on in high school swimming competitions automatically repeated in my head: *This arm then that arm then this arm then that arm*. Now though, in the spaces between each beat, I thought her name—*This arm, Amber, then that arm, Amber, then this arm, Amber, then that arm, Amber*.

When I reached the concrete wall, I flipped and did another lap. I wouldn't let on that I knew he was there. I needed to control this situation, and for some reason, denying his presence made me feel like I'd gained another measure or so. Focusing on Amber, remembering she was the reason for what I was doing, made concentrating easier. At first, anyway. Until I began to tire and the awareness of his nearness began to win the tug-of-war with my attention.

I forced myself to complete three more laps, the anticipation of finally being near him, talking to him, bubbling up inside me like a butterfly waiting to escape its cocoon. I had my reasons for not acknowledging him—but what were his reasons for ignoring me? What if it wasn't even him, but one of his security men? No, anyone else would have kicked me out already for sure. Then why had he let me continue my swim?

Soon the wings of curiosity fluttered and scratched with such distraction that I could no longer resist the urge to poke my head out.

At least I managed to complete my lap.

Then, after wiping the water from my eyes, I started to look around.

I'd expected him to be sitting to my side at the head of the pool, so I was truly surprised when I spotted him in the lounge chair directly in front of me. His face was chiseled and serious underneath near-black hair. Metallic sunglasses paired with a layer of scruff made him appear both more laid back and more dangerous than the pictures I'd seen on the Internet. Even dressed in a standard hotel-variety plain-white robe, he was intimidating. His feet were bare and crossed at the ankles. His elbow was propped on the chair arm, and his thumb and index finger framed the side of his face as he, without a doubt, bore right into me with his gaze behind designer eyewear.

My heart flipped. He was infamous, famous, and if the rumors were to be believed, dangerous—a multibillionaire luxury resort owner and legendary bad boy. But my reaction wasn't fear; it was excitement. Not because he was ten times sexier in person—though he was—but because he was *here*.

Reeve Sallis.

Sitting mere yards from me. After all the work I'd done to make it happen, here he was. Step one. Success.

"Oh!" I weaved the thrill I felt into my lines hoping it passed as simple alarm. "I didn't realize I wasn't alone." An innocent smile curled my lip with a few flirty blinks. It was a look that had bought me quite a few drinks along with a fur coat and a nice piece of jewelry or two. But that was years ago. I was rusty, and I prayed under my breath that he didn't notice.

His stare had a texture I could feel on my skin. "And I *did* realize I wasn't alone when I very much should be. I imagine it's a similar feeling of astonishment."

I swallowed. "Yes, probably so."

"I'll help you out." He stood, swiftly. In two steps he was at the side of the pool, leaning down to offer his hand.

My gut told me that the smart thing to do would be to get out of the pool. I was trespassing on the property of a very powerful man.

But my heart told me I couldn't give up so easily. So I ignored the tightening in my stomach and stood my ground—or, rather, treaded my water—and said, "No, thank you. I still have a few more laps to do."

His lip curled up into a half-smile. "You don't. You're done." Again he reached his hand toward me.

Ignoring his offer, I broadened my smile and turned up the charm. "Ah, you're one of *those* kinds of men."

He let his hand fall and tilted his head questioningly. "Which kind is that?"

Behind his lenses, I felt the command of his stare, and even in his crouched position, he held himself with utter confidence. My eyes chased the broad muscles in his neck that disappeared under his robe. They, along with his entire demeanor, demanded my respect or, more likely, my capitulation.

Yeah, I knew his type. "The kind who gets what he wants when he wants it."

"Well. Yes." He chuckled as he, yet again, extended his hand out for me.

I was tempted to swim another lap. But I didn't have enough sense about him yet to know if that would piss him off or intrigue him. So I said, "I got it," and refused his hand, pulling myself up over the side on my own. I did know it was too early for physical contact. My exit of the pool was on his terms but our first touch would be on mine.

"Oh, you're one of *those* kinds of women." He stood with me and handed me a towel with SALLIS embroidered along the edge in gold.

I took it. I was dripping all over his bare feet, after all. And while I'd felt covered in the clear water, I now felt nearly naked in my salmon-colored bikini. Which was the point, but still. "Okay," I said, as I wrapped the terrycloth around the ends of my hair. "I'll bite. What kind of woman is that?"

"The kind who won't take help from a man."

There had been a time when nothing could be further from the truth. I'd been very dependent on men, relying on one or another of them to put a roof over my head, keep me fed and clothed and entertained.

But that was years ago. Now I only counted on myself. That was perhaps the hardest part of the role I had to play—giving up the control I'd gained. Submitting.

If that was what it took to get the answers I needed, I'd do that and more.

I tilted my head to squeeze the moisture from my hair onto the ground next to me. "That's not so. I took your towel."

His eyes were still hidden, but I knew he was checking me out. I could feel his gaze skidding across my skin, sending goose bumps up my arms. "That's nothing." His attention landed on my breasts. "There are hundreds of towels stacked around here."

My cheeks heated, sure that his choice of the word *stacked* was purposeful. Because there was no denying that's what I was—stacked. My breasts had come in early and grew rapidly, swelling until I filled a double-D cup. They'd embarrassed me as a teen. No one else flopped and jiggled like I did in gym class. So I hid them behind baggy shirts and sports bras. It wasn't until I'd met Amber that I realized the power I'd been given through genetics. She taught me how to embrace my body, how to use it for my benefit.

With those lessons in mind—with *Amber* in mind—I pushed away my discomfort and bent over to run the towel up and down my limbs, exposing my cleavage. "That's proof that you're wrong. I could have easily gotten my own. I accepted it from you."

"You have a point there."

I had two points, actually. My nipples were standing tall and proud. It was the morning chill, of course, more pronounced after the heated pool, and I wanted to fold my arms over myself when I stood back up. But I forced myself to follow their example and rose up as tall and proud as they were.

When I did, I was met with my shoes. Reeve must have gotten them while I was swimming. He held them out to me now.

With a sigh, I took them from him. "You really want me gone, don't you?"

"What can I say? I like my routine. Swimming alone is part of my routine."

"Huh. I didn't take you for a man who was rigid." The media made Reeve Sallis out as impulsive and erratic. I was familiar enough with the difference between public perception and reality, but knowing Amber as I did, it made more sense that Reeve was that guy than the one he was playing at now.

He clicked his tongue at me like he was chiding a naughty child. "Now look who's making premature judgments."

"Touché." I sat on a deck chair to buckle my sandals. Leaning over to do it would have just been gratuitous at this point.

"But while I've got you here . . ."

I tensed as he undid the belt of his robe. *I can do this, I can do this,* I chanted to myself. This was what I'd come here for—to do what was necessary, no matter how much I didn't want to. Back then, I would have done far more for far less. And, I noted as Reeve discarded the item of clothing on the chair behind him, with far less attractive men.

Goddamn, Reeve Sallis was hot.

Like, sizzling hot. He wore nothing but trunks—thank the Lord it wasn't a Speedo—revealing a perfect swimmer's body. His arms and torso were long and sculpted, his shoulders broad, and his waist trim. The six-pack he sported was nearly an eight-pack, and the muscles around his abdomen were so defined, so hard that I barely resisted the urge to lay my hand across them. My mind couldn't process how solid they would feel beneath my palm and wouldn't it be amazing to just find out?

While I was ogling—and probably drooling and definitely not breathing—he sat on the chair and faced me. "I hope you don't mind. I was getting a little warm."

It *was* getting a little warm. More than a little. And it wasn't the modern fire pit running nearly the entire length of the pool behind our deck chairs that made my skin scorch on the inside.

"Uh, of course I don't mind." Though, it sort of sounded like I did mind. Really, I was just disappointed that was the reason he'd undressed.

Jesus, Em, what the fuck? You're bummed that he didn't want you to blow him? Really, I was disgusted with myself. I mean, it was great that he wasn't unattractive considering what I'd probably have to do with him eventually, but what kind of bitch would I be if I looked forward to it?

Maybe old habits died harder than I had thought. I couldn't decide if I wanted that to be the case or not.

Reeve was apparently unaware of the battle going on in my head. "Good," he said. "Then we should probably talk."

"Interrogation time? I suppose that's to be expected." With his newly exposed body, I wasn't sure I'd be able to concentrate. And he had yet to take off those glasses, which was unnerving. Perhaps that was exactly why he kept them on.

"I'm glad you see it my way. If you didn't, this would be a whole lot less fun."

I finished fastening my shoe and sat up. "Is it fun now?"

His forehead wrinkled as he tapped a long finger against his lips. "I haven't entirely decided yet." His declaration came out low and raw, and it seemed, more honest than he'd intended.

Immediately, he changed gears, moving his hands to grip the arms of the chair. "But back to the interrogation. Why exactly are you here?"

It wasn't what I thought he'd ask first. I'd been expecting "Who are you?", but that he'd chosen the other question spoke volumes about my progress with him. He didn't care who I was. He only cared that my actions interfered with his own plans.

Dammit.

If my plan was going to work, Reeve had to want to get to know me. At least he hadn't dismissed me yet. I still had a chance to reel him in. "I'm here because I wanted a morning swim."

A hint of a brow peaked up over the frame of his glasses. "I assume you're a guest at this resort."

I bit my lip and nodded slowly. Even after our banter, there was a chance he could have me kicked out. A very good chance. Maybe the lip bite could make me seem virtuous.

Who was I kidding? He'd seen the girls. Once my chest was displayed, I'd lost all shot at claiming innocent, even if I truly was. And I wasn't.

The interrogation continued. "There are six other pools open to the public. This is the only one reserved in the morning for my personal use. Why did you choose mine?"

"I wanted the privacy."

"Wrong." He said the word as though he were buzzing a player out on a game show. "This wasn't about privacy. It couldn't have been easy for you to get in here. You went to a lot of trouble."

My shoulder hitched up in a nonchalant shrug. "It really wasn't that much trouble." That was actually the truth. I'd discovered pretty easily that any manager had the power to program my resort key card to let me in to the pool during Reeve's reserved time. A few days of prowling and I'd found a night manager who seemed he would be vulnerable to my seduction techniques. He was twice my age, balding, with a ridiculous hairpiece. I'd been prepared to give him a hand job. Turned out he could be bought with a hundred. That had surprised me. I'd grown up with my body as my only asset, and I'd learned to use it. I was still getting used to having money as an alternative.

He frowned. "That doesn't speak well for my staff."

"Or it speaks well for me."

"Ah. You don't want to get anyone in trouble." It wasn't a question.

Teasingly, I tapped my own lips and threw his words back at him. "I haven't entirely decided yet."

He laughed. It was a good sign.

"You see," I said, lacing my hands and stretching them above my head, "I'm not loyal to the person who helped me. But on the other hand, I'm not loyal to you either."

He leaned forward, a smile dancing on his lips. "You'll tell me if I ask you."

"Maybe. Are you asking?" I'd totally throw the manager under the bus. But not yet. It was information that he wanted that I had—it kept him engaging with me. I'd likely keep the secret until the next time we met, no matter how much he asked.

That was the idea, anyway. Then Reeve surprised me. "I'm not asking. I don't really care about my staff at the moment. I'm more interested in you."

My pulse kicked up like I'd downed a shot of espresso. Because it was a victory. Because it was a moment of triumph. There was no other reason I cared. No other reason his interest keyed me up.

Reeve steepled his hands together then pointed them toward me. "Why this pool?"

I mirrored his leaning, lacing my fingers together and resting my chin on top. "I wanted to meet you." *Needed* to meet him. I had a long list of questions and as far as I was concerned Reeve Sallis had the answers.

"The truth comes out. Why would you want to meet me?" He seemed honestly perplexed.

"Are you joking?" There were certainly thousands of women who wanted to be his bimbo of the month. Word was he treated his sex toys well. He had enough money to lavish on them without even noticing a dent in his wallet. Then there were those who likely wanted to meet him just to claim the brush with fame. Plus he was, well, hotter than a man had a right to be.

But if it was flattery he needed . . . "You're a very interesting human being, Reeve Sallis. Not to mention, you're easy on the eyes. More than easy on the eyes, actually. Who wouldn't want to meet you?"

"I can name quite a few people, and I'm sure there are many more that I can't name. You could have met me in other ways." Though he'd verbally ignored my comment about his appearance, his mouth twitched ever so slightly letting me know it had pleased him.

Why did that make my belly flutter?

It didn't. It was nerves. It had to be. I transferred the emotion to my words, letting my voice get breathy and unsteady. "I wanted to meet you alone. Without your goons and your public."

"A lot of people would be scared to be with me alone."

"Who said I wasn't scared?" I should have been scared. He had a reputation that, as far as I could gather, was either completely fabricated or totally underplayed. The former was more likely, but what if it was the latter? What if I was truly unsafe in his presence?

It was also possible that I *was* scared. In all honesty, it was probably the core of his allure. But I couldn't let fear or captivation take over. I had no other choice but to see my plan through. For Amber.

Reeve tilted his head. "That's an interesting combination of traits—a stalker who's scared."

"Only scared enough to make it fun." Strange that I once lived for that kind of scared. "And not a stalker, Mr. Sallis. I merely have a curiosity that gets away from me."

"I like your curiosity. And your philosophy on fear." He shifted gears again. "I think I may have started off with the wrong line of questioning. I don't even know who you are."

He removed his sunglasses, and I couldn't help but gasp. His eyes . . . At the surface, they didn't seem special on their own. A common blue and gray that could be easy to overlook. His brows were the prominent feature, what most people likely noticed. They were thick and arched. They darkened his expression and distracted from what lay in the icy pools below them.

But his eyes caught me. There was something I recognized in them—a sorrow or a longing that was both gripping and haunting.

I saw myself in those eyes.

Reeve noticed. As soon as he did, he looked away, scanning the horizon. I didn't blame him. Small as it was, it had been a revealing moment. Far too intimate for strangers.

When he turned toward me again, he'd hidden whatever it was that I'd seen. "There's something familiar about you, though. We haven't slept together, have we?"

I laughed. "No, we haven't."

"Good." He clarified before I could feign indignation. "I mean, I'd hate myself if I'd forgotten you."

"You haven't. And you won't. Forget me, I mean." I meant to allude that we'd sleep together eventually. It was as close to offering myself as I'd get. Anything more would be slutty and set me up as one-night-stand material. I needed to be more like flavor of the month.

More important, at the moment, was the delivery of my name. I had to be honest—I was too recognizable not to be. There was no reason to be deceitful about it anyway. If Amber had mentioned me ever, she would have used my real last name, not the one I'd taken on when I'd reinvented myself. There was a chance, of course, that she'd figured out my new identity. A possibility she'd mentioned it in passing—*Oh, that girl? You know, the voice on that sitcom? I used to know her. . . .*

It was a risk I had to take. I extended my hand. "It's Emily. Emily Wayborn."

Reeve hesitated—was he as determined to be in control of our first contact as I was?

Whatever his reluctance, he quickly overcame it, taking

my palm in his. His grip was strong and sure and aggressive. Almost too tight, but just barely not. He held it without saying anything for several seconds, and, I don't know how—somehow, though—I knew he was making his own allusion. His own promise. He wanted me to know what he'd be like.

In bed.

With me.

He'd be powerful and controlling and forceful, even. Almost too forceful, but just barely not.

Was that how he'd been with *her*? Did *almost* become *too much*?

I couldn't let myself go there. So instead of entertaining the thought further, I entertained a new one—Reeve Sallis had good hands. Really good hands.

After what seemed like ages and yet not nearly long enough, he let my hand go. "A qualified pleasure, Emily Wayborn. Qualified because you did interrupt my swim time."

"Qualified pleasure is the only kind I seem to give." That had come out dirtier than I'd intended. Or maybe exactly as dirty as I'd intended. God, my confidence in flirting was nil. "Anyway, I get the familiar thing a lot."

"It wasn't a line."

"I know." Though for half a second I worried he found me familiar for other reasons. Because I was like Amber. We'd been inseparable and so much alike at one time, everyone thought we were sisters. But that was years ago. I'd changed so much, even if she'd stayed exactly the same.

No, it was the other reason he found me familiar. "It's because I'm famous." I sounded embarrassed because I was. "My voice is famous. I'm the computer on *NextGen*."

"You're joking."

"Nope." I took a deep breath and then repeated my

famous catch phrase in the lilting tone I saved for the show. "User error."

He laughed. Heartily. Like, full belly laugh.

Really, it *was* funny. All the years I'd worked to keep my figure, going to audition after audition trying to land my big break, and when I finally did it was in a role that only utilized my vocal cords. The hit show of the past two seasons, *NextGen* was the story of a family living in the not-too-distant future. Pitched as the movie *Her* meets the old cartoon *The Jetsons,* I played the part of the household mainframe—the computer that controlled each and every aspect of their lives. Practically overnight I was recognized by thousands, but only when I spoke.

Funny thing was I had a knockout body. A knockout body that no one ever saw. I got the humor in it. Really, I did.

When he'd stopped laughing enough to speak, he apologized. "I'm sorry to say I've never seen it. But I've heard about you. The show, I mean. It's quite a hit."

"It's . . ." There was nothing to say except, "Well, it pays the bills."

He smiled again, and this time I noticed the hint of a dimple. "At least I can be assured you aren't after me for my money."

It was my turn to laugh. "I don't make that kind of dough. And who said I'm after you?"

"Aren't you? Well, if you're not, that's a shame."

My belly flipped again. I had him intrigued. It was time to make my exit. Next time I'd bump into him more casually, more seemingly accidental, and then, if I was good, he'd ask me out. "I'm sorry for intruding on your morning, Mr. Sallis."

"Reeve," he corrected.

"Reeve." His name slid off my tongue a little too easily. "I'll let you get to your swim now."

I stood, and he followed. "After all the trouble you went to, you're not going to stay and watch? I'm disappointed."

It was tempting. I scanned his amazing body once more. He probably looked like a God in the water.

But I had to leave with the upper hand. Leave him wanting more. "Is it a lofty goal to want you to learn you can't have everything you want?"

"It is lofty. And not true." His voice grew deep and certain. "I want you to join me for dinner. And you will. Won't you." It was a statement—plain and clear.

And, damn, I hadn't predicted that. "When you put it that way, I suppose I will."

"Tonight. Seven-thirty. In the Cherry Lounge."

"I thought the Cherry Lounge was closed." I'd been at the resort for more than a week and the room had been off limits the entire time.

"It's closed when I'm in town. It's where I dine. It's where *we'll* dine."

Though he hadn't moved, it felt suddenly like he was closer to me than he'd been only a second before. As though his presence had extended out from his body, invading my own space. It flustered me, but I managed, "Formal or casual?"

"You can't come as you are?" He grinned a grin so wicked that I knew he meant the double entendre, and, though I shot him a disapproving glance, I also smiled. And I shivered. Because, while I had ulterior motives for getting close to him, Reeve Sallis got to *me*. I'd read about his natural charm and sex appeal, but nothing had prepared me for the fullness of it in person. It was indescribable. Any adjective I tried to pin on him felt contrived and unoriginal. He was magnetic and provocative and commanding.

And he did scare me. There was a possibility he'd done terrible things to people—things that would frighten anyone with half a brain. Still, were it not for Amber, I might be able to overlook the rumors. Might be tempted by his charisma. That might have been the scariest thing of all where Reeve Sallis was concerned.

He shook his head. "Don't answer that. It was inappropriate, and anyway, there's no way you'll respond the way that I want you to."

He was wrong. I'd respond however he wanted me to if it got me what I wanted. What I needed.

But not yet. I couldn't go that far *yet*. "That sounded like an apology until you tacked on another thing you probably should be apologizing for. So how about I ignore everything you've said in the last ten seconds and we try this again. What should I wear to dinner this evening, Reeve?"

"Nothing too fancy. A dress, though, please. It would be a shame to hide those lovely legs of yours." But he said that with his eyes on my rack.

It was where I wanted his eyes. Another moment of triumph. A minor one. Partly because it meant he was attracted to me, but mostly because if they were elsewhere, if they met mine instead, I wasn't certain I could keep the advantage.

Thankfully, it was hard for anyone to look elsewhere. I had a nice rack.

I pushed my chest up and out just enough to let him know the attention was welcomed. "I know exactly what I'll wear. Until tonight."

His gaze rose to meet mine and lingered just long enough to threaten my control. Just long enough for me to glimpse the burden of his own restraint. Then, without a goodbye, he turned and dove into the pool, his form so tight and perfect that he barely splashed.

Despite my intentions to leave, I stayed long enough to see him swim the length and back. He was mesmerizing. His body was strong and lithe all at once, his arms gorgeous as they flexed and stretched, cutting through the water with powerful strokes. His tight ass could hold my attention for hours.

Though he never looked up, I'm sure he felt my presence, just as I'd felt his. There was an attraction between us. An electric pull that made the air crackle and twist around me even at that distance. It was something that I couldn't have faked, and I was grateful for it. It would make it easier to take the steps I needed to take next.

At least, I hoped that was the reason I was grateful for our connection. I didn't want to believe the alternative.

CHAPTER
2

I turned my face to look at first one eye and then the other in the bathroom mirror of the luxury suite I'd checked into a week before. I'd applied two different shadow techniques to my lids—one soft and natural, the other bold and sultry. Normally putting on makeup wouldn't have been so stressful. I should have easily been able to choose which look better suited the occasion. But it had been so long since I'd dressed up for a man. The shift in thinking put me on ground both familiar and foreign. Instinctively I tried to fight it, clinging to the woman I'd become, a woman who'd grown fiercely independent.

Yet there was that voice echoing through my head, the voice that had been with me constantly since it was resurrected in my memory from the sound of Amber's message. She guided me now like she'd guided me back then. *"Which would Reeve prefer?"*

My gaze stayed steady in the mirror, but I wasn't seeing myself anymore, lost to a memory so vivid it was as if it were happening now. It was Amber's eyes in the reflection, squinting as she applied thick mascara to her long lashes.

"Find the thing that makes him notice you and put all your attention there." She smacked her glossed lips together and then turned her focus to me. *"If he's only interested in your ass, wear a pair of tight jeans and you're done. He won't care what's on your face if he's only looking at it until he can get a peek at your behind."*

She'd been seventeen when we met. Vibrant, beautiful, daring. Wise, I'd thought. Aware in ways that I wasn't. I didn't know yet that the uncle she visited on the weekends wasn't a blood relative or that his gifts were what she lived on. I didn't know that the reason she'd turned up in my life, the reason she'd moved onto the couch of the dealer next door was because she'd run away from home, from the man who'd taken her virginity at the age of nine—her father. I only knew that she'd shown up in my dull, lackluster, impoverished world and she'd glistened. I was fascinated with her instantly. Awestruck. Enamored. Fuck, I was practically in love. I would have followed her anywhere.

And I had. I'd followed her everywhere, through everything. Until, I couldn't anymore.

I blinked my eyes, dismissing the memory before the guilt started to taste sour in my mouth. Not for the first time, I wondered if the clarity of my recollection of Amber meant that she was no longer in this world. If she was . . . gone—I couldn't bear to think the actual "d" word— then I would expect her to haunt me. She was good at that in life, how could she not be in the after?

Her pseudo presence was a double-edged sword. It both helped and distracted. Reminded and ridiculed. I needed her because she'd created the person I was before, the person I needed to be now. I just couldn't let those thoughts overwhelm me. Couldn't let *her* overwhelm me. Not again.

I cringed as I spoke to the air—spoke to *her*. "I'm sure

you're going to be with me a lot, Amber. But you've got to give me my space." I caught my eye in the mirror and shook my head. "Now I'm talking to invisible friends. Twenty-nine is a fine age to go crazy, isn't it?" It would be funnier if mental disorders weren't in my genetics.

At least I knew what I was doing about my lids.

Sighing, I reached for a makeup remover towelette and wiped away the shadow and liner from the more sultry eye. Reeve had already shown himself to be a tits man. The seductive eyes were overkill as long as I wore the right clothes. Which I would.

I finished up my look with a very subtle blush and a pale lipstick before stepping into my dress. I'd told Reeve earlier that I had the perfect outfit in mind for our date, but it was a lie, and not the first that I'd told him. I'd figured out enough about him to know just what *would* be perfect. A few hours spent at the outlets and I'd found it—a simple peach A-line that hit low thigh. With its full skirt, it looked more flirty than slutty except where the neckline dipped at my bosom. It wasn't a very low plunge, but it didn't take much to make my breasts stand out, which was the goal. It had been a carefully thought-out purchase, yet it was plain enough that it seemed it might be something I'd plucked from my closet.

After I had it on, I checked myself once more in the mirror. My hair was tied up in a casual knot, my lips done in a long-lasting matte, and my skirt moved easily. I looked casual and chic, but I was one hundred percent dressed for sex.

Shoulders back, Amber's memory whispered at my ear. *You look good. He'll be putty in your hands.*

"I hope so," I said out loud again. "For your sake." Whether I was talking to my reflection this time or the memory that clung to me in recent weeks, I wasn't sure.

Although the Sallis Palm Springs Paradise Resort

boasted over 250 acres, it was only a five-minute walk to the Cherry Lounge from my suite. I left early so that I could take my time getting there. Still, when I arrived, my forehead was damp and my heart rate elevated—but it was just as likely that was from nerves as it was from the activity. At the door, I paused at the sign that read CLOSED FOR PRIVATE ENGAGEMENT wondering if I should knock or just walk in. Not wanting to appear tentative, I settled on the latter. I wiped my brow with my palm, took a deep breath, and tried the handle. It turned.

As soon as I stepped inside, I was greeted by one of the henchmen that always seemed to accompany Reeve Sallis. They appeared in several pictures that I'd seen of him when I'd scoured the Internet for any bit of information I could find on the man. This particular guard was tall and serious. Hard. The edge of a dragon tattoo snaked up his neck from under the collar of his dress shirt and there were two noticeable scars that decorated his face. His dark suit jacket was tight enough that I could make out the bulge of his holster at his hip. An earpiece dangled from his ear like jewelry, but I imagined the device networked him with all the other Sallis minions.

"That way, Ms. Wayborn," he said without any welcome in his voice, gesturing across the restaurant. "Mr. Sallis has asked for dinner to be served on the outdoor patio."

I nodded, then set off in the direction he'd indicated. That had been yet another of Amber's lessons. *"You have to set yourself apart from the help. You have to show that you're different. That you're worth more than the people who scrub the floors and cook the food and drive the cars."*

And wear the guns, I added silently to myself now. Bodyguards weren't new to me. They were a staple among the rich, paranoid men who'd supported my earlier life. Most security had been just for show, though, while the man behind me had definitely seen action. I snuck a peek back over my shoulder at him. He was watching me, as I'd figured he would be, but he glared, harsh and menacing. As though he'd decided I was an enemy. I was—but could he know?

My chest tightened at the panicked thought that I might be walking into some sort of trap. The man I'd just left could shoot me in the back several times before I even registered the first shot.

Even if it wasn't too late, even if I was walking into a trap, I was determined to see this through. I hugged my arms around myself and turned my focus back toward the patio. Not that the man I was about to meet was any less frightening. In fact, he was definitely more so. Why that thought sent butterflies scattering in my stomach, I had no idea.

Nerves. Just nerves.

The backside of the restaurant was a wall of windows and I could see as I approached that the outdoor dining space was corralled by another wall of glass. Beyond, the last hints of the sun tinted the sky above the mountains and the city cradled in the valley below was lit for the night. A fire blazed in a large pit, keeping the dark at bay and pinning my attention to its vibrant reflection in the glass behind it. I was out the doors and halfway to the burning beacon before I noticed Reeve standing to the side, looking out over the view.

My steps stilled while I took him in. I was exponentially grateful that he hadn't noticed me so that I could catch my breath privately. Because all air had left my lungs at the sight of him. He stood at an angle, and the profile view enunciated the strength of his jaw and the sharpness of his bones. His hands were buried in his pants pockets causing his jacket to hug the sculpted shape of his swimmer's ass. Even like that—his features half-hidden, his body buried underneath the pale gray suit he wore—he was captivating.

I studied him. Light from the fire danced shadows across his cheek, the effect haunting. Not haunting—haunt*ed*. My thoughts started to spin. Did Amber cling to him like she clung to me?

Without turning, he spoke, surprising me. "Are you going to join me or do you prefer skulking in the background?"

A smile pressed at the line of my mouth. Of course he'd know I was there. Ignoring the lingering tickle of stage fright, I started toward him. *Showtime.*

"I'm joining you," I said with the confident voice of the character I was playing. "I just got distracted with the view."

He shifted in my direction, and I was sure to keep my focus on him so that he'd know that *he* was the view I'd been talking about. Then our eyes caught. My breath hitched as a shock of electricity jolted down my spine. The slight lift of his brows told me he felt it too and that knowledge sent a flood of warmth rushing through me. It had been such a long time since I'd been so entirely attracted to a man. So long that I'd forgotten what it felt like, how consuming it could be. How confusing. How comforting.

It perplexed me. I was an actress and surrounded by beautiful faces and perfectly toned bodies, yet not a one of them had the effect that Reeve Sallis had on me. There was irony in it, I was sure. A sick play from karma.

Or maybe it was all in my head. Maybe it was *Amber* in my head—my interest in the man simply transference of what she'd felt for him. Perhaps her emotions had stained mine the way a restless spirit stained the cherished places it had left behind. Despite its basis in the paranormal—despite how crazy it might make me—that was the most comfortable explanation I could come up with, and I went with it.

But then he said my name. And the sound of it—"Emily," rough and sinful on his tongue—branded me. I was Emily

Wayborn, formerly Emily Barnes, and no one else. There was no space for Amber in the syllables he uttered.

He appraised me, his look smoldering. "You look fantastic."

My heartbeat ticked up a notch at the compliment, but I still recognized his odd inflection. "You sound surprised."

A smile slid across his lips as he closed the distance between us. "I didn't think you could look more attractive without wearing less. I was wrong." His tone said that he'd given this thought. That he'd thought about me wearing . . . *less*.

Goose bumps perked up on my skin while contradicting heat ignited in my belly. "I'm flattered."

"No, you're not."

"Excuse me?"

He put a firm hand on my elbow and leaned in toward my ear. "Let's not start out with lies between us, Emily."

My muscles went rigid and my pulse sped up for a different reason than it had a moment before. "I don't know what you—"

He cut me off. "You know you're attractive. Own it."

I smiled, the knot under my shoulder relaxing. "Beauty is subjective, Reeve. Yes, I'm aware that many people find my looks appealing. I work hard to make sure they do. It doesn't mean that you will. I'm honestly flattered to hear that you do."

He pulled away, but his grip remained. "I do. You wouldn't be here if I didn't."

It was a moment of victory that felt much more like relief. All of this, my whole charade, depended on Reeve's attraction to me. Though I'd felt confident after our morning exchange, the hours in between had given me time to doubt.

A waiter appeared seemingly out of nowhere with a wine service cart. There were two glasses already filled with a light liquid. Reeve acknowledged his servant with only a dismissive nod, and the waiter retreated immediately. Reeve released my arm and picked up a glass. "I thought a Meursault Chardonnay would be appropriate." He held it out for me.

I paused. Five years ago I would have taken it without a second thought, but my current self was cautious and worried about accepting a drink that I hadn't seen poured. From what I'd gathered about Reeve during our few interactions, he was cautious and controlling. He would want to sample his wine before accepting it. So why had it been poured before? Paranoia began to creep in.

He caught my hesitation. "We're having salmon. I assure you it pairs well. Or is there something else wrong?"

I couldn't improv fast enough so I settled for a bit of honesty. "I was trying to decide if you'd be the type to roofie me."

He studied me with a flat look and searing eyes. "Now, Emily. We both know that drugging you wouldn't be necessary to get you in my bed." He seemed pleased by the flush that spread across my cheeks. "But I'd be happy to switch glasses, if you prefer."

With a shaky hand, I took the one he'd first offered. "No. This will be fine."

He chuckled. "Come. Our first course is waiting for us."

He escorted me to the lone table set in the space. The pressure of his hand on my arm wasn't threatening this time—it was warm. Solid. Comforting.

Careful, he could still be a dangerous man. Even if your panties are starting to soak.

It wasn't Amber's voice behind the warning; it was mine. Still, I thought of her as Reeve helped me with my chair. Thought of her as he took his seat across from me. Thought of her as I placed my napkin in my lap and took a bite of the salad that was waiting on the table. I let her become heavy in my mind, a dark moon eclipsing any light of desire that

Reeve kindled. With that and another few sips of my wine, my nerves settled and the only warmth I felt was from the fire at my side and the alcohol in my veins.

We finished our salads without speaking. When he was done, Reeve pushed his plate to the side. Immediately, three waiters descended upon us. One refilled our wine, one took our plates, and the last replaced them with our main course—an herb-encrusted salmon fillet on a bed of rice. Silently, they retreated again.

They continued to watch us. Our every move carefully observed. They'd probably seen a lot in their time working for Reeve. I made a note that they could help me find answers, though I would need to build their trust first. People who worked this closely to Reeve Sallis would not divulge secrets easily. If at all.

Still, they could be a backup plan.

When my focus returned to my date, I realized he'd been watching me. "Your staff is well trained," I said.

"Very."

"It's admirable." I took a bite of my dinner, hoping that would change the subject. Reeve continued to watch. "Mmm," I said letting the sound reverberate in my throat as fish melted on my tongue. It was actually quite delicious even if I didn't have much of an appetite.

Reeve held his study for another long minute before picking up his own fork. "Tell me about yourself, *Emily Wayborn*." He said my name as if holding it out to examine. Or as if he didn't really believe it was mine.

"Emily Barnes, originally," I offered. He'd learn that easily enough on his own from one look at my Wikipedia page.

"Why did you change it?"

"Oh, I don't know. It seemed everyone in Hollywood had a nom de plume so why not me? *Barnes* is so flat and unattractive." And I'd thought that a new name would make it easier to disappear from my old life. Not that anyone would have come looking. Amber had been the only one who cared, and she'd told me with absolute conviction that she wouldn't be following after.

"I suppose Emily *Wayborn* does flow better off the tongue. What else?" As he ate, he kept his eyes on me, his focus intent.

"About me? What do you want to know?" It was an expected conversation for a first date and for that reason it should have been easy. But I'd been with plenty of men who didn't care to know anything about me other than whether I was on birth control or not. If that was really what Reeve was looking for, it was best to just skip to the point.

He shrugged. "The interesting things. The things I can't learn from Google."

"Did you already do a search? Or are you planning to later on?" I presumed that a whole background check had been done on me before I was allowed on the premises.

He leaned forward as if he were sharing a secret. "I'll never tell." He took a swallow of his wine then grinned guiltily. "Okay, I already searched. I don't dine with just anyone. Don't let it go to your head."

The idea of Reeve Sallis Googling anything himself, instead of having someone do it for him, made me smile. Plus, he'd dropped the wariness that had accompanied the start of his questioning and, even while I kept my attraction at bay, I much preferred the flirtatious banter.

"Well, then. You're already an expert," I teased.

"I'm not. Tell me." His eyes were light, but his tone authoritative, and the simple two-word command shuddered through me.

"Okay." I dabbed my napkin at my mouth. "I'm an only child. Born in Fresno. Grew up in Bakersfield. My father ran off when I was in elementary school. My mother was— *is*, I mean—not well, mentally. She functioned well enough when I was growing up, but just barely. My childhood was average. I got average grades. College was out of my price range and, honestly, I wasn't interested. So I started modeling, which turned to commercial acting, and then *NextGen* was my big break." It was all true. For the same reasons I'd decided to use my real name, I'd decided to use my real backstory. I expected Reeve to dig, and with as much power as he had, I knew he'd find out what he wanted to about me. The trick, then, was to tell him enough of the truth that he didn't feel like he needed to dig much further.

He nodded a few times as I spoke, as if confirming each piece of information before he filed it away. Much like I would with anything he shared with me. I had my reasons to be cataloging; I wondered what his were.

He's cautious, I told myself. *He's a man with enemies. He has to ask questions. You got this.*

"What else. . . ." I bit my lip as I thought of how to cap my self-summary. "I'm here at the resort by myself for a much-needed rest before we start shooting again the second week of January. Oh, and I'm a natural blonde."

His brow rose. "There are ways to verify that, you know."

A hum began between my legs. "Are there? Tell me more about that."

"Maybe later." The darkness in his eyes said he was definitely considering it.

Good.

Or not good. I was torn on the issue. If I didn't have to have sex with him to find out what I wanted to know, the better off I was. Right? It just wasn't really likely that I could get as close as I needed without getting him off. In which case, good that he was considering it. And good that my body seemed to be into that. Because it would make it easier, of course.

The talking was essential though, too. Maybe even

more than sex. Reeve would never let me into his life if he didn't trust me. I needed to seem transparent. Step one in the Find-A-Man game that Amber and I had played was how to appear vulnerable. Men liked vulnerable women. Rich men paid a lot to fuck vulnerable women. Paid a lot *to* the vulnerable women they fucked.

A lot of the time, I hadn't actually been vulnerable with them. But I could play the part. It was the reason I'd become an actress—because I already knew I was good at pretending.

Back then, of course, the roles were well-defined. The lies straightforward. *Yes, I'm twenty-one. Yes, you're my first. Yes, it feels good.*

Now the lies were ones of omission and that made things trickier. Instead of being clear-cut, everything became half-truth. It meant walking around in grays. It meant I had to screen my life and filter out what I would and wouldn't say, all the while praying that I came off as an open book.

At least the dividing line was unambiguous. I could tell Reeve that my childhood was average but I wouldn't tell him that, at seventeen, I met the friend who would finally get me out of my average life. I'd tell him I'd dated rich men, not that I'd spent several years as what some would call a glorified prostitute. I'd tell him I was at his resort to relax, not that I'd come to try to find the one person I'd been so determined to leave behind.

The dividing line was Amber. I'd answer Reeve's questions, but I'd leave out anything that had to do with her. Eventually, I hoped he'd tell me *everything* that had to do with her.

CHAPTER

3

"Are you still close to her?"

I looked up from my meal, panic rising in my chest. Reeve couldn't be asking about Amber. He had to mean someone else. I quickly replayed in my head everything I'd said in the last few minutes, trying to find a "her" that I'd mentioned. "You mean my mother."

He nodded and I let out a silent breath of relief.

"No, not really. She still lives in Bakersfield and I'm in West Hollywood. I visit when I can. The rest of the time I pay for someone to take care of her."

"That's no substitute for daughterly love."

His judgment irked me. "And the shell of a human she's always been isn't a substitute for a mother." I immediately regretted the sharpness of my words. They were counterproductive and really, he hadn't said anything I hadn't thought myself on a million guilt-laden occasions. Besides, it shouldn't matter what he thought of me.

It shouldn't matter and yet I found myself needing to explain. "She doesn't even know me most of the time now.

Alcohol-induced dementia. Possibly undiagnosed schizo-phrenia. The specialist I took her to said it's hard to be certain and there's not a lot to be done at this point. I visited her last week, on Christmas. Took her out for Chinese. Halfway through dinner she accused me of trying to poison her. She'd forgotten who I was. Said she'd never seen me before in her life. Got belligerent. Combative. The restaurant owner called the police."

My jaw clenched remembering how much it had upset me. "It wasn't the first time she's been that way with me, and I should have expected it. Just . . . when I'd seen her last, at Thanksgiving, she'd been good."

She'd greeted me that day with bright eyes and a tight hug. I'd been the first to let go for once. Then she'd remembered the voice message on her machine. *"From Amber, honey. I've been saving it for you."*

I'd thought she was confused, but I had humored her and listened to the message. And there was her voice. Amber's voice. Then it was as if only hours had passed since I'd seen her instead of years and every feeling, every memory was alive and present within me. I'd spent the rest of the day consumed with Amber. Missing Amber. Wondering about Amber.

I realized now that that day may have been the last I'd ever see my mother well. And I'd spent it thinking of Amber.

Suddenly my throat felt tight and my eyes wet. I didn't get upset easily, but I'd been edgy and emotional for weeks. There were only two women I'd ever loved, and both of them were lost to me in such different ways. My mother was gone for good. But Amber I might still be able to find.

Reeve shifted in his chair, reminding me of my surroundings. I peered out over the valley and attempted to compose myself. Damn, how had I managed to get so worked up? Well, thinking of Amber had caused me to look vulnerable. I silently thanked her.

When I turned back, I offered a shaky smile. "Anyway. She'd been better. And I guess I forgot that wasn't who she was most of the time."

"That sounds terrible." His tone was sincere and tender. "I'm sure you're doing the best that you can with her. Don't be too hard on yourself." Even after knowing him for only five minutes, I was positive this was the closest the man came to an apology.

It moved me.

I nodded, afraid to say anything else.

Reeve pushed his plate out of the way and stood. I hadn't eaten much but was more than happy to stop. I stood as well, following him to the stone bench near the fire pit. We could sit right next to each other here, but I left a space between us when I sat, not sure if closer was necessary. It was completely dark now except for the few lights that hung around the patio and the blaze from the pit. The ambiance was beautiful, romantic even. Maybe a little eerie as well, but strangely, I was finally feeling at ease.

I pretended to be lost in watching the flames flicker and spurt until the waiters finished clearing our dinner plates. When they were gone again, I turned the tables on Reeve. "What about you? Were you close to your parents before they died?"

He hesitated, and I wondered if his reluctance was because of the subject matter or because he didn't like to be in the hot seat. Finally he answered, "Yes. I was."

"You were sixteen, right?"

"Looks like I'm not the only one who knows how to Google."

I avoided the comment. "So you were a kid, basically, with a huge empire. That must have been overwhelming."

He pinned me with his eyes. "Emily, I'm not someone who is easily overwhelmed."

It was a warning. Yet I ignored it. "Even as a teenager? You don't have to fake bravado for me. I'm impressed whether you were strong and stoic or sad and over-your-head."

He held the silence for a moment then let out a sigh. "I was a little bit of all of it. But I'd been trained for the hotels. My father was a lot older than my mother and was a workaholic. He had already had one heart attack. I knew this would be my future, sooner rather than later. And it helped that I didn't inherit everything right away. The board ran the company until I was twenty-one."

"What did you do with the time in between?" These answers weren't ones I needed. I'd asked mostly because I wanted him to feel comfortable telling me things. But also because I was shockingly genuinely interested.

"Lived with my grandparents in Greece." He noticed my surprise. "I'm guessing your Internet searching didn't tell you that."

I shook my head.

"It's not widely known. My mother's family is . . . well, complicated. So I don't speak about them often because the media will undoubtedly twist it and make of it what they will. And frankly, I don't think it's anyone's business but my own." He paused and I thought he might not say any more on the subject, including me in the people whose business it wasn't.

He surprised me. "I lived there until I was eighteen and then came back to the States for college."

"Stanford, right?" I waited for him to nod. "And your grandparents—are you close to them?"

"Nope. My grandfather died a few years back. And I haven't seen my grandmother since I left. Though I do send her a card every year on her birthday."

"A thin piece of mail is no substitute for a grandson's love," I teased, or challenged, rather.

Reeve glared, but a smirk played on his lips. "No, it's not. But since her parting words to me were, 'If you leave, don't ever come back,' I feel like a card is more than expected. Or deserved."

I took that in. "It sounds like there's more of a story there."

"There is." He stood and moved to lean on the concrete edging of the pit, facing me. "But I'm not willing to tell it."

I sat back on my hands and studied him. I wondered if under different circumstances he would be the kind of guy I could like. The kind that I could truly care for. The kind of guy that would destroy me.

More importantly, was he the kind of guy Amber could like? Or had he really been just another one of her sugar daddies? And if so, what exactly had Reeve gotten out of the exchange?

"What are you thinking?"

I didn't even blink. "That you certainly know how to be intriguing. I'm guessing you're also intriguing in fluent Greek."

"Intriguing in Greek," he said, amusement lining his words. "I speak the language, yes."

"Say something for me."

"Another time." He swept a heated gaze over me. "You know what's intriguing?"

Yes. This. I liked this. Liked how his stare felt coarse and predatory.

I played coy. "What? *Me?*"

"Very." There was the expression again, his eyes meeting mine, intruding into me, into places deep and sacred and delicate. Places I'd filled so compactly with secrets and memories and Amber that they felt crowded with him there too.

And when he looked at me like that, I had an unexplainable urge to make room for him. For only him.

My instinct was to look away, but I forced myself to bear it. And then I noticed he was struggling too. My breath grew fast and shallow. "No way. I'm boring, mostly." But there was nothing boring about this. Nothing dull about the shine between us. It was strong and hot like a wire that only became live when we both held an end.

Then he shifted, and the fire was directly behind him, putting his face in shadow. "I wouldn't call any woman who chases after a man boring." Though I couldn't read his features, his tone seemed suddenly harder. Accusing even, and the electricity between us notched up a degree.

"I didn't chase after you exactly. I didn't even know you'd be at the resort when I booked the trip." Lies. I'd chased him. And though I hadn't been positive he'd be at his Palm Springs resort, I'd suspected based on his previous habits around the holidays. It took more than a week to figure out how to get him alone.

"Then when you learned I was here, you decided to . . . ?"

"I decided to meet you." It was another interrogation, like the one at the pool, but more intent. I pretended I didn't notice and tried to return us to the easiness of the moment before. "This surely isn't the first time you've been come on to, Reeve. How do you normally meet women?"

Even though his expression was indifferent, his eyes reached everywhere—the insides, the outsides. Touching me, tickling me in ways that made me flush and squirm and burn. "Normally, I don't meet women unless I want to," he said. "Normally, I initiate."

God, he was alpha male through and through. If I didn't know without a doubt that Amber would never have put up with a true dominant then I might have pegged him for the master/slave type. My guess was that, at the very least, he was bossy when it came to his women, just like it seemed he was bossy with everyone in his life.

"*You* initiated dinner," I offered, hoping that would console his obvious irritation. Hoping it would relieve me from the violation of those eyes.

It didn't. "You *wanted* me to ask you to dinner."

"I wanted to see you again." My voice wasn't as sure as I would have preferred. I was losing ground. I felt it slipping away underneath me. Desperate to gain it back, I added boldly, "I wasn't necessarily aiming for dinner. I was more interested in *dessert*." I skated my gaze down his body, accentuating my point.

"To be blunt, Emily, I'm usually uninterested in women who are so forward."

But forwardness had gotten me the date in the first place. And despite his words, his shoulders pushed back and his chin lifted, obviously pleased with my interest.

Besides, my body was really the only weapon in my arsenal that I knew how to use. "Usually," I repeated, standing as I spoke. "That means not always."

He cocked his head. Watching me.

Then I knew with absolute certainty that he wanted to kiss me. That if he did, he'd take every last bit of power I had.

I couldn't let that happen. I had to act first.

With a burst of resolve, I closed the space between us and settled my palm at the front of his pants. My breath caught as my hand closed around the thick outline, surprised he was already hard. "It seems it also means not right now."

His cock twitched as I tightened my grip, but otherwise Reeve remained still. It was a stark contrast to the way I felt inside—nervous, agitated, infested. Aroused. I stroked the length of him, my heart pounding as he grew harder beneath my touch. Falling to my knees was natural and my hands fumbled at his buckle with a desperate urgency that had little to do with finding Amber.

I'd barely undone the clasp when my upper arms were seized and I was pulled roughly to my feet. I struggled to get loose, but my hands were pinned securely behind me. I managed to twist enough to see the person holding me was the bodyguard who'd met me at the door.

I turned toward Reeve who still leaned calmly against the pit wall. The hint of a wicked smile on his face sent a bolt of trepidation through me. Had this been planned? Was this a trap after all? Or was Reeve a kinky guy who let his staff participate in his sexual acts?

After a moment, he spoke. "I probably should have warned you this could happen. My men usually insist on doing a body search on anyone who spends time alone with me. I told them to skip it with you, but that, of course, made some of them even more wary."

A misunderstanding, then. My pulse settled slightly. "I wasn't going to hurt him," I said over my shoulder. "Just the opposite, actually."

"That may be true," Reeve said. "But as I'm not used to having women come on to me, neither are they. Like I said, I always do the initiating."

Reeve exchanged some words with his bodyguard in a foreign language—Greek, if I had to guess. Perhaps that was why he hadn't wanted to speak it to me, because it was the language he used to communicate with his security team. I waited for them to finish, for Reeve to explain and for the guard to let me go.

Instead, the grip around me tightened.

Reeve stood, the corners of his lips turned down in an insincere frown. "I know this is awkward, Emily, but Anatolios insists on having you patted down now. To make you more comfortable, he's agreed to let me do the honors."

At the moment, I would have preferred the bodyguard.

Even just the thought of Reeve's hands wandering over me made my belly twist and flutter, and right now I didn't want to be turned on by him; I wanted to be pissed. I *was* pissed. Because I didn't buy for a moment that this wasn't all part of Reeve's game. I didn't buy that anyone could ever *let* Reeve do anything. He was a man who did what he wanted.

So, as he crossed the two steps between us, I tried to find comfort in the fact that he wanted to be touching me. Like I wanted to be touching him.

His guard—Anatolios—shifted his hold, pushing me forward as if he were a loyal servant presenting a gift to his master.

Reeve looked me in the eyes. Oh yeah, he was enjoying this. "This will only take a moment, Emily. No need to be worried."

I didn't speak. Anything I had to say would likely only get me in trouble. Best to just let the man do as he pleased and hope that my cooperation would earn me more of his trust.

He started with his hands at my neck, his touch fiery on my skin. Then he swept them down over my collar and outward across the line above my chest. Under his fingertips, my nerves awakened, spitting into flames that licked and burned in the tracks of his path. He glided down the sides of my torso, cupping under my breasts, lingering before he drew back to my waist. Then over my hips. Down the outside of my thighs, his eyes were heated and never left mine. He didn't pat down like the security at the airport looking for a hidden weapon. He caressed. He teased. He tortured.

He bent to continue his trail to my ankles. There he paused, throwing a glance to Anatolios. Next thing I knew, my legs were kicked apart from behind, forcing me to widen my stance. I swore under my breath, but didn't fight. Reeve resumed his torment, this time moving up the insides of my shins, past my knees, higher, to the sensitive section of my inner thighs where each centimeter of skin crossed made me fidget and squirm, finally landing at the crotch of my panties.

I drew in a shuddering breath. I was on pins and needles, my arousal so spiked that it was itchy and agonizing and infuriating.

Reeve straightened to his full height while keeping one hand positioned at my center. His eyes glistened as he registered the dampness of the material. "I like this, Emily. It makes me happy to know that at least a portion of your interest in me is sincere."

Fucking asshole. "It's all sincere," I said through gritted teeth.

He stepped even closer so that his breath whispered across my face. "I want to believe it. I really do." He slipped his fingers inside my panties then, ignoring my throbbing clit and moving lower where he circled my entrance before plunging inside of me. "Ah, soaked. I like this a lot."

I struggled to suppress a moan, struggled to be as stoic as he'd been when I'd touched him.

But it was impossible. The storm was already gathering, my belly tightening as the pleasure built and I couldn't help the small, breathy cries that echoed from the back of my throat.

Reeve sighed heavily, pressing his forehead against mine. "You're very tempting, Emily Wayborn. So very tempting." Desire clouded in his expression, but—in his stance, in his form, in the way he held himself firm against me—I saw restraint. Which would win? Which did I want to win?

He brushed the thumb of his free hand across my lower lip. "Tempting. But as I told you, I'm not easily overwhelmed." He pulled away suddenly, leaving my body wound up and wanting. "I've just remembered some business I need to attend to. Thank you for an entertaining dinner, Emily. Anatolios can see you back to your suite if you'd like him to."

Then he was gone, exiting as quickly as his waiters had come and gone all night long.

Again, I cursed under my breath. I didn't dare look at the guard who had finally let me go, aware that he was likely gloating in my humiliation, and I certainly wasn't letting him escort me out. Without another word, I straightened my skirt and started out the way I'd come in, my head high despite Anatolios's eyes heavy on my backside. It certainly wasn't the walk of shame that I'd expected to make at the night's end, but I handled it with as much confidence as I could muster.

Back in my room, I collapsed on the bed, my fists balled at my sides. "Dammit," I said, punching the mattress next to me. "Dammit, dammit, dammit." I was frustrated and turned on. And worried that I'd never hear from Reeve again and that I'd fucked everything up in my search for Amber. I punched once more for good measure.

But really my turmoil at the moment had little to do with Amber and all to do with what I'd learned that evening: Reeve Sallis liked to be in control.

I'd met that type of man before. I knew what they liked. They were the men who liked to fuck, but on their terms. They were the men who liked giving gifts and praise almost as much as they liked taking them away. They were the men who liked to hurt. To humiliate. Manipulate. They left bruises. They left scars. They were the men that induced fear. The men who debased and defiled. They were the reason I'd left that life in the first place.

And this was why, where Reeve Sallis was concerned, I was fucked. Because these were the men that I could never stop craving.

CHAPTER
4

My cell phone ringtone woke me the next morning. I considered ignoring it, but the thought that it could possibly be Reeve had me reaching across the bed before it stopped ringing.

"Emily. It's Joe Cook."

I rubbed a hand over my eyes, trying to convince myself I wasn't disappointed. Reeve didn't even have my number, not that that would matter.

Then I registered what the caller had said. I sat up. "Joe. Hi. Do you have news?" He wouldn't have called if he didn't.

I'd hired Joe Cook after the police had been utterly unhelpful in my search for Amber. It wasn't their fault really. I didn't have enough for them to go on, plain and simple. I'd argued. I'd pled. I spent all of Black Friday in the station, in fact, trying to get someone to take my report seriously. Finally, an older detective called me into his office. Patiently he listened to my entire story. He listened to the message that I'd recorded onto my phone from my mother's answer-

ing machine. He listened to me explain how, even though
Amber never once asked for help or stated that she was
in trouble, I knew there was something wrong because
she'd said "blue raincoat"—our code.

Then just as patiently he explained the reasons he
couldn't do anything. "There is simply nothing that you
have presented to justify a missing person," he had said.
"I'm not saying that nothing happened to your friend—I'm
only saying that we can't help you find her."

I opened my mouth to argue when he added, "But I do
know someone who *can* help you. He's pricey, but worth
it if this is that important to you."

It was *that* important to me. I left the station ten minutes later with Joe Cook's number.

Joe had arranged to meet at a hole-in-the-wall diner in
Hollywood—his choice, not mine—and at first sight I
knew he wasn't like anyone I'd spent much time with. The
men I'd known best were suave and charming, at least on
the outside, their hands manicured, their suits pressed,
their cars expensive. Half bounty hunter, half private investigator, Joe had shown up on a Harley, decked from
head to toe in black leather and sporting colorful tattoos
over every bare inch of his arms and neck. His hair was
buzzed and he wore dark glasses that he never took off,
even inside. As gruff and gritty as he was, I wouldn't have
been surprised if he knew the detective who'd pointed
me his way because Joe had a record of his own.

Despite my first impression and the fact that his resume
was simply, "I find people who are hard to find," Joe was
professional. He took my business seriously, gathering details of my friendship with Amber for nearly three hours,
never doubting or questioning my reasons for hiring someone like him rather than one of the hundreds of PI's I
could find on the Internet for a third of his asking price.
I wasn't an idiot and Amber knew how to hide. I needed a

tracker with skills that included more than taking pictures of cheating spouses and locating children after they'd been put up for adoption.

Joe was that guy. It was a gut feeling more than anything, but I believed it enough to hire him on the spot. When he'd given me his first report that included mention of past events that I'd been convinced were buried, he'd more than proven himself.

"I found the parents," he said to me now. "Actually spoke to the mother. She's a real fucktard. Lived in the same house for all these years in Santa Clarita, only an hour from where Amber was staying in high school, but I'd bet money she never bothered to look that far. She rolled her eyes when I mentioned her daughter's name. Said she hasn't heard anything from her in over a decade. Said she'd figured Amber was dead. Didn't seem interested even when I'd shown her pics of Amber from after she'd run away. I see people do shitty things on a daily basis so it's with authority that I say she had a bad family life, Em."

I nodded even though he couldn't see me through the phone. "Yeah, I know."

Amber had never spoken much about her parents, but what I had gleaned from the few things she'd slipped over the course of our friendship was that her mother had been a jealous bitch. Jealous of her own daughter. Her dad was the worst kind of scum and had been sexually abusing her—his child—on a daily basis, and instead of defending her, Amber's mother resented her.

At least my mother had tried to love me. "Well, that was a long shot anyway. Did you see her father at all?"

"Now, that's an interesting thing. He wasn't there. He's been at Folsom for the past several years."

"State prison?"

"Yep. He was sentenced to twenty-five years for aggravated assault on a child. Some kid in the neighborhood.

Seems he would often give the girl a ride after school and by ride I mean a trip on the baloney pony, not his car. Now here's where it gets fishy. Back at the beginning of October, he got himself murdered."

The thumbnail I'd been absentmindedly chewing fell out of my mouth. "Wait . . . did you say murdered?"

"Uh-huh. Assaulted with some sort of 'slashing-type weapon.'" The quote marks were evident in the way he said it, as if he was reading from his notes. "Pronounced dead on site."

"Wow." It sounded appalling to hear it told so plainly, but I also felt a stab of vindication. If someone had slit his throat with a "slashing-type of weapon" years ago, how different would Amber's life have been? I wondered if she knew. Wondered if she felt the same sense of victory. Wondered if she was feeling anything at all these days.

I shook that last thought off. "I guess it's not uncommon though for pedophiles to get offed in jail, right?"

"'Offed.'" Joe seemed amused at my use of slang, as he often did when I tried to talk the lingo. "Not uncommon, no. But keep listening. It gets weird. The cops never fingered anyone with the job, but I have a source there telling me that everyone knows who did it. Nick Delatano. He's a mob fall guy." Joe paused. "That means he took the blame for something or other or protected someone more important than him and he'll get rewarded for it somehow. Basically, he works for mafia, even in prison. And not just mafia, Emily—a special branch called the Philadelphia Greek Mob. Heard of them?"

"I haven't." Though my skin was already prickling with the mention of the word "Greek."

"They've been what some call 'dormant' for the last decade or so, but what that really means is they're just operating under the radar. They're like the Italians, you know, um, specialists in money laundering, tax evasion, extortion, drug trafficking. Murder. Only they're from Greece."

I swallowed. It had to be coincidental. "Mob guys can hate child molesters too."

"Not denying that. But supposedly Nick didn't even know James Pries was a sex offender. So why was a mafia guy taking a hit out on a child predator?"

Even though the thought had already taken up residence in my mind, I wasn't ready to believe it. "There could be a hundred reasons. Maybe they fought over toilet paper. Maybe James fought back when Nick was making him his bitch. This probably has nothing at all to do with Amber."

"Maybe." Joe's tone said he didn't believe that for a second. "It's just interesting considering the last man she was seen spending time with was Reeve Sallis, who also has mob ties."

"*Rumored* mob ties." Jesus, even to myself I sounded defensive.

"Yeah, yeah, 'rumored.'" He was quiet for several seconds. "I just can't get that picture out of my mind, the one of Sallis with Vilanakis. Not many people can get that close to Vilanakis."

I knew the picture. It had been one of the earlier things that Joe had uncovered about Reeve. I'd seen the picture myself on the Web, but hadn't known the significance of the second man. His name wasn't even labeled on the post. It was a crappy phone pic taken at a family dinner and shared on a personal blog. I'd thought nothing of it until Joe had emailed it to me almost two weeks before Christmas with a simple message: *"Michelis Vilanakis. Known crime boss. What's the connection?"*

It was the moment that the plan I'd been knocking around in the back of my mind seemed to become necessary.

Then why was I so eager to dismiss the connection between the mafia and James Pries now?

If I was being honest with myself it was because of Reeve. Because now I'd met him. Because now I didn't want to think of him as *that* dangerous. Because I didn't need any reason to be more attracted to him than I already was.

But Joe was right. "I know. I know. Just, there hasn't been anything to prove that and I don't want to make connections that aren't based on anything verifiable in case it causes us to neglect other important facts that will help us find her."

"Find out what happened to her," Joe corrected. He made sure I never forgot that he believed we were looking for a dead person.

It was one of the first things he'd said when we'd met. "You know, after forty-eight hours missing, the odds are that the victim is deceased."

"Amber's not a statistic," I'd said firmly. "I know her. She knows how to lay low, how to disappear. In fact, I don't even know that she's missing. Just that she needs my help."

"No one can find her. That means she's missing. She's been missing for several months. She's not going to be alive."

"Well," I'd said. "We'll just agree to disagree." I'd realized I was lucky to have someone help me at all. If we had different bets on the outcome, that was fine. The search process was the same either way.

Still, I reminded him of my stance as often as he reminded me of his. "What will you do when you find her alive and well?" I asked him now.

"Let you say, 'I told you so.'"

"Oh, I will." I chewed my lip as I debated whether or not to share the information I'd learned since last speaking to Joe, knowing he'd want to know my source. Since any detail could prove important, I settled on disclosure. "On the topic . . . did you know that Reeve lived with his maternal grandparents in Greece for a couple of years after his parents died?"

"No. Where did you hear this?"

It was the question I'd been dreading. I hadn't told Joe what I was doing, nor did I plan to. Whether or not he tried to talk me out of it, he certainly wouldn't approve. "It doesn't matter where I heard it. But it's credible. Maybe that's where the rumors of ties to Greek mafia started?"

"Huh. Maybe. Or that's when he started working with them." Joe sounded like he thought the latter was more likely. "You didn't happen to learn the maternal grandparents' surname?"

"Isn't it Kaya?"

"Well. Short answer—I don't think so. His mother's marriage certificate lists her maiden name as Kaya, but there's simply no record of her existence before that. Every bio that Sallis has published says she grew up in Athens and met her husband at the opening dinner reception of his resort there. She was supposedly just out of school. Problem is, that event was invitation only and there's no Kaya on the list. So say she came as a plus one. Ignore the question of who'd take a nobody kid to an important political event. Because that's what it was—a dinner to schmooze the officials. It was a big deal for one of Greece's own countrymen to bring his success back to his homeland. There would have been tight security. Elena would have been on the list, even as a date. Kaya has to be a fake name or that wasn't where she really met Daniel Sallis. One of those is a lie. Which begs the question—why?"

Probably because where she really met him wasn't suitable for discussing in polite company. I was jaded where very rich men were concerned, though. It was my experience that most of them bought their women. Why wouldn't that be the case with Reeve's father?

I hoped it was the case with Reeve as well or I was wasting my time at his resort.

But I didn't say that to Joe. Instead I let his question hang.

"Well. That's all I have right now. Do you have anything else you need to tell me?"

It was my opening, my chance to tell him that I'd decided to go after Reeve on my own. The smart thing would be to tell him, to tell someone.

But could I really do this if anyone else was involved? Reeve had too many resources. I couldn't shake the feeling that he'd find out if I pulled Joe into the mix, and the last thing I wanted to do was endanger anyone else. "Nope. That's all I've learned too."

Joe sighed. "Then you'll hear from me when I have more."

"But Emily." He caught me just as I was hanging up. "Remember the girl is as far as I go. I'll do what I can to find your friend, but if all roads lead to Sallis, I'm out. That's a death wish."

He'd given me a similar warning the day he'd agreed to work my case. *"You won't find anyone who will take on a man like him. And if you find someone who says they will, run."*

I was tired of running. And, fuck, maybe I did have a death wish.

I'd known that Amber had started seeing Reeve long before her phone call. I'd seen a picture of them together in the Star Tracks section of *People*. It wasn't even a magazine I read very often, and when I did, I skipped over the section that featured photos of celebrities out in the world doing celebrity things. The fact that I'd seen it at all had been a giant fluke. It was a few weeks after the first episode of *NextGen* had aired, and both critics and audiences were hailing it as the best new show of the season. Paparazzi began waiting outside the studio and showing up at network events. Though my face wasn't that recognizable, I'd find them hanging around my neighborhood on occasion. Sometimes I'd catch a flash out of my peripheral vision, a cell phone held up in my direction. I'd heard from a costar that I was in that week's *People*, so I picked it up.

In my tiny one-bedroom apartment on the hillside of West Hollywood, I had poured myself a glass of wine and curled up on my couch before opening the magazine. Her photo caught my eye first—ironically it was directly opposite where mine was featured. The shot had been taken at a star-studded gala event held at Reeve's hotel in Santa Monica. His hands were stuffed in the pockets of his tuxedo, much like they had been when I'd arrived at the Cherry Lounge, and she clung onto his arm flashing her perfect smile.

She looks thin, I'd thought, *and she's dyed her hair a lighter blond.* Funny, I had too.

I was transfixed for a long time before finally reading the caption. SALLIS'S LATEST FEMALE COMPANION, it read. It didn't even mention her by name. Until that moment, I'd thought I'd come so far from where I'd left her half a decade before. Seeing us paired on two facing pages like that, where even in a photo I could see the who I was compared to the who she was, I realized that I hadn't gone anywhere. Her with no name, me with no face. At least she had a "companion."

After I hung up with Joe, I opened the room safe and pulled out the accordion file organizer that held all the information I'd gathered regarding Amber, including the clipping from *People*. That was where all of this had really begun—when I'd seen her face and realized that she was still alive. Not that I'd thought she was dead before that. She'd just been dead to me, and in that photo she'd been resurrected. I didn't pay any more attention to her after that than I had before, didn't look for her on the Internet or try to track her down. But, still, something was different. Memories surfaced more easily. Her name was closer to the tip of my tongue. Her face seen in crowds she wasn't in.

After making sure the deadbolt was locked and the DO NOT DISTURB sign was on my knob, I laid everything out on my bed as I searched for it now. When I found it, I studied it, wondering when exactly it had been taken. I always referred to it in my mind as "January 27" since that was the edition of the magazine, but that wasn't the date of the photo. Reading through all the copy on the page, I discovered a reference to New Year's Eve that I hadn't noticed before.

It was just a year ago, then. *One year. NextGen* had aired just after the holiday as a midseason replacement show, changing my life entirely. Had Reeve Sallis done the same for Amber?

On a whim, I decided to put everything in chronological order so that I could cement her timeline in my head. I placed the *People* photo in the top left corner of my bed. A few seconds later, I changed my mind and scooted it in so I could put something before it.

Joe's research had found the piece of information that I wanted to put first. She'd been living in a hotel. A Sallis hotel. On October 19, a little more than a year before I'd heard her message, she'd let her room go and there was no record of any address after that.

"Because that's what she does," I'd told him. *"She pegs the man she wants. She gets near him. She moves in. October nineteenth is when she moved in with Reeve."*

"Huh. She moves fast," Joe had said.

I intended to move faster.

Using a piece of the hotel stationary from the bedside table, I wrote down, *August 30 to October 19—hotel*. This I placed in the first spot on the bed.

Besides *People* magazine, Amber had only been photographed with Reeve a few times, and those I'd had to search the Internet for hours to find. I'd printed them all for my file, and now I laid them out on the row in no particular order since none of them referenced a date except one. I put that one last. It was captioned MEMORIAL DAY AT THE PALM SPRINGS RESORT—the very place I was staying. It was the last reference to a location that Joe and I had been able to find for her. Though he'd said he'd only investigate Amber, Joe had gone so far as to learn that Reeve's Beverly Park home had been undergoing renovations and had been completely uninhabited for most of the previous year. Joe figured Reeve had been resort hopping during that time. Currently, he was in the process of tracking down Reeve's travels for the summer months, trying to determine where he'd gone and if Amber had been with him. It was a slow task since Reeve traveled a lot, always using his own jet. Private flight manifests weren't always easy to find, it turned out, nor were they always accurate.

After the Palm Springs resort pic came the transcription of Amber's message. I'd typed it out so I could refer to it easily. The date on the answering machine had said August 17. Three whole months after she had last been photographed. Three whole months before I'd heard that cryptic message. I wanted to blame my mother for that, wanted to believe she'd been too lost in her head to remember to tell me she had a message waiting. But it was just as likely she didn't tell me because I hadn't visited her in months, and what was the urgency of calling me to ask about a blue raincoat?

I tried not to think too much about the lost months. It would be too easy for the guilt to overwhelm me.

The message was the last time anyone had seen or heard from Amber. She'd simply vanished after that. When Joe had called a PR representative of Reeve's to inquire about how he might get hold of her, he'd been given a scripted response: "Mr. Sallis and Ms. Pries have ended their relationship. We are unaware of Ms. Pries's current whereabouts." The woman wouldn't even say when they'd broken up, but when Joe asked if Reeve was seeing anyone now, he'd been given a definitive no.

Reeve was photographed mid-September at an event with another woman and again at a Halloween party with yet another woman, both unnamed. These pictures started a new row on the bed. Next to them, I placed the paper that I'd written the statement from Reeve's PR on. On another piece of stationary I wrote the newest information: *James Pries murdered—October*. This I held onto as I studied everything laid out in front of me, hoping it would connect with something, anything.

But no matter how I tried to look at it, I couldn't get James Pries's murder to fit. Amber called me in August. Reeve was seen dating others by September. Common sense put her disappearance between the call and the first event he attended without her. Her father's death was after that.

But despite what I'd said to Joe, my gut told me it was relevant. When I returned everything to my file folder an hour later, the paper with James Pries's murder was included.

I ordered brunch from room service and spent the rest of the day in my suite reading anything I could find about the Greek mafia on the Internet. I learned about the Philadelphia Greek Mob and all the key players. I hunted for any connections to the Sallis name. When I'd exhausted the topic, I ordered room service for dinner. Then I looked again for Amber, hoping for something I might have missed in previous searches.

And then Reeve. I scoured the Web for pictures of him, for articles. I read everything I found, even though I'd read it all before. Then I read it again.

When night fell and my eyes couldn't stare at a screen another minute, I shut my laptop and peered into the mirror above the desk I'd been working at. "Well," I said to my red-eyed reflection. "Time to face what you've been ignoring for the last twenty-four hours. I fucked up with Reeve."

I'd told myself that I'd cooped myself up because I had to research. The truth was, I'd wanted to be in my room in case he'd called. I'd convinced myself he'd reach out, that he'd give me a second chance. Hell, to be honest, I wasn't even sure what I'd done wrong. Too many years had passed since I'd last seduced anyone, and I just didn't know what I was doing anymore. Didn't that deserve another shot?

The idea that he might not give me one—that he likely wouldn't—was unbearable.

I rested my face in my palm and willed the emotions to stay below the surface as I said the words over and over, "I fucked up, Amber. I fucked up."

It was my imagination, no doubt about it—the words were even direct from a memory, and not new—but I heard her voice clear and soothing in my head. *This is only today. Tomorrow's going to be something else entirely."*

CHAPTER
5

The next day, I revised my plan. Reeve may have wanted nothing to do with me, but Amber was still missing, and I was still determined to find her. There was less than a week before I had to be back at the studio in Burbank, which meant only a handful of days left at the Palm Springs resort. Though I didn't know how long she'd stayed, I did know that Amber had spent some time here. Surely someone on the staff had to remember her? The trick was finding the right staff.

Along with my accordion file, I had stuffed a few items I'd worn for different shoots in the room safe including brown tinted contacts and a brunette hairpiece. The wig was professional and nearly impossible to detect, especially when I wore it under a hat, which I paired with a sundress over my swimsuit and headed out. First stop, the pools. Amber had always loved the water, almost as much as I did. She liked to drift and float and dry off by lying in the sun. Then repeat. Reeve's pool was a lap-only pool except in the mornings when it was reserved only for him. I doubted there was any way he'd have let her splash around during his laps. Also, not only was his early swim time not the best hour for sunning, but Amber usually wasn't even awake at that time of morning. Lucky for her there were six other pools on the property that were open all day. I decided to start at the one farthest away from my suite and work my way back.

The hotel didn't provide lifeguards, so I set my sights instead on the towel boys. At pool number one, I sat in the hot tub for fifteen minutes first to make my approach seem ordinary. Standing in front of the attendant dripping wet didn't hurt either. I was a woman who knew how to use her wiles, after all. My prep was wasted, though. The towel boy there hadn't worked at the resort long enough to be helpful. I repeated the same routine at the second pool only to find that towel boy was new too. Pool three's towel boy was a woman who grunted at me when I tried to talk to her. Pool four was the family pool— Amber wouldn't have been caught dead in a place over-run with children. I went through the routine anyway, in case the towel boys rotated where they worked. Though that one had been there the summer before, he'd been working in housekeeping then.

By number five, I was starting to get frustrated. This was a quieter pool. I dipped my feet in, which calmed me down. Centered me. I was ready to perform when I stood up and made my way to the towel bar.

The attendant was young. Probably early twenties. His eyes were glued to his phone as I came walking up so he didn't see me at first. "Hi," I said, dripping in front of the counter.

He didn't look up. "Need a towel?"

"Yeah."

He grabbed one off the stack of linens beside him and scooted it across the counter.

"Can I have an extra one, please?"

He glanced up at me. "Uh, sure." I had his attention now. He pocketed his phone and reached into a bin of unfolded towels behind him. "Here, take one of these. Just came from the dryer."

He tried to brush my hand as I took it from him, but I didn't let him. He had to work to get rewards from me.

"Oh, thank you. That's . . ."—I held the towel like a cape behind me, making sure the attendant's eyes were where I wanted them before wrapping it around me—"nice." Okay, maybe he didn't have to work that hard.

"Can I get you anything else?" He smiled, completely accommodating now.

I pretended to consider. "Have you worked here long, uh, Eric?" I asked, reading the name on his tag.

"Going on three years."

"Then maybe you can help me with something else." I leaned forward over the counter, hoping I appeared flirty instead of eager. "My friend spent some time here last summer. She was my age. Blond. My size. I was wondering if you might remember her. Her name's Amber."

He seemed truly disappointed. "I'm sorry. There's way too many girls that come through here for me to remember—"

"I have a picture." I fished into the oversized beach bag at my feet and pulled out the Internet photo I'd grabbed from my file before leaving my room that morning. I'd chosen the one taken at the resort. Though I had some original pictures from a long time ago, I wasn't ready to admit that I'd known Amber in my youth, in case—God, I was paranoid—my questioning somehow got back to Reeve. Besides, the resort shot was more recent, and I thought seeing her in context might be helpful.

The attendant peered at the photo. I watched as his face changed to recognition. Then to concern. He was fidgety when he pushed it back toward me. "Uh, no. Definitely not. I don't know anything about her."

He wasn't a good liar. And why was he lying anyway?

I leaned in a little farther hoping a view of the girls could persuade him to tell the truth. "Are you sure? I know she was here. She was dating the resort owner and—"

The attendant began shaking his head before I'd even finished speaking. "Nope. Don't know her. Excuse me but I have to get back to folding these towels. Have a nice day." He turned completely so that his back was to me.

I stood there for another minute before picking up my bag and heading for a nearby deck chair. I slumped down and shot a glance back at the towel bar. The attendant *had* acted weird, hadn't he? Or was I just imagining things again?

"You're one crazy woman," a voice said behind me.

I turned to find a man wearing a Sallis resort shirt picking up a used towel off the empty seat beside me. "Excuse me?"

The man gathered another few towels from the ground, speaking to me without looking at me, his voice low. "You can't ask about Sallis's women and expect anyone to tell you shit."

My brow creased until I realized he must have overheard the exchange at the counter. And if my interest hadn't been piqued before, it was now. "Does he tell you not to say anything?"

"Sallis? Not exactly. It's unspoken. His women are not to be touched, not to be talked about. End of story. Not an out-and-out rule. The staff just knows." He said it like the subject was over.

It wasn't. "But *how* do you know? There has to be something that began the idea in the first place." Like, Reeve planted it. It would be so typical of him with his control-everything-yet-seem-aloof desire. I wouldn't doubt it for a moment.

But the attendant simply shrugged. "No idea."

He shot a look over at me and must have seen the determination on my face because he stopped what he was doing and sat on the chair next to me. Perhaps overdramatically, he looked around to see who was watching us, then leaned toward me and said in a hushed voice, "Okay, you didn't hear this from me, but there was an incident. Once. A cook who made a not-nice comment about the lady Sallis was dating."

Though I felt silly doing so, I lowered my own voice. "What happened to him? Did he get himself fired?"

"He got himself dead."

My stomach dropped. "Dead? For a simple comment?" Then I realized the guy was laughing. "You're making this up."

He grinned, straightening. "Yeah, I am."

"Jerk," I said playfully, returning his grin. I looked him over now, discreetly behind my sunglasses. He was cute. A nice-guy sort. Clean-cut and well mannered. He probably didn't try anything on the first date. Maybe not the second either. He'd probably be someone that would be really good for me.

And I wasn't interested in the slightest.

"Sorry," he said, not at all sorry. "Couldn't help myself. Really, there's no story to back up my point. Just trust me—Sallis is a good employer, but he's not the guy you want to cross. He's the kind of guy you respect. There isn't anyone here who will fuck that up."

"You sound pretty confident about that." I narrowed my eyes. "You must have worked here a while. Were *you* here last summer?"

He laughed. "Seriously? After what I just said?"

"You gave me no reason to be afraid of the question." My tone was serious, but I let the teasing show in my expression. "Come on. I won't tell anyone. Just . . . did you? You did, didn't you? Work here."

He laughed again, shaking his head. "Shit. I can't believe I'm doing this. Let me see the picture." He looked around once more before taking it from me. After only a second of studying it, he returned it. "That's Ms. Pries."

"Yes! Yes, that's her!" It was surprising how overcome I was just by the simple sound of her name. How happy I was to find someone who had, so far, only verified that Amber had been there. A fact that wasn't at all new to me. "So you knew her?"

"I knew *of* her. Everyone knew of her. Never talked to her or anything, but I saw her around."

"Okay, okay." I was too excited to think. "Do you know anyone who did talk to her?"

"I don't know. Maybe someone at the spa. I heard she was there a lot. But no one's going to tell you shit there, so don't bother."

I made a mental note to book a massage and admonished myself for not thinking of that already. "Do you know when she left?" He was shaking his head again so I encouraged him. "A ballpark time frame. The season. Anything."

His knee bounced as he considered. "She left in June maybe. Probably. Same time as Sallis did. Before you ask, no, I don't know where they went. Sallis didn't come back here until Halloween."

"With her?"

Another head shake. "Alone."

I bit my lip. "And you don't have any idea where he went? No guesses?"

"You don't give up, do you?" He laughed again. "I honestly don't know. Doesn't Sallis have a home somewhere?

Maybe there. Or another resort. I'm sure he stays in some of his other places throughout the year like he does here."

There were nearly a hundred Sallis resorts around the world. Saying he could be at any one of them provided no help. "Who would know what his schedule is?"

"Beats the shit out of me. And probably not a good idea to go asking around about *that* either."

"Well, thank you. I appreciate this." I fished in my bag for my wallet and pushed a hundred toward him.

He waved my bill away. "No way. It was bad enough I was saying things I shouldn't say. I don't want to be accused of taking money for it. I'd rather have my excuse be that I was dazzled by a beautiful woman."

"You flatter me." Part of me wished I could be charmed so easily. Wished I could be charmed at all by someone like him.

"Nah. I still think you're crazy." He hesitated. "But if you're into a crazy good time, come by here when I get off work at seven. I'm Greg, by the way."

"Trish." I didn't shake his hand. And I wouldn't meet him. I'd gotten everything I wanted from him already. But he'd been helpful so I said, "I'll consider it. Greg."

I wondered if he would have asked me out or been as forthcoming if he'd known I'd been on a date with his boss just two nights before. Did that put me in the unspoken category of untouchable? I decided it was best not to ask.

I sat back on the deck chair and considered my next move for several minutes after Greg left. According to him, there wasn't any reason to continue my interviews of the resort staff since they wouldn't tell me anything. Of course, *he'd* still given me information even after he'd said asking anyone was pointless. Which meant that I might still have a chance to learn something. If I got lucky. Or if I played my part well.

Either way, I was too tired to keep at it that day. A growl of my stomach led me to La Cabana, the poolside cantina. Not wanting to wait for table service, I settled at a counter seat and ordered chicken street tacos and a glass of Sauvignon blanc from the bartender—Lucy, according to her name tag. I kept the wig on, but took off my hat, careful not to disturb the piece underneath, and set it on the counter. While I waited to be served, I pulled out my cell phone from my purse and looked up the number for the resort spa. By the time Lucy returned with my food, I had an appointment at ten the next morning for a massage.

As I ate, I realized that though speaking with Greg felt satisfying, I really hadn't learned anything useful. I knew before he'd told me that Amber had been at the resort the previous summer. Now, I supposed, I knew she was gone by the end of June. Maybe. Probably. He'd also told me that by Halloween she was no longer with Reeve. But I'd already guessed that because of the picture from September that showed Reeve with another woman. Actually, the most interesting thing I'd discovered from the conversation was that at least some of Reeve's staff believed that he wouldn't want them talking about him.

And that information was definitely not helpful.

Sighing, I pushed away the remainder of my tacos and laid my head on the counter.

"Looks like you need a refill," Lucy said.

I followed her eyes to my empty wineglass. "Yeah. I think one more."

"I'll have to open up a new bottle. Give me just a minute."

She left and I propped my head up with my elbow and dazed absentmindedly at the wall only a handful of feet away from me. One section of it was covered in framed pictures, a variety of sizes. As I continued to stare, I realized the pictures were of people, sort of like the display found in the home of a grandparent, not a bar. Intrigued, I rose to check it out more closely.

They were candid shots. From this very restaurant. Reeve was in several of them, wearing a casual button-down shirt and khaki shorts, his hand clapped around the shoulder of someone in one. Raising a bottle of an imported beer in another. He wore the same outfit in each of them, so I guessed they were all from the same event. I just couldn't tell what the event was or when it took place.

But if they were recent . . .

Though my eyes naturally went to the pictures with Reeve in them, I studied the other faces now looking for Amber, hoping she might be in one. And also the ones with Reeve in them. He was too photogenic not to. Too beautiful. Too captivating.

"He's a real looker, isn't he?"

I peered over my shoulder to find Lucy, her hand outstretched toward me with my glass of wine. I took it from her, nodding my thanks. "He's not bad on the eyes," I conceded, returning my focus to where I'd been looking a moment before. It was in a smaller frame, a white matte surrounding it so that only a three-inch picture showed. Reeve was in it, with two women in bikini tops and long skirts. Several buttons of his shirt were undone as if this was later in the evening. His smile was bright, his eyes sparkling. He seemed to be enjoying himself, and while I was drawn to the serious expression that I'd seen from him most often, this look was awfully appealing too.

I pointed to the display on the wall. "When were these taken, anyway?"

Lucy had returned to her place behind the bar, but she answered as she wiped down the counter. "His thirtieth birthday. It was quite a party. Not too big. A hundred or so friends and family. We closed the pool outside and he held the whole thing in here."

Reeve was thirty-six now. Amber wouldn't be in these pictures. I kept looking anyway, fixating on one of the women. She had her head turned away from the camera, her hand covering her mouth as if she was laughing so it was hard to really see her face. "Oh, wow," I gasped, when I recognized who she was. "That's Missy Mataya."

Missy Mataya was at the center of Reeve's dangerous reputation. They'd dated for a while. Or fucked. Whatever it was that he did with his female companions. Much like all the women he was seen with, he'd never claimed her as a girlfriend, and if they'd ever demonstrated public displays of affection, they weren't caught on camera. Also like Reeve's women, Missy had been gorgeous. She'd been an up-and-coming supermodel. Exotic. Young. Well loved.

Then—probably soon after the picture I was looking at had been taken—she'd fallen from a cliff edge and died. Or jumped. Or been pushed. No one was ever sure. Some people said she'd probably committed suicide. A few believed it had been an accident. Many pointed the finger at her lover. They'd been at his private island in the Keys, after all, and every other person with them on that trip said the last they'd seen her she'd been with Reeve.

Reeve had never been one to address rumors or accusations of any kind, and this occasion was no different. He didn't release a statement. He shared his story with no one. Every reporter that attempted to get an interview was denied. The police claimed they'd questioned him and declared he wasn't a suspect in the incident, but when no one was charged at all, people weren't happy. It was Missy's fans that began the public attacks against Reeve, flocking to social media to proclaim him a murderer and a liar. Soon others joined the cause. There were all sorts of people ready to hate a man like Reeve. Business opponents. Middle-class citizens who felt that the rich were inherently evil. Conspiracy theorists who were sure Reeve had paid off the police. Members of the Christian right who were more than happy to crucify a man who lived such a tawdry life.

Reeve publicly ignored these accusations as easily as he'd ignored any others in his life. It wasn't as if the claims would turn into anything. As far as the law was concerned, Reeve Sallis was innocent. A good part of the nation's people, however, believed he was just another rich man who had used his money and power to get away with his crime.

I'd never had an opinion on the matter. Even after Amber went missing, I'd refused to take Missy's death into consideration. There was no proof that it had been anything but an accident. I needed tangibles, not hearsay.

"Missy's up there?" Lucy asked. "Huh, I thought I'd gotten all the pictures of her taken down."

I turned toward her. "Why? Did he ask you to?" The answer didn't matter, I realized after I'd asked. It wouldn't tell me if he'd done it or not.

Lucy shook her head. "Oh, no. Not him. But there's too many . . . you know. Her photos just beg for people to say things and that girl's had enough of that already. Let the dead rest, I say."

"Of course. That's the right thing to do." I debated whether or not I should do the same and let the subject go.

But I couldn't. I hadn't been interested in her before, but this was an opportunity to learn more and I might not have it again. "Do people—guests, I mean—ever say anything about him"—I nodded at the picture of Reeve—"and her?"

"You mean do they call him a murderer? Oh, yes. Not as much as they did. But sometimes." Unlike Greg, Lucy didn't seem at all cautious about what she said, which surprised me. Though the cantina wasn't very crowded, there were still ears that could overhear.

If she wasn't worried, neither was I. "Do you think it was really an accident?" It was only slightly more polite than the question I wanted to ask, which was, *Do you think he did it?*

She looked as if she might be offended even with my nicer version, but then she said, "Hell, I don't know. Probably. If anyone could get away with it, he could. But then again, that girl was wild. For that matter, so was he a little back then. More so than now, anyway. They partied a lot. Accidents happen easier when you're not being responsible, if you know what I mean. I suppose I wouldn't be surprised if I found out he did or he didn't. Though he never did really grieve for her. Not around here, anyway."

Lucy waved her hand, snapping out of her memories. "But whatever happened, the resort doesn't need all the talk that could be stirred up with the picture. Would you mind handing that frame to me? I'll put another picture in its place. I've got some other snapshots somewhere around here from that night."

I took the frame off the wall and gave it to her as I sat back on my stool. "You've been here awhile, then." As long as Lucy was feeling chatty, I had other questions I wanted to ask. "Did you ever meet his other women? The one he dated last summer, for example? Amber Pries?"

"Ms. Pries? She came in here a few times." The bartender peeled the notches back from around the back mat of the frame as she spoke. "I never talked to her much personally except to take her drink order. She was another wild one. Liked to drink. I'm sure she liked doing other things as well. Especially liked to flirt with the boys, even when she was here with Mr. Sallis."

"I bet he didn't like that." It was typical Amber. The men she'd usually paired up with generally liked how social she was. Enjoyed that she was so willing to be shared.

But I didn't need to be told how Reeve felt about it and I hated the part of me that jotted that reason down as a possible motive.

"No. He didn't like it at all. They'd fight about it some-times in here. But he was real fond of that one so I think he would have put up with anything from her. When he came back last fall without her, he definitely seemed more somber. I wouldn't be surprised if the girl messed around in front of him one too many times, and he finally broke it off."

Or worse.

No, I couldn't think that. Even if it did give Reeve rea-son, it didn't mean he'd . . . *hurt* her. Did it?

"That's quite interesting," I said when Lucy seemed to be looking for an acknowledgment of her statement.

She gawked at me for a second. "You know, I just fig-ured out who you remind me of. Your voice. You sound just like that computer in that sitcom, *NextGen*."

For a brief moment I considered admitting the truth, considered delivering the "user error" line I knew she was wanting, but ended up delivering my usual response—a smile and, "I get that a lot." Even without my current dark thoughts, I didn't love dealing with fans.

Her expression fell ever so slightly. "Fun to be a celebrity sound-alike though. Such a great show." Her eye caught on a customer flagging her down at the bar. "Excuse me a minute." She set down the photo, now out of the frame, and left to attend to the patron.

I took a sip of my wine and picked up the picture ab-sentmindedly. It had been bigger than the matte. Now, un-framed, I saw the whole picture. And in the part outside the three-inch square, the part that had been hidden when it was on the wall, was another familiar face.

My pulse quickened as I glanced down the counter to make sure the bartender was occupied. Careful to not at-tract any attention, I dropped the picture into my bag. I left a fifty to cover my tab and slipped out.

Back at my room, I pulled the picture from my bag and

studied it again. Then I compared it to the one I had on my phone that Joe had sent a few weeks before. Without a doubt, the man beside Reeve in both pictures was the same—Michelis Vilanakis. The two together on one occasion was easy to dismiss as coincidence. They were important people at the same function. No big deal. But for them to be together twice, and at an event as personal as Reeve's birthday party . . . I had to accept that the two absolutely knew each other.

So what exactly was Reeve's connection to the Greek mob boss? They both had a bit of a playboy reputation, but Vilanakis was at least two decades older than Reeve. If they were friends, they made an odd pair. Business associates seemed more likely. And if Reeve was doing business with Vilanakis, it meant Reeve was doing business with the mob.

I sank down on the edge of my bed and tried to decide how that information made me feel. It *should* have made me feel scared. Cautious. And it did.

But also it didn't. Because it didn't change anything in regard to Amber's disappearance. And it didn't make Reeve someone different than the man I'd already met. A man who was powerful with or without mafia ties. A man who commanded as easily as he charmed. A man who had put his hands on my body, had touched me on his terms, had excited me and turned me on while he'd made a fool of me.

Dammit, why did I come on so strong?

I rolled my shoulders, trying to loosen the rocks that had taken residence there, while I lamented my situation. Nothing I'd learned today made up for what I would have learned if I hadn't fucked up my original plan to get close to Reeve. I was disappointed to the point of heartbreak.

I fell back on the bed and curled myself into a ball. *Tomorrow,* I tried to tell myself, but didn't find it as soothing as I had the night before. At least tomorrow I was getting a massage. That was something to look forward to.

CHAPTER

6

The first time I shared a man with Amber had been on my seventeenth birthday.

She'd been hanging around the neighborhood for the better part of the six months before that, and we'd become friends. We'd had the same taste in food and music and movies and, unlike the other girls we'd known, we both preferred a line of coke to a bowl of weed. "Champagne taste," Amber would say. "That's us."

Though we were the same age, our lives had been very different. I'd gone to school during the day, trying to pretend that my grades were salvageable as she'd watched the Home Shopping Network and ate Cheetos on the neighbor's couch. Amber had dropped out of high school, and since she'd also run away from home, no one was pushing her to go, while graduation was the one thing my mother demanded of me.

I'd hated everything back then. School. My mother. My neighborhood. My body. Everything but Amber. She'd been fun. Sassy. Sexy. She was electric and electrifying and everything I wanted to be. And she cared for me. Maybe even loved me. If I had gone to a shrink they probably would have said that was why I latched on to her—that I thought of her as the mother mine had never been. I knew how screwed up everything seemed. But who could ever know why a person fell for another? I only knew that I had been dull and dim and that Amber made me less so.

She'd also had things I didn't. Things that money bought. The clothes she wore were designer, her nails were always done. She'd lowered her panties once to show me her Brazilian. Whenever I'd asked how she paid for things, she'd always answered simply, "My uncle." Even as we'd grown closer to each other that was all she'd tell me about the mysterious relative.

"For your birthday," she'd said two days before, "I've got a surprise. Plan to spend the weekend with me."

So that Friday, I slipped out of school early and met Amber at the bus station where she purchased two tickets to Santa Monica. Though I couldn't get her to give me even a hint as to where we were going or what we were doing, I spent the two-hour bus ride buzzing with excitement. Whatever Amber had in mind, I knew without a doubt that this trip would be the beginning of the next phase of my life. I was ready. I was so ready.

Outside the station in Santa Monica, Amber bummed a smoke off a street musician and I scanned the street, taking in the sights of a place I'd never been. A red convertible parked nearby caught my attention—more specifically, the man leaning against it. He was older, maybe as old as my mother, but attractive. Not because he was all that good-looking, exactly—though his body was definitely fit and trim—but because of what he exuded. Confidence. Assurance. Money. He drew my attention, and in the way that a restless, sexually charged young girl often did, I found myself wondering about him. What it would be like to kiss a man like him. What it would feel like to be beneath him. I'd had plenty of sex before. With boys from school. I'd yet to meet one who knew what he was doing, and though I would never have admitted it out loud, I was dying for it, thoughts of it never far from my mind.

When Amber followed the line of my sight, she dropped her cigarette with a squeal and exclaimed, "There he is, Em! Come on."

"There who is?" I asked as she tugged me toward the very man I'd been staring at.

"My uncle!" After throwing her duffle bag into the backseat, she jumped into the man's arms, wrapping her legs around his waist. Then she proceeded to make out with him like I'd done on more than one occasion with the boys under the bleachers at school. Never out on a public street. Never with a man who had to shave every day.

When they had finished their display and Amber was back on her feet again, she made introductions. "Rob this is Emily. Em, Rob."

He may have said something to me. I didn't really know because I'd been too busy staring at her, my jaw gaping.

"Oh, Emily, he's not really my uncle," she told me as she jumped into the passenger seat. "Get in."

She'd misread the cause of my surprise. I grinned— only one of the many times I'd grin that day—and climbed in the backseat. If Amber hadn't been the coolest person I'd ever met before that moment, she'd certainly proven herself now.

Rob took us to a fancy restaurant and fed us fancy food and snuck us fancy expensive champagne. Though his hands were never far from Amber's body, he didn't leave me out of the conversation, asking me what I thought of the oysters, if I knew that they were an aphrodisiac, if I knew what that word even meant. He was very nice. Interesting and witty. Sexy. The way he touched my friend, the way

I caught him looking at me in my baggy T-shirt and loose jeans, as if he could see what they hid. As if he were interested.

In a bathroom stall, Amber laid out a line of coke on her pocket mirror. "Happy Birthday from Rob," she'd said, holding up the bag of white powder. "He's married so I only see him when he can get away from her for the week-end. Then we meet here. His other house is in Riverside. He likes you, you know."

So many questions I wanted to ask—how had she met him? Why hadn't she told me? Wasn't their age difference a problem legally? And did she say *wife*?

But all those thoughts were eclipsed by the compliment from a deeply attractive man. "I like him too," I'd said, wondering if that was weird to say about my friend's boy-friend, or whatever he was. Wondering more if it was weird that she'd said it to me in the first place.

Then the coke kicked in and I didn't wonder much about anything after that.

Later, he'd taken us back to his house, a gorgeous Mediterranean-style home with floor-to-ceiling windows that gave a panoramic view of the bay. Rob encouraged us to change into something more comfortable so we'd slipped upstairs to the master bathroom where Amber donned a pair of boy shorts and a tank. All I had to wear was another boring T-shirt, so Amber loaned me one of her tanks and then found a pair of boxers from one of Rob's drawers.

"He won't mind?" I asked, already putting them on.

She laughed. "No. He definitely won't mind."

Back downstairs Rob waited for us with his shirt un-buttoned and his feet bare. Over and over, I found my eyes pulled to skate the naked skin of his chest and the trail of hair that led beneath the band of his jeans. Over and over,

I felt his eyes skim the abundant curves of my breasts pressing at the thin material of my shirt.

He served us more champagne and more coke. When we turned giggly and giddy, he pulled out his video camera. "Get in close together," he said. Amber moved close to me on the couch, really close, throwing her arm around my shoulder. "Yeah, just like that." He moved in with the lens, kneeling down on the floor in front of us. "Can you touch each other? Amber, put your hand on Emily's gorgeous tits."

My body zinged from his praise. Amber had tried to encourage me to flaunt the girls before. She had a smaller chest and frequently told me how jealous she was of my DD cups, but all I'd ever felt about my boobs was embarrassed and self-conscious. Until then. Until a man out of my league said that they were gorgeous and my best friend put her hand on one. My nipples hardened as Amber squeezed.

"Damn, Emily. You like that, don't you? Your body says you do." Rob's voice was gritty. Tight. "Now, kiss each other."

I hesitated for only a second, but when Amber's mouth met mine, I'd been ready. It was strange and different— softer and wetter than the kisses I'd had before. The actual kissing didn't turn me on the way that Rob groaning and rubbing at the crotch of his jeans did. It was my first taste of the power of sexuality. I could do that to someone. I could bring a strong, self-assured man to his knees. Where a similar realization might overwhelm me in other circumstances, having my best friend at my side only bolstered my new confidence. It was singularly the most electrifying moment of my existence.

Amber pulled away suddenly. "I have to pee," she announced. She wavered as she headed to the bathroom, but she glanced back over her shoulder before disappearing around the corner and winked. At me or at Rob, I wasn't sure.

Rob put the camera down and looked at me with clouded eyes. Then he took Amber's place on the couch next to me. His hand drew lazy circles on my knee, sending my pulse skyrocketing. "You look really good in my boxers," he said as his fingers drew up my thigh. "I bet you look really good out of them too."

Goose bumps scattered along my skin and I stiffened slightly. Not because he scared me, because he didn't. But the way he made me feel scared me, and that he was Amber's boyfriend.

"Have you ever been with a man?" he asked, his touch nearing the hem of my shorts—*his* shorts.

"I'm not a virgin." I didn't think it was what he was asking, but I didn't know what else to say.

He leaned in closer and grazed his teeth along my collarbone. "But have you been with someone who knows what to do with his cock? Have you been with someone who can make you come?"

I shivered. Did he know? Was it obvious how much I yearned for a more grown-up sexual experience?

He moved in to kiss me, and I forced myself to pull away. My eyes glanced toward the hallway. "Amber."

Rob paused but he didn't retreat. "You know why Amber brought you here, don't you?" His thumb caressed my lower lip as his other hand found the elastic ribbing of my underwear.

My hips instinctively bucked up, begging for him to touch me there, touch me where he was so close to touching me.

"She brought you here for me."

I should have been repulsed. I should have been terrified. I should have been pissed at my friend for luring me out on the pretense of giving me a birthday present when she really only meant to bring me as a gift for her pervert of an "uncle."

But I didn't feel that at all. I felt exactly the opposite. Beautiful. Wanted. Special enough for Amber to be okay with sharing her lover with me. Special enough that she'd known I would be a prize.

It was enough. I was sold. I was ready to strip off all of my clothes and let Rob do whatever he wanted to my body.

Except he had more to offer. "What do you want, Emily?" His fingers slipped under my panties and through the wet mess of curls to find my clit. I hadn't been touched there by anyone but myself. I gasped at the pressure of his thumb against the sensitive nerve center, certain I'd explode.

And he'd asked me a question. . . . How was I supposed to answer? All that came out was a breathy, "Please."

"I'll give it to you," Rob said between kisses along my jaw. "Whatever it is. Amber likes to be pampered. Spa trips. Beauty salons. Is that what you want?" The strokes against my clit grew more intense while a finger reached down to dip into my entrance. "Or what about clothing? I'd prefer to see you in items that fit you better. Showed off this beautiful body of yours." He bent to suck my nipple into his mouth through the tank top. "Tomorrow we'll go pick out a whole new wardrobe. Does that sound good?"

"Yes." I would have said yes to anything he offered at that point. Yes to what he was doing. Yes to how he was making me feel.

Rob took it as the green light. As soon as I'd gotten the word out, his lips were on mine. His tongue fucked my mouth like his fingers fucked my cunt. When I came, it was fast and intense and amazing.

That was just the beginning.

Amber joined us eventually and we played like that all

night long, all weekend, taking turns kissing and petting and stroking and making each other come. It was hot and naughty and like nothing I'd ever imagined sex could be. And maybe it was wrong. Because Rob was married. Because Amber and I were half his age. Because Amber and I were *under*age. Because Rob bought us presents in exchange for letting him stick his cock into our pussies and our mouths.

But as far as I was concerned, it was the first time anything in my life had ever felt right. Though the full potential of my newfound sexuality wouldn't manifest until later, I already knew that this would be my way out. Who cared if my grades wouldn't get me into college? Who needed a degree when I had the power of my body? Who needed a job when I could be taken care of by a man?

And how much better that my best friend was with me through it all?

CHAPTER

7

I sat forward, rubbed my forehead, and stared at the clipboard in my lap. I hated intake forms. They were such an awful part of spa visits that I often wondered if the point of it was to get you tense so that the massage would seem extra relaxing. But maybe not everyone hated them as much as I did. While I filled them out honestly at doctors' offices, I couldn't ever figure out why half the information was necessary for someone to simply rub lotion into your skin.

The new-client paperwork at Reeve's spa was just as irritating. Stating that I was on birth control was okay, I supposed, but other questions made me cringe. *Have you ever been pregnant? Have you ever done illegal drugs? Which ones?* As I often did when I felt the answers weren't pertinent, I lied.

"I did my best," I said as I handed the clipboard to the masseur who called me back.

"I'm sure you did fine, Ms. Wayborn. I'm Geoffrey and I'll be attending to you today." He spoke with an affected accent that emanated the snobbery of a luxury spa. Or of a flaming homosexual. I didn't really care either way. Geoffrey looked like a man with strong hands and that's all that mattered to the knots in my back. "Do you have a specific area you'd like to focus on today?"

"No. Everywhere." I couldn't remember the last time I'd felt truly relaxed. Even now I couldn't let go of the source of my tension. I asked the question I was there to ask, the one I knew I probably shouldn't. "How long have you worked here, Geoffrey?"

He proceeded to give me his résumé, probably thinking my reason for asking was due to a lack of confidence in his skills. I heard very little after he'd said he'd been at Reeve's spa for four years.

"Last summer—did you ever see a client named Amber Pries?" Had she been in this very room? Had Geoffrey been her masseur?

Geoffrey's expression clouded. "I'm sorry, Ms. Wayborn. Client/therapist privilege prevents me from sharing that information."

"Of course. I wasn't thinking." I probably should have slipped him a hundred. Maybe it wasn't too late. Though, what could he know? The spa experience wasn't designed for chatting. If Geoffrey had worked on Amber, he would have seen her body but what could he tell me that would be useful about that?

"If there are no other questions . . . ?"

I considered leaving. I considered asking for another masseur. I considered trying harder to get something more from Geoffrey, like a key to the file room. But I was tired of dead ends and the massage sounded good. God knew I needed one. "Nope. I'm ready."

"Well, then. Get undressed to the level you're comfortable. Then lie on the table under the sheet, chest down, face in the cradle. I'll be back in a few minutes."

Having been to plenty of spas in my lifetime, I knew the drill. I stripped completely, took my place on the table, and closed my eyes.

Then, as they always did when I had a silent moment, my thoughts went to Amber. Where was she now? Was she better than how I left her or worse? Did she forgive me in the end? Did she ever realize I needed forgiving?

With no warning knock, the door opened and I heard Geoffrey come in. He didn't say anything as he began, first running a light path up my spine from my ass to my neck with the palm of his hand. I always liked that part of a massage—the initial touch. The hello. This hello was firmer than others and dared to go lower on my behind. It was confident and in charge, just like I'd expect from a Sallis spa. Despite feeling off-balance the last few days, this simple action helped me regroup. And finally I began to relax.

Geoffrey pulled down the sheet to my waist, and though the cool air sent goose bumps parading on my skin, I was soon warm from the lotion and the rhythm of his hands. He continued to work my back and shoulders for long, silent minutes, loosening the tightest knots, smoothing out the rocks in between my ribs. Then he moved to my arms, then legs, magically relieving the tension in first one limb, then another.

He's good, I thought as my mind went empty of everything but where I was. *This is exactly what I needed.* Then I began to drift.

Thoughts returned, hazy, dreamlike. The touch of my masseur morphed into touches from the past. Touches from Amber and Rob. Then Amber and Reeve. Then just Reeve. His caress became erotic, forceful. He kissed me—hard—and it felt like a scene I'd been in before, except different. False. Because I liked it and I wasn't supposed to. Because he was supposed to be awful and mean. He was supposed to hurt me. I pushed away, confused, and saw Amber at the door. Then came familiar words, words that had stained themselves into my memory. *"You fucking bitch. You knew I loved him, you fucking bitch."*

"No," I tried to say, as I always did in response. *"I didn't. He did this."* When I finally got it out, though, it was wrong. Because I didn't deny. I didn't refute. *"Yes,"* I said. *"Yes."*

Reeve chuckled through the fog. "Good dream?"

Had I said something? *Yes.* I'd said *yes.*

Then he said, "Time to turn over."

I blinked, rousing from my sleep. Lifting my head, I found the sheet held in the air above me. It blocked Reeve's face. He wanted me to change sides, I realized. He was covering me so that I could make the shift without being exposed.

And it's not Reeve, silly. It's Geoffrey, I said to myself, scooting down so my head wasn't lying on the face cradle.

Except when he let the sheet fall again, it actually was Reeve's face that stood above me. What the fuck? When the hell had he come in?

"Uh, hi." I sat up suddenly, clutching the sheet to me, disoriented from my dream. When had Geoffrey gone? Had I slept longer than I thought? Spoken in my sleep? How embarrassing. I wiped my mouth, hoping I wasn't drooling.

Reeve smiled in that devilish way he often did—the way that made the insides of my thighs tingle. "Hello. Did you enjoy your nap?"

"I enjoyed the massage *before* the nap. Geoffrey is really—" I cut myself off, noticing Reeve was wearing suit pants and a dress shirt, but no jacket. His sleeves were unbuttoned and rolled up to his elbows, and his tie was missing. Clarity bolted through me. "That was you the whole time, wasn't it?"

He answered with a question that was all the affirmation I needed. "Ready to go on?"

"Sure." It was still the dream. It had to be. I lay back on the table and closed my eyes.

The sheet was tucked around my upper thigh, exposing my leg. I heard the pump of the lotion dispenser. Reeve picked up my foot and began rubbing at my ankle, working his way down to the sole. At my heel, he used just his thumbs, alternating them up and down with medium pressure.

I fought against the moan that threatened. It felt good. So good. *Too* good.

Too good to be a dream.

Fuck, this *wasn't* a dream. My eyes flew open. Peering down at him, I found him watching me with a satisfied grin. As if he'd been waiting for my gaze to meet his. Or as if he'd been watching my expression.

I propped myself up with my elbows. It really *was* Reeve. He *really* was there. "I'm sorry. I'm sort of out of it."

"I hadn't noticed." His face was somber, and I couldn't decide if he was teasing or not.

Mostly, I couldn't decide why he was there in the first place. Reeve wasn't a man to do things without motive. Was this a friendly surprise? Was this his way of making the first move that he insisted he always did?

I hoped it was. Because that would mean I hadn't fucked up after all. That would mean that plan A was back on. It would mean that there could be more between Reeve and I, and that was increasingly becoming very important to me.

But after the way he'd left me the night of our date, I was almost sure that a friendly surprise was wishful thinking. And something about his tone felt icy. Ominous. Or was that my imagination, fueled by cobwebs remaining from my dream?

"You're thinking too much," Reeve chided, as if he could read my mind. "Lay down. Let your mind go."

His eyes left mine to concentrate on his hands. He moved up to my calf now, digging into the sensitive knots with a walk of his knuckles. His touch was so specific, so concentrated. So in tune with what I needed.

I resigned myself to it and lay back down. But there was no way I could let my mind go again. Not now. There was too much tension between Reeve and me, and as he kneaded and stroked me into a listless puddle, the tension between us wound tighter. It was a much different experience than it had been when I'd thought it was Geoffrey hovering over me. Now the massage didn't just feel good, it felt sensual. Now the firm pressure from Reeve's hands wasn't just good technique, it was intimate. Now the sheet didn't seem modest, it seemed skimpy. Now I wasn't relaxed, I was aroused.

Especially as his hands got higher. And higher. When he bent my knee. When his kneading met the muscles of my hips. When his fingers worked the inside of my thigh, up, up, the tips brushing the outer lips of my pussy.

Heat boiled in my veins. Want. Need. It took every ounce of my strength not to fidget and squirm. Everything not to beg for him to . . . what? More. That was all I could articulate. Just, more.

To keep myself centered, I watched him intently as he invaded the landscape of my body. He was focused. Restrained. Professional, when this wasn't even his job. Controlled. Always controlled.

But his quiet intensity gave him away. I saw the effort it took. Saw the desire cloud his features. Saw his eyes sweep along my skin. I stopped wondering what this was and started wondering what it could be.

He tugged at the sheet and I hoped. But he merely

covered my leg and moved to repeat the process on the other side.

Except this time, he spoke. "I hope you're nice and relaxed, Emily. Because we need to have a chat."

Apprehension fluttered in my belly. Chatting was definitely not the direction I wanted to go in from here. Whatever he had to say, I couldn't possibly listen. I was too agitated.

But without him spelling it out, I knew those were the terms of this arrangement. He'd touch me—in his way. And I'd listen, whether I wanted to or not.

So I propped myself up again and gave him as much of my attention as I could.

"It's interesting," he said, his thumbs doing that amazing thing on the bottom of my foot, "how people respond to you when they believe you've gotten away with murder."

My stomach dropped. No speech that started with murder had a happy ending.

"Most people are frightened of you," he said as his hand stroked up my shin. "They pull their business. They stop attending your events. They certainly won't let themselves be seen with you. It's not really anything to fret over, losing those connections. You don't want cowards in your court. Good riddance to them."

"I'm not a coward," I managed to say defensively. Though I wasn't sure why I was defending myself. Or why I was anxious that he might mean good riddance to me when that was probably exactly what I should be wishing he meant.

He glanced up at me, amusement in his features. "No, you're not. You're not scared. Or you're not scared enough."

I barely fought the shiver that begged to stutter through my body. It was a menacing statement, and I wanted to deny it as well. Tell him that I was definitely scared enough.

But what the hell did that mean, anyway? Considering how turned on I was despite everything I'd learned about him, still turned on despite the foreboding in his tone, well, maybe he had a point. I really wasn't scared enough.

The amusement transformed to what looked more like awe. Then his attention fell back to my leg and I couldn't see his face well enough to read him. But after he pushed my ankle back so that my knee bent, his touch changed. A single finger traced the line of my inner thigh. Softly. Sweetly. Just as he got to where I so wanted him to go, he abruptly stopped. One second passed. Two.

Then he resumed the firm pressure from before, re-claiming his restraint. For now.

I could wait.

His speech continued, his voice firm, icy. "There are other people, too. Those that respect you. They aren't nec-essarily your friends, because they're also scared—probably even more so than those who keep their distance. They con-tinue their financial support of your endeavors. They invite you to their parties. Their children's weddings. They look out for you. Because, you see, they're afraid that if they don't . . . well . . ."

My heart hammered in my ears. Suddenly I was feeling vulnerable in a way that had nothing to do with my nudity and everything to do with the frailty of my small frame compared to the strength of his much larger one.

As if to prove that point, Reeve increased the pressure of his kneading, digging his fingers into the flesh of my thigh with a bite that sang and stung. "It's a very intense form of power, actually. Much like having money. I'm sure you've gotten a taste of that with the recent success of your show. Imagine that but multiplied by a billion."

"Mm-hmm," I said, a response that served as an answer though it was mostly an involuntary reaction to his hands.

He'd reached the top of my limb again. Like before, the tips of his fingers brushed against my folds.

Goddamnit, I was wet. And trembling. And overwrought with anticipation. This time, would he let his touch wander farther up? *In?*

His hands left me. He pushed my leg down, pulled the sheet back over my leg and pinned me with narrowed eyes. "It's also not unlike the power of being a very attractive person. Another privilege that you understand." He scanned the length of my body, the sheet still a barrier between us, and let out an audible breath. "I imagine you must understand it very well indeed."

It was an accusation. The grit in his voice and the weight of his stare said so. Fucker. Whatever hopes I'd had for this whole scene of his, it was clear now that his intent was not friendly. Punishing, more like. I still wasn't sure for what exactly. For being in his pool. For using my beauty to draw his interest. For coming on to him without his permission. I'd thought his humiliating body search had been all the reprimand I was getting. Guess I'd been wrong.

My eyes fell. However, a glance at his crotch gave me the slightest smidgeon of satisfaction. He was unmistakably hard. He might be punishing me, but he was punishing himself too.

Reeve headed toward the door, and I feared suddenly he was leaving. Instead he grabbed the stool in the corner and brought it back with him to set above my head. I kept my eyes down. Not closed, but lids lowered because if I looked anywhere but toward my feet, I could see him—he was *that* close—and it was intimidating. Why had he sat, anyway? Why give up the ability to tower over me? Though when he'd stood, he felt less menacing. It was this new position that made me feel the most vulnerable.

Every one of my senses magnified as I tried not to panic.

My mouth tasted like iron, as though I'd bitten my tongue. Maybe I had. The stool creaked—he'd moved. Why? The pump of the dispenser sounded. Then his hands were on me again, massaging my shoulders in small firm circles of his fingertips. Like before, his pressure was perfect, his attention to my knots, precise.

I closed my eyes.

After several long minutes of silence, he spoke again. "There's one more group." His voice was low. Soothing. "They're small and they seem to be . . . how do I put it? *Attracted,* that's it. They're attracted to the idea of danger. The mystery of it. The intrigue. It's glamorous to them. I encounter them often." His hands pushed lower, to the muscles above my breasts. "They want to friend you. They want to fuck you. They want to be fucked by you."

My eyes flew open and I tilted my head back to see him better. *You think that's me?* I wanted to say. *You think I'm attracted to you because I think you're dangerous?*

But I said nothing. Because possibly he was right.

Though I was looking at him, his eyes remained on his hands. They trailed together up my sternum to the hollow of my throat, where his touch lingered and I wondered if he could feel the rapid beat of my heart.

When his fingers moved again, they separated outward to slowly glide up the sides of my neck. Every nerve ending in my body whirred with terror. I was still with fear.

"I assure you, Emily, that it's not nearly as romantic as it all seems." His voice was so hushed and the blood thrumming in my ears so loud that I had to strain to hear him now. "It's a façade. It's the power that attracts you. The idea of violence. Not the actual act." His hands splayed to lightly cup the sides of my throat. His touch barely there. Tickling at my skin.

Yet I knew . . . God, he could break me. He could squeeze and that would be all.

"In reality, Emily, murder is messy and final. And it hurts."

My teeth clenched together. Every muscle in my body went rigid. I wasn't prepared for this. Finally, I was afraid.

In a sudden movement, he swept his hands back down over my shoulders and I let out a heavy sigh of relief.

Then he began the rhythmic kneading again. His fingers pressed painfully into my tissues causing tears to gather in my eyes. Though it hurt, I preferred it to the soft touch at my throat.

"You asked around about me, Emily," he said, and again the air left my lungs. This was my crime, I realized. For the second time, I'd fucked up. Fucked up big. Had I really thought that my questions would go unnoticed? Had I really thought Reeve let *anything* go unnoticed? "That didn't make me happy."

I couldn't help it—I whimpered.

"Aw, Emily. Shh." He ran a hand over my hair, petting me. Maybe it was supposed to be soothing but I guessed he meant it to be as chilling as it was. "I understand, beautiful girl. I can't blame you for wanting to find out about the women I've been with. It's smart. You want to know if you could fit in where they did. Want to know if you compare. Want to know why they are no longer with me. If it's because I really am as dangerous as people say. That's it, right?"

I nodded, my throat too tight to speak.

"I need to hear it, Emily. That's why you were asking, wasn't it?"

My yes came out on another whimper, but he accepted it. "Good." He ran the tips of his fingers around the edge of my face from my chin to my forehead, stopping to massage my temples. "The problem with men who are actually a threat, though, Emily, is that you don't ever find out how unsafe they are until it's too late."

I shuddered. But even though my breathing was now laced with soft sobs and my lip was trembling, I was still undeniably aroused.

I hated him, I decided. I hated him and I hated me.

Reeve's hands fell audibly into his lap. "Tell you what. Since you were so curious, I'll give you this: each relationship I've had has ended for a reason. There's no need for you to know any more than that."

If he were going to kill me, I thought, *he wouldn't say that. He'd tell me everything. Right?* It wasn't a bet I'd put money on, but I was clinging to it.

He leaned his face down toward mine and rested the bridge of his nose on my cheek. A tear slipped down my face as he whispered at my ear. "As for whether or not you compare—yes, Emily. You are one of very few women who actually do."

He nipped my lobe, sending a buzz of fear/excitement to scatter through my already trembling nerves.

Abruptly, he stood and smiled. Fucking bastard had the nerve to flash me his devilish grin. "Nice chat, Emily. I think this went well, don't you?"

Thankfully he didn't press me for an answer because I refused. I was too frightened. Too pissed. He'd never intended to hurt me, just intimidate me. And he got off on it. And that made him a goddamn asshole.

He started to leave and I held as still as I could, waiting for the sound of the door to shut so I could get up, get dressed, and get the fuck out of there.

But before I heard it, he spoke again. "Oh, and I think you made a good choice not to meet up with my former pool boy last night. As his title implies, he's just a child. What you're looking for requires a man."

That was it. I was furious. He'd fucked with me. He'd scared me. He'd belittled and chided. Now he'd implied he was the only person who could give me what I need, yet he'd made sure I knew he was completely off limits. His weakness was me. He wanted me and he hated that maybe as much as I hated him.

I sat up and twisted toward him, purposefully letting the sheet fall around my waist. "You sound jealous, Reeve."

He turned back to me, his eyes sparking at the sight of my naked torso. His expression was hot and primitive, drawing my nipples out to sharp points. He placed his hand over the thick bulge at the front of his pants and stroked himself. "Maybe I am jealous," he said, his voice strained. "But I've learned from experience not to let jealousy inform my actions."

With his hand still pressed against his cock, he delivered one last statement. "Leave my resort, Ms. Wayborn." Then he was gone.

I let out an exasperated groan.

Then, I left too.

I dressed as fast as I could and hurried back to my room where I packed in a flurry. Within an hour after leaving my massage, I was checked out of the hotel and on my way home. Done. I was done with him. The whole thing had been a bad idea. The man was a psycho. A fucking manipulator.

For the entire two-hour drive back to Hollywood, though, as well as the days that followed, Reeve's words stayed with me, haunting me as effectively as Amber did. He'd been warning me, yes. Proving he was a threat. Making sure I knew who he was and what he could do. And it worked—I was thoroughly convinced.

But I couldn't stop remembering that look in his eyes— the one that wanted to devour me. The one that said his control was on a thread. That blazed as he stroked himself through his pants.

He'd threatened me, but that look made me wish I'd called his bluff.

CHAPTER

8

The backstage assistant smiled in recognition when she spotted me. She was dressed in a black, long-sleeve shirt and black jeans and looked out of place next to all the stars decked in evening wear. Leaning forward, she covered the mike of her headset and whispered, "Ms. Wayborn, you're up in ten."

I couldn't hear her over the applause in the background but her lips were easy to read. In case I had any doubt, she held all ten fingers up.

"Thanks." I nodded then turned to check my lipstick in the backstage mirror and tried not to vomit. Live performances scared the crap out of me. I preferred a camera, a clapboard, and the option to do over.

For the fifteenth time in as many minutes, I wished I'd declined the invitation to present an award. My agent had thought it would be good for exposure, as did our show's publicist. The only reason they'd asked me in the first place was because Ty Macy, my costar in *NextGen,* was up for Best Actor in a Comedy Series. Ty had decided early on that the SAG Awards weren't worth his time even though he was a shoo-in for the win. So they'd chosen me to present it so that, if he won, I could also accept his award on his behalf and not waste time with climbing out of my chair and approaching the stage.

Less time meant less money spent from the budget. Hollywood was all about keeping as much in the producers' pockets as possible. I was economical. Woohoo for me.

I was also crabby. And restless. While I'd expected to easily get back in the rhythm of filming, I'd been on the set for two weeks and it hadn't happened. I blamed it on Amber—still missing, still occupying my mind. I refused to credit Reeve Sallis for my distraction. The fact that I'd been counting the days since I'd left his resort—nineteen to be precise—didn't mean anything either. That was simply the number of days since I'd abandoned my original Find Amber plan. That's why I knew the count.

Of course, I didn't have a new plan yet. Which was another reason I was in such a perma bad mood.

"Your forehead wrinkles when you're pissy." Amber had told me that more than once during our friendship, and sure enough I saw the crease now. Taking a deep breath, I forced my shoulders back and my face to relax. I swept another coat of gloss over my lips and stuffed the tube into the pocket of my designer dress—the absolute best thing about the evening. Pockets had been my only requirement for the evening's apparel. I hated being tied to a purse.

As I put my hand in, I felt my phone buzz. I didn't intend to answer it, just see who was calling. But it was Joe.

"She was spotted," he said without a hello.

It took a few seconds to register the meaning of his words. "You found Amber?" I was so excited, I forgot to hush my voice.

The stage assistant glared at me with a finger pressed

to her lips. I mouthed an apology and plugged an ear so I could hear Joe better over the show in the background.

"No, I haven't found her. But she was spotted. Sallis is off the hook."

Electricity pricked at the back of my neck but I refrained from getting my hopes up without more information. I stepped farther back into the wing so I wouldn't disturb anyone. "What does that mean exactly? Spotted by who?"

"Don't know. Someone texted me a picture. She's standing in a casino in Colorado and she looks good. The photo is date stamped and there's a sign in the background that mentions a Halloween Slot Fest. I'll send it to you when we're off the phone."

"Halloween." I went through the dates in my head. We'd guessed Amber's disappearance had occurred sometime between August and September when Reeve had been seen with another woman. "Could he have gotten back together with Amber in October? Is there a chance we have our timeline wrong?"

"I don't think so." Joe's quick answer told me he'd already been through all these possibilities before calling me. "And Amber's with another guy in this pic."

"What guy?" There was applause again behind me. I glanced back to make sure it wasn't time for my entrance and saw there was still one more presenter before me.

"Don't know who the guy is. Can't see his face. It's not Reeve, though. He wasn't in Colorado at Halloween. He was at a Day of the Dead charity event that Sallis Resorts and the Four Seasons sponsored in Hawaii."

"And you're sure that the picture wasn't doctored to make us think it was taken later than it was?"

Again, Joe's tone was sure. "I'll send the pic to you. You'll see."

Other excuses begged to be spoken, reasons why Reeve couldn't possibly be innocent in Amber's disappearance.

But, really, why did I think that? Because he'd threatened me? Because he'd had a shaky relationship with her? Because I didn't want to stop thinking about him, even if it was only in terms of this case?

It's not him. This is a good thing. "Well, okay then. I guess we can drop the investigation regarding Reeve."

"I've already pulled the resources that were allocated to researching him further. I'll keep a loose eye on him in case something comes up, but this is a pretty good sign. And now you don't need to play amateur Nancy Drew and can drop whatever insane investigation you were doing on your own."

"What are you—?" Except, as soon as I thought about it, I knew exactly what he was referring to. A humiliated blush crept up my neck. "How did you—?"

Joe cut me off. "It's my job, Em. I have a loose tail on the guy. How did you think I wouldn't find out?" He didn't wait for my answer, which was fine because I didn't have one. "And this isn't my job, but I feel I need to tell you that what you did was beyond stupid. Not only did you put yourself in the circle of someone who is very probably a dangerous man, but you didn't tell anyone what you were doing. What would have happened if Sallis had discovered the reason you were at his resort in the first place?"

I wasn't exactly sure Reeve *hadn't* discovered the reason I'd been there. But Joe's question implied that he didn't know the extent of what had happened on my trip, at least. I carefully worded my response so as not to volunteer anything new. "He would have kicked me out," I said.

"Or worse. And who would know where you'd gone missing to?"

The thought had crossed my mind more than once. "Well, you would have, Joe. But, I hear what you're saying. I'm sorry I went to the resort. It was a lapse of judgment. I won't do it again."

"Good. Because you can't count on me to bail you out if you get into trouble. I might not get there in time. Especially if you haven't told me what you're up to. And even if you had, I'm not a match for that man." His frustration with me was evident in the number of words he'd devoted to his scolding, even if it was absent in his tone.

It made me feel guilty. Not guilty enough to stop me from doing something like that again, but he needn't worry about a repeat venture. Reeve had ended that himself.

Another round of applause sounded and I turned to see the stage assistant gesturing to me. There was a commercial break before my presentation, so I knew I had at least another minute. "Joe, I have to go. But I get it. And thank you." Just as I started to say goodbye, I thought of something. "Oh, wait—who did you say sent you the picture?"

"I didn't. Anonymous. I've had a bunch of feelers out though. It probably came from one of them."

"Ah. Okay." If the anonymity didn't bother him, I wouldn't let it bother me. The assistant waved a frenzied hand toward me. "Going now, Joe. Thanks again." I clicked "End" and took my mark at the curtain.

The assistant was visibly relieved that I'd put away my phone. "You have one minute, Ms. Wayborn. I'll count down when we're at ten seconds."

It was only a moment later when another buzz came from my pocket. Knowing it was the photo from Joe, I pulled out my cell and opened the message immediately, angling myself so that the assistant wouldn't get uptight about another peek at my cell.

As it always did when I encountered pictures of Amber, my heart skipped a beat. It was definitely her in the frame. And Joe was right—she looked good. She was only visible from her hips up, and the smirk she wore was distinct, confident.

It was an expression I recognized very well. It was the

same one she gave to Rob the time she saw him after he'd left us and we'd moved on to someone richer, more virile. She gave it to the wife of a New York businessman when she discovered us in her husband's bed. She gave it to me when I lay in the hospital, chilled from shock, bleeding. It was her victory smile. As though she'd won the ten-thousand-dollar jackpot mentioned in the banner above her in the picture—a feat that would please her, but would hardly impress her. It was probably pennies to the man who stood next to her with his arm at her waist. Though the image was cut off, the edge of his suit was clear and the hand he had pressed low at her hip suggested an inti-mate relationship. It was almost fitting that his face was hidden. Didn't matter who he was, anyway. As long as his credit card had a high limit, his name, his features, his per-sonality even, were irrelevant.

Seeing her so smug left a bad taste in my mouth. I was good at ignoring the memories it brought back, but now I felt silly having worried about her for so long. She was ob-viously fine. As always. She didn't need me. She'd never needed me.

My thumb hovered over the reply on the text. I could tell Joe to drop the investigation. Save myself money and frustration.

But Amber's phone message. The safe word. And some-thing else niggling at me—what was it? Something about the picture.

"Ms. Wayborn. Ms. Wayborn!"

I startled at the assistant's prodding. Dammit, I was late for my cue. Dropping my phone in my pocket, I threw back my shoulders and put on a smile before accepting the en-velope from the security rep and walking out to take my place on the stage. My knees were wobbling, but my face gave the impression of confidence. The energy surging from the audience applause told me they bought it.

That was the funny thing about smiles—if you flashed the right one, no one knew there was more going on inside. I couldn't drop an investigation just because I'd seen one picture. There wasn't enough information to know if it told an honest story. Amber appeared just fine. But she always knew which smile was *right*.

"Ty is such an asshole." Chris's voice was low, looking out over the party as he talked to me. "He knew he'd win that award. Not being here was his way of claiming superiority over everyone. He's such an asshole."

"Mm," I sounded in agreement, sipping from my champagne glass, wishing I could have skipped the after party. Usually I did well with fancy occasions, but my mind was too knitted in Amber and the picture and the question of why it had left me so unsettled.

Chris Blakely didn't need me to be *on*, at least. He was as near to a friend as I had these days, and lately we really only saw each other at show biz events. We'd met almost three years before on the shoot of a national commercial for dog food. The whole premise of the ad was ridiculous, but Chris had made the day fun and when it was over I'd let him take me home. Then I'd let him take me to bed. Sometimes after that too, when I'd been lonely and couldn't stand it, I'd call him up and take advantage of the benefits he freely offered.

Besides Chris, I hadn't been with a man in six years. Men were my drug. Staying away from them had been the only way I knew to stay clean. The only way to reinvent myself. Sleeping with Chris had even been a risk. I hadn't learned until after he'd taken me that he wasn't my drug of choice. Lucky for me.

Lucky for him, I still enjoyed an occasional romp in the hay.

Now, he had a fiancée and I had a hit TV show. Casual hookups were off the plate.

"You gave a good speech, though," he said, referring to the acceptance spiel I'd delivered when Ty had, in fact, won the award I'd presented. "Much better than that shithead would have."

"You're just upset that he landed that role and you didn't." Was it shitty that I was glad for that? I had no relationship with the actors on *NextGen*. I could do my thing and go home. If Chris had been cast, it would have been harder to stay detached.

"Damn right, I'm upset. Doesn't change that he's a douche. I'd have done a better job and shown up to receive my accolades. You know what? I'm glad he didn't show." His eyes stroked down my body. "You looked much better giving that speech than he would have too."

"Stop it. Megan's just in the bathroom."

He shrugged, not seeming to care that his future wife could potentially catch him ogling another woman. "You're a wet dream, Em. I don't mind telling you—when I'm not in the mood and Meg is, you're my go-to fantasy."

"God, Chris. Are you sure you aren't the one who's the asshole?" Amber's philosophy had been that men would try to get under a skirt no matter what. *"Might as well charge them for it."* I'd hoped she was simply jaded, but in the years that had passed without her, her point was made more than once.

I lived in Hollywood, though. That did qualify my experiences. The environment was only a step away from a whorehouse on so many levels.

As if to demonstrate my thoughts, Chris leaned in close, whispering in my ear, "Can't help it. You inspire the naughty. You're that kind of beautiful."

I groaned inwardly as I pushed him away. I'd gotten it

my whole life. I'd exploited it, even. But I'd gained some self-esteem in recent years and now the comments and the looks rubbed me in ways they hadn't before. It was shitty to be valued for genetics. It was shitty to be treated as though it were my fault men were horny pigs.

You sure didn't seem to mind it when the remarks and heated glances came from Reeve. The chiding voice in my head sounded more like Amber's than my own. Which made it a hell of a lot easier to tell it to fuck off.

Chris read the disgust on my face. "Too much?"

"Yes."

"Sorry. I'll behave." He studied me, without any sign of desire this time. "Seriously, though, how are you? I was disappointed when you didn't come to our New Year's get-together."

"It would have been weird." When he started to refute, I added, "Besides, I was out of town."

"Nice. Where did you go?"

And now I regretted the admission. Because now I had to tell him. "Just to the Sallis Resort in Palm Springs." And now I was thinking about Reeve, an ache settling low in my stomach. Lower.

"God, I haven't been there in ages."

"You've been, then?" It was meant as small talk. Easy words that didn't require much focus.

"I used to spend a lot of time there. With Missy."

Required or not, he had my attention. "Missy? Mataya? I didn't realize you knew her."

"You didn't? I guess that was before I met you. I did some modeling gigs with her when she was starting out. We hit it off and stayed close right up until she died."

"She started out at fifteen. Oh, my God. You could have been her father!" Not that I hadn't slept with my share of older men.

"I wasn't banging her." His eye twinkled with a wicked gleam. "Well. Not regularly, anyway."

I shook my head. Honestly, I couldn't have cared less if he'd been fucking a teenager or not. What I did care about was what Chris might be able to tell me. If they were friends when she died, if Chris had visited her at the Palm Springs resort, did he have any insight into her death?

I was still searching for the best way to ask when he said, "Look, it was back in my cokehead days. I was a mess back then. So was she for that matter. But *shh* about Missy, because there's Megan, and I don't like her knowing much about that part of my life."

I made a mental note to call Chris sometime for coffee and gossip without his significant other and turned my focus to my greeting. "Megan," I said, maybe too brightly. "I absolutely love your dress. It's Terani, isn't it?"

"Thank you, Emily." Her voice rang with possession. Her carriage was guarded. Although we were the same height, she peered down at me. "And you—don't you look . . . *cute* . . . with those pockets."

The only thing shittier than the way men treated a pretty woman was the way women did. More often than not, the catty remarks and jealous eyes made me want to show how easily I *could* steal their men if I wanted to.

I swallowed against the desire to be malicious. "You're too kind. I went for comfort. I figured no one would notice me anyway." Okay, I was a little snarky after all. Because people noticed me. They always noticed me. "But don't let me interrupt your evening. It was good seeing you, Chris." I leaned in and gave him the faux hug that was popular in my crowd. That was spiteful too. While it played as genuine, the contact was only to irk Megan. I nodded to her. "Next time."

I glanced at the clock on my phone. It hadn't even been

an hour since the party had started and I'd promised my agent at least two hours of "presence." When I'd protested, he'd said, "Everyone assumes you're ugly. If you want your next role to be more than a voiceover, you have to show them that you're not."

But a scan over the Shrine Expo Hall told me that his plan was pointless. There were at least a couple thousand people in front of me—all of them trying to show that they weren't ugly too. A flood of inadequacy poured over me, a feeling of I-don't-belong, but if not here, then where?

The room began to close in around me, blanketing me with acute heaviness. I drained my champagne in one swallow then set it on a waiter's tray as I pushed through the crowd and out to the overflow area that had been set up in the parking lot. Once the chill night breeze hit me, I gasped in a deep breath, swallowing the air in long gulps, as though I'd been underwater and had finally reached the surface.

With Amber, I'd been a glorified hooker. In Hollywood, wasn't I pretty much the same thing? I'd simply left one bed to move to another. I chuckled at the paradox. It deserved a laugh, at least.

Footsteps sounded behind me, and I stifled the last bit of humor threatening to escape. Without looking over my shoulder, I felt the air change. The hair at the back of my neck bristled and the sting of electricity huddled around me.

I turned, somehow knowing what I'd find—*who* I'd find.

He leaned against the concrete doorframe watching me with eyes that pinned me in my place. He was captivating and magnificent, his tux fitting him better than clothing had the right to fit a person, better than any one of the pretty men that filled the room beyond him. Those men, my peers, they were a sea of beautiful—calm and serene. Reeve was the ocean, dark and commanding and turbulent. They moved in gentle waves. Reeve stood still and set the world crashing around him.

That easily, the breath I'd just managed to get under control was knocked from my lungs.

He spoke before I could regain my composure. "What a coincidence that you'd be at the same event that I'm at."

The boldness of his accusation shocked me into response. "I'm not following you, if that's what you're insinuating." My pulse fluttered in fear, in excitement. In irritation. I didn't like the way he agitated me. Maybe I'd deserved it at his resort, but this? This was my turf.

With a surprising display of fierceness, I locked my eyes to his. "I'm the one who belongs at this event. Not you."

He laughed and the sound of it fueled my indignation. It also sent heat rushing up my thighs, heat that turned my rage inward as well as out.

Hands in his pockets, Reeve stepped toward me. "Calm down, Emily. I was only teasing. Of course you aren't here because of me. Perhaps *I'm* here because of *you*." He paused long enough for panic to jolt through me with reminders of the ominous words he'd delivered to me the last time we'd seen each other. "Perhaps this time I'm the one who's examining."

My anger stepped up another notch, overwhelming my unease. "Examining me? Like, why—to scare me? To see if I'm as fun to mess with when you're outside the home field? How dare you? Come here, into my world, and prod at me just because you feel like it. Proceed to make it your playground. How dare you?"

His lip curved into a chiding smile. "Now you know how I felt."

I refused to acknowledge my humiliation, though the flush that swept down my neck more than likely gave it away. "Thank you for the lesson, Mr. Sallis," I said, my voice surprisingly steady. "I assure you that I have more than gotten the point. You won't be having to give me any further demonstrations." I started toward the venue doors, praying I could manage the walk. High heels and weak knees did not make for a good combination.

I circled widely around him, wanting to keep as much distance between us as possible. But I could still feel the warmth pulsating off him like the driving beat of a dance club. It trembled through me, coming up from the ground, shaking me, gripping me. I fought through it, forced myself past him.

"Emily." His address caught me midstride. Five more feet and I'd be back in the Expo. Just a few more steps . . .

I couldn't help myself—I stayed. I didn't turn toward him, though. That was my single act of restraint.

"What I did to you at the spa—" His voice was silk and stubble all at once. The texture of the sound, as much as the mention of the spa, was bait on a hook. I practically leaned into his next words. "It wasn't very nice."

I spun toward him. "You think?"

"I like my privacy. I was mad." It wasn't an explanation so much as it was a reminder. *You provoked me,* he was saying. *You deserved it.*

"So you made me think you wanted to kill me?" Admittedly, I had earned his admonishment. I hadn't earned a death threat.

"Eh. I never said I wanted—"

I cut him off with a point of my finger. "You did. In every way you could without the specific words."

He opened his mouth as if to defend himself further. Then his expression changed, his features darkened, his eyes gleamed. "Did it scare you?"

"What do you think?" A shiver ran down my spine. He knew he'd scared me. It had been his intent to rile me up, make me afraid. What I hadn't realized was how much he liked that he had.

He moved closer. "But did it scare you enough?" His voice was sandpaper—abrasive, rough, yet it smoothed away a layer of my desire to run. "It didn't, did it?"

I wanted to say yes. It was almost true, after all. His last speech had made me leave his resort. He'd frightened me away. I'd abandoned my plan.

But I had regrets. I'd convinced myself they were entirely because of Amber, but that was a lie. He'd intrigued me. I hadn't stopped thinking about him, and now, even as he towered over me, even as he pressed in closer, even as he set a tornado of trepidation spinning in my gut, I didn't leave. I didn't *want* to leave.

He considered me for several seconds, his head cocked, his eyes narrowed. The heat pulsing off of him was even hotter when he faced me straight on like this, his stare searing through me. And just like sitting in front of a blazing fire, it was pleasant yet intense. Too intense.

Still, I didn't leave.

"Should I tell you what I think, Emily?"

Walk away. "Actually, I don't really give a fuck." I tried to pretend I wasn't completely hypnotized, but even I could hear the failed pretense in my tone.

"See, but I think you do. You came looking for me first, remember?"

"Then you told me to go. And I did. Now who's doing the looking?"

Reeve reached his hand out and toyed with a loose tendril of my hair. "I'm going to tell you what I think, Emily." His fingers kept me mesmerized as he rolled the strand between them, his pull gentle, so gentle. "I think you liked it. I think you liked being scared."

Each word was like the tickle of a feather against

sensitive skin, making me itch and squirm under the graze of their truth. I wanted to pull away. Yet I also yearned for an increase in pressure, ached for his fingers to tug, hungered for his words to turn hard or for his mouth to stop talking all together and crash against mine instead.

"I think it turned you on."

My gaze flew up to meet his. "You mean like it turned you on to threaten me?"

He dropped his hand. Darkness crossed his eyes, and I suspected he was angry that I dared to challenge him. Or angry that I knew something so personal about him. Or maybe angry because it was honest, and maybe that pissed him off as much as his truth afflicted me.

Or maybe it wasn't anger at all but something else, something more primal and raw and base. Slowly, he smiled. "I can't deny that it turned me on."

The tension between us stretched taut. We shared that. However not-very-nice his demonstration, however sick and twisted it had been—we'd both been aroused. And now that we'd both acknowledged it, the dynamic between us changed. Now the door was open. Now one of us just had to walk through it.

Reeve was the one to cross the threshold. He reached out and took my hand in his and caressed his thumb across my knuckles. Goose bumps took perch along my skin as his touch sent electricity shooting up my arm and down to my core.

"Look"—he fixated on our hands—"I'm not going to tell you that I would never hurt you."

Alarm skidded through my nerves with a delicious thrill, rousing my want, heightening my desire.

"Besides, I don't think that's something you'd want to hear from your lover."

"Lover?" The term caught me off guard. It also brought

me to my senses. What the fuck was I doing? I pulled my hand from his and took a step back.

Reeve's expression gave nothing away. "What exactly did you think we were talking about?"

I hadn't been thinking at all. That was the problem. There was a pull between us—that much was obvious. I'd meant to take advantage of that when I was using him to find Amber. If I had a reason to still believe he was involved in her disappearance, this would be a victory. But now there was no reason to pursue him. There was no reason to involve myself with a man who was at the very least dangerous if not also a killer.

Yet I still wanted him. "I don't know, Reeve. Because you do a lot of talking, and all I hear are mixed messages."

"I'm unmixing them now. Listen. This is the one I want you to hear."

And what exactly was it he was saying? That he wanted to take me into his bed? That he wanted to scare me and possibly hurt me and I was supposed to be okay with that?

The horrible part was that I *was* okay with it. But to what end? It had been men like him that I'd run away from all those years ago. Because, even though I desired them, I knew they weren't good for me. I knew that I didn't have the capability of determining how much pain, how much fear was too much.

What was it that Reeve had said to me at his spa? *"The problem with men who are actually a threat is that you don't ever find out how unsafe they are until it's too late."*

It was a wise warning.

He was waiting for me to respond, his eyes questioning.

"I hear you," I said. Then with effort, I shook my head. "Your last message was louder."

It was satisfying to be the one to turn away this time. The one with the last word. It didn't make it any easier.

Just as I was about to step into the Expo, though, Reeve was at my side. He stretched his arm in front of me like a barricade, bracing his hand on the doorframe. He didn't touch me, but he stood close enough that I could feel his exhale skate across my skin, the rhythm of his breathing a song that brought another layer of goose bumps to the surface.

"I don't know what it is about you." His voice was strained, the only sign that he wasn't completely in control. "But I can't get you out of my mind. You contaminate my thoughts. I keep remembering your body under my hands as I touched you. The parts of you I didn't touch. The sounds you made. The look in your eyes. You haunt me, Emily."

My knees were jelly, my insides a puddle of want and need and trepidation. But warning bells underscored Reeve's words. *"You haunt me,"* he'd said. *"Contaminate my thoughts."* I recognized the sentiments. I'd been there. I was there—with him, yes. With Amber.

She was the reminder I needed.

I swallowed, and without looking him in the eye said, "Now you know how I felt."

He let me leave this time. Let me have the final word. Part of me wished he hadn't.

It was later, in the dark of my apartment when I was drifting in the space between consciousness and sleep, that the niggling thought stirred by Amber's picture turned into something concrete and shaped. I bolted upright in my bed. Had I been dreaming? I was pretty sure I'd been lucid, but just to be sure I reached for my phone from the nightstand. The picture of Amber was still on the screen. I pinched my fingers across the surface to make it bigger and zoomed in on the man's hand at her waist.

There, on his middle finger, was a large ring. It was

ornate; the red jewels across the face were laid out in a distinctive V-like pattern. I closed out of it and scrolled back through my messages from Joe until I found the first picture he'd sent me, one with Reeve at an anonymous dinner function. The one where he was with a man. A man who also wore a ring. I magnified the image. My breath caught as I saw it clearly—it was the same ring.

Michelis Vilanakis, the mob boss that I'd seen in two separate pictures with Reeve, was the man with Amber at the casino in Colorado. This finding solved nothing, raising more questions than answers. One thing for certain, it put Michelis on the investigation list. And because of their connection, Reeve was back there as well.

And only three hours prior, I'd walked away from him. *Goddamn it.*

But before disappointment suffocated me in its grasp, I had another realization—Reeve Sallis was not the type to let just anyone walk away from him. Why would he do that unless he intended to follow?

So all I had to do was wait.

I fell back to sleep easily, strangely more at peace than a person being pursued by a man like Reeve should have been.

CHAPTER

9

The next day, he sent me flowers. They were waiting at the studio when I arrived—a bouquet of white lotus blossoms, a plant that symbolized both female sensuality and potential for enlightenment. It was also often associated with death.

I tossed them in the trashcan in the conference room where we did our weekly table read without bothering to open the note.

The day after, a bottle of red wine came. A 2004 Barolo Cannubi, an expensive Nebbiolo variety with an oaky flavor that was supposed to heighten women's arousal.

I gave it to Ty Macy as a congratulations gift for his Sunday night win. Again, the note went unread.

Wednesday brought chocolate-covered liquors, which I ate—there are only so many temptations in a week I can withstand.

Thursday, a first edition copy of *Peyton Place* was added to my bookshelf.

Friday, Reeve was waiting for me on the front porch of my apartment when I got back from my morning run.

I nearly tripped over myself when I saw him.

I'd been confident he'd show up eventually, but honestly, I was surprised to see him so soon. I thought it would be another week of extravagant gifts before he came in person. I'd left the porch light on when I'd left the apartment so I spotted him when I was still half a block away. He sat in my wicker patio chair, half-illuminated, half-shadowed. Without seeing his face, I knew who it was. I could tell by his carriage, by the way he held himself even as he lounged. Besides, who else would it be? No one ever visited me.

He wore a suit and tie, and I wondered for the first time what he did with his days when he wasn't dropping in on his various resorts around the world. Did he go to an office? Sit behind a desk? Did he always wear a suit? At the end of the day, did he remove his tie and loosen the buttons of his starched dress shirt, revealing just a hint of the solid planes he hid underneath? Or did he often work at home, in sexy sportswear with a phone glued to his ear as he barked orders to lackeys and made capital-D Decisions that influenced the lives of many?

Wherever he worked, I doubted he was usually up and dressed for business this early. The sun wouldn't even rise for another hour. It was impressive. *He* was impressive. And as gratifying as it was for me to have captured his attention, I was fully aware that I was in over my head.

I'd slowed to a cool-down pace before I saw him, but now I walked the last fifty feet so I had time to gather myself. To catch my breath. To still my beating heart.

"You jog?" he asked when I was close enough, skipping the formality of a hello.

I climbed the step and moved past him, pulling the door key from the chain on my wrist. "I prefer swimming." I especially preferred not sweating. Hopefully, I didn't smell too bad. I'd keep my distance from him just in case.

Except, I didn't want to keep my distance. The charge shooting between us was crackling and sparking, and we'd barely exchanged two words.

I opened the door and stepped inside. Though I didn't invite Reeve in, he followed. *I have a potential killer in my house. I have a man who's said he might hurt me. In my house.*

Suddenly I wasn't so sure the moisture pooling between my legs was just sweat.

I hung the wristband on the peg by the door and looked over my shoulder to see him blatantly surveying my apartment. There wasn't much to see. Less than a thousand square feet, it was basically a kitchen that opened up to the living/dining area and then a bedroom. My walls were bare except for a few random art pieces. It was clean if maybe a little dusty. The good thing about long days on the set meant that I wasn't home enough to mess up my house.

Most importantly, there was nothing to connect me to Amber. I had things from her—photos, mementos. Leaving her out of my décor had been intentional.

Apparently having seen enough of my apartment, he turned to face me. "I have a pool."

"I'm sure you do." I did too, technically. There was a community pool for the apartment building. But I rarely used it since it was kidney bean shaped, meant for leisure, not laps.

"You should come over to swim. Naked."

"Naked, huh? Is that a requirement?" I'd been naked under the sheet at his spa. The memory of it set my stomach fluttering. His hands on me had been beyond amazing, but even just being bare in his presence, being stripped, vulnerable—that feeling was amazing as well. Amazing and terrifying, without his threats, but also because of them.

Reeve leaned against the back of my couch and braced a hand on either side of him. "It's a preference."

"Of yours." I toed off my tennis shoes and set them in the hallway to my bedroom.

"I believe of yours too. Except, you're playing games with me."

"No. I'm not." Since he was watching, I pulled my tank over my head and tossed it past him to the back of the couch. The sports bra I wore underneath was supportive but revealing.

"Uh-huh." He grinned, but the look on his face suggested he despised my teasing as much as he welcomed it. Eyes locked with mine, he picked up the sweaty shirt, brought it to his nose, and *sniffed*.

Some people would find that disgusting. Some people would not be turned on by the way his pants seemed tighter than they'd been a moment before. Some people would not be fantasizing about the other vulgar, vile things that a man like Reeve got off on.

I tried to pretend that I was one of them. "Perv."

He grinned and gave me a pointed look. "You were the one who looked about to come just now."

"Oh, honey, don't even think that you can imagine what I look like when I come." I only thought to regret the words when I heard them hanging in the air after I'd said them. Reeve's expression twisted, dark and sinful, and I knew he felt provoked. Why wouldn't he? That was exactly what I'd been doing—testing him. Baiting him. Daring him.

He stared at me intently, like a lion hunting its prey. Studied me so long and so hard that I could swear he saw past my façade, past my skin and bones and internal organs. Saw past whatever it was that made up my physical structure and into the parts of me that were cryptic and complicated and concealed. Saw into the parts of us we had in common—the dark parts, the broken parts, the Amber parts.

Maybe it was too ugly to look at for long because he turned away first, circling around the sofa toward my bookcase. "Tell me something," he said, overtly switching gears. "What's with you and Chris Blakely?"

He'd been watching me at the Expo, then. Before he'd come outside after me.

His question about Chris was spoken casually, but it was purposeful. A more naïve woman might have missed it, but I was too experienced with men like him. He wanted me to know that I was in his sightline. That this was what it meant to be part of his life. That he would monitor me, if he felt like it; he'd rule me. And he expected me to submit.

I couldn't decide if that freaked me out or thrilled me.

So I played coy. "He's an actor. We've worked together on occasion. I guess we're friends."

I walked into the kitchen and got a glass from the cupboard. Chewing my lip, I filled it with filtered water from the sink and debated full disclosure regarding Chris. On the one hand, Reeve might be asking about him because he already knew I'd had a past with him and he wanted me to admit it.

But no one knew about that.

And there was the other reason he might be asking— maybe he didn't want me to find out what Chris knew about *him*.

It was a long shot, but since I hoped to contact Chris for more information about Missy at some point, I decided the less I said the better.

I drank some of my water then set the glass down and leaned across the counter to watch Reeve. His fingers trailed across the spines. I couldn't see the exact books, so I tried to think what was there. My Katherine Hepburn autobiography. My copy of *Rebecca*.

He stopped and pulled one from the shelf then flipped through it lazily. This one I recognized from the cover. *PostSecret: Extraordinary Confessions from Ordinary Lives*, one of my coffee table books. I collected them and had so many that most lived on my bookshelf rather than on my coffee table. This particular book was a printing of blog posts that shared secrets anonymously. Parts of it read like my diary, and I'd marked several pages with Post-it notes so I could easily come back to them. Reading it had always felt comforting.

Seeing it in Reeve's hands, though, wasn't comforting. He flipped through the pages, stopping on the ones I'd tagged. Chuckling at some. Growing somber at others. At one, he lifted his head toward me and nodded slightly as if confirming what he'd just thought, what he'd just read.

I ran through several confessions I knew by heart, trying to imagine which it had been:

Again and again. Used.

I'm more scared of court than I was when he almost killed me.

I would do absolutely anything in the whole world if I thought it would make her happy.

Whichever ones he was reading, any of them—all of them—were private. Too private for him to know they spoke to me. Yet, I didn't stop him. I let him sink one layer deeper under my skin.

It was bad enough that he was in my apartment—in an apartment that I paid for myself. His presence reminded me of a time when everything I owned had been given to me by men. The things I had now, though small in number and worth, were all mine.

Trying to distract myself from the anxiety Reeve's invasion caused, I asked, "Why do you want to know about Chris anyway? Do you want me to fix you up? He's got a fiancée, you know."

Reeve shot me a glare. "Cute."

He put the book back on my shelf and moved toward me. When he reached the counter, he said, "Chris doesn't look at you like he has a fiancée."

Ah. I'd forgotten Reeve was a jealous man. Or I'd underestimated the depth of his envy. Strangely, it was a fairly common trait of the kind of men I'd involved myself with in the past, the kind of men who had everything. I knew how to pander to them, knew what to say to put their insecurities to rest. *No one could ever be man enough to compare with you,* I'd say. It might have been what Reeve was looking for in regard to Chris.

But I couldn't bring myself to give it to him. "A lot of men don't look at me like they have a fiancée."

Reeve leaned across the opposite side of the counter so we were face-to-face. "I don't like that."

Jealousy was generally boring, yet on Reeve, it was fascinating. And, I suspected, dangerous. "You don't? What are you going to do about it? Lock me up and never let me out in public?"

"I have some nice secluded resorts I think you'd like. My island properties are so beautiful you'll forget you're in a prison."

He flashed his dimple. It was subtle, only noticeable when he smiled in a certain way, the way he was smiling now. And his eyes . . . I'd thought they were blue, but now I saw green flecks. They caught in the light. They caught me in them, made me feel warm. Made me feel trapped.

I stood up straight, distancing myself without moving away. "Look at you. Acting as if you have some claim to me. I think I already blew you off the other night."

"Look at you, acting as if I'm a person that you blow off. I think I already warned you about me." He was teasing as I'd been. But he wasn't all at the same time.

My heart skipped a beat. "Another threat?"

"If you want it to be." He looked at me like he had earlier—that intent way that saw through me, into me. Saw all my dark parts.

In a way, he was showing me his darkness as well.

My lip quivered, but I wasn't scared. Well, not scared enough. "I do."

His eyes sparked, and with that simple phrase, we entered into an agreement. He would have me. He would fuck me. He would bring me into his world.

And in return I'd let him break me.

I took in a shuddering breath as I fell under the heaviness of our unspoken understanding. He saw it and straightened.

Now, I thought. *He's going to make his move now. He's going to take me now.* He'd strip me but he'd keep his own clothes on, undoing his pants only far enough to release his cock. He'd be coarse and crude and he'd make me late for the set. *Now.*

I wasn't prepared. I was so ready.

He walked around the counter to join me in the kitchen. At the frame, he paused. "Then why have you ignored every invitation I've sent?"

"Your notes? Huh." I wrung my hands together, more nervous than I wanted to be. "Maybe I should have read them before I threw them away."

His eyes narrowed to incredulous slits. "You threw them away without reading them?"

"They felt detached. Impersonal gifts sent by one of your minions. Did you even select them yourself?" I'd planned to say all this to him eventually, but now the words seemed tedious. Seemed like obstacles dotting the couple of yards between us. *Now.* I willed him to close the distance. *Now.*

"I did select them myself. Every one of them. They would have felt less detached if you'd read what I'd said."

God, now I wished I had.

But I shrugged, pretending to not care. Pretending that the hum of attraction around us was normal. "Maybe. I still prefer personal invitations."

"You're awfully confident. Some might go so far as to say egotistical."

I laughed. "That's fitting coming from you."

"With me, it's not ego." There wasn't a trace of humor in his delivery. "I simply know what I'm worth."

"And I know what I'm worth, Mr. Sallis."

He appeared amused. "Okay. I'll bite. What are you worth?"

"More than generic gifts and dictated notes." This speech was not impromptu. If I expected to gain anything about Amber from Reeve, this was an important part of the plan. I had to be more significant than a passing curiosity. I had to tie him to me. And to get that guarantee, I'd have to push him as much as I dared.

It helped that I actually believed what I said. "I'm worth more than the flyby in the night that I know you're counting on. I don't do pump and dumps. I also don't do romance."

He crossed his arms and leaned his shoulder against the wall. "What is it exactly that you do then, Emily?"

I steeled myself. I'd made similar arrangements so many times. It had been so much easier when I was younger. When I didn't care. When I was with Amber. *"Value for value,"* she'd say. *"Nothing short of total needs met."*

My life was different now—I met my own needs. But the first part was still reasonable. "I do the exchange system, Reeve. I give you something you value in exchange for something I value."

He pushed off from the wall and divided the space between us in half with one step. "Emily, when I fuck, it's of value to both parties. No exchange needed."

A rush of arousal burst through me so fast that I felt

dizzy. *Now,* I was silently begging, ready to skip the negotiations. *Now, now, now.*

He held his place.

My nerves pulsed with frustration, buzzing like a fly at a window that could see the outdoors—that could *be* there if only it could break through the glass.

If he wouldn't reach for me . . .

I wanted so badly to pounce, to feel my lips on his, to ease the ache between my legs. But besides having learned my lesson in Palm Springs, this game was always best played from the stance of indifference. I couldn't show him how desperately I wanted him. I'd let him call the shots. I'd let him initiate the moves. I'd let him make the offers. I'd wait.

I didn't have to be happy about it, though.

I picked up the glass of water from the counter and turned to the sink to pour it out. "I'm sure you like to think that you're God's gift to women, Reeve. But that's not how it works with me. I need to be taken care of. Otherwise I can be perfectly happy with my vibrator, thank you very much."

He was on me in half a second. Less, even. He spun me around, gripping me at the elbows. He searched my eyes, always searching. Always studying.

"I can't figure you out, Emily." His words were tight yet even. "I don't know if I like you or if I just want to fuck you."

He pressed me into the point where the counters met and one of his hands moved to palm the back of my head. Then—*now*—while he held me forcibly in place, he crushed his mouth against mine.

At first, I tried to reciprocate. As he nipped at my bottom lip, I attempted to suck on his upper. As his tongue thrust inside my mouth, I moved mine along his teeth. But everything I did felt awkward and out of rhythm, and eventually I stopped trying. I gave in. I surrendered.

And that's when the kiss became earth-shattering.

He took me where he wanted me to go, showing my lips how to move with the slightest turn of his head, coaxing my tongue with the silky licks of his own. It was a kiss that took—took my desire, took my passion, took my will. It was selfish and singularly choreographed for Reeve and Reeve alone.

But as he took, he also gave. The way he held me still, the way he set the tempo and chose the dance, the way he pressed and pushed and sucked and stroked so that I wouldn't have to decide any of it, so that I could simply be present and cared for—those were gifts that he gave without hesitation or restraint.

He presented me with a freedom that I'd once had and taken for granted. And, damn, how I'd missed it. So even though this kiss was for him, about him, I took and took and took.

My lips felt bruised and swollen by the time he pulled away. I was dizzy and disoriented. I wanted him to keep kissing me. I wanted him to slip a hand down my shorts and bury it in my cunt. Then I wanted him to follow with his cock.

But his kiss had returned me to a role I knew well. A role I enjoyed more than any other. A role of submission.

"You'll come over to swim Sunday morning," he said. "Nine o'clock. I'll text you the directions."

He kissed me again—shorter, but rougher. More demanding, pressing all of his body against me, grinding his thick erection against my abdomen.

Then, abruptly, it was over.

He stepped back from me, his eyes wild as he wiped his mouth with the back of his hand. With a satisfied nod, he said, "Consider that your personal invitation."

And he left.

CHAPTER

10

The relationship Amber and I had with Rob lasted nine months, until his wife hired a private investigator and found out about his naughty weekends. He dumped us then, saying he wanted to make his marriage work, but left us each with a nice parting gift in the form of a check.

"Severance," I'd called it.

But the next time we saw him he had a sixteen-year-old on his arm and a wedding ring still on his finger. That's when I learned my first hard lesson: Men Never Change.

I was still too naïve to realize that the axiom didn't apply just to men.

When he ended things, I took it as a sign. My mother was on my case about not having a job. It was time to grow up, get a job, get an apartment.

Amber had other ideas.

At first she cried, as she always did—I'd learn that later too. She claimed she was heartbroken and would never love again. After a week of this, she woke up confident and resolute. *"Time to go hunting,"* she'd said.

Less than a month later, we were living in a two-bedroom apartment in West Hollywood with Liam, a thirty-year-old copyright lawyer we'd met at a coffee shop. Our arrangement with Liam was different than it had been with Rob. He was nice, decent. He didn't give us presents because we were having sex with him, but he did take care of us.

And we took care of him. We did the grocery shopping and the laundry and lounged by his pool while he went to the office. When he came home, we fed him a home-cooked dinner and rubbed his shoulders. Then he'd take one of us to bed. He didn't feed us drugs. He wasn't married or rich in any sense of the word, but he made more than enough. He liked one-on-one sex as much, if not more, than threesomes, and he always chose Amber as his solo partner. Which was fine with me. She "loved him madly"—her words—and he seemed genuinely fond of her as well. They were an adorable couple. I was the best girlfriend with benefits.

Part of me thought our happy family could last forever. Another part was smarter than that. Not just smarter but itchy for something else, something I couldn't name. Restless, I took some acting workshops and a couple of jobs modeling for stock photographers. Amber, on the other hand, gave all her attention to Liam and her assumed role of housewife, which included, in her mind, spending his money.

One Friday, Amber was out on an all-day shopping spree when Liam came home unexpectedly early from work. He'd been at court all morning and decided there wasn't any point going into the office at that time of day, so he took the afternoon off. I fixed him a sandwich and set him up in front of the TV—what Amber would have done if she'd been there.

"Drinking so early? I shouldn't," he'd said when I brought him a cold beer.

"But you will."

He'd taken it from me, saying, "You're a bad influence. I should tie you up and punish you."

It was innocent teasing, nothing meant by it at all, but I'd been on my way back to the kitchen when he'd said it, and I'd turned back to him, surprised. Not surprised by the teasing—that was common between us—but by how the thought made me feel. *Being punished.* I hadn't thought about it before, really. I'd been spanked before. By Rob. But it had always been playful, never as a consequence. And the idea of it, the idea of being humiliated and disciplined, was strangely exciting.

Liam must have read my thoughts from the expression on my face because he'd said, "You'd like that, wouldn't you?" Said it like he'd finally understood something about me that he hadn't before. Said it like this understanding interested him. Said it like *I* interested him in a way that I hadn't before.

Then, before I had a chance to answer—as if I *could* answer such a strange question without having longer to think about it—he'd said, "That reminds me. I got you a present."

"Really? What is it?" I wasn't as surprised about a present as I'd been about the idea of punishment. He'd bring us things on occasion. Nothing expensive. Costume jewelry, mostly. DVDs of the latest chick flick.

"It's nothing much. Just something I saw and thought of you. There's a bag in my briefcase by the door. Get it out, will you? But bring it here before looking inside. I want to explain it."

"Okay." I went to the foyer and found a blue plastic shopping bag in his briefcase.

When I'd just entered the living room, he'd stopped me. "Wait." He had that same look on his face that he'd had when I left him—the interested look. Intense and warm.

It had made me feel intense and warm and interested, and my heart pounded with anticipation as I'd waited for him to say something else. It felt like a lifetime spanned in those seconds.

"Put the handle of the bag between your teeth," he'd said, finally. "And crawl to me."

It was such a strange request, so out of the blue and uncharacteristic. It should have sparked questions or an argument, even. I should have said, "Hell, no, I'm not crawling to you. You weirdo." I was barely eighteen. I'd had a handful of sexual partners who were mostly teenagers and beyond the threesomes with Amber, I'd never gotten especially kinky.

But I'd also never been very interested in sex. It had gotten me what I'd needed and was certainly fun. I just wasn't easily turned on and the payoff wasn't always worth the effort for me.

Until that moment, when Amber's boyfriend lay sprawled across the living room couch, his feet bare, his jacket off, his tie loose, and told me to crawl. Instantly, my mouth grew moist and my belly knotted with the firm ball of arousal. Because being told to do something so demeaning, so perverted, so shameful . . . it thrilled me.

I put the bag in my mouth and started to bend down, but he stopped me again. "First, take off your clothes."

I did. Without hesitation.

He watched me as I stripped. "The other day," he'd said, "you mentioned hating how sweet and nice modern-day romantic heroes are. I saw that"—he'd nodded at the bag from the briefcase—"and thought you might appreciate it instead."

His statement piqued my curiosity, but I soon forgot about it. Because when I'd gotten down on all fours, the ceramic floor had hurt my knees and the bag had pulled at my teeth. It swung as I'd crawled, and the way it hit my breasts had been uncomfortable and humiliating.

But the more uncomfortable I had felt—the more humiliated, the more sick and twisted—the more I had been aroused.

Liam's expression had only added to my desire. He'd watched me like I was an animal, like I wasn't a person but a pet, meant to be dominated and lorded over.

"You aren't like Amber," he'd said, and I hadn't had to ask what he'd meant. Amber wouldn't have gotten on her knees on a hard floor let alone gotten wet between the legs from such a degrading act. Amber wouldn't be turned on by the prospect of pain or submission.

No, I definitely wasn't like Amber.

I never did make it to the couch. Liam pounced before I'd even crawled midway across the room. He pounced and he bound my hands with his tie. He spanked me. Hard. Punitively. He fucked me roughly, mercilessly. When he'd finished, he'd left bruises on my wrists and arms and breasts.

He'd marked me in other ways, ways that couldn't be seen. With the truth he'd taught me about myself. With the names he'd called me as he'd pounded into me, the names that had sent me over the edge. *"Whore." "Slut." "Bitch."* He'd marked me as dirty. He'd marked me as submissive. He'd marked me as *not Amber*.

And that terrified me.

I'd cleaned up by the time Amber got home. When she'd knocked on my bedroom door to ask if I wanted to go out with her and Liam to grab dinner, I'd told her I had a headache. Later, when she'd left Liam sleeping in their bed, she'd come to check on me.

"I think it's time to move on," I told her. "Liam is fine, but he can't buy us all the things Rob could. Is this what we want for our future? We could have so much more."

She'd been reluctant, but she was a good friend and said she wanted me happy more than she wanted Liam. I suspected she also believed she really did deserve more than he could give her. We were gone within the week.

It was longer before I got around to looking at the gift he had bought me, the one I'd carried across the room in my mouth. It was an early copy of *Rebecca* by Daphne du Maurier. For a long time, I refused to look at it. I hid it under my bed and pretended it didn't exist, pretended that the things that had happened with Liam, the things he'd shown me about myself, weren't real. Weren't true.

Turned out it wasn't as easy to run from those revelations as I'd thought it would be. And when they came to the surface again, they were even more painful—physically and emotionally—than they'd been coming from Liam.

CHAPTER

11

My legs were jelly as I drove to Reeve's house Sunday morning. I'd left more than an hour early even though he was only thirty minutes from my house via Mulholland Drive. I had a feeling he wasn't the type to keep waiting. When I found his place, I turned around and parked a block away. Then I waited.

Patience had always been one of my strong suits. It was required when hunting men the way Amber and I had, and somewhere along the line I'd learned that anticipation paid off sexually. But anticipation was not to my benefit with Reeve. I'd already lost two nights of sleep thinking about him, about his kiss, and despite what I'd said to him, my vibrator had done nothing to relieve the throb between my legs. While it was helpful to be genuinely interested in a man I wanted to get close to, I recognized that the intensity of my attraction to Reeve was a weakness. It distracted me. It made me vulnerable.

It didn't help that I was wearing nothing under my maxi dress. I was bare, easily accessible, and it made me sensitive and horny just because of the naughtiness of no panties. And it was only going to get worse when I stripped completely to get in the pool. Though he hadn't specified that he wanted me naked when he'd delivered his invitation, he'd suggested it earlier, and I refused to play cautious. I wanted him to see me as strong. He needed me to be a challenge. I'd be of no interest to him if I were easy to break down.

Had he broken Amber down as well? Or had he restrained from dominating with her? It seemed unlikely to think he'd ever hold back, but on the other hand, Amber and I had shared more than one man who loved her one way and fucked me another.

But Reeve hasn't even fucked you. What if he wasn't what I thought he'd be in bed at all?

I chuckled at myself. Man, I was sure making a lot of assumptions. He could very well be all bark with no bite and all my anxiety would be for nothing.

Funny how disappointing that thought was.

At exactly ten to the hour, I turned my car on and headed back to Reeve's house. He was at the end of the cul-de-sac. The driveway curved so I couldn't see the house from beyond the entrance gate. I pulled up to the intercom and rolled down my window to hit the buzzer.

Before I touched it, though, the gate opened. He was waiting for me. A small shiver ran up the back of my neck. Followed by an internal eye roll at myself. I was so fucking pathetic—being delighted because someone who knew I was coming was looking out for my arrival. As if it meant he was excited for my visit instead of just that he knew how to be a good host.

I continued to chide myself as I followed the drive around the bend. Then the house came into view and the shiver that ran through me had nothing to do with Reeve and all to do with the magnificence standing before me. It wasn't the largest home I'd ever been in, nor the

most extravagant, but it was exactly the style I loved best—
modern with clean lines and lots of windows.

My Prius felt out of place in front of the multicar garage that likely housed Aston Martins and Bentleys. Being in this environment, I realized I'd forgotten how much
I enjoyed the *stuff*. I'd spent years with the luxury—jewels,
boats, clothes, cars. While I'd never loved material things
like Amber had, there were certain luxuries I had gotten
used to. And even though I had the pride of knowing everything I owned now was mine outright, I couldn't say I
didn't miss nice things. Which meant there was yet another
level to my excitement as I followed the walk up to the
front door. Reeve was a very rich man. And so far, it
seemed he had very nice things.

He also seemed to like feeling safe. I'd spotted two
suited men with guns patrolling the yard, and if I saw two,
it meant there were four. Plus the guards he likely had inside. It was one thing to have a security system, but this
was overkill. I'd been at A-list celebrity parties with less
people packing.

Like the gate, the door opened for me automatically. A
butler—who wore a gun at his waist—greeted me and took
my purse before leaving me in the company of one of the
henchmen from Palm Springs. The same one who had held
me as Reeve had body searched me—Anatolios.

"Ms. Wayborn. Please, come in. Mr. Sallis is waiting
for you. Follow me." His tone, like last time, contradicted
his welcoming words, but this time he looked at me with
more interest, his expression lewd and ugly.

"Thank you," I said, stepping after him, but really what
I meant was *Please don't stay with us at the pool*. It was
stupid to even wish it silently because I knew from experience that he'd at least be watching from a distance, and
from the look he'd just given me, I could tell he got off on
the voyeurism. Once again, I wondered what he might

know about Reeve's other women, about Amber. That was a question I'd never have an answer to, though. While I was pretty sure now that I knew the price to get him to talk to me, it was not a price I was willing to pay.

From the foyer, the house's design became apparent. It was long and narrow with large rooms stacked side-by-side so that each looked out at the canyon beyond. The entire back wall, in fact, was made of floor-to-ceiling windows. And the views were breathtaking. The kind of breathtaking that made me pause midstep so that I could look without the distraction of moving at the same time. From every direction, there was something to look at, the far side peering out over Franklin Canyon Park, the windows to the right revealing Fryman Canyon Park, and to the left, the Sunset Strip.

Then, when I acclimated to the grand scene, I saw another view that made my pulse speed up and my breathing uneven—the pool. More specifically, the man in red swim trunks sitting on a deck chair next to the pool.

And fuck if all the windows didn't have perfect sight-lines to every inch of the backyard.

"This way, Ms. Wayborn." Anatolios stood ahead of me pointing not toward the yard, but toward an open door.

I raised a questioning brow.

"If you'd like to change."

Change. Into a swimsuit. I hesitated.

It wasn't that I was uncomfortable with nudity. I'd done modeling and bit parts on cable television that called for no clothing. Before that, with Amber, I'd done so many things beyond stripping that being naked had become no big deal.

My apprehension now came from another angle entirely. I'd be naked. With Reeve. In front of the butler and Anatolios, who'd probably get a hard-on over it, and who-ever else was in the house, as well as anyone who might have binoculars in the houses across the canyon.

The whole scenario was an epic turn-on.

It was another check against me in the vulnerability category. If I did this, if I walked out there and let the scene unfold the way I so very much wanted it to, I wouldn't be able to turn back. It would be like going down the rabbit hole. There would be no way I'd come out the other side the same.

But it wasn't like I could change my mind about wearing a swimsuit—I hadn't brought one with me at all. And really, turning back had stopped being an option a while ago now.

With revived determination, I turned down Anatolios's offer. "Nope. I'm good, thank you."

If this surprised him, he didn't let on. He pointed to the glass door ahead of us. "Right that way then."

He wasn't accompanying me any farther, which meant he'd been told to stay behind. Been told to leave Reeve and me alone.

My stomach fluttered. Oh, God. I was a goner.

It felt like miles from the door to where Reeve sat in his chair, reading from a tablet of some sort. Nervousness spun through me, dizzying me. Keeping me frozen in place.

Then, he looked up. Looked right at me as though he sensed I was there.

It was all the invitation I needed. Focused on him, the walk became easy. He wore sunglasses, but the tilt of his head, the stillness of him told me his eyes were glued to me as I made my way toward him. He was an incubus, calling me with a seduction song so well known to me that I didn't have to hear it to respond. My body hummed with it naturally. The air vibrated with the tune, the rhythm of it growing stronger with each step I took.

When I reached him, I realized I'd been smiling since I walked out of the house.

"You made it," he said, with a smile of his own. The

radiance of it competed for attention with the bronze, toned planes of his chest. I wanted to touch them, follow the dips and ridges with my fingertips. Trace them with my tongue.

But I also wanted to keep staring at those lips.

"Did you have any problem finding me? I realized too late that I should have sent a car."

"No. It was fine. No problem at all." I didn't add that I would have turned him down if he'd offered. I preferred the freedom my own vehicle gave me.

He must have read between the lines. "You wouldn't have accepted it anyway. I get that, I suppose. You could have come in earlier, though. Instead of parking down the street."

A blush crawled up my neck. "I suppose I should have expected that." But the embarrassment quickly passed when I realized he'd been waiting for me. Watching for me. It should have been irritating to have my movements so scrutinized. Instead, it made me ridiculously thrilled.

"Probably." He never stopped looking at me. I didn't want him to. I couldn't stop looking at him either, both of us with grins that bordered on goofy.

It was that damn kiss, I realized. It had moved us from flirtation to action. From the place where we just imagined what it would be like to give in to our attraction to a place where we knew. It turned something that had only existed in our heads into something that lived, something that burned and throbbed in our sense memory.

Or maybe it was just me. It would be best if it were. Because the only thing worse than falling under Reeve's spell would be me believing that he'd fallen under mine as well.

I forced myself to look away. "It's beautiful here. Your house. The view. I bet you never get tired of looking at it."

He didn't move his focus from me. "I haven't so far."

It doesn't mean anything. It doesn't mean anything. Of course he'd like looking at me. He'd already admitted to wanting to fuck me, which he wouldn't want to do if he didn't find my appearance pleasing. And anyway, this was the type of line I'd heard before and never thought twice about. So why when Reeve said it? Why, of all the men I'd been with—all the rich, attractive, adoring men—why was this guy the one who made me weak in the knees?

"Get out of your head, Emily, and join me." Even in my thoughts, he watched me. "Sit. Or were you planning on taking up my offer for a swim?"

I *could* sit. There was a space heater between him and another deck chair, and the idea of curling up there was warm and inviting.

Except, I didn't think that was what he really wanted. For that matter, it wasn't what I really wanted. I wanted to push things along. I wanted to show him that I was up to the level, that I could deliver what he preferred.

I *wanted* what he preferred. "I'm guessing the pool is heated?"

He nodded. "Did someone show you where you could change?"

"Anatolios did." Well, it was now or never. I took a deep breath and turned to him. "But I seem to remember you saying it was your preference that I didn't wear a suit. Was that wrong?"

"Not wrong at all." Was it my imagination or did his grin widen ever so slightly? Those damn sunglasses—if only I could see his eyes. "It's not exactly secluded back here."

"I noticed. Funny how you hadn't mentioned that before."

He leaned forward, his elbows on his knees. Daring me. "Is that going to be a problem?"

Ah, this game. The one where he set the challenge high and expected me to back down. This game had once been my favorite, and, though it had been ages since I last played, adrenaline surged through me without hesitation, as if it had been simply waiting for the cue.

Any doubt I had disappeared. Confidence underscored my movements.

"You're the one who gets jealous." I reached back to the knot that held my dress up at my neck, and paused. "So you tell me. Are you okay with other people seeing me?"

"As long as *seeing* is all that other people get to do without my say-so, then I'm fine with it." He leaned back in his seat. "In fact, I'm more than fine with it."

"Then we're good." I pulled the tie of my dress and let it fall to my feet, leaving me completely bare. It was tacky to watch Reeve's reaction, but I couldn't help myself. He kept most of it behind his glasses anyway, but there were some reactions he couldn't hide. The bob of his Adam's apple as he swallowed, for one. His hands curled around the end of his armrests, his knuckles whitening. The emerging outline of his cock through his trunks.

I bit back a satisfied smile. "What about you? Are you swimming naked as well?"

"I'm not swimming at all." His voice was controlled, but just barely. "I'm watching."

Watching. That changed things. Not a lot, because I liked being watched, but I had gotten myself set on the idea of being watched *with* Reeve, not *by* him.

I turned my back toward him as I moved to the edge of the pool, letting the new scenario digest. Before I dove in, I cocked my head at him. "Why do I feel like I'm on an audition?"

"Maybe you are."

The water wasn't quite as warm as I'd expected it to be, or perhaps it was Amber that brought the chilliness over me. She was an anchor—holding me down, making the ascent back up from my dive more difficult than it should have been.

He liked watching me too, she said.

The thought stirred me to be defensive and jealous,

chasing me through my laps. Each breath I took, each stroke was an effort to shake her from worming into my head. It was unexplainable, considering how often she and I had shared men in the past. Ridiculous because I was only there for her in the first place—to find her. To protect her.

It rattled me. Why should I care what she and Reeve had been to each other?

By the end of twenty laps I had no answer. I only knew that Reeve didn't mind if there were other people watching me, and for that reason, neither did I. But I wanted to be the only person he saw.

The realization made me come shooting out of the water, gasping for air. I clung to the ledge and willed myself to calm down.

"You look good out there."

My eyes rose to find Reeve's pinned on me, his sunglasses now gone. The compliment warmed through me, making my limbs tingle. He couldn't have ever said that to Amber since she didn't know how to swim.

It was petty. *I* was petty. I smiled anyway. "I usually do another twenty."

"Don't." It was sharp, commanding. "Skip it. Come be with me."

The tingling spiraled through my body, intensifying to a rhythmic pulse. I was naked and watched and turned on. And even though my long game remained Amber, I wanted Reeve. I wanted Reeve to want me.

I lifted myself to sit on the side of the pool then nodded at Reeve's neck. "I don't suppose I can use your towel?"

That grin. His grin. It undid me every time. "You could. But I'd prefer to watch you drip dry."

I frowned, squeezing the water out of my hair. "Of course you would."

"Ah, stop with the face. You like it."

My nipples were tight beads because it was chilly but

also because I *did* like it. I liked everything about it. Reeve knowing it, acknowledging it, only undid me further. I lost the frown. But I didn't stand. I wasn't sure my feet could move.

Maybe he understood that too. He stood, took the towel from around his neck, and spread it on the lounge chair next to him like a blanket. Then he came to me and held out his hand. "The heater will warm you up fast enough. Come."

His fingers around mine sent shockwaves through my system. Or maybe it was the way he raked my body with his eyes. He lingered on my breasts, lingered longer at the apex of my thighs, his gaze touching me so thoroughly as though it were his hands instead. As though he'd already rubbed his thumbs across my nipples, pressed the pad of his finger to my clit.

He led me to the chair and it took everything not to pull him down with me. Then he let go of my hand, but he stayed peering over me while I silently wished for him to lower himself on top of me.

Finally he asked, "Would you like anything? Coffee? Water? Mimosa?"

"Would it be brought out by one of your henchmen?" I knew the answer from his grin. "I'm good. Thank you."

"You're not interested in company?" His tone said it wasn't a question about whether or not I cared about being seen naked—we'd already been over that. He was confirming whether or not I wanted the sexual activity to be between me and him and no one else.

I should have told him it was up to him. I should have been willing to do whatever he preferred. That was how to snag a lover. I knew the drill.

But the reason I couldn't say it was the one I'd discovered in the pool—I wanted Reeve to myself. I wanted to only be Reeve's.

Could he guess that as well as he guessed everything else about me? The idea made me cringe, made me have to look away, but I simply couldn't force myself to change my answer. Instead, I lifted my shoulder into a half-shrug, hoping I appeared nonchalant about it. "I'm more interested in the company I already have."

He chuckled and I feared I'd answered wrong, especially when he returned to his own deck chair. I bit back a disappointed sigh and clenched my thighs together hoping for some relief.

Reeve scratched at his chest and stared into the distance. "You're stunning, Emily. I know you know that. Incredibly gorgeous." The admiration felt calloused and cold, delivered like statistical data. "But beautiful is a dime a dozen, especially around here. It doesn't make you special."

"Then I've failed my audition?" The bulge in his shorts kept me from worrying too much.

He twisted toward me. "Au contraire. You wouldn't be here if you weren't beautiful. That was the first round. You made it to callbacks." His hand swept down to his lower abs and stopped just above the band of his trunks. "I'm very attracted to you."

I ticked my head toward his erection. "I see that."

"I didn't try to hide it. In fact, that's how you pass round two."

"I passed that a while ago then."

"Yes. You did." He placed his palm over his cock and my insides turned to molten lava. I wished it were my palm on him. He only had to say the word, and I'd take him in my mouth.

But Reeve was a master of patience. A master of willpower.

He dropped his hand to his side. "God, I can't stop looking at you. You're perfect. Your breasts are fantastic. Real, aren't they?"

They felt heavier under his stare. "Yes. You can touch them, you know." It was desperate and pathetic. Only a step away from begging.

"Yes, I know." But he didn't move. "And the rest of your body . . . your long legs, your tight ass. Your pretty pussy." He sighed with an *mmm* that made my thighs quiver. "I'm really quite happy looking at you."

He listed my attributes like someone trying to decide whether or not to buy a show pet. It was blatant objectification and should have disgusted me, should have turned my stomach.

It did just the opposite. I felt hot, every nerve in my body awake and wanting. So why the hell were we still sitting apart?

I curled on my side to face him better. "I like hearing that. Thank you. Should I tell you that I'm happy looking at you as well?"

"It doesn't matter. But out of curiosity, are you?"

Most men expected to hear it, even when they knew it was a lie. I was particularly good at making them believe it. But it was with complete sincerity that I answered this time. "Yes."

Reeve considered. "Huh. Maybe it matters after all."

We were flirting. After everything we'd danced around. I was naked and he was hard and instead of touching, instead of kissing, instead of sating ourselves in each other, we were flirting.

I sat up and turned, placing my feet on the tiled ground. "Is that the purpose of today? Just looking? Or do you have further intentions for me?"

Reeve rubbed his hands together. "So many questions. So eager." He dropped his hands to his lap and tilted his head toward me. "Honestly, I haven't decided yet."

"Any other man would have cast me by now. Can you tell me what else you need to decide? I'm dying here." I rubbed my thighs together to accentuate my statement but also in an attempt to soothe the ache that had taken residence between them.

Reeve sat forward and pierced me with a look that made me still. "You want to know what I need, Emily? I need you to acknowledge that you know who the director is."

I didn't even blink. "You. Of course. What else?"

He shook his head. "We're not done with that one. It's the sticking point right now. You say I'm the director, but we both know that you fight that. You like to direct as well."

I opened my mouth to protest but stopped myself. Why wouldn't he see it that way? It was what I'd shown him all along—I'd pushed and bullied and tried to do things my way because it was the only way I thought I could get close to him. How ironic that it wasn't at all what I wanted? That what he really wanted from me in return was exactly what I wanted to give? Something I hadn't let myself give to anyone in a long time.

I wrapped my arms around myself and studied my pedicure. "No," I said finally. Honestly. "That's not true. I've just had my trust betrayed in the past and now it's harder to give up the control." My voice was thick and on the verge of cracking, yet the next words came without force. "And maybe it's not fair to ask you to be patient with me, but I promise I can be worth it. Because I want to be directed." I lifted my eyes to his. "I want to be directed by you."

Even though I'd taken off my clothes just minutes after I arrived, this was the first moment I truly felt naked.

Reeve stared at me, unflinching. Nothing softened or changed in his features, but when he spoke, his tone was grittier, more threadbare, as if my plea had somehow made him more vulnerable too. "In that case, all that's left is the screen test."

I searched his eyes looking for the invitation that I assumed his words gave. When I wasn't sure whether I found it or not, I took a guess and dropped to my knees in front of him, reaching for the drawstring at his waist.

He brushed my hand away. "No." But before I could let frustration take hold of me, he clarified. "I'm certain your mouth feels good. I've kissed it and I have a good imagination. I'm more curious about your cunt."

Then I *had* read him right. Hallefreakinlujah. Because I didn't want to wait anymore. My body was ready and needy and I wanted him inside me more than I wanted my next breath.

I leaned back on my elbows, spread my legs, and trailed one finger up the length of my bare slit. "Well, here it is," I said with a naughty smile.

Reeve's eyes grew dark and narrow.

Then, without warning, he was on me, holding me down on the rough concrete, my arms pinned at my sides as he hovered inches above me. His expression, though filled with lust, was hard and angry. "Don't tease me. Don't ever tease me. I take what I want, when I want, how I want. Don't ever believe that anything you do can influence my actions. Is that clear?"

I swallowed, fear and excitement coursing through me with equal ferocity. "Yes."

"Who's the director?"

"You." I barely managed not to stutter, and hell if I wasn't wetter than I'd been all morning.

He nodded once, sharply. "I'm going to fuck you now. I'm not going to wear a condom. I've seen your health records—"

I was too surprised to think before cutting him off. "You've seen my health records?"

He clamped his hand, hard, over my mouth. Then he loosened his grip, letting his fingers tug at my lower lip. "I'm not sure you understand who I am yet, Emily."

My heart pounded in my ears. "I'm learning."

Reeve trailed his fingers lower, down my neck, over the space where my pulse fluttered in my throat. "No. You aren't yet. But you will."

But you will. The words were a promise I ached for him to fulfill. I wanted him to show me and teach me and correct me. I wanted to learn to please him with a desperation I couldn't explain.

He pressed his pelvis into mine and I could feel the throb of his cock against my center through the thin barrier of his trunks. "Still want this?"

"More than ever."

His lip turned up in an appreciative grin while his hand reached down to undo his trunks. "I'm not concerned whether it feels good for you or not."

"What happened to your fucking being of value to both partners?" As soon as I said it, I realized I was pushing my limits.

But Reeve only smirked. "This isn't *my* screen test. It's yours. I don't give value until I know it's deserved."

Perhaps it wasn't the best time to throw his words back at him, but out they came. "Awfully confident, aren't you? Some people might call it egotistical."

"Emily—" It was a sharp warning, but I swore I saw amusement behind his eyes.

Still, I'd gone too far. And I didn't even know why. I just couldn't help myself, as though I thought that if I fought against him until the very last moment that I'd somehow hate myself less for it when I finally gave in.

Or maybe that wasn't it at all. Maybe I simply knew how good it would finally feel to submit, how rewarding. And it scared me. Scared me almost as much as the idea of not having it at all.

I was so aroused. Every cell in my being was on fire,

ready to combust. And Reeve was there, on top of me, telling me he would have me and all I had to do was let him. "Okay, okay," I said, serious now. "No teasing."

"Good girl." He braced his elbows on the ground at either side of my head, then nudged my thighs apart with his knee and settled between them. I could feel the tip of his cock at my entrance, could feel it twitch as his eyes scoured over my lips and breasts—lips he had yet to kiss today, breasts he had yet to touch or lick.

That was when I understood that he wouldn't. Not this time. He wouldn't caress or explore my body, wouldn't indulge even though I could tell he wanted to. He was going to make this as sterile as possible, for what reason, I didn't know. To say that he denied himself? As some sort of self-challenge? To prove a point?

Whatever his motive, I couldn't go along with it. I needed release. I was too wound up, too painfully turned on. At the risk of crossing the line again, I asked, "Any problem if I concern myself with it? With feeling good?"

He hesitated only a fraction of a second. "By all means, go ahead."

One hand clutching to his shoulder, I lowered my other hand and pressed my thumb to my clit just as he shoved up and inside me. I cried out in surprise, but also in a bit of pain and a whole lot of pleasure. I hadn't been exactly prepared, and damn, he was hung. Or he just filled me in the right way. I didn't know since I hadn't actually seen him.

Reeve locked his eyes with mine. Though he said nothing, I could see that he was just as shocked as I was by . . . by what? The initial contact? The fit? The electricity that radiated in waves from where we were finally joined? Jesus, he wasn't even moving yet.

And then he was.

He was moving, thrusting in deep, even strokes. Each time he entered, he buried himself to the balls. Each time he pulled out, he withdrew to his tip. His long, languid tempo ensured that I felt every part of his cock each and every time he filled me and released me. The tension in my belly knotted and tightened. With the added pressure on my clit, I'd be over the edge soon. *Too* soon.

Reeve's expression didn't change. He was restrained, in control while I was spiraling out of it.

I started to move my hand away.

"Put it back," Reeve said, the gravel in his voice the one indication that he was affected. "Keep touching yourself."

"Thought you didn't care. If it felt. Good for me." My words were breathy and my phrases short.

There was a glint in Reeve's eye. "I don't. But if you come, it will feel better for me."

I resumed the swirling of my bud, cautiously, but even with the half-hearted effort, my orgasm began to build. It was so erotic—Reeve's detached attitude, the primal way he rutted into me, the fact that we were in plain sight of everyone in his house. My fingernails dug into his shoulder and I bit my tongue, trying to remain as stoic as he was and failing as tiny sighs of pleasure escaped behind my closed lips.

Reeve pushed forward, inching my hips back so that he hit even deeper. Then he increased his speed, rocking my backside into the concrete in a way that scratched and stung. "Since this is all self-serving"—his voice was even grittier now, husky and raw—"you don't need to tell me that it feels good. Because I don't care."

"Right." Damn, though, it was too much. It felt so fucking good. "Ah, God. It's so. Ah."

"Don't say it." The warning that laced his words only inched me further toward the pinnacle. "Don't you dare say it."

"I'm not. Saying. Anything." But I was there, I was bursting and now only sounds left my mouth, syllables with no meaning but when put together said very definitely how fucking fantastic it felt. My entire body shuddered as my orgasm ripped through me. I squeezed my eyes shut and let it take me.

Somehow I could still hear Reeve talking. "You're coming," he said. "I can feel it. Fuck, Emily, you clench so hard." He forced through my tightening walls, continuing to pound into me with fierce determination. Then he was coming too, jabbing against my pubic bone as he spurt inside of me.

When I calmed, I opened my eyes to find him still hovering above me, still staring at me with intense scrutiny. I still couldn't quite get a read on him, but there was a question in the furrow of his brow. Or confusion. Irritation, even.

I took in a shaky breath and wondered what he saw on my face. Disappointment, I imagined. I hadn't expected to rock his world but I'd wanted to at least know I'd pleased him.

Then again, he was still inside of me. Maybe I had.

We stayed like that for what felt like an eternity. Finally, he sat back on his knees, pulling his trunks up over his cock as quickly as he left me. He trailed one solitary finger down my naked pussy and said, "Leave a landing strip next time you go into the salon. I don't like feeling like I'm fucking a little girl."

He left me. I dressed quickly and followed him into the house but neither Reeve nor Anatolios met me. The butler retrieved my purse and I was escorted to the door.

CHAPTER

12

I'd just stuck the key in the door when my cell rang. Though I was already balancing my mail, the next week's script for the show, and the Diet Coke I'd gotten from a gas station on my way home from the day's shoot, I fumbled to answer when I saw Reeve's name on the caller ID.

"I want to see you," he said, without preamble. Just the sound of his voice made my stomach flutter and dirty thoughts invade my mind.

"You do?" I braced the phone on my shoulder and pushed the door open. Inside, I dropped everything but the phone and my drink on the floor and turned around to push the door shut, eyeing a gray Bentley that pulled up across the street as I did. My neighborhood was swank but not Bentley status. It was something that drew attention.

But it didn't have nearly the hold on my curiosity as Reeve did.

"I wouldn't say it if I didn't mean it." There was an undercurrent of playfulness in his tone that had me breathless and wanting.

Be chill, Emily. "Huh. Does that mean I passed my audition then?" Having not heard from him since I'd left his house several days before, I'd waffled back and forth between thinking he was taking his time and thinking I'd fucked up. Either way, the week had seen me more than a little distracted, not to mention burning out a set of AA batteries.

"Was there any question?"

I fell into the front room armchair and thought carefully about my words. It wasn't a time to get clingy, after all, but I wanted to be considered for a role that was more significant than fuck buddy. "There were lots of questions," I said finally. "The audition was Sunday. It's Friday and you're only now calling. You play it awfully cool, Sallis."

"You know how casting decisions can take time." His grin was apparent through the phone. "Here's an answer to your lots of questions—you passed. With flying colors. And now I want to see you."

"To see me," I repeated. "For clarity that means . . . ?"

"I want to fuck you."

God, how did he make me blush so easily? "And when exactly would you—?"

"Now. There's a car waiting outside."

The Bentley. "How thoughtful. But why don't—" I cut myself off before refusing his ride. Though I hated the idea of being stuck at his house without my own transportation, I needed to make an effort to do things his way. "Okay."

"Excellent."

I was already heading to my closet, worried about what I'd come up with to wear on such short notice. "Tell your driver to give me ten."

"No."

"No?"

"Whatever you think you need to do before you see me

is unnecessary." His eagerness had me giddy. I had to bite back a giggle.

"At least let me put on something that I haven't been wearing for a twelve-hour shoot. I need five." My black-and-white A-line skirt was clean. I could pair it with a red tank and a white jacket. Throw on my black four-inch-heel Louboutins with the red accents.

"Five then," Reeve conceded. "Honestly, Emily, don't spend too much time choosing an outfit. Whatever you're wearing isn't going to be on for long."

Having a driver to Reeve's turned out to be a good thing. My body hummed the whole way over making it hard to hear my thoughts, and my thoughts desperately needed to be organized before I had another encounter with the man. Not having to drive gave me time to focus elsewhere.

You have an agenda, I reminded myself. *An agenda that doesn't have anything to do with stopping the reverberation between your thighs.* I'd spent a lot of time on my get-close-to-Reeve plan so I had a basic idea of what to do next, but since it was a mission that relied on improvisation, I didn't have everything entirely ironed out. I'd look for signs of Amber, of course, and, ideally, I would earn Reeve's trust to the point where he would let something slip.

Yeah, real likely with Mr. I'm N. Charge.

Maybe if I got in his inner circle—if I got him to take me to dinners with Vilanakis or even other friends of his—maybe then I could find a solid lead.

So much time had passed, though, and even Joe hadn't delivered any information recently. There was a good chance that I was chasing after a trail that was long dead.

But even if I was too late to rescue Amber, I had to know what happened to her.

Or you want the excuse to wrap yourself in Reeve. There she was again, her voice ringing in my ear as clear as if she were sitting next to me.

"Maybe that's true, Amber," I said quietly. "But it's about you, too."

"Did you say something, Ms. Wayborn?"

I looked up to find the driver looking at me in his rear-view mirror. "Sorry. Just talking to myself."

He smiled awkwardly, probably unused to conversing with the people he drove. It was an opportunity for me, though, and while I was sure that Reeve had spies in all of his employees, there had to be something I could glean from him.

I leaned forward. "It's Emily, by the way."

He nodded with another awkward smile that told me he'd never call me anything but Ms. Wayborn.

"And you are . . . ?"

His eyes darted from the road to the mirror and back to the road. Finally he said, "It's Filip."

Reeve seriously had his men trained. Getting even a simple name shouldn't be like pulling nails.

And now that I had his name, I'd reached a dead end. I considered a second. "Is that an accent I hear? Where are you from, Filip?"

He answered with less hesitation this time. "Egaleo, Ms. Wayborn."

I'd never heard of it, but I made a guess. "Is that Greece?"

He nodded. "Just outside of Athens."

Reeve either really liked being able to communicate with his employees in a language most people didn't know or he liked surrounding himself with people from his homeland. His parents' homeland, actually. It was hard not to immediately want to say the whole thing smelled of mob. I grew up on Hollywood stories, though, and was smart enough to realize that the most scandalous of options was not always the most correct. So I had to give it the benefit of the doubt.

Except then we were at Reeve's house, and Filip opened the door for me to climb out of the back. He wasn't wearing a tie, and as I passed by, I caught the edge of a tattoo peeking out from under his shirt.

I stopped and bent toward him. "That's an interesting tattoo. What is it exactly?"

Filip tugged at his collar, covering the design. "It's nothing. Mr. Sallis is waiting for you inside, Ms. Wayborn. Just go on in."

But I'd seen it before it had been hidden. A *V*, stylized to match the ring of Michelis Vilanakis.

No one greeted me at the door and the handle turned when I tried it. I headed through the foyer, the heels of my shoes resounding in the quiet house. Once the walls opened up to the main living space, Reeve was there, dressed in a sleek gray suit with a black dress shirt and gray tie and I forgot all about Filip and his tattoo. Reeve was so striking, so overwhelmingly captivating—I needed a moment to catch my breath.

I didn't get it.

He came to me immediately and pulled me to him, setting one hand on my hip and threading his other in my hair. Holding my head like he had that morning in my kitchen, he kissed me. Claimed me. Devoured me. He licked into my mouth with bold, possessive strokes, painting his presence with his tongue, stealing the air from my lungs, spinning my world on its axis.

Soon, he moved his hand off my hip and up, up my torso where he finally—*finally*—clamped his palm around my breast. His grasp was strong, his fingers kneading into me as he squeezed and released, mirroring the way my pussy begged to clench around his cock. I clutched to his lapels for balance, ready for him to push me to the couch, to the floor, to the wall. Ready for him to ruck my skirt up around my waist and plunge into the warmth of my body.

Just when I was thoroughly dizzy and lust-swollen, he pulled his mouth away. "Thank you for coming." His smile lit his face, matching the one I was sure was on my own lips. "And before you make some tacky joke about not having come yet, I'll assure you that you will."

I half-giggled, half-groaned. Half-melted in anticipation. "Well, glad that's out of the way."

His hand was still at my breast, his thumb teasing over my nipple now while his other palm wrapped around the back of my neck. He studied me, his eyes taking in my features with such intensity, as if despite all the time he spent looking at me he'd never truly seen me.

"I'm an awful host," he said eventually. "I should tell you to make yourself at home, but all I care about is making myself at home inside you."

Why don't you? What came out was, "Uh-huh."

His mouth found mine again as he grabbed my ass and drew me into him. If the last kiss had been intense, this one was consuming. My face burned from the scruff of his five o'clock shadow and my lips stung from his nips. I threw my leg around his upper thigh, opening myself, practically grinding against him.

Then, out of nowhere, the ability to think came rushing back, and thoughts, though jumbled, flashed through my mind, competing with my senses. Thoughts like, *Wow, I wasn't expecting that.* And, *Would it be out of line to start undressing him?* And, *Wasn't there something I was supposed to do when I got here?* And, *If this is how he makes me feel with this kiss, how the hell am I going to survive tonight?*

I began shaking my head, disconnecting myself from his mouth as I pressed my hands against his torso.

I was almost afraid Reeve wouldn't accept my retreat. I was also totally afraid he would.

Tonight, he was a gentleman though. Cupping my face, he asked, "What is it?"

My eyes darted from his collar to his ear to his chin— everywhere but his distracting lips. *We'll get back to that,* I promised myself. I had to remember Amber first. Remember that I was here on false pretenses. I might need to be able to make demands from Reeve eventually, which meant I had to well-establish the part I was playing now—a woman who was looking for a sugar daddy. I needed to ask for . . . something . . . to set the standards of exchange in our relationship. I had to do it now while he was in a good mood. But what to ask for?

I had no answer yet, and here he was waiting for a response.

I cleared my throat. "I'm trying to decide if this is a good time to bring it up." It was partly true. Mostly, I was stalling, trying to remember what I'd asked for from men in the past. Back then I'd needed everything from clothes to housing. Now I *needed* nothing.

"Unless you're talking about my cock, then it's never going to be a good time to bring it up." He was teasing though, his tone light. "So might as well get it over with. Come sit with me."

He took my jacket and purse and set them on an armchair. Then he wrapped his fingers in mine and pulled me after him to the couch. He sat down and I moved to sit next to him, but Reeve tugged me instead onto his lap. He pushed my knees apart so I'd straddle him then ran his hands up and down my thighs, sending electric sparks across the surface of my skin.

I watched his fingers disappear under my skirt and return on their next sweep down. "This is awfully distracting."

"It's meant to be. Tell me what's on your mind."

"Okay." *What had I wanted to say?* I swallowed, letting my weight settle on him as I gathered my thoughts. "So." Something stiff rubbed against my inner thigh. I looked down to find his pants tented. "Oh."

Reeve's pupils were dark. "Yes, I'm hard. You're sitting on my lap, what do you expect?"

"Nothing less. Just." I tried to adjust myself so that I wasn't pressing quite so intimately against him, but his hands flew to my hips, stilling me. The heat of his cock radiated through his pants, heat that was also reflected on his face. "Like I said, distracting."

He wrapped his arms around my ass and brought me in tighter. "Well, let me help make things clear. If you don't tell me what's up in about three seconds then you're going to lose the opportunity entirely."

God. His hands. On my ass.

But, focus! "Your audition," I managed. "I've passed it. I'm not sure you've passed mine." Lies. He'd passed. Passed and then some.

"Ah. Of course." His tone was stiff, but he began massaging circles on my backside through my skirt. "You want to be taken care of in a currency other than orgasms."

"Well . . ." *Did it have to be one or the other?*

His lip turned up in a knowing smirk. "Correction—in addition to orgasms. Why do I have a feeling you're going to be an expensive girlfriend?"

I took a deep breath in, flustered by his touch, empowered by the label he'd given me. "Because I am. But I'm going to try to be worth it."

"Oh, you'll be worth it. That's not an option." He spanked me. On my ass cheek. Hard.

I jumped from surprise, my face reddening with a flush that ran hot, straight to my core.

His expression darkened, saying he liked that. Liked spanking me. Liked my reaction. Knew that I liked it too. Unlike me, he was able to stay on topic. "So what's this going to cost me, Emily? You have a good paycheck, so you're going to have to tell me what you have in mind."

"Yes, I have a good paycheck." I nodded as I spoke, conscious that his hands were moving again along my backside, trying so very hard to keep focused.

And I still hadn't thought of anything to ask for so I was forced to improvise. "I can afford my apartment and living expenses. But I take care of my mother too so I don't have the extras, and I really like extras. Designer clothing is a weakness."

"If I had my way you wouldn't ever wear clothes." Forget what his hands were doing because now Reeve leaned forward and bit my nipple.

My panties went from damp to soaked. "Ah." *Concentrate.* "And I'm a shoe whore."

His head popped up, suddenly intrigued. "Now shoes I can get behind. Can't you just wear shoes"—he glanced back at the ones I was wearing—"like those, and stockings? Those thigh-high things."

Damn, I liked it when he got flirty. He still had that undercurrent of dark, but was also fun. Like he'd been when I first met him at the resort.

His other resorts. If I could get him to take me to some of his other resorts, maybe that could lead me to Amber. "Mostly, I want to travel. I want to see places, first-class style, and I don't want to travel alone."

"And that's the reason you targeted me."

"One of them." I ran my hands up and down his chest, digesting the words he'd just said. " 'Targeted,' " I scoffed. "As if I were a sniper."

He leaned back in the chair, distancing himself from me. "Aren't you?"

It bothered me that he thought that. Bothered me because there was resentment in his tone. Bothered me because his mood seemed to have changed with the statement.

Bothered me mostly because it was true.

I dropped my hands. "You really don't like me do you?"

"I still haven't decided." He didn't even try to pretend he was teasing.

It stung. More than I wanted it to. More than it should have.

I scooted off of him, awkwardly because of how I'd been sitting and because it was stupid for me to be hurt by what he'd said. He made it even more awkward when he didn't try to stop me.

Folding my arms across my chest, I walked to the windows overlooking the pool. It was almost prettier at night. The lights shone on the water, making it glimmer. Making it glamorous.

Much like this life.

I'd forgotten how sparkly it appeared on the surface, how it was really only smoke and mirrors.

"Emily." Reeve sighed softly. I watched his reflection in the glass as he stood and came up behind me. He gathered my skirt up and squeezed my ass. "I *have* decided I want to fuck you," he said at my ear. "Do all sorts of dirty things to you."

He could push me against the window and bang me right there. That would be plenty dirty. And probably a fitting way to fuck a woman that he didn't even like.

The thought made my chest feel hollow. How sick that it also turned me on?

Reeve watched me in the glass. "That's what you want too, isn't it Emily?" He pressed the length of his body against mine. "For some reason, I want to give you things as well. Which works out for you because I wouldn't ever give anything out of obligation alone."

I turned my head slightly toward him, showing him he had my attention. Wishing I could tell him that I didn't really want anything from him. Wishing I could be "liked," for once, instead of "paid for."

"Here's what I'm going to do," he said, pressing kisses to my neck in between his words. "When you leave here later, you'll take one of my cars. I'll leave the keys on the coffee table for you. It's yours. I'll have the title transferred to your name tomorrow. Will that do?"

Only if it will help me find Amber. "It's a start. I suppose beggars can't be choosers."

"I think you'll find in this case that beggars actually can."

I pulled away and spun to face him. "Are you saying that if I beg I'll get to travel?" I'd do it. I'd do whatever it took to find the truth and get away from this man. This man who was very much the flame to my moth. Already I feared that finding answers wouldn't be enough to sever his pull on me.

He put his hands in his pockets and straightened his stance. "I'm saying you get a car. I'll think about the rest." His wicked grin returned. "And also, begging is more than welcome."

Welcome, not necessary. If it wasn't necessary, he wasn't getting it.

After a beat, he said, "I'm going to get the keys and pull the car out of the garage. You will wait for me in my bedroom. Up the stairs, to the right, end of the hall."

I took a shaky breath. This was it. Yes, I'd already had him inside me, but I was certain that I hadn't yet been introduced to what things would really be like between us. If I wanted out, if I had any doubts at all, this was my window, before he put the keys in my hand.

Out was what I should have wanted. I didn't. And

suddenly, I was scared. Not of what Reeve would do to me, but of what I'd *let* him do to me.

I forced myself to make an effort toward self-preservation. "Reeve. Is there . . . do I need to know anything? Like what you expect from me . . . ?"

His eyes darkened. "You'll know." He paused, probably waiting for me to do as he'd told and go upstairs, but I didn't move. "What?"

"Do I need a safe word?"

His eye twitched, but he met me dead on. "You either trust me or you don't, Emily. If you need a safe word, you probably shouldn't be here."

He was right—I shouldn't be there. Especially when I was clearly walking into a questionable situation without being given any tools to get out if I needed to. If I'd learned anything from my past, I'd have run about now.

Except my past also told me that I was incapable of running from danger. "Well, isn't it lucky that I've never been really good at doing what I should."

This time I did move. I walked toward the stairs, taking off my tank as I did. I peered over my shoulder at him as I tossed it to the floor, smiling when I saw him fixed on me, crazy with desire. That eased me ever so slightly. I may have been walking into the fire, but there was a chance I wouldn't be walking in alone.

CHAPTER

13

I dropped my skirt in the upstairs hallway and my bra at the door to Reeve's room. Like the rest of the house, his private space was magnificent and modern. It expanded the entire width of the house and was broken up into two spaces with an entertainment area on one side and the sleeping area on the other. I went left, to the bedroom. The room was furnished with a king-size bed, chair, ottoman, bench, nightstand, and dresser, yet it was so large that it looked sparse. The clean lines and open space let the spectacular view of the canyons take center stage through the floor-to-ceiling windows that carried from the main floor to this one.

I pulled the ponytail holder from my hair, which I began to twist it into a bun as I walked to the glass. This area was on top of the living room and overlooked the same scene. Being higher up, though, the perspective was different. Grander. The emphasis wasn't on the landscape of the yard but on the opposite canyon wall and the night sky beyond. Instead of the sparkle and glimmer of fabricated light, there was the faint bleed of stars through the LA smog and shades of dark that extended on and on.

This was a more accurate view of this world. This was what was under the outer layer of glamour—endless dark. I could sink back into it so easily, embrace it, live for it, hoping for that occasional burst of star shine. But I knew from experience that sometimes—*often*—the light didn't ever get through.

And I was a girl who would let the dark swallow me up whole.

I couldn't do that. Not this time. I couldn't care if Reeve liked me or not. I'd fucked plenty of men that I hadn't liked. Hell, things would have been easier if some of them hadn't liked me as much as they did. I needed to look at his indifference as a gift. Needed to find my own apathy.

From now on, no attachment. Distance. Callousness. Minimum of pleasure. I'd fake my orgasms. My smiles would be superficial. I was an actress. This was just another role.

When he came into the room a few minutes later, I was sitting on the ottoman with my legs crossed, in only my panties and heels.

"I wasn't wearing stockings," I said. "This was the best I could do on short notice."

He surveyed me as he tossed his jacket on the dresser. "I approve." He stayed where he was and worked the knot of his tie, loosening it, his eyes never leaving me. "Take off nothing else. But get yourself ready."

Shit, this was going to be hard. He was already shredding me to pieces with the way he was looking at me. With the way he'd taken command of the room the moment he walked in. With the way my every cell wanted to fall down at his feet and obey.

How the hell was I supposed to only pretend to submit when that was exactly what I wanted to do?

Disengage, that's how. Self-denial. It couldn't be any harder than dieting. I just had to gather my willpower and stay in control.

I pasted on a sexy smile. "I'm guessing teasing is allowed when you ask for it."

He raised a curious eyebrow and began working the buttons on his shirt. Slowly.

"I'll take that as a yes." I spread my legs apart, hooking my ankles around either side of the ottoman. Then, making sure I had his attention—which I did—I licked the tip of my index finger and slipped it under the band of my panties.

His face remained stoic, but as his eyes slid down my body, they darkened and sparked. Was that even possible?

His shirt open now, he moved to undo first one cuff then the other. "Tell me what you want, Emily."

"Besides everything I told you downstairs?" The strip routine was killing me. Thank God for the masking of my panties. It hid that I wasn't actually rubbing my clit. There wasn't any way I could watch him while touching myself and not explode.

He eyed me predatorily as he removed his shirt and set it on top of his jacket. "No. Here. Now. From me. What do you want?"

"You."

"More specific."

"Your cock." I knew these lines. They were the ones every man wanted to hear. "I want your cock."

He moved to his belt now, undoing the buckle with deliberate care. "Too vague. What do you want me to *do* to you? Tell me."

Anxiety fluttered in my chest. "I want whatever you want." But my voice sounded meek. Tentative.

Reeve pulled his belt from his pants and flicked it with frustration. "Stop pandering."

I jumped at the snap of the belt, at the snap of his tone. I'd already dropped the façade of playing with myself. Now I dropped the sugar in my tone as well. "I'm not pandering. I'm trying to do what you want. You're the director. Remember?"

He smiled tightly. "And right now your director wants you to tell him what you want. In detail."

I stared, wide-eyed. Nothing was coming to mind except the truth, and saying that would make me too vulnerable. Too exposed. I needed another answer. Anything.

The silence dragged out too long.

"If you can't say it, then this doesn't need to happen." He turned his back to me, walking away as he spoke. "The car key is on the counter. You can let yourself—"

I bolted up. "I want you to fuck me!" The words tumbled out. "Hard."

Reeve spun back to me. "Where? In your mouth, in your cunt?"

"There." I shook my head, erasing my last response, knowing he'd want a more definitive answer. "My cunt."

"On the bed?"

"No. Against the window. From behind. I want you to strip me and press me hard to the glass. So it will feel like anyone can see. And anyone who does will know that I'm special because I'm the one you're fucking."

He crossed to me in four strides. Gripping my upper arms, he pushed me back against the window. "And you don't want me to be gentle. You want me to fuck you rough. You want me to leave you raw so that tomorrow you won't be able to forget for one second that I was in you tonight."

Yes. That. Yes. I nodded.

"Say it," he demanded.

"I don't want you to be gentle. I want it rough and raw. I won't forget that you were in me tonight." God, saying the words—the words that said what I really truly wanted from him—it did something to me. Made me even more aroused.

He knew that, I was sure. That man, I swear he could see inside my mind. Inside my soul. Knew just what it would take to make me come undone.

His grip on me loosened. "Take out my cock, Emily."

My hands shook as I undid the button and slid down the zipper to his pants. Then I drew in a sharp breath, surprised to find he wasn't wearing anything underneath. He was, exactly as I'd thought from our first time together, well hung.

Despite my promise to myself to remain detached, I was desperate to touch him. I had to do it anyway. He'd expect it. I closed my grip around his hard, thick length and stroked him. My eyes darted back and forth from my hand to his face. I couldn't decide what I liked looking at more—his steel erection or his heated expression. So many times, the enjoyment I got from pumping a man was the power it gave me, and there was this, too, with Reeve. But even more predominant was the anticipation of what that expression said this man planned to do to me. Of what his hot shaft of flesh would feel like inside of me.

No. I didn't care about that. It was inevitable, but I couldn't look forward to it. I could not.

Without warning, he flipped me around so that I faced the window. He positioned my arms above my head. "Don't move," he said in a way that made it impossible to disobey even if I wanted to.

He reached around to cup my breasts and I let out an involuntary moan. They'd been begging for his attention since his eyes first lingered on them. Having them finally touched, finally fondled and caressed, was more erotic than I'd imagined. More pleasurable than I wanted it to be. I decided I would die if he ever stopped.

God, how I needed him to stop.

But that asshole took his time—squeezing, kneading, pinching my nipples—all the while sucking and nipping at my neck, my jaw. Something in his approach made it obvious that this was for him, for his pleasure. For his satisfaction. Was he simply enjoying my body? Or was he claiming me? Because I'd be marked when this was all over. Maybe it was a good thing I didn't actually have any screen time. It would be a hell of a lot of hickeys for makeup to cover.

I was panting and on fire when he moved his touch lower, but, amazingly, still in control of my senses. I took that as a victory. One round down without losing myself to him. Could I make it through the next? My heart hammered in my chest as I braced myself for his fingers to find a new sensitive spot on my body to torment. Prepared for it to be my clit, I was surprised and relieved when, instead, he curled his fingers around the waistband of my panties.

"Thank you for telling me what you wanted, Em." He shimmied my underwear over my ass, slowly. Teasingly.

The canyon, I thought. *The lights. Focus on the lights.*

But I couldn't block out his voice.

"I won't always ask for your input," he said next, bending as he pulled my panties down to the floor. "And I won't always take it when I do." He maneuvered the material over one shoe, spreading my stance as he lowered my foot back to the ground. "But you will always give me what I ask for."

Give me what I ask for. They were trigger words for me. Words that turned me from a strong, competent woman to an addict begging for her drug. *The lights. Count the lights on the houses.*

Leaving my panties dangling at my other ankle, Reeve rose, trailing his fingers up the outsides of my legs until he was at his full height. He met my eyes in the glass. "While I won't promise that you'll always like what I do to you"—he pressed in closer, letting the tip of his cock tease at my hole before gripping my hips with both hands— "I will promise to take you where you need to go."

He thrust into me, stretching me, filling me completely. My eyes blurred and my throat went dry. It felt so good. So right. He plunged in hard and fast. Unrelenting. Unforgiving. Everything inside was tightening, building, gathering. I had to make it stop. Had to keep counting the damn lights. *Seventeen. Eighteen. Oh, God . . .*

I held on. Just barely. My eyes latched onto one spot on the canyon wall and I clung to it, focusing on it so intently that I was able to dull the amazing things that Reeve was doing to me. Even when his hand reached around to work my clit in quick, pressured strokes, I held to my focal point.

I added breathy gasps then. For his benefit. It was easy. All I had to do was open my mouth a little and out they came, my body sensing the pleasure despite my head's distinct denial of it.

The pulsing knot of tension in my belly remained, an orgasm ready to release as soon as I gave it permission, which I wouldn't. I could do this. I *was doing* this.

Time got lost in the haze of barely held control. I didn't know how long Reeve had been moving in and out of me, how long I'd been fighting the mounting storm inside. The sweat that layered my skin and the wobbliness of my legs suggested it had been a good while, but the exhaustion I felt may have been from the effort to keep my climax away just as much as it could have been from the physical activity.

Whatever the time span, I was wearing out. I needed him to be finished, and soon. I laid on the vocals, increased the breathiness in my sighs, raised the pitch of my moan, hoping these efforts would move him along. In my experience, men were always triggered by the sounds. They loved believing they'd affected a woman so much that she was reduced to communicating through gasps and groans. Maybe it would work for Reeve as well.

Except then he slowed his tempo and tugged sharply at the knot in my hair, bringing my face back toward his so forcibly I cried out.

"I'm not going to come tonight," Reeve said quietly at my ear, "until you're gripping me like you did last time. So either you decide to let yourself orgasm or I can keep at this for a pretty fucking long time. It's up to you. Just be forewarned—I'm not going to make it easy for you to withhold."

My grasp on the haze gave out. Sensation came reeling back into full awareness. Every part of me, every inch, every molecule was ignited and ready for takeoff. There would be no more fighting it. Not just because I'd been called out but also because of the way he'd done it, threatening and demanding. Blatantly reminding me who was in command. I couldn't control anything anymore if I wanted to. I was putty in his hands. I was the criminal who'd been cornered. Now all I had to do was surrender.

So I did.

I closed my eyes and let my body take over. My body that was currently owned and operated by Reeve Sallis. Now when he pinched at my nipple, I felt every zing it sent to my center. And when his other hand reached between us, drawing moisture from my cunt to my other hole, when he dipped a finger in and massaged the overly sensitive walls—the cries he elicited then were real and raw. The tension had built so long and so abundantly that even at its onset, it overwhelmed me. It shuddered through me with agonizing leisure, thundering through every nerve, gripping me with fierce control.

Then, finally, release. Blissed release. Stars shot across my vision and I fell, weak and boneless.

Reeve caught me and carried me to the bed where he

dropped me on my backside. Kneeling before me, he lifted my lower body up like a bridge, and entered me with a punishing stroke. Over and over he pounded into me, fucking me with fury and ferocity. I hadn't yet recovered from the last orgasm and this one was already starting to consume me.

My vision was glossy and unfocused, but I searched for his eyes, hoping to plead silently for relief. When I found them, when our gazes locked, something passed between us. Something without name or label. Something brutal and honest and undeniable.

That's when Reeve surrendered as well. He groaned and tensed. His whole body contorted as he ground into me, burying his cock as deep as possible, coming as hard as I had. It set my next orgasm off and I clenched around him, even as he fell on top of me in exhaustion.

As soon as we recovered, he rolled off of me, away from me. He put an arm over his eyes and said, "You can stay if you want. Or leave. Your choice." Then he went to sleep.

I lay silently, my body wanting to pass out, my head wanting to dissect and study. My emotions were what won out. They were mixed and intense and all over the place. They wanted me to run.

As I gathered my clothes, I tried to convince myself to stay. *You need to get closer to him. This is your opportunity. Accept his invitation.*

But soon I was dressed. And no matter how strong the argument, I couldn't bring myself to go back to Reeve's bed.

I found the keys he'd left on the coffee table by my purse and jacket. Outside, a gray car had been pulled out of the garage and was waiting in the drive. My already weak legs nearly fell when I saw it. I didn't know enough about cars to know the model, but I knew enough to know that Jaguar Coupes were pretty pricey. And it was mine. Reeve had given it to me in exchange for what had happened upstairs.

Which was what, exactly?

I didn't want to think about it, but the thoughts kept rolling unwelcome through my head. Even as I climbed into the car and familiarized myself with the controls, I was reflecting on him. On us. As I started the engine and pulled down the driveway, as I wondered how I'd get through the gate and as I sighed with relief when it swung open automatically, as I drove down Mulholland in a car that took every curve with such ease and beauty it was art—through it all, I was engrossed with Reeve.

Eventually, I let the thoughts take precedence. I said to myself what I didn't want to admit—I'd set out to capture him and instead he'd captured me. I couldn't fight it. It was done.

And though I'd keep searching for Amber—always— she no longer mattered in my relationship with Reeve. Without her, I'd still be consumed with him, obsessed with him. Owned by him.

I pulled to the side of the road at the first opportunity, and I sobbed.

CHAPTER
14

I'd read the same paragraph in my book three times and still had no idea what it said. Honestly, the only reason I had my Kindle open was to keep others from bothering me during lunch. A voice star doesn't require a dressing room, which meant I had no place to hide away on set. At least the catering area was big enough that there were other tables for those who wanted to be social. A mobile device in front of my face said that I was not one of those people.

Today, though, I couldn't even bother with the pretense. There was too much on my mind. Too much *Reeve* on my mind. It had been four days since I'd left him in his bed, and I hadn't heard a word from him. Even the title to the Jag had no accompanying note when it arrived the day before and I was riddled with doubts. Had I done the right thing in leaving? Had I fucked up in some other way? Did he decide that he didn't like me after all?

I picked at my tuna salad, so wrapped up in my head that I didn't see Joe walking toward me until he was practically at my table.

The set was a closed one with strict security. And I hadn't put Joe on any clearance lists. "How did you get—?"

"It's Vilanakis," he said, cutting me off. He sat across from me and threw a manila envelope on the table in front of him. "In the picture. She's with Vilanakis."

"Wow." I knew he'd get up to speed eventually. But I hadn't prepared myself with a reaction. "How, um, did you figure it out?" Mostly I wanted to ask, *Does this mean that you're going to tail Reeve again?* Because then I'd need to prepare more than a reaction. I'd need a defense.

Joe shook his head. "Doesn't matter. The question is how did *you* figure it out?"

"I . . ." *Fuck.*

Joe pulled a document from his envelope and placed it in front of me. "This came through my reports yesterday."

I glanced at it, not needing more time to study it to recognize it as a copy of the official title that had been delivered to me by courier the day before. Guess that answered whether or not I needed a defense. Unable to look at him, I focused on moving my fork around on my plate.

Joe leaned forward, forcing my attention. "Emily. Why is Reeve Sallis signing over the title of one of his cars to you? One of his expensive cars, at that."

I swallowed. "I thought you weren't watching him anymore."

"I'm not. But I still have a few flags out for suspicious behavior. This"—he pointed at the paper—"is definitely suspicious behavior. Want to tell me what's up?"

"Just. He. It's." I ran a finger down the bridge of my nose. "It's complicated."

Joe muttered something under his breath then leveled me with a stern look. "It would be easier to work for you, you know, if you weren't always working against me."

"I'm not working against you, Joe." My volume was higher than I meant it to be. I caught myself and both lowered my voice and leaned in closer to make sure no one could hear me. "This isn't about Amber. It's about me. Mostly. I can't explain or defend myself. All I can say is don't worry about me and Reeve."

"Dammit, Em," Joe said, hitting his fist on the table hard enough to make my plate jump. "He's not a good man. I can't protect you from the things he might do to you."

I covered my face with my hands. "I know." Then I threw them in the air. "I know." I didn't need Joe to tell me Reeve's faults. I knew he wasn't a good man. At least, I knew that he wasn't good for me. It was the same thing as far as I was concerned. "And I'm not expecting you to protect me. I'm in this on my own."

Joe shook his head. Then he sat back and shook it again. "Jesus, Emily. I don't even know what . . . Are you even still interested in what happened to Amber?"

"Yes." When he didn't look convinced, I said it again. "Yes. I am. More than ever." I searched his face, looking for understanding or at least acknowledgment. There was nothing. Joe was excellent at hiding his emotions. I bet he was a great poker player.

I sighed. "I don't expect you to understand. But hopefully you can do your job without having to. I have to know where she is. And if I get lost on the way to finding her, then that's what has to happen. Just . . . we have to find her."

Joe scrutinized me for several seconds, his knee bouncing against the table leg. Finally he cursed under his breath and pulled another paper from his envelope. He turned it so it faced me and set it in front of me.

I picked it up. It was stapled in the corner, several sheets of what appeared to be a list of phone numbers. I flipped through, finding some were highlighted, some crossed out. One was circled several times. Not understanding, I raised a questioning brow.

"Her last call was made from Sallis's ranch in Wyoming."

"What?" I looked down at the paper again realizing it must be a copy of calls from the ranch. "So that's where they were when she called me? Are you sure?"

"Apparently, it's one of his favorite resorts. He spends a lot of time there. They were there all summer after leaving the Springs."

I have to get there. It was the most prominent thought I had even though I wasn't sure what I could do or find out once I got there.

I set the paper down and looked at Joe. "What are you doing with this information? Are you following up on it?"

"I took a trip up there. Did some poking around but all I really got was confirmation she was there. Now I'm dropping this lead." He picked up the phone list and slipped it back into his folder. "She's been seen since then. This isn't necessarily relevant."

"But you told me anyway. Knowing I think it is." He also had to know that I would try to do something with the information myself. Did that mean he supported me even if he didn't understand?

Joe closed his eyes and circled his neck around, stretching the muscles. Then he cracked his knuckles and said, "Actually, I think it might be relevant too."

"You do?"

"There's some information that says Vilanakis might be involved in trafficking."

"Trafficking women?" I felt sick.

"Yes."

He gave me a second to process that, but he could have given me an hour and it wouldn't have been enough time. How could it be? The things that Amber did, the way she was—call her a whore or a slut and it would be offensive and also not far from the truth. She sold sex.

There was no denying that. But it was at her discretion. It didn't mean she deserved to be pushed into anything against her will. It didn't mean she deserved to be a slave.

"It takes a huge network to run an operation like that," Joe said, tentatively. "I wonder if Sallis isn't involved."

"God. No!" This time I had to cover my mouth. I hadn't taken that leap yet. Hadn't put Reeve into the Vilanakis/trafficking equation and the thought of it now repulsed me.

I tested the idea carefully. Reeve was cold and dominating, and I suspected that he could be rather cruel in the bedroom if he wanted to be, but did I think he sold other women to men who would do much worse?

"No," I said again, firmly. "That's not what this is." My own submission had been with consent. He demanded it from me but he'd never forced it.

"Are you sure?" Joe let the question settle. "Maybe he isn't involved with the worst of it. Maybe he simply provides financing. Maybe Amber found out. Tried to let someone know, called you. And when Sallis discovered it he turned her over to his partner."

I shook my head, unwilling to believe it. Was that naïve? Bile gathered in the back of my throat and I pushed my salad away. It was a horrible thought, but wasn't it the first scenario that made sense?

There was no way I could accuse Reeve without the proof, but defending him was equally out of my reach. I took a shaky breath. "Reeve's personal staff, the ones closest to him—they seem to all be Greek. They have the accents. They speak the language. Does that mean anything?"

"It could."

"One of them, a driver named Filip, has a tattoo on his neck that looks like the ring in the picture with Amber. Vilanakis's ring."

"Emily—"

I didn't want to hear his warning. "Maybe it's Reeve's people that work for Michelis. Did you consider that? Maybe it's his staff that turned Amber over to their boss. Maybe Reeve has nothing to do with it at all."

He reached his hand out toward me, his palm flat on the table. "Emily, you have to extricate yourself from this man."

"I . . ." He was right. Of course he was right. But. "I can't, Joe."

"Why? Has he threatened you? Tell me and I can help you." Joe stood and came around the table to sit next to me. He lowered his voice, and said, "Whatever threat he's made, Emily, if he told you not to tell anyone, you can tell me. I'll get help without jeopardizing you. I know people. We can take care of this."

"I thought you couldn't protect me," I sneered, uncomfortable with his closeness and his show of concern. Both were unexpected and unfamiliar.

"More like I don't want to have to."

"You *don't* have to. Reeve didn't threaten me." Not in any way I didn't want him to. "And I can't leave him. Can we just leave it at that and please, don't ask me to again?"

He seemed to wrestle with himself for a moment. "Okay. I won't. But tell me you'll be careful."

I forced a smile and met his eyes to reassure him. "I will." It wasn't exactly a lie, but it certainly was an impossible thing to agree to. Being with Reeve at all was, by the very nature of him, not careful.

It was better not to remind Joe of that. I changed the subject. "So what are you doing now? About Amber?"

"With the Greek mafia in the mix, it's an even bigger investigation than I first guessed."

"Are you saying you can't do it?" Until that very moment, I hadn't realized how much I was relying on Joe even as I conducted my own investigation.

"No. I can do it. It's just going to take a little more time

to get the leads we need. If Amber's been pulled into trafficking—" He caught himself, realized it was too grue-
some for me to consider. "Well. Anyway. It might take a
while to find her. But I will. We will."

"Thank you." I meant it so much that I said it again.
"Thank you."

"I'll let you know when I find anything new. And don't
call me. I don't trust that your new friend isn't watching
your phone. I'll have a burner couriered to you here tomorrow that we can use for future communication." He stood
and started to walk away.

After only a few steps, he called back to me. "Hey, Emily, if you got lost, I'd come looking for you too."

I was still reeling from everything else he'd told me. I
didn't have room for this as well.

Thankfully, he didn't wait for a response, and he left as
abruptly as he'd arrived.

The next several days passed without hearing from Reeve,
giving time for Joe's revelations to become a played-out
soundtrack in my mind. The new information scared me,
yes. For Amber. But it didn't change my curiosity about
Reeve. I'd already accepted my draw to him and it was
with the terms of "no matter what." He could be the worst
thing I ever imagined, and I'd still be pulled to him. And
until it was proven that he was actually a bad guy and not
just a rumored one, I didn't plan on fighting it.

I wasn't sure I could fight it even then.

By Saturday, I was desperate to hear from him again.
So far he'd proven himself a weekend lover, so if he was
going to call, I knew it would be today. Or maybe I just
hoped it would be today because it was that dreaded
February holiday. The one that saw chocolates and wine
overstocked in all the stores. At least those items were as
appropriate for self-soothing as they were for gift giving.

I was pouring my second glass of wine when the phone rang, and it was only a little past noon. Maybe that's why my chest felt funny when I saw the caller ID, but probably not.

"I didn't expect you to be the leaving type," Reeve said, skipping a greeting yet again.

"I was eager to take my new car for a ride." I curled my feet up under me on the couch and delivered my excuses with enough sugar to hopefully hide the truth. "And I had an interview scheduled the next morning. Besides, I figured you for the type to want your space." None of it was a lie, but mostly I didn't want him to know that I'd actually panicked and run.

"I appreciate that. But I don't mind you staying the night. It's nice to have someone to wake up and fuck on occasion."

Then he *had* wanted me to stay. Or he wanted me to in the future. It was sort of charming that he couldn't say it outright.

"Just no cuddling," I teased.

"Cuddling allowed on my terms."

Jesus, how did a reference to cuddling make me so wet? "I'll stay next time then."

"Tonight. You'll stay tonight."

My heart possibly somersaulted in my chest. "Okay."

"I have an event I have to attend first. A Valentine's Ball thing."

"Yes." Was he inviting me? He had to be. Who else would he go with and why mention it if he wasn't going to take me?

Still, Reeve was unpredictable. I held my breath, waiting.

"I can either pick you up on my way home or you can meet me at the house."

I wasn't sure whether he meant home from where he was now or if he meant something else. "Pick me up?"

"Yes. It starts at seven so I should be able to leave by eleven. I'd be by your house around eleven-thirty."

I let out a slow breath, surprised at how let down I was to be the after party instead of the main event. "Uh, I'll meet you. At your place."

"Are you sure? You'll be on my way."

"I'm sure." Could he hear the disappointment in my voice? "I have a beautiful car. Shame not to drive it."

He didn't have any obligation to me, romantic holiday or not.

Even though Reeve hadn't claimed me as his date for the night, I dressed up for him. I figured he'd be wearing a tux and it was a holiday. Or maybe I just wanted him to see what he'd missed out on. Either way, a low-cut black sheath cocktail dress seemed appropriate.

It was almost midnight when I arrived and both the gate and the front door opened for me automatically. The employee who greeted me at the house, someone new this time, sent me in then went out the front door behind me.

There was no one in the living area when I walked back, and, except for the light coming from the dining room, the rest of the house was dark. On the table was a coil of rope and a black velvet box. Even several feet away, I knew what kind of box it was. And that made me beyond curious.

I crossed to the table and flipped the top of the box open. My breath caught at the piece of jewelry inside. The chain was silver and simple, but the half-dollar-size sapphire-and-diamond pendant was like something I'd never seen. Something gorgeous and unbelievably expensive.

"Do you like it?"

I startled at Reeve's approach. Then I stammered because

I loved it, and I was sure it wasn't for me but not sure at the same time.

He reached around me and took the piece from its box. "It's yours. Turn around."

Stunned didn't begin to describe my reaction. Speechless. Dumbfounded. I spun so my back was to him.

He brushed my hair over one shoulder and I held it to the side as he fastened the clasp around my neck. I felt his lips on my bare shoulder where he left a solitary kiss.

"Happy Valentine's Day," he whispered. Then he took the hair I had gathered and tugged it back with a painful yank. "Now you have to earn it."

He stripped me naked except for the necklace and blindfolded me with a towel he found in the kitchen. He tied me to the dining room table with the rope and spent the next hour—or longer, maybe—teasing me, taunting me. Bruising me, spanking me. Bringing me so close to orgasm then denying my release. I could barely speak, barely form coherent words when he finally climbed on top of me and notched his cock in my cleft.

"Beg," he said. "You have to beg."

"Please," was all I thought I could manage, over and over, but it wasn't enough for him, and he rocked against me, closing in on his own orgasm without having entered me.

"I'm almost there, Emily. If you want to come with me, better tell me now."

I fought through the haze of exhaustion and frustration, desperate. So, so desperate. Desperate to the point of rage. "Reeve, you motherfucking asshole. I'm pleading with you for the love of all that is holy, please! Please, put your goddamn cock inside of me and let me come."

He let out a low chuckle that vibrated through my body. Then he bent down to my ear. "Not what I had in mind, but fucking hot all the same." He slid inside me and pushed his hips forward so that he knocked against my clit. It was all I needed to send me soaring.

I passed out, completely drained and sated. I didn't remember him untying me or gathering me into his arms, but I did wake up briefly as he tucked me into his bed. I felt the kiss he left on my forehead and heard the words he whispered: "I wasn't supposed to want to keep you, Emily."

Despite my exhaustion, the words imprinted. They were both sweet and ominous at the same time. I wanted him to keep me too. I was more than happy to be kept by him. Was he implying that there would be a reason that he couldn't? Or wouldn't?

But I was too tired to think about it any more than that. I fell into a deep sleep that lasted well into the next morning.

CHAPTER

15

I woke to sunlight streaming brightly through the wall of windows. Reeve wasn't there, but the other side of the bed had been slept in. Too bad I didn't remember it. I considered pulling a pillow over my head and going back to sleep, but my brain was already at work with a million thoughts that wouldn't let me shut down. One thought in particular I couldn't ignore any longer: now that I was in with Reeve, how the hell was I going to help Amber?

It had to be my priority. Reeve could be more to me than my connection to her, but he couldn't be *instead* of her. That wasn't a promise I was going to break.

So it was time to search for answers, and I wasn't finding any under the covers.

Besides, the smell of bacon wafting through the house was a siren I couldn't deny.

Since my dress hadn't made it upstairs, and since I preferred to not give Reeve's staff a show if I could help it, I searched through some drawers until I found a plain white T-shirt. I threw it on and headed downstairs.

I didn't expect to find Reeve in the kitchen, but the sounds and smells of coffee and cooking were the only signs of life in the house so I went there first.

To my surprise, it was exactly where I found Reeve. He was standing behind the island stovetop, turning bacon in a skillet with a pair of cooking tongs. A medium bowl on the counter had the remnants of an egg mixture and just as I walked over, four slices of toast popped up from the toaster.

"Morning," I said with a silly grin that came out of nowhere.

He returned the smile, his expression heating as he ran his gaze down my body. "I like you wearing my things."

"I like wearing your things." The giddy voice that spoke sounded like a freaking teenager. I cleared my throat and came to stand across from him, the island between us. "You're cooking. Where's your staff?"

"I gave them the day off."

"Really?" Everything about the situation was surprising—no staff, Reeve cooking. The last man that had cooked for me had been Liam and that had only been burgers on the grill. That was a decade ago. So much had changed. So much hadn't.

Thinking of Liam made me feel off balance, and I kicked my toe absentmindedly against the wood base of the counter. "I like it. Like being really alone with you." Whoa. Where had that come from?

Reeve set down the tongs. "As much as you like it when we're *not* really alone?"

I swear my blush extended to my toes. How did he know those things about me? How did he just understand what dirty things turned me on?

"That shade of red looks good on you," he teased. "Come here."

I couldn't look at him as I circled around the island.

When I was within arm's reach, he pulled me into him and I licked my lips, expecting a kiss. Wanting a kiss.

But it didn't come. Instead, he fingered the jewel at my neck. "I knew this color would bring out your eyes. But it looked better when it was all you were wearing."

"Such mixed messages you give, Sallis. You like me wearing your things, you like me not wearing your things. You're awfully confusing."

"And you're awfully distracting. I changed my mind—go back where you were." He swatted my behind and turned his focus on his meal. Or maybe he was as thrown by the tender undertones in the air as I was.

Come to think of it, "awfully confusing" was an understatement. I had a feeling that no matter how much time I spent with the man, he'd always be completely perplexing. I wondered if Amber had felt the same about him or if she'd managed to crack his code. I wondered if he'd given her jewels that brought out the color of her eyes and called her distracting. I wondered if he'd given his employees the day off and made her breakfast, kissed her in the kitchen while she wore nothing but his things. While she wore nothing.

They weren't the kinds of Amber questions that usually pushed for my attention, and it shamed me. It also reminded me that I needed to be asking other questions. Ones that would gain useful information and as many as Reeve would allow.

"So, is this something you do often?" Okay, I was weak. It was the only door I saw open, though, so I slipped in. Maybe it was just the only door I saw.

"Breakfast? I do it every day." He walked to a cupboard and brought back a stack of plates.

"Cook, I mean. Send away staff so you can be alone with a girl."

He seemed to think about his answer. "I can't say that I do."

"Don't worry. I won't let it get to my head. I remember; I'm not special." I added a wink so he'd think I was only regurgitating his words and not digging for the reassurance that I was somehow suddenly desperate for.

"I'll say this, Emily—I've dated my share of actresses and you're the only one who hasn't bent over backwards to try to keep me entertained. Outside the bedroom, I mean." As he spoke, he placed a paper towel on one of the plates and started moving strips of cooked bacon to it from the pan.

"I'm pretending that's a compliment." I wasn't sure what it was, to tell the truth.

"It actually might be."

He'd said it easily, with no complaint in his tone, but the more I thought about it the more the comment unsettled me, made me question if he wanted me to be something different than I was with him.

I thought of Amber. She was practically the definition of entertaining. She was the one who could never sit still, who wanted to go out to the bars and sing karaoke at the top of her lungs. She was loud and boisterous and color-ful, and while I'd always felt like I was too when I was with her, they were not attributes that had remained in my years without her.

Did Reeve wish I was more like her? I'd been focused on the sex, but did I need to be that for him to get him to open up to me?

It wasn't something I knew how to blatantly ask.

I crossed my arms and leaned my torso on the counter. "Did you not want your other girlfriends to be entertain-ing?"

His brow knitted slightly in the middle of his broad

forehead. "Usually I'm quite drawn to entertaining. But sometimes it can be exhausting."

"What about your last girlfriend? Was she entertaining?"

"She was both entertaining and exhausting."

"Is that why you're not with her anymore?" I hadn't even realized I was going to ask it before I did. And after I had, while I recognized that it had come purely from a place of insecurity, I hoped his answer would tell me things I needed to know.

He glanced up at me before turning to plate the toast. "It's complicated." When he turned back, he said, "And yes."

I could relate to the exhausting as well. Amber had been so much of both and, in the end, it was a lot of the reason it had become impossible for us to stay friends. Though she'd been the one to suggest it, I was the one who had actually walked away. I was the one who'd abandoned her. I was the one who was always looking back.

For all the reasons I'd always told myself I'd left, maybe that was why I'd actually been able to do it. Because by that point, I'd been tired.

It was entirely possible that Reeve had a similar story. "Then did you break up with her? Or was it the other way around?"

Again, his answer came after a pause for thought. "Not sure anymore."

I studied him, trying to interpret his answer. For the most part, what I'd seen of him had been stoicism and detachment. If he'd been the same with Amber, then maybe he could have cast her off without hesitation. He may have taken up with her for the fun, for the sex. She was certainly good at both. Then, maybe Joe was right. When it got to be more, when it got to be too much—an easy thing to imagine if Amber was still strung out and wild like she'd been the last time I'd seen her—did Reeve hand her over to his business partner? A man who sold such women to people who would pay a lot of money to break unbridled passion?

That was possible too.

But sometimes with Reeve, I'd seen sparks of something else that hinted at true emotion underneath his aloof exterior. It may have been in my head, a desperate need of my own to find humanity in the depraved way I allowed myself to be treated. *Enjoyed* being treated. But I sensed it now in his tone as well. In the way he'd said, "It's complicated." In the way he'd said, "Not sure anymore." The words were laced with sadness. Regret.

Maybe that just meant he felt bad for what he'd done to her, but it echoed so much of my own remorse that I had the urge to say something consoling. "Maybe it was a mutual decision then. Best for both of you. Though, I can't imagine anyone wanting to leave you."

Once said, the words sounded honeyed and hollow rather than earnest, and I couldn't blame Reeve when he treated them as such, cocking his head with incredulity. "What flattery, Ms. Wayborn. Are you trying for another present already? I'm surprised you're not still worn out from earning the last one."

No, I mean it. I can't imagine ever wanting to leave you.

I also couldn't imagine ever saying that to him outright. Because what if I found out that he really did hurt Amber? Wouldn't I want to leave him then?

I would. Of course I would.

None of that thinking was relevant now, anyway. And until I found her, until I knew the truth, I couldn't know what I really meant at all.

So I said, "I'm very happy with both the gifts I've been given and the methods you've chosen for repayment. That said, I'm quite a greedy woman. You're feeding me—I'm sure that's all I need to refuel."

"Greedy woman, indeed. And yes, refuel."

His grin, the subtle command, the promise in his subtext—they did things to me, made me want to move from investigation to flirtation. From flirtation to conjugation.

Amber, though.

I ran my thumb across an imperfection in the slate countertop and turned the conversation back to her. "Are you still friendly with her?"

Really, this was the question I should have asked a long time ago. Even *Do you still see your exes?* would have worked. I'd refrained from it because I hadn't felt like Reeve would talk to me about his past. Not after the way he'd threatened me after digging around at his spa.

I also hadn't asked because I'd known the answer wouldn't be conclusive of anything. If he said no, would that mean it was because he couldn't talk to her anymore? Or that it had ended badly enough that he didn't want to? On the other hand, if he said yes, I wouldn't very well be able to ask him to hook us up so I could know for sure. And how would I know it wasn't a lie?

He didn't look up from the orange he was peeling. "Who?"

Here I was fretting and he wasn't even following the conversation. "Am—um, your last girlfriend. Do you ever see her now?" Shit, I'd almost said her name. I had to be more careful.

Reeve separated the orange onto two plates and then turned to me, his brow furrowed. I tensed, thinking he must have caught my slip. But he said, "What's with the interrogation? Are you going somewhere with these questions?"

I pushed off the counter to stand upright, as if the posture would make me sound more genuine. "No interrogation, Paranoid Boy. I don't really know much about you. I'm trying to learn."

"You're trying to learn about my ex-girlfriends," he said, wiping his hands on a dish towel, "not me."

I peered past him at the sun's reflection on the oven door. "I guess I also want to know what I can expect for my own future."

"Let's get something straight here." He was forceful enough to draw my eyes back to him. "Women before you have nothing to do with you, Emily."

He may have meant it to be encouraging. But it wasn't, because he was wrong. The women he'd seen before had everything to do with me. After all, if it hadn't been for one woman before, I wouldn't be here now.

He couldn't know that, but I replied spitefully nonetheless. "In other words, don't ask questions."

"In other words, ask questions about *you*."

I didn't skip a beat. "Are you ever going to take me to any of your resorts?" But what I really wanted to ask was, *Do you wish I were her?*

He didn't answer, his face giving nothing away.

"Uh-huh. That's what I thought."

His expression softened slightly, but if he'd intended to say something useful, the buzzing of the oven timer cut it off. "The frittatas are ready. If you sit over there, I'll bring you your food."

I'd been dismissed. But only to the counter behind us. This second island had no cupboards or appliances built in and was lined with bar stools along one side. I took a seat at one in the middle and watched as Reeve spooned the eggs onto our plates, any desire to pout dissipating. For one thing, he was too delicious to look at with his sculpted bare chest and sweatpants that rode low enough to highlight the sexy V where his torso met his thighs.

For another, he'd said that he didn't do this often. What did that mean about me? I'd lied to him when I'd said I knew I wasn't special. There were too many subtle signs from him that suggested not exactly that I was, but that maybe I could be. In the bedroom, though. Outside of there, I wasn't so sure.

And what about Amber? Had she thought she was special? Had she been?

Perhaps it was best that he'd ended my line of questioning, because there were some answers I wasn't sure I wanted to know.

I let out a weary breath and was ready with a grateful smile when Reeve set a plate in front of me, and another at the spot next to me. He didn't sit yet, grabbing utensils and napkins next and making one more trip for mugs and the coffee pot.

As he filled my cup, I nodded to the unopened *LA Tribune* that was also on the counter. "A newspaper?"

"What's wrong with a newspaper?"

"Nothing. Except the death of trees. Welcome to the modern age, Reeve, where you can get your news on an environmentally friendly device called an iPad."

He shook his head emphatically. "It's not the same."

"No, it's not." I took a sip from my mug. "It's better."

"My father used to read the newspaper," he said, sliding onto the stool at my side. "As time goes by, my memories of him fade, but him and his Sunday paper—that's a constant. As long as they continue to print, I'll subscribe."

"I take back everything I just said. I'm a bitch." It wasn't like I could have known, but I couldn't help being disgusted with myself as I stuffed a bite of frittata in my mouth. "Holy shit. This is really good, Reeve."

"You're welcome. I'm glad you like it."

"Thank you for making it," I said, better late than never. "Where did a guy like you learn to cook?"

"My grandmother. She believed that every good Greek boy needed to know his way around a kitchen."

He was tender when he talked about his family, reverent even, and I had a feeling he'd tell me more if I prodded. There were things I could learn from the conversation, but I couldn't bring myself to pursue it. I would only use the information for gain, and while that was my agenda with him, it felt wrong to defile that now.

So I said simply, "You can feed me any time you like."

"Can I, now?" He reached over and picked a piece of orange off my plate. "Open." When I did, he placed it in my mouth but didn't let go, holding it there with his finger and his thumb. "Now suck."

I slid my tongue under the slice and sucked both the fruit and his fingers until he was moist and sticky and the space between my thighs wasn't far from the same.

"I may have to remember this for the future." His voice was huskier than it had been a moment before.

"Please do."

Reeve reached for the business section as we dug into the meal, which I took to mean he preferred to eat in silence. I decided to give him that, picking up the entertainment news.

"Are you actively auditioning right now?"

I turned my head toward him and found him peering at me sideways. "No. The show's going strong. I figure I can be happy with that for the time being." Or content. Or maybe just not miserable. Besides, my career wasn't really my focus at the moment.

Reeve made an *mm* sound, returning his eyes to his paper. I might have assumed he was bored with my answer, but I heard something else underneath. If he had something to say, I wanted to hear it.

I swiveled toward him. "Do you not approve? After all the other women you've dated, it's probably embarrassing to be seen with one who plays a silly robot's voice on network television."

He threw me a sharp look of disapproval. "Don't do that. You aren't that girl."

Not what girl? I wanted to ask. Because all I could think was that he meant I wasn't Amber. And I knew that.

He lowered his paper. "You just seem to not be entirely satisfied with your role on the show. When you talk about it, you're always demeaning it."

I started to refute him, but I couldn't. So I sighed. "It's not a dream part, no. But the show's a hit. And next year the producers have talked about making me a simulated life form instead of just a voice that comes from the walls."

"So you'd be on screen but you'd be playing a robot?"

I probably imagined the mocking in his voice, but if I didn't, could I blame him?

I let out a groan and covered half my face with my hand. "I know. It's not much better." My hand fell to the counter. "But neither are the roles my agent is suggesting for me. They're all fluff. Pretty face, valley girls with no substance. They're just as humiliating. Only in a different way."

"The curse of being beautiful," he said, and this time I knew he was mocking me.

I wadded up my napkin and threw it at him. "Not a curse. But being attractive doesn't always put me in a position of power despite what it does for you."

He'd suggested that at his spa, and while I'd understood what he meant, I enjoyed being able to throw his judgments back in his face.

Except it didn't work quite the way I'd hoped. "I don't know about that. I bet you could get the roles you want. You simply aren't going about it the right way."

"You're right," I said tersely. "I should invite myself

over to my agent's house some Saturday and swim naked in his pool, and I'll probably get my pick of scripts."

His eye twitched, the only indication what I'd said bothered him. "You could also demand that he give you better parts. Remind him that, yes, you could play those bimbo roles, but since you're also smart and talented, it would be a waste of your time. If he fails to acknowledge that truth, then you need a new agent. And with the success of your show, I'm sure finding someone else to represent you shouldn't be a problem. If that's what you really want, you should go for it."

It had been an idea I'd tossed around more than once, always deciding against it for no other reason than habit. I was used to being told what role I was supposed to play. By men.

But here Reeve was telling me something different. Telling me I had options. Encouraging me to make my own decision.

I didn't know how to respond, so I faltered and dismissed him. "You don't even know if I'm talented. You've never seen me act."

But he wouldn't let me get away with that. He tilted his head and said, "There are some things you just know."

There were layers to his statement, and in the back of my mind I wondered what other things he *just knew*. What things he *just knew* about me. But more dominant than those questions were the strange emotions surging inside me, noisy and bright and overwhelming like a carnival. Maybe I wasn't fun or sassy or "entertaining," but I was here. He'd made me breakfast. He'd given me options. He'd fucked me like I liked. And maybe he'd hurt my friend.

But he made me breakfast.

I picked up my coffee and sipped it, swallowing down the tight knot forming in the back of my throat. Reeve was still staring at me, and it made me feel both self-conscious and prized. Threw me off balance.

Needing something else to steal my attention, I glanced toward the rest of the newspaper stacked in a pile next to us.

The lifestyle pages were on top and as soon as I saw the featured article, my grip tightened on my mug. It recapped the Valentine's Ball that Reeve had been at the night before, and, fittingly, his picture was front and center. He looked fantastic in his black-on-black Dolce & Gabbana tuxedo, almost as stunning as he'd looked when I'd seen him in it the night before.

"I would have gone with you," I said, nodding toward the paper. The offer wasn't coming from disappointment or a need to push forward in our relationship, but from a genuine want to be that for him. To be his plus one.

It surprised me and immediately I tried to think of a way to take it back.

Before I could, he spoke. "Thank you. I appreciate that." His smile slipped away. "I've actually been meaning to talk to you about that." His tone was serious, and I braced myself for whatever he was setting me up for. "I can't date you right now. And I'm not going to take you out in public."

My chest tightened and the knot in my throat returned, and I felt like crying or screaming.

I couldn't do either. So I sat up straighter. "When you said I wasn't entertaining, I didn't realize that you meant I was miserable to be with."

He laughed. " 'Miserable.' Very funny."

I scowled, hurt by his declaration, humiliated by his amusement, on the verge of deeper, more intense emotions that I refused to reveal. I stood, ready to gather my things and leave.

"Sit down," Reeve ordered, suddenly sober. He waited

until I, reluctantly, did. "I meant, I won't take you out *yet*. I don't appear in public with women I'm seeing until I've been with them at least two months."

"You don't?" I was astonished as much as relieved.

"No. I don't. No exceptions."

I did the math in my head, calculating my own two-month graduation date. "So you won't take me out in public until the end of March?"

His lip turned up, teasing. Challenging. "If you're still around."

"I will be." My words were resolute.

"I kind of think you will." He angled toward me and ran his hands up and down my bare thighs.

It was distracting, but not so distracting that I couldn't ask, "Why the rule?"

"Lots of reasons. Mostly because, despite popular opinion, I don't think that the media has any right to my private life. They can speculate all they'd like, but I'd rather give them as little to feed on as possible."

There were actors and actresses I knew who felt the same, sneaking around the paparazzi for first dates and booty calls. It was completely reasonable for Reeve to adopt that sort of guideline for himself, even if having a set-in-stone probationary period was a bit inflexible.

Then I realized what that meant about getting to his other resorts, getting to Wyoming. My stomach sank. "And that's why you won't take me traveling yet either."

"Correct." He sounded almost sorry about it. "It's also why we'll only see each other on weekends until then. Weekdays are filled with business and promoting and since I work a lot from home, there's no telling who's going to be around here at any given time."

Dammit.

Two months until I had any chance of getting where I needed to be most.

Dammit, dammit, dammit.

I scowled, wishing he weren't touching me like he was. Wishing I had only my frustration to focus on. I gathered what I had of it up against him. "It would maybe have been useful to tell me some of this."

"Why?"

The cocky glint in his eye irked me more. "Because then I would have known what to expect. It could have saved a lot of agitation on my part." I pushed his hands off of me and swiveled so my knees were toward the island, away from him. *Two months.*

Dammit.

"You're right," Reeve said quietly at my side. "I should have told you."

I turned my head slightly toward him, surprised by his admission of guilt. "Then why didn't you?"

He looked like he wanted to turn me back to him, but he refrained. "Maybe I like seeing you agitated."

Yes. I was sure that was true. "Maybe you're just an asshole." The damn man simply smiled.

Then his expression slid into something more serious. "Maybe I didn't tell you because I hoped I could be a person who did make exceptions." He let a beat fall by. "But I'm not."

I knew what he was saying. Knew in my skin, in my bones, and while I didn't know why he hoped he could be someone other than he was or what—or *who*—had driven him to that desire, I understood exactly what it was to want to change. To try to change. To find it impossible.

And I knew what it was to expect that the people around you could live with that.

My annoyance and resentment dulled into a mournful acceptance. I was committed to finding Amber, even if it took longer than I'd originally planned. Even if each step of the way I found more common ground with my adversary. Even if I discovered he wasn't an adversary at all.

I let out a silent breath, determined to make sure he wasn't leaving out any part of his no-exception rule. "What about the women you're only seen in public with once?"

"Means I was with them for at least two months. Then when I took them out, they probably failed the night in public. Or I was just over them."

"You're so cavalier. Like I said, 'asshole.'" But I was thinking about what else he'd said. *"Failed the night in public."* So there were more unwritten rules I didn't know about? Would there be other hurdles I didn't expect?

He leaned toward me and whispered in my ear. "Stop worrying, Blue Eyes. I'm not going to throw you to the wolves. I'd rather be the one to devour you."

That, I was also sure, was true. And I didn't think he meant "devour" in just a sexual connotation, which made it even sexier that he'd said it. My body was already humming from before when he'd stroked my thighs, and now, though he'd sat back in his chair, his breath on my skin had left me heated. Even under everything else going on in my head, that always stayed constant—the simmer of arousal in my blood, stirred simply by his presence.

The discussion was over, but I wasn't quite ready to let it die. "Are there women who never make it to the two-month mark?"

"Many. There are women who never make it past night one."

But I had. And so had Amber. Plus all the women I'd seen him photographed with over the years. To think there'd been more.

I planted my elbow on the counter and propped my head up on my hand, pivoting to face him. "Huh."

"'Huh'? What does 'huh' mean?"

In that way that it was sometimes easier to point fingers at other people for the faults I didn't want seen in myself, I laid out my hypocritical judgment. "It means you're an even bigger slut than I thought you were."

"Did you just call me a slut?" Now I was sure he wanted to spank me.

I grinned. "If the shoe fits."

"It doesn't. It's your shoe."

"Now you're calling *me* a slut?" I deserved the turnaround, but I didn't deserve the term . . . not anymore.

"Yeah. I am." He stood and closed in on me, pulling me to the edge of my seat so that I had to open my knees around him. "What's more, you like it."

I put my hands on his chest like two stop signs, not pushing him away, but not letting him get closer until I made this clear. "When we're having sex, yes, Reeve, I like it. A lot, in fact. But not just in regular conversation. Mostly because it was true at one time, but it's not anymore. At all. You know, I can count the men I've been with in the last five years on one hand?" I could count them on two fingers, to be precise.

"Really?" He didn't bother hiding his surprise.

"Yes, really."

"Huh." He also didn't bother hiding his satisfaction. "I guess I'll have to save the slut reference for when you're underneath me."

"That would be preferred."

Without any warning, he picked me up and threw me roughly on the countertop, pinning my arms above my head with his hands.

"Like this?" His eyes danced with dark pleasure. I squirmed, trying to get loose, but his hold on me only tightened. "Is this what you wanted, slut? Such a fucking dirty girl. Such a greedy little whore."

Yes. Exactly like this. His tight grip on me hurt and the

counter edge dug into my lower back where his hips pressed against me, but I was instantly aroused, my breathing heavy, my mouth and pussy ready for invasion.

His gaze went to my lips, and then slid up to my eyes. He kept my hands pinned, but his pressure loosened and I stopped pretending to fight him. And the way he looked at me—with interest, with adoration—it stirred goose bumps to poke from my skin and made my chest flutter.

"Emily," he said, and I realized I liked my name when he said it. "Stay over every night you come here."

A lump formed in my throat. "Okay."

I wanted him to kiss me, thought that he might, but he stood up instead. "Now look what you did." Following his gesture, I found his pants tented.

He nodded his head in the direction of the stairs. "Come shower with me so you can take care of this and prove how miserable you make me." He left, completely sure I would follow.

I did. Of course I did, and as I took each step behind him, I remembered what I'd known since the day he'd shown up at my apartment and kissed me for the first time. What I'd somehow let myself forget. Whether or not Reeve was an actual killer didn't really matter. Whether or not he'd pushed Missy Mataya from a cliff or ordered someone to do it, or—*God, please no*—done anything that had gotten Amber killed, Joe was right to be concerned for my safety.

Because, little by little, moment by moment, without any shred of doubt, Reeve was certainly going to kill me.

CHAPTER
16

The consequence about a pleasant Sunday with Reeve was a Monday filled with guilt. My stomach ached as I drove into my incredible job in my amazing car given to me by an enthralling man who should be my enemy rather than my lover. If I was going to spend my weekends with him, then I needed to do my best to keep the rest of my free time focused on other ways to find Amber. Not that I had a lot of free time. With twelve-hour production days and limited avenues of investigation, it wasn't like there was a lot I could do.

But by the time I'd checked in at the lot, I had an idea of *something* I could do—I could talk to Chris Blakely. Frankly, I should have followed up on it before and if I hadn't been so consumed with my fascination about Reeve, I would have. Though Chris hadn't known Amber, he'd known Missy. He'd spent time at the Palm Springs resort with her. Surely he could tell me something new about Reeve during that time. Give me some inside dirt about the couple. His theory about the cause of her death would be worth a conversation alone.

While I wasn't as certain as Joe was that my phone calls were monitored, I decided it didn't hurt to be cautious. Also, Chris hadn't given me any indication of his opinion on Reeve. That meant I needed an excuse to reach out to him. I could bring up Missy as an afterthought. Luckily, a suitable cover story came up at that morning's table read.

As soon as I had a break, I called him on the cafeteria phone. I'd considered using the disposable but suspected Chris wouldn't take a call from the unknown number. A call that showed up coming from the studio, however, he'd surely answer. No actor could resist those calls.

He answered on the first ring.

"Hey, Chris, it's Emily."

"Emily. Hi. Wasn't expecting you. What's up? Did you lose your cell?"

"No. Stupid me, I left it at home, and I couldn't wait to talk to you so I'm using the phone on the lot." It was almost disturbing how easy it was to lie to him.

"Well, this sounds promising. I don't know how Megan will feel about it, but—"

I cut him off. "Stop it. That's not why. I have a lead for you. Just found out the show is introducing a new male character next season, and I knew you'd want to know ASAP." Really, I didn't think Chris had a chance in hell of getting the part, but he didn't need to know that.

"Serious? A cameo or what?"

"A recurring role. It's the mom's brother. I thought maybe we could get together, and I could give you some hints on prepping for it." Hopefully I could pinch one of the writers for some inside scoop so that I could back that up.

"Fuck. I'm out of town. When's the audition?"

"Not until after hiatus. They haven't even announced it

yet. So we have time." I'd just have to figure out how to meet with him without it interfering with my Reeve time. "Maybe you could even come to the studio. When will you be back?"

"Last week of March. I'm in Canada shooting the next *Warrior Wick* until then."

"They're making another one?" The first movie had been the worst thing I'd ever sat through.

"It's indie. It didn't have to make much to break even." He had a point there. "So we'll hook up when I get back?"

For a minute I considered just asking him on the phone. But I wanted the real dirt. The kind of dirt you got face-to-face with no time constraints. "Yes, when you get back. Maybe I can get my hands on a side by then."

I was disappointed it wasn't sooner, but it wasn't like I was going anywhere before my two-month probation period with Reeve was up. And since *NextGen* would be done filming the season around the same time, I could likely slip away on a weekday to meet with him.

I stayed at Reeve's both Friday and Saturday that weekend. And the next. It became our routine. Sometimes I worried about the passing of time, worried about Amber. Besides meeting with Chris, I couldn't think of anything else to follow up on and Joe was working any leads that came in. He was more and more certain she'd gotten wrapped up in Vilanakis's sex trafficking and that would take time to break.

I, on the other hand, was more and more *un*certain. About Amber. About Reeve. About everything. I saw no signs of mob engagement when I was with him. I also saw no signs of Amber. But I did see signs of me—the woman who I'd been. The woman I'd run away from. The woman I'd forgotten I loved being.

Each week that passed by I felt less like I was playing

a part with him and more like the act was what I put on the other days of the week. I'd lie to Ty Macy when he'd badger me about the origin of my hickeys. I'd dodge my agent when he tried to set up auditions for me, wanting to keep both my weekends and my break from filming as time to be with Reeve. I'd drift through my days, plastic and perfect on the outside, simmering with shame on the insides. Friday nights when shooting was over, I put Emily Wayborn to sleep and let Emily Barnes wake up.

It was early March when I woke up in Reeve's bed alone in the middle of the night. When I couldn't doze off again right away, I decided to get up and look for him. I put on one of Reeve's T-shirts from his dresser and padded into the hall. It was dark and a peek downstairs over the hallway bridge told me that there wasn't any light downstairs either. The house was quiet, and I realized it was the first time I'd truly been free to explore. Usually either Reeve or his men were around and I'd never had a reason to go into any of the rooms on the wing opposite the master bedroom.

But now I did. If I got caught, I was simply looking for him.

The first two rooms I went in were standard guest rooms, each with a bed and a dresser and a bedside table. The third room appeared at first glance to be the same, but then I noticed magazines on the nightstand. The last person to stay there had probably left them, but when I picked up the top magazine, I discovered it was the *People* magazine from a year before. The one that had my first celebrity photo. The one with Amber and Reeve in it.

It could mean nothing. It could also mean something.

Not wanting to flood the room with the overhead, I switched on the bedside lamp and looked around. There was a jewelry box and a hairbrush on the dresser. Strands of pale yellow hair clung to the teeth of the brush. I opened the top drawer and found women's underwear. The next drawers were jeans and T-shirts and lingerie. The closet was filled with more clothing—evening dresses, blouses, shoes, slacks.

Reeve had been with plenty of women. The items could have been left by anyone. They could have been left by several different women, collected and stored in here over time. They could be things he kept for the use of the current flavor of the moment.

Why, then, was I so sure they'd belonged to Amber?

Because she was the last woman he'd dated, probably. But if they were her things, why were they still there when she wasn't with him anymore?

The hair on my neck stood up and a chill ran through me. I didn't want to be in there. There was no way I would ever know why the things were there without asking, and the longer I stayed, the more my mind ran away with possibilities. I turned off the light and went looking for Reeve for real this time.

Since the downstairs was too quiet for me to think he was there, I went back down the hall and started up the stairs to the third floor. I'd never been up there either and had no idea what I'd find. I heard him before I finished my climb. He was talking to someone, and while that should have been a reason to stay away, I needed him. Needed him to reassure me that there wasn't any reason to believe he'd done anything to hurt anyone. Reassure me that what he'd shown me was the real part of him as much as what I'd shown him was the real part of me.

The stairs opened up to a single loft-style room. It was dark except for the moonlight coming in from yet another wall of windows. There was enough light to gather that the room was an office from the bookshelves and file cabinets along the inner wall. Reeve sat at a long sleek desk in the back corner, his face and bare torso illuminated from the large computer monitor in front of him.

"Fuck you," he said, and I froze. But his eyes were on his screen. "You're just pissed because I cleaned you out."

"That and other things," a male voice said in response, followed by something in Greek.

I couldn't tell if he was on speakerphone or Skype. Whichever, what kind of a man would Reeve be talking with in the middle of the night?

I wrapped my arms around myself and huddled in the cloak of darkness, watching him, not because I was snooping anymore, but because I had an innate curiosity where he was concerned and I was pretty sure that whoever he was talking to, whatever he was talking about, it wasn't the kind of conversation he'd want me to hear. Maybe I should just go back to bed.

"It's the family way," came the voice from the computer, "to hold a grudge."

"And Nikolas is especially good at it," Reeve said. His eyes never moved from the screen. "Why don't you come over here?"

"Come there? Me? Or Nikki?"

"None of you." He looked directly at me now. "Emily." He'd known I was there all along. Of course. He held his hand out for me to join him. Because that was what I wanted to do, because I'd do whatever he asked, I went. When I got close enough he pulled me onto his lap and wrapped an arm around my waist.

And instantly all my fears and doubts were calmed.

Now I could also see the computer and the whole scenario became clear. Three men's faces showed on the screen in three separate frames. Another frame showed an animated computer table with playing cards laid out in the middle and one more frame showed a hand of two cards.

There was also a box with names, current bet amounts, and total winnings.

"Online poker?" It was sort of charming to see Reeve involved in something so regular-guy.

"With real money, of course. And you're my good luck charm." Looking at his earnings, though, it didn't seem like he needed a good luck charm.

The current bet amount changed for the name *Nikki* and an indicator lit up to show it was now *Pet*'s turn. It was this latter man who acknowledged me first. "Who's this pretty thing?" He was about my age with dark features that suggested he was from the Mediterranean. The bright natural light that filled his screen suggested he was in a far different time zone.

Reeve dismissed him. "As far as you're concerned, she's no one. Make your bet."

"Watch her, though," one said. *Nikki* according to the screen. He was older than Reeve, by ten years I'd guess. His features were very similar to Pet's. Relatives, maybe.

The third one, *Gino*, studied me. "Yeah. Good point."

I tugged at the shirt I was wearing, knowing I was covered but feeling exposed with all the eyes. Without moving his focus from the screen, Reeve said quietly, "You know they're looking at you to figure out what my cards are."

"Oh." I hadn't even thought about them trying to read my face. It was hard to think at all with Reeve's thumb brushing up and down on my bare thigh. He probably didn't even know he was doing it, and it was sending electric bolts of want straight up to my core.

Pet's eyes narrowed. "Seriously, Reevis? You're already winning. Couldn't you have given us the girl for a tell?"

"That would be a bad idea," I said. "I can see his cards, but I know shit about poker. I'd lead you astray." It was totally not true. I'd played cards since I could count to ten. Reeve was currently rocking a flush and if the river card was a two or seven of hearts, he'd have a straight flush.

To him, I asked, "Reevis?"

It was Pet that replied. "As in Beavis and Butthead. It's been his nickname since he was, what? Fifteen?" Since the scoreboard listed *Reevis* as well, I presumed that all of the names were nicknames.

Gino nodded. "About that."

"And you're the butthead, Petros. Make your fucking bet."

Petros said something in Greek that sounded like cursing and entered something in the computer. Pet showed on the screen as having made his bet and the indicator moved to light up *Reevis*.

His hand on my thigh moved higher, under my shirt to where my leg met my torso and his caress here made it nearly impossible not to squirm. Maybe he knew what he was doing after all.

He turned his head toward me and his breath felt hot on my ear. "What do you say, Em? Should I bet high or low?"

Gino interjected with something I didn't understand and Petros responded with more Greek. Then he asked, "What are you helping Reevis for anyway?"

Reeve also said something I didn't understand. I looked at him, questioningly.

"They're trying to convince me not to take your advice since you know nothing about poker." The look he gave me said he knew full well that I understood the game. "I told them I trusted you anyway."

It was probably just something to say but it both thrilled me and gutted me at the same time. I wasn't someone he could trust. And as much as I wanted to, he wasn't someone I trusted either.

But I wanted to. I wanted him to trust me too, no matter how undeserved it was.

It was for that reason as much as because he had good cards that I said, "Then I say go all in."

He brought his other hand up to stroke his thumb across my cheek. "Can't win if you don't risk, can you?"

I nodded, not sure we were still talking about the game, and my chest felt tight and funny.

"All in it is." He dropped his hand to the keyboard to enter his bet. The animated dealer turned the river card. Two of hearts. Reeve took the pot with his straight flush.

The men groaned and complained. It was easy to make that out even without understanding the language. Reeve rubbed his nose against my cheek. "Appropriate card." He moved lower to suck on my neck.

He means appropriate because he won, I told myself. *Not because of its suit and number.* Because how could he say such a sweet thing and be genuine when he had a woman's wardrobe in his guest room?

The computer got ready for another round, and each man had to click in. Gino said something that seemed to be addressed to Reeve.

Reeve pulled his mouth away from me just enough that he could talk. "No. I'm out."

More groans. More complaining. It was Nikki who made the comment that got Reeve's attention. All the words sounded so much alike, but I would have sworn he'd also said "Michelis."

Or it could have been "Nikolas." Maybe that was Nikki's real name.

Whatever it was, Reeve didn't like it. He snapped something back. Something that made everyone else *ooh* in response. Then he leaned forward and turned the computer off.

"What did they say?" I asked. "And who were they? Friends?"

Reeve shifted me so that I straddled his lap. Straddled

his erection. He ran his hands down the sides of my torso sending chills skating down my spine. For a moment, I thought he wasn't going to answer me, and considering where he was going instead, I didn't mind not talking. Considering how much I was beginning to fear the truth, maybe it was best to avoid it.

But then he said, "They're my cousins. Nikolas is my uncle." *See, it* was *Nikolas*. "They asked me if I'd consider sharing you." He bent down and took my nipple in his mouth, sucking it to a taut bud through the T-shirt.

Both his mouth and his words had my heart rate spiking. Being shared had been standard once upon a time. It hadn't bothered me then. It really didn't bother me now. I'd still do it if Reeve asked me to. I just wished that he didn't want that. Wished he wanted me all to himself.

I wanted to know if he was planning that for me, but, like all the questions burning on the tip of my tongue, I couldn't bring myself to inquire.

"Have you done that before?" I asked instead. "Shared? With them?"

"Yes."

"Glad I put a shirt on." I hated the edge to my tone. Hated that his answer brought disappointment when it wasn't even about me.

Reeve released my breast from his mouth and rolled my nipple between his fingers. "I wouldn't have called you to come over here if you didn't." He seemed far less interested in the conversation than my body. Either he didn't notice I was affected or he didn't care.

"Right. Even though you've shared with them before. Even though you've let your entire staff see me." I was burdened with apprehension regarding him, but this, this one silly issue, if he could make this good, it would make all of it good. It would be a sign that he really wasn't what I feared.

He tugged the hem of the shirt and nodded for me to lift my arms. When he'd pulled it over my head, he met my eyes. "I don't mind what my staff sees because I know you like it." He kissed the surprised O off my mouth. "And yes, I've shared with those fuckers but only occasionally. And not ever before I was done."

It was enough. It was more than enough. Because I wanted it to be. Because I needed it to be.

He trailed his lips down my jaw and neck, heating my blood until it coursed through my veins like a river of lava, until I was scorching and in need of relief that only he could give.

Reeve leaned back from his kisses and pulled his swollen cock from his sweatpants. He urged me up on my knees and gripped my hips, positioning himself under my cunt, which was pulsing and eager and wet.

This was good. Sex with Reeve was always good. The things he did to my body were beyond fantastic. Beyond what I'd ever known my body could do or feel.

And this thing he was doing to my heart?

I shouldn't want it. Shouldn't acknowledge it.

But I couldn't help the breathy query that sailed off my tongue. "So what did you say when they asked about me?"

He buried his gaze in mine. "That I wasn't sure I'd ever be done."

And with those words he turned *enough* into *more*. He pulled me down as he lifted himself up, burying his cock deep in me, sending my hormones flying into the "feel good" stratosphere. Sending another part of me soaring there as well—the part of me that was more emotion than sensation. The part of me that was more soul and essence than pleasure receptors.

It was good that, even with me on top, Reeve controlled our rhythm because I was too overwhelmed, too in the clouds to be in charge of anything but the attempt to remain present. It was tempting to let go of that as well. To let myself drift and be taken care of. Let the pleasure buoy me until it crashed over me and swept me under.

But I stayed with him, because that's where he wanted me to be—*with* him. It was like he expected me to release and enjoy, but first I had to take the ride. With him.

Admittedly, I almost missed it. He gripped my hips and lifted me up and down, stroking his cock with my cunt, almost as though I didn't even need to be there. As though I were a sex toy, a warm body. So why did it even matter if I used him the same way?

Except, that was only one element of our fucking. There were also the words that had preluded. And, when he stood and pushed me back against the desk, bracing me between his body and the edge, when he lifted my thighs so that he could pound into me harder, deeper—that's when I was sure that the other element actually existed and wasn't in my head. The element that kept me anchored to him.

It was his eyes. More specifically, the way he never broke contact. He looked at me the entire time he moved inside my body. Looked at me with an intensity that didn't falter. Looked at me as though I were of value. A man had never looked at me like that while he was fucking me the way I liked to be fucked. I liked it rough and dirty. I liked to be debased and humiliated and commanded. Liked to be manhandled like a doll with no apology for how the sharp wood edge of the desk dug into my back or how the unbridled thrusts of his cock felt like they were ripping me apart.

How could someone do those things to me and still gaze at me with appreciation? With something akin to affection?

How could I let someone do those things to me and feel better about myself than I ever had? Feel more for him than I had for anyone I could remember?

Most of the time before this night and after, Reeve didn't show that to me. Usually he took me from behind so we never had to look at each other at all. Often, he'd make me come. Hard. Again and again. And sometimes it would be base and primal and only about him. He was always rough. Always raw. He fucked me however he wanted—fucked my tits, my mouth, my cunt. He'd tell me when he wanted my ass in the future, he'd take that too.

And then sometimes, rarely, in the middle of the night, he'd be sweet. Pulling me into his lap, kissing me, caressing me. Letting me fly but anchoring me with his eyes. Speaking words he'd never dare say in the light of day. Words that I'd never dare say in return.

It was these times that I felt the most connected to him. It was these times that he scared me most.

CHAPTER

17

After Amber and I had left Liam, we'd spent a couple of years in Mexico at a luxury resort. We had gotten a permanent room by banging the manager, and, on occasion, his son. The rest of the time we'd bang the men who stayed there. Retired men with loose pockets who were ready to sleep with anyone for the night. Finding a blond young thing was the highlight of their trip.

We were no longer a package deal, at that point. Sometimes we would share men. More often, we wouldn't. It had been riskier than staying with one man the whole time. Being a mistress. There were times during low season when we didn't get as much attention as we would have liked. The all-inclusive meal plan at the hotel kept us eating, but we hadn't always had money for other things. Things like waxes and pedicures and birth control. Once every couple of months we'd had to splurge on antibiotics from the local clinic to clear up whatever STD we'd managed to contract. Twice, I'd sat with Amber until they took her back to terminate a pregnancy, waited until she came back out so I could walk her to our room. Then we'd take a couple of nights off, sit on the beach, drink. And not talk about what it was that we did.

But as risky as it had been to our health, I'd thought it was safer. Emotionally safer. No one could get too close. No one could know me enough to really know anything about me at all. Or so I had told myself.

I'd been twenty-one when Amber first rescued me from a bad situation.

It had happened the way many hook-ups had back then—at the bar. Amber and I would go to the lobby for the nightly shows and then sit at the counter and wait for someone to approach us. Someone always did. The men were usually older than my father, but one night a preppy college boy named Aaron had found me instead. He told me he was spending the summer selling risky stocks for his daddy to the rich old guys at the resort, and I'd thought, *We're so alike. Both preying on the deep-pocketed wrinkly Republican men in different ways.*

I had liked feeling a kinship with someone. And Aaron seemed to like me as well. He bought me pretty things from the gift shop. Took me out on his father's yacht. Took me to bed. He was cocky and conceited, an asshole really. But I liked him, liked the kinky things he did. Sometimes he'd tie me up or put clamps on my nipples. Sometimes he'd put a collar on my neck. Sometimes he had hit me, and it was really sensual when he did. Sometimes he had hit me, and it only hurt.

Other times he had invited other men to take me to bed. Men who were possibly interested in going into business with him but needed an incentive. Aaron made *me* the incentive. When I didn't want to, when the men were too eager, too arrogant, I'd tell him no. And he'd tell me to do it anyway. More than once I came back to him bruised and bleeding, and he'd tell me he loved me, tell me what a good girl I was, tell me how I'd earned him another hundred thousand. Then he'd throw me a washcloth and tell me to clean myself up.

When I was staying with Aaron, Amber and I would meet by the pool each day, and I'd smile and explain away the marks on my body. At any point I could have told her what was going on, but what would I tell her? It wasn't like my relationship with Aaron was abusive. At least, not most of the time. I had loved a lot of the things he did to me personally. I had craved them. The rest, I figured, was what I should expect to live with if this was the person I truly was.

As summer had come to an end, Aaron became more desperate to make as much money as he could. His father had given him some goal that should have been impossible, but with me as his secret weapon, he was closer than he'd imagined he could be. He became obsessed with reaching it. Which meant he was more forceful with his demands for me. He pushed me to entertain more clients. He pushed me to let them do more and more depraved things to me.

And when I wasn't enough to win their accounts, he took it out on me. One night, his abuse pushed me to my limits. He used me in ways that a woman should never be used. I screamed, but I wasn't sure I ever said no.

I spent the next day in Aaron's room, curled in a ball on top of sheets that were bloody and soiled. When he left to do some work, I didn't leave. If it had occurred to me to get help, I was in too much pain to do so. Then when he returned that evening, he was apologetic. But cruelly so. In the way that I would have loved if I weren't so wounded.

I was barely conscious when Amber appeared. I wasn't even sure how she'd gotten there, but I heard her yelling and crying. "Get off of her," she'd shouted, over and over.

Her voice brought me to lucidity and for the first time in hours I was aware of what was happening to me. Aware that I was being hit and beaten and tortured while being fucked.

Amber wasn't a threat to him. He had no reason to stop. "She likes it," he had said. "Didn't you know that about your friend? She loves to be hurt. And she's better than a whore because she takes it for free."

She had pulled at him. Clawed at his shoulder and I'd remembered thinking I should help her. Or I should explain that Aaron was right. This was what I liked. And even when it wasn't, it was what I accepted.

But then his weight became heavy on top of me, and his movements still. I looked up over his shoulder and saw her standing with a nearly full bottle of tequila, blood dripping from the glass. Blood dripping onto me. Blood that wasn't mine but his.

She'd rolled his rigid body off of mine, not bothering to check his pulse or if he was breathing before she'd wrapped me in a blanket and took me to our room.

I went in and out of sleep for the next two days, but each time I had woken up she had been there, taking care of me. She fed me, brought me painkillers she'd swiped from someone or other. She cleaned me up, wiped away the blood and semen from my skin with a warm washcloth that she never let get cold.

And she had talked to me. "When you're well, we'll go back to the States," she had said. "We'll be partners again and nothing like this will ever happen again."

When I could talk, I asked her, "Do you think he's dead?"

She shook her head, but her words were honest. "I don't know."

Later, I told her that it had been going on all summer. She spooned me in the bed and cried, stroking my hair. "Why didn't you tell me?"

"I couldn't," I told her. Which had been true. All the

opportunities I had to tell her, I'd thought about saying something and the words never made it past my lips. Because I'd wanted parts of it. Because I had been too addicted to the thrills Aaron gave me to know when he'd gone too far. Much like how she was addicted to the cocaine that the hotel manager supplied her with on a regular basis.

Amber misunderstood me, thinking that it must have been Aaron threatening me that kept me silent. "We should have a code," she'd said. "A safe word. Something we can say to each other that means we need help, but no one else will know what it means."

I got silent after that. What was there to say? She'd saved me from something that I'd willingly put myself into. Someone that I had desired beyond anything explainable. Someone that she'd possibly killed, and, if she hadn't walked in, I might have let kill me.

I loved her for it. But, I hated her a little bit too.

Her iPod played in the background, something moody and unfamiliar that she'd put on repeat, something she did whenever she discovered a new song that she loved.

"What's playing?" I had asked, more interested in changing the subject than finding out.

"Do you like it? One of the men I met last week introduced me to it. It's a Leonard Cohen remake called 'Famous Blue Raincoat.'"

"It's pretty," I'd said. Then I'd closed my eyes, wanting to drift back into a never-ending sleep.

But Amber shook my shoulder gently. "I'm serious, Emily. We need a word. Anything." She paused, waiting for me to agree.

When I said nothing, she said, "How about 'blue raincoat'? We'll remember that from this song. How does that sound? Em?"

"Yes," I'd said, not opening my eyes. "That's good."

"Then that's what it will be."

She sounded comforted by this decision, as if it fixed everything bad that might ever happen to us.

It was ignorant thinking on her part. "Blue raincoat" couldn't help me. Because what good was a safe word if I knew I'd never use it?

CHAPTER 18

We wrapped up the season for *NextGen* on the last Friday of March, the same night Chris Blakely texted to say he was back in town. I used the burner phone to call him and made plans to see him the following Monday.

The weekend was spent with Reeve, as was every weekend. I left him Sunday night not expecting to hear from him again until Friday. But just as I was getting ready to leave for Chris's house on Monday afternoon, Reeve surprised me with a phone call.

"I miss you," he said, and tingles ran down my spine. "Since you aren't shooting anymore, I should have had you stay the night last night." There was never an invitation with him—he told me when I'd come over; he told me when I'd leave.

Was it wrong that that turned me on about him?

I cradled the phone on my shoulder so I could throw my hair in a ponytail. "But the rules," I teased. "I still have two days before I can be seen around your house during the week. My two-month probation isn't up until April first." I was actually down to counting the hours. Not just because I was eager for him to take me places, but because I was tired of balancing two lives.

Also, with each day that passed without looking for Amber, it was getting easier to forget that I meant to be doing that.

"Fuck two days," Reeve said.

"What exactly does that mean?"

"It means that my ranch manager from Wyoming happens to be in town along with some of his crew."

I nearly dropped my phone at the mention of Wyoming— the last place Amber had been with Reeve.

"I have meetings with them throughout the day," Reeve continued. "But I've also invited them for dinner at my house. I've decided you'll join us."

"Really?" I was almost as excited about him showing me off as I was about whom he wanted to show me off to.

"And afterward, if things go well, I'm going to fuck you in the ass. Prepare for that however you see fit."

I let out a laugh that showed more nervousness than I wanted it to. "Thank you for the warning."

"My pleasure." His tone was low and gruff. "And yours, of course."

After we hung up, I clutched my phone to my chest, heart pounding, trying to process the news. After all the time waiting, time that took me farther and farther away from finding Amber, I'd finally gotten a break. While it was entirely possible that I might not get the chance to ask any of the Wyoming staff anything useful, at least it was an opportunity. An opportunity that I planned to make the best of.

The acceleration in my pulse wasn't just because I was looking forward to dinner though. The *after* plans also had me anxious. I wasn't opposed to them, necessarily. I might even be excited about them. I'd been with men who'd given me the best orgasms of my life with a backdoor entry. I'd also been with men who'd hurt me so bad that I'd blacked out from the pain. It was never a position I agreed to without trepidation.

Honestly, it was never a position I agreed to at all. But since I seemed to have no willpower with men, I didn't ever refuse either. Sometimes that worked out in my favor. Most of the time . . . well, most of the time when it came to anal sex, my favor wasn't part of the equation.

So far, Reeve hadn't taken me too far, but I believed he could. I believed sometimes he wanted to. The question was did I trust him to be careful with me in this area? And did it even matter if I didn't? Because I knew damn well not to trust myself to know my limits.

Chris and I had spent the last hour talking about the part on *NextGen*. I'd advised him on his resume and listened to him read through the audition piece. Now it was time to segue to the topic of Missy.

I just hadn't figured out how to do that yet, whether I should casually drop her name or plunge straight in.

"Hey, I appreciate all this, by the way," Chris said. "Let me get you a beer as a thank you." He scooted out from the banquette and headed to the fridge.

I took a deep breath. "Hey. There's something I've been thinking about since the last time I saw you." Plunging in it was then.

"Shoot." Chris shut the door with his foot and started back with two Coronas.

Here I go. "Missy Mataya." I braced myself, not sure if the subject was a sensitive one or not.

He slowed his steps, his expression suddenly reserved. "What about her?"

A sensitive one, then. I'd have to tread lightly. "Well, she's the mystery of the century. I've never met anyone who actually knew her." I paused, hoping my curiosity seemed innocent. "And you said you visited the Sallis Resorts with her—does that mean you were around when she was dating him?"

He twisted the cap off a bottle and handed it to me. "Yep. I was."

"Damn." I took a swig and let the pause hang, hoping he'd volunteer more. When he didn't, I pushed. "So?"

"So . . . what?" Chris studied me. "You want to know if I think he did it?"

His tone said he was annoyed, but there was no backing down now. I lifted my chin. "Yeah. I do."

He scrutinized me. Then, with a huff, he shook his head and took a swallow of his beer.

I felt like such a scandalmonger, ready to feed on the gossip like every other person you meet in Hollywood. The press hacks, the paparazzi, the starfuckers, the wannabe celebs. I was as disgusted with myself as he was.

All I could do was own it. "That's really tacky, isn't it? I'm sorry. I'm too curious for my own good. I really don't mean to be that asshole."

The acknowledgment seemed to be all Chris needed. "It's fine. People used to ask all the time and it was bothersome, but I haven't thought about it now in a while, so it's really fine." He slid into the seat across from me. "It was rough back then, though."

"I'm sure it was. Losing a friend is never easy. No matter what the circumstances." At least this part came naturally when improvising, so much of it stolen from my own life script.

Chris took a long pull on his beer. "I was lucky though. I wasn't working a lot then and I got to spend a lot of time with her those last months."

"That's why you were at the resort in the Springs?"

He nodded. "She'd call me and tell me she was lonely

so I'd drive down there. Hang out until I had another audition. Drive back. Good times."

I allowed him a moment for the memory before asking, "Why was she lonely? Wasn't she dating Reeve Sallis?" It felt strange to say his name in such a detached way, as though I had no connection to him. As though he were someone I knew from infamy rather than someone I knew intimately.

It almost seemed like a betrayal.

"Yes." His tone was laced with barely restrained hostility. "And that dickface was most of the reason she felt that way. He was hardly ever around and when he was, he treated her like she was his property. Like she was a toy that he brought out for social events and blowjobs. The rest of the time he forgot she even existed. Left her with real strict instructions to not go anywhere, not talk to anyone. I was one of the few on the approved list of friends."

Now it definitely felt like a betrayal. This was Chris's version of their relationship. I knew full well how things looked different on the outside. There were things I could say, ways I could defend, but I bit my tongue.

"Oh, and she'd tell me about stuff he liked to do—kinky stuff." He said the word "kinky" as though it were repulsive.

"Like what?" I asked through gritted teeth.

"God, I don't remember now. But it seemed like it was some pretty fucked-up shit." He leaned back and put his arm along the top of the bench. "He'd bring other people into the bedroom. I remember that. Sometimes to watch. Sometimes for big orgies. And he liked to have her blow him in public. The worst, though, was when he wasn't around. He loaned her out to his buddies. Let them have their way with her."

It was funny how I hadn't noticed how straightlaced Chris was until that moment. He was alpha in the bedroom—a little rough, a dirty talker. But besides that, he was straight up vanilla. I'd detached myself so much from my past that I'd allowed myself to think his style was enough for me.

It was blaringly obvious now that it wasn't. Nothing he'd said sounded especially kinky, and all of it sounded pretty hot. I was irritated at his judgment. I was also unreasonably jealous of a dead girl.

I forced myself to take a breath before I asked, "How did Missy feel about that?" That was the only thing that really mattered, after all.

"How do you think she felt?" He probably didn't really want to hear my answer. Thankfully, he didn't wait for it. "It was horrible and degrading. But she wouldn't fucking leave him either. I could never get why."

Because she liked it, I thought, but I wasn't about to go there unless he did. This conversation was about getting insight, not pointing out Chris's closed-mindedness.

"But she also could have just been paranoid from all the drugs she took. That was another reason she stayed—the drugs his friends fed her. All the time they kept feeding her with coke. Giving it to her before she even asked."

Wasn't that familiar? "They do that so she'll be more into the sex."

"Yeah. That's what I always said." He sounded glad to be validated. "But she never saw it as a problem."

Another thing I knew way too much about. Amber never thought it was a problem either, and by the time I forced the issue, it was too big of a problem to do anything about. As trite as it sounded, I shared the only wisdom I had for him. "It's hard to see when you're in it."

He nodded but his expression was dismissive. "She fought with him about it though. Fought with him all the time, really. About everything. Fight and then they'd fuck. Sometimes with everyone watching."

I twisted my lips, trying to stand back and look at the

situation objectively. For many sex-driven couples, fighting was simply foreplay. If Missy had really been afraid, I would have pictured her docile and ready to please. The picture Chris painted portrayed her as feisty and willing to speak her mind.

In my experience, those weren't the signs of abuse.

"They fought that last night, too," he added, pulling me from my thoughts.

My pulse ticked up a notch. "You mean the night she died? You were there?"

"Yeah. I was. Crazy, right?"

"Um, yes." This was so beyond what I'd expected when I'd contacted Chris. I reached my hand across the table, grabbed his arm, and pleaded, "You have to tell me more. I'm dying here." If he'd had any thought of not telling me more, this would change his mind. Chris could never resist the spotlight.

"There's not much to tell," he said in a tone that suggested his words were falsely modest. "Reeve used to throw big parties. He was famous for them back then, and that weekend he had a huge one on his compound in the Pacific. Everyone was there—all Missy's friends. Reeve's friends. Friends of their friends. And everyone was pretty much drunk or high the whole time."

He took a long swig of his beer, his eyes catching on a space somewhere beyond me, and I suspected he was lost in memory.

I forgot to breathe, waiting for him to go on.

Finally he did. "That last day, Reeve and Missy went at it from the moment they woke up."

"Do you know what about?" Though fighting didn't indicate abuse, it could suggest a motive for murder.

"Everything. Nothing. The clothes she wore. The girls he hung with. His work. He didn't like how many drugs she did, but like I said, it was his friends who gave them to her. And they fought about his friends. They could hardly stand to be with each other. I'll tell you what, if she had come home from that trip, he would have dumped her within the week. I promise you."

"So you think he did it. You think he killed her." It was obvious from what he'd said, from the way he'd said it, that he thought Reeve did. But I wanted to hear him say it. Wanted to hear him tell me why.

Chris seemed to consider, working his jaw as he did, though I knew he had to have an opinion without thinking about it. Maybe he was considering whether or not to share it.

And while he considered, I considered too. Considered whether or not anything Chris had said made a difference to me. He'd painted Reeve as possessive, commanding, powerful, particular. All of that only turned me on. Even if Chris gave me proof that Reeve had killed Missy, pushed her off the cliff in a fit of passionate rage, would that matter?

No. It probably wouldn't.

Reeve was right. I wasn't scared enough.

Chris stood and went to the window, remaining silent so long I decided I'd crossed the line in my questioning. I cleared my throat, wondering if I should apologize or if it was time for me to go.

Before I could decide, he spoke. "The last time I saw her was around three in the morning." He stared out over the courtyard. "Reeve was nowhere to be found and she was going on and on about how she was going to find him and tell him. Tell him 'what she'd done.' I don't know what it was. She kept saying it was a secret. She was pretty drunk. And high. And I was too. She wasn't making sense, but no one was at that point. So I didn't pay attention. Even though she was worked up. And agitated. Maybe scared too."

He turned back to me, leaning one shoulder against

the window frame. "Do you know what I did then? While she was freaked out and afraid? I went to bed. I was sleeping while she was desperate. I was sleeping while she maybe struggled. Maybe cried and screamed. Sleeping while she fell to her death."

Chris squeezed his eyes closed tight and it seemed I should maybe say something. Except I had no idea what that would be.

And I was too lost in guilt of my own. *What was I doing when Amber needed me?* I wondered. *When she maybe struggled. Maybe cried and screamed. When she maybe found her death.*

"I woke up late the next morning." Chris's voice brought my focus back to him. "And I didn't have time to look for her to say goodbye before I caught the boat back. If I'd tried, maybe the search for her would have started sooner. Maybe people would have been questioned before they went home. Before it was too hard to remember what was said and who was there. Maybe I would have remembered more of what she said in her crazed state. Maybe I could have been more helpful if I'd tried to recall things then, instead of two weeks later when the police approached me. I'll never know."

"You can't live on what if's," I offered. It sounded as hollow as it felt.

He ignored my comment and sat back down with a finger pointed to the sky. "But those circumstances, those mistakes on my part don't change what I do know—that there was something that was off. Something big." He was fired up, intense. "Even when the Coast Guard tried to tell me I didn't remember things correctly. When they told me my story couldn't be corroborated, I never changed my tune. She was upset about something. So, yeah. There are people who say she probably fell. Because she was a mess and it was dark and no one was paying attention to anyone anymore. But you want to know if I think he did it? Yes. I do. Without a doubt. She told him something that he didn't want to know, and I don't know what it is, but I believe in my gut that's how it happened. So he silenced her. No, I didn't see him do it. No, I can't prove it, but he did it.

"And if by some crazy chance he didn't actually push her off that cliff, it was still his fault she died. All his. It was his fault she was there. It was his fault she was in a mood that sent her away from the house, away from safety. It was his fault his fucking friends kept feeding her coke like it was water. It was his fault that she thought she had to stay with a douchefuck like him. He took a precious human and he turned her into used, Emily. Turned her into a possession. He ruined her and then he killed her."

It was a beautiful moment, in so many ways. Watching a man speak with a conviction that I'd never seen. Hearing the desperation and pain under words of accusation. It was a testimonial. A baring of his soul. And instead of finding myself in it—instead of wondering whom I could blame for Amber, wondering if I would blame Reeve—instead of looking in the mirror for once, I looked at Chris.

And I saw him. Saw what he was really saying. "You loved her," I said, the realization complete now that I spoke it.

"Of course I did."

"I mean, you were *in* love with her."

"Yeah. Yeah. I guess I was." He leaned back, letting the admission drift from him freely.

"Damn." I wasn't sure if this changed his story or not. Did it make it more tragic? Did it bias his blame? Did it mean anything to my interpretation of the details? "Did she know?"

A grin danced on his lips. "I told her every chance I got." His somber expression returned. "Which wasn't as often as I would have liked when she was with Reeve. We were hardly ever alone. Always with those Greek cronies of his."

"His bodyguards and staff, you mean." I hadn't been out in public with Reeve yet. Once I was, would I even get the chance to dig where I needed to? Or would Anatolios always be on my heels? "I hear he's never without them."

"And he definitely never leaves his women without them. If not them, his friends."

"The ones who fed Missy the coke?"

"Yeah."

As of yet, I hadn't seen any of Reeve's friends. It was possible he'd removed himself from the drug world after her death. Though Amber would also have been attracted to those kinds of friends. Maybe he just didn't think he needed that to keep me around.

Or maybe I had seen them around and didn't realize it. "Who are his friends? Celebrities? People he works with?"

"People from Greece. I guess he grew up with them or something?"

"He grew up in the States. But he lived in Greece for a couple of years. Did they live with him? Or just visit?" My mind immediately went to the men from the poker game. They were the only people I'd seen him interact with—cousins, not friends.

"Just visited. A few of them were around a lot. At the resort too and they had rooms of their own. Five or six of them—all one family. All with the same last name, at least."

"Which was . . . ?"

His face screwed up as he tried to remember. "Give me a minute. It will come to me." He tapped his fingers rapidly on the table, as if the beat could trigger his memory. After a minute, he groaned. "Nah. It's gone. Wait! Pet. One of them was called Pet."

Petros. From the poker game? Reeve couldn't know more than one Pet. "Was there a Nikki or a Nikolas, too?"

"Yes. Nikki. Older guy."

"Gino?"

He nodded.

Reeve's cousins. He'd never said from which side, though. "Their last name wasn't Sallis?"

"Nope."

Joe had already stated that he thought Reeve's mother's maiden name was a fake, but I tried it anyway. "Was it Kaya?"

"Definitely not. And what's with all the questions?" He eyed me curiously. "Have you been hanging around with Reeve or something?"

"I . . . um . . ." I'd been prepared to say I was simply curious, but once I started naming names, it got trickier. I'd have to give something—or appear to give something. "I have a friend who's gotten mixed up with some people who might know Reeve. Really, I'm just grasping at straws."

"Geesh. Scary. But it doesn't sound like those are the same guys, fortunately."

"Yes. Fortunately." But if that was a dead end, there was still one more person to inquire about. The one I knew for sure had been in pictures with Reeve. "There's one more guy named Michelis. Was he at either the party that night or the resorts? Michelis Vilanakis?"

Chris slammed his palm on the table. "Vilanakis! That's it!"

"He was there?" I'd asked in case, but I was still shocked to find I'd made a hit.

"Yeah, maybe." Chris wrinkled his forehead trying to remember. "I don't remember him for sure, but Vilanakis. That was the last name of all Reeve's friends. Pet and those guys."

My heart pounded in my ears, certain I'd heard him wrong. "Pet's last name was Vilanakis?"

"Yes. Definitely. I remember Missy used to tease him about having 'villain' in his last name."

The room seemed to tilt and the light was suddenly too bright. I thought I might even throw up. I stood and took my beer to the kitchen sink where I poured the rest out. Then I flicked some cold water to my face. It didn't help. The world was off. Disrupted. In upheaval.

Reeve wasn't just connected to Vilanakis. He was related. His mother—it had to be the reason her real name was covered up. Because she'd been a Vilanakis. And if Reeve had stayed with his maternal grandparents after his parents died, he may have become close to them. May have become privy to their dealings. May have become involved, as well.

This changed everything, I was certain. Though I couldn't quite articulate how. Not yet.

"Emily, are you okay? You're worried about your friend now, aren't you?"

"Hmm?" I suddenly realized Chris had been talking to me. "I'm fine. The beer just got to me."

"There's cold water, if you want it."

In the fridge, I found a small bottle. I'd just taken a long gulp when Chris asked, "What do you know about the Vilanakis family, anyway?"

I hesitated, not wanting to say but knowing he'd Google as soon as I left. "I don't know anything, really. Except that they're part of the Greek mob."

"Are you saying that Reeve Sallis is connected to the mob?"

I crossed back toward him. "No," I said definitively, desperately. "*I'm* saying nothing. *You're* saying you saw him with some people named Vilanakis, and I'm saying there's a Vilanakis who's a mob boss. There's no reason to think they're the same people. Especially since you said you don't remember the one who's the mob boss actually being there."

But I knew they were the same people. Knew it in my marrow. And now I was scared. Not for myself, but for Chris. It was one thing to risk myself. Putting him in the mix was not fair.

The guilt was already forming a tight knot in my gut.

"Those guys were totally mob. It makes so much sense. They and Reeve acted like frat brothers." Chris was barely listening to me, his expression lighting as he began to put this revelation together with his past. "They were really sketchy dudes, Em. I wouldn't want to meet them in a dark alley. You need to get your friend away from them."

"I'm trying, believe me. But that's total conjecture. If you didn't see—"

"And, Em!" He cut me off, practically bouncing in his seat. "Missy mentioned Interpol. In her rambling, she'd said something about getting Interpol involved."

"She said she was going to get Interpol involved?"

"Yeah. I even told that to the Coast Guard. They said no one else reported that and it was just hearsay coming from me with no one to back it up. And even if they could back it up, her own words weren't reliable because of her chemical state."

But if what Chris said was true, if Missy really had tried to get authorities involved, and if I was right about Reeve being a Vilanakis—and I knew I was—then there was suddenly a very real motive for her to die.

I needed to sit down.

As I slid back into the banquette, Chris went on. "I told them about the fighting too. Everyone verified that and Reeve still got off. I used to think he probably paid his way out of a charge, but now I'm wondering if he didn't use the mob to strongarm the investigation."

It was exactly what I was wondering. "Any chance any of the mafia had anything to do with her death and not Reeve?"

"No way. They all left earlier in the day. That was one of the things he and Missy fought about. She wanted them to stay; he wanted them gone. He won. They flew out on a copter before noon."

"She wanted them to stay? Doesn't it seem like if Missy had info on them, she would have wanted them to leave?"

"Hmm." He frowned. "Maybe she was planning to lead Interpol to them on the island. With them gone, she might not have known where to send them."

"Yeah. Good point." Really, there wasn't enough to make solid conclusions, but there was more than enough to have pursued a prosecution. Well, enough if the police knew about the mob connection. It sure appeared like they didn't. If they did, they'd definitely been bought off.

"You know, it did seem like Reeve's friendship with those guys was strained after. I saw a group of them talking to him outside the church on the day of her funeral. He told them they needed to leave. At the time, I assumed it was because he was done with the drug scene. Now, though—"

"You think maybe he was distancing himself from them so that his ties to them wouldn't be discovered." I finished for him.

"Uh-huh."

We sat quiet for a minute. I was sullen and processing. Chris, on the other hand, seemed to be excited about the new angle on an old mystery. When he was excited, he talked. That had to be nipped in the bud, and now. "You can't talk about this, Chris. You know that, right?"

"What do you mean? We have to tell someone."

"No, we can't." After I said it, I realized that wasn't going to work. He was too determined to have some sort of justice for Missy. "I mean, I already have an investigator on the case. For my friend. I'll fill him in with all this. Then, I'm telling you, he'd say to lay low about it. Any spreading of this will draw the wrong attention."

He ran a hand over his face. "I don't know."

"Chris, trust me on this. This isn't something you want to be involved in. And my friend could be endangered from anything we say." I thought of something that would speak to him personally. "Think of your career."

"Yeah," he conceded, hesitantly. "Okay. You're right. You'll update me if anything happens?"

"If I hear anything. But it's a slow process and, honestly, it might never go anywhere."

"Justice for Missy isn't happening as a closed case either. At least this gives her a shot."

Don't count on it. I swallowed the last of my water, swallowing with it my guilt for deceiving a friend.

I set the empty bottle on the table and looked at my watch. I needed to get going so I would be ready for my dinner with Reeve.

I'd just opened my mouth to announce my departure when Chris said, "I'm sure you have other things to do. But before you go, want to get naked?"

"Chris!" I wasn't just disgusted with his timing. "You have a fiancée."

He smirked. "I had a girlfriend the last time we banged."

"You didn't tell me."

"It didn't come up."

"No. I don't want to get naked. I won't do that to another woman." I stood up, grabbing my purse from the bench next to me. "Besides, I really do have to go." And sex with Chris was not something that was ever happening again, not just because of Reeve's appearance in my life.

Fuck. Reeve. I wasn't sure what I was going to do about him now that I knew what I did. It wouldn't be figured out here with Chris, though.

Chris followed me to my car to say goodbye, sweeping me into a tight hug and kissing my cheek before pulling away. "Thanks again. And talking about Missy was good. Maybe I can get some closure. Overall, good afternoon, even though you refused my bedroom invite."

"I'm ignoring that comment," I said. Then I narrowly glared, giving him one final warning. "Remember, not a word, Chris."

"I got it."

"Good." I opened the door of the Jag.

"This is what you're driving?" He whistled. "I have to get on that show."

I cursed myself for not parking around the corner. Though, if I wasn't paying for my mother, if I was less conservative with my spending, I suppose the car *could* have been purchased with my own salary.

Deciding not to comment, I smiled and climbed into the car. I started the engine, and with a wave, I drove off.

CHAPTER
19

Three blocks away from Chris's, I pulled into a drugstore parking lot and let out a long, shaky breath. I massaged my temples, sorting through what I knew and what was merely a guess. What was still unknown, what actually mattered.

As horrible as it was to admit, I didn't care two figs about justice for Missy. She was dead. It was sad. But I didn't know her and it was in the past.

What I did care about was why she died. Or how she *might* have died, because it was still possible that she'd really just fallen. However, there was also a very good chance she'd been pushed. Silenced before she could lead authorities to the Vilanakis family. To *Reeve's* family.

No. I didn't know that for sure. But I would have bet money that if I called Joe and told him to look for Reeve's mother as Elena Vilanakis instead of Elena Kaya, he'd find something.

Then he'd tell me to get the hell away from Reeve. He'd tell me again that searching for Amber was a lost cause.

He'd tell me he'd do what he could, but it wouldn't be much considering whom we were dealing with.

I closed my eyes and tapped my head on the steering wheel. "Dammit, Amber," I said out loud, talking directly to her for the first time in weeks. "What the hell did you get yourself into?"

Seeing no other options, I gritted my teeth and pulled my burner phone from under the driver's seat where I kept it. I hit dial on the only contact that was programmed.

"What's up, Em?" There was concern laced in Joe's voice. It made me paranoid for a second. Made me feel like he knew where I'd been and what I was doing.

But then I realized he was probably only anxious because I never called him. "Not much," I said with as much cheer as I could muster. "Just . . ." God, Chris was going to kill me. Well, he'd never know. "I want to pull the investigation. Can I do that?"

I'd still keep looking for Amber, but I couldn't lead Joe or Chris to the same possible fate as Missy. It wasn't fair to risk so many innocent people. As for myself . . . I hadn't really been innocent since I'd first joined her and Rob in the bedroom. And she'd walked into the fire for me. She deserved my reciprocation.

Joe was silent a beat. "Why?"

I knew he'd ask, and it still caught me off guard. "Because I finally realize it's a waste of time and money." *Please, let that sound honest.*

"Did Sallis threaten you?"

"No!" That was the last thing I wanted Joe thinking, especially since it wasn't true. I had to be more convincing. "Reeve isn't a threat at all, Joe. In fact, the more I've gotten to know him, the more I see he didn't do anything. The rumors about him are exactly that—rumors. He's all bark and no bite. If Amber's still in trouble, it's with

Vilanakis and not Reeve. And I'm not getting mixed up with the mob." It was basically all of his previous points regurgitated. I couldn't get more convincing than that.

But he still didn't buy it. "This is fishy, Emily."

I leaned back against the headrest and stared out the front window. "I know it *sounds* fishy. It's not. Things are going really well and my relationship with Reeve is now more important than this investigation. I don't want to mess it up." My voice cracked on the last line as I realized it was actually true. Yes, I was more fearful than I'd been before about my involvement with him, but mostly because I couldn't bear to give him a reason to leave me.

Jesus, I was fucked up. I pinched at the corners of my eyes. "Sorry. I'm really feeling guilty about going behind his back."

"I can see how you'd feel that way," Joe admitted. "You're sure he's safe?"

"He's very safe. A kitten in lion's clothing." More lies, but it didn't feel as far from the truth as it could have. As scary as he'd made himself out to be, he hadn't ever hurt me.

Funny, how I could still comfort myself so easily. My gut knew it was false security and a little voice inside my head repeated the words I'd said to Chris earlier. *"It's hard to see when you're in it."*

"All right." Joe still sounded hesitant. "If you swear that—"

"I do. I swear. You can send the final bill to my accountant and I'll get you paid." I wanted to be done with the conversation. Even if he wasn't convinced, he wasn't going to keep up his digging if he wasn't getting any more checks.

"I'll do that."

"And, Joe, I appreciate all you've done. Thank you." I

took another shuddering breath, afraid the real crying would start any moment.

I was about to hang up when I remembered. "I'm tossing this burner phone now. Is that good?"

"In a Dumpster some place you never go. Erase all your texts and history first."

"Got it."

The call ended and I gave myself exactly one minute to let the tears fall. I didn't even know why I was crying exactly. Because I was afraid for Joe and Chris? For Amber? For myself?

More likely because I was alone in my search now.

As it should be, I told myself. No matter what men had come and gone in our lives, it had always really only been Amber and me. It was almost wrong to have involved anyone else.

I moved the car out of park, intending to drive behind the drugstore to throw the phone in the bins there. But a black car a few rows down started up at the same time and even though it left the lot ahead of me, I was suddenly paranoid. Because I was almost sure that car had followed me in the lot to begin with.

I waited to toss it until I found a car wash Dumpster a few miles away, when I was certain I hadn't been followed. Then I drove home.

When I got there, I found Reeve waiting for me on my front porch, sitting in the same chair he had when he'd shown up the first time, dressed in a suit, as he had been that day. I smiled as I came up the walk. It wasn't even forced. He did that to me, sick and sad as it was. He made me happy. He made me want to be transparent instead of hidden.

But Reeve didn't return the expression. His body remained still, his face even. And I knew before I put the key in the lock, before I even got close enough to feel the rage radiating off of him, that I was in real trouble.

The urge to run passed through me with lightning speed—there one second, gone the next. It wasn't even a thought I could feasibly entertain. I couldn't run from someone like Reeve Sallis. Even if he weren't standing five feet from me, he could hunt me down.

Besides, there was no logical reason to think that he knew anything about my afternoon, knew what I'd discovered about him. Sure, he was obviously angry, but maybe he'd simply had a bad day.

God, I was good at lying to myself.

Or you're just excellent at survival, my head said, in that voice that sounded an awful lot like Amber's.

If that were true, I wouldn't be letting this probable killer into my house. And I was. I even held the door open, gesturing for him to go on inside.

Reeve moved behind me and took the door from my grasp. "No. After you."

Only three words spoken and yet they said so much. They said, *I'm in control here. I'm the one who's calling the shots. And you're the one who agreed to follow them. What's more, you like it.*

Did I still like it? Now that I knew what I knew?

Fucked up as I was, I still did.

So though dread curled in my stomach like the remnants of a bad meal, I walked past him into the house, leaving him at my backside where I was vulnerable.

I heard the door latch close. The next thing I knew, he had me pinned to the wall with my hands held firmly behind my lower back.

"Hey," I said, wriggling to get loose. "You're hurting me."

He only tightened his grip. Without a word, he leaned in. Leaned in toward my mouth. Relief flooded over me, and I lifted my chin to meet his lips, more than a little turned on by his rough greeting.

But he didn't kiss me.

Instead, still holding my arms behind me, he slowly knelt, dragging his nose down the center of my body. When he was on his knees, his face in my crotch, he *sniffed*. Several times. Smelling my cunt through my clothing. Sniffing at me like a dog seeking out its bitch. It was weird and vulgar and depraved.

And damn if it didn't make me weak in the knees.

Then, just as suddenly as he'd grabbed me, he let me go. He stood and backed away, distancing himself from me as though he were Superman, and I was his kryptonite.

I stared at him, dumbfounded. "What the hell, Reeve?"

"No," he snapped. "You don't get to ask any of the questions here."

"If you don't want questions, you better start talking." Maybe it wasn't a good idea to pick a fight with a member of the Vilanakis family, but I had a feeling we'd fight eventually whether I did or not. His anger was palpable, and if he was going to be mad at me, I at least deserved to know which of my transgressions had set him off.

His expression was ice cold, his eyes sharp-pointed swords. "Chris Blakely."

My stomach dropped with the weight of a boulder, but somehow I managed to keep my composure. "What about him?"

Except, he wouldn't have asked about Chris if he didn't already know about him, so I might as well give Reeve what he wanted. "I spent the afternoon with him, is that what you're after?"

He rushed back toward me and pounded his fist against the wall by my head. "Yes, that's what I'm fucking after. What the hell did you think you were doing?"

He'd been calm before, in control despite his mood.

Now he was raving and rabid. His hands shook. His voice rumbled.

He's jealous, I thought. At least I hoped that's what this was. I could defend myself easily enough for that, since I hadn't actually committed any crime that warranted jealousy.

I forced sugar into my voice. "I was just helping him go over his audition, Reeve. He's a friend and he's trying to get a spot on *NextGen*. I gave him some pointers."

"At his house? Alone? Wearing that?"

I looked down at the jean shorts and long-sleeve V-neck T underneath my duster. It was casual wear and not particularly sexy. "What do you want me to be wearing?"

"Something that doesn't have your breasts falling out on display." He was pacing now, seemingly more agitated with each thing I said.

I crossed my arms over my chest. "I have big tits, Reeve. There's very little I can wear that doesn't put them on display. And if you're suggesting that something happened—"

He cut me off. "I'm suggesting that it wasn't appropriate for you to be at his house, alone in the middle of the day, regardless of what happened."

I'd definitely been with men who were controlling, but my circumstances had changed so much since then that I was out of my realm now. Reeve gave me presents, yes, but he didn't keep me, and with several years of independence under my belt, I wasn't prepared to have someone telling me what I could and couldn't do.

It pissed me off.

"Jesus, don't you trust me?" I threw my purse and duster on the couch so I could do some pacing and pointing fingers of my own. "You go lots of places with gorgeous women surrounding you and I can't spend a day helping a friend? I didn't fuck him."

"That isn't the point."

"Then what is the point? That you just want a say in what I do? That wasn't something you ever spelled out as part of our relationship." It was strange that he wasn't that concerned with whether I'd messed around with Chris, just that . . . Unless . . .

I spun toward him, hands in fists. "Is that why you were sniffing me? You were trying to see if I *smelled like sex*?" The idea made my blood boil hotter even though it was also admittedly provocative. "You could have just asked me."

Reeve shrugged dismissively. "My way was faster and more conclusive." He picked up the purse I'd dropped, and opened it.

I gaped. "Um, excuse me. That's mine."

"Do you have something to hide?" He continued rifling through my belongings, and I said a silent prayer of thanks to whatever God existed for telling me to toss the burner phone.

"It doesn't matter if I have anything to hide. It's *my* purse."

At least Reeve seemed calmer now, preoccupied as he was with his snooping. After a minute, he pulled out the sides I'd taken for Chris and skimmed them before tossing them and my purse back on the couch.

I smiled smugly, happy to have proof about the reason for my afternoon visit. "That was the script I worked on with Chris. Happy now?"

He ignored my comment and took a menacing step toward me. "The point is that you shouldn't have been with that guy, no matter what you were working on. So why did you think it was a good idea to go?"

He wasn't calmer after all, I realized now that I was eye-to-eye with him. In fact, he might have been even angrier, his rage pulled in and controlled, ready to unleash in a concentrated fury.

It would have been wise for me to back down, but I had to know if my crime was because I'd been with a guy or that I'd been with *that* guy. Did Reeve know what Chris knew about Missy? Did he worry Chris would tell me?

"Why shouldn't I be there?" I asked, not quite as confident as I had been a minute before.

"Emily," he warned.

"Because you don't like him? Because—" Something suddenly occurred to me. "Hey, how did you even know I was there?"

"That doesn't matter. Answer."

"Like hell it doesn't matter. Are you having me followed?" God, oh God, what if he was? The black car from earlier—that had been him! Or one of his men. *What if he had my phone tapped too? My house bugged? Who had I called? What had I said? What could he know?*

"Only when your Jag shows you somewhere you shouldn't be." He took another step toward me. "Answer my question."

Sometimes I didn't know when to stop. "Is that the real reason you gave me the Jag? So you could track my whereabouts?" How the hell had I not thought about that before?

As quickly as he had the first time, Reeve pushed me back against the wall. He wrapped one hand in my ponytail and yanked it roughly to the side. Then he clamped his other across my mouth, silencing me. He leaned in so he was only inches from my face and in a quiet, eerily controlled voice said, "Stop with the questions, Emily, or so help me I am going to lose it with you."

My heart clamored in my chest and my eyes widened. His hand over my mouth was disarming. Meant to keep me from talking, it felt close to smothering. For a moment, I considered biting his hand, but then decided it was probably not in my best interest and instead forced a deep, calming breath through my nose.

"Now." Reeve wound my hair tighter around my ponytail, getting a better grip. "Like I said, I'm the one who will be doing the asking. So I'm going to remove my hand, and you're going to tell me why the hell you thought it was a good idea to be at a man's house—a man who will fuck anyone he can and Hollywood knows it, a man who most certainly wants to fuck *you*—alone, hugging him in the street where any asshole with a camera could get a picture of you together."

He removed his hand, and I opened my mouth to answer. But I was distracted by what he'd said about Chris. Was he concerned about the paparazzi then? And not about Chris himself?

The question slipped out. "Does this have anything—"

Reeve pulled my hair tighter, snapping my head to the side and cutting off my words. "Take your time if you need it, but I want an answer to be the next thing that leaves your mouth. Nothing else."

Fuck. I was in trouble.

I was arguing with a devil. A man with money and power. A man who wasn't happy with me. It was exactly the time to be scared and cautious and indulging, and I was scared. But I wasn't being cautious or indulgent because the dominating bad boy type was my weakness. I liked seeing him come out to play. I wanted to keep him around.

But I also wanted to submit to him. Wanted to please and gratify and charm him. I wanted to say the right thing, more than I'd ever wanted to say the right thing in my life, but I wasn't sure what the right thing was. I'd have to make a guess. And from what he'd given me, I'd say it was being seen alone with a man like Chris was the error. The situation could easily put me in the most unreliable of gossip rags as his lover. I hadn't thought that Reeve cared about public opinion.

Maybe I was wrong.

"I wasn't thinking about what it looked like," I said finally and his grip loosened. "He hugged me, and I didn't think to stop him."

"You shouldn't have been with him alone in the first place." He moved his face in closer, his lips a mere whisper from mine now. His eyes, hard and cold, level with mine.

"I shouldn't have been alone with him in the first place," I repeated as he cupped my breast. "Even though it was completely innocent."

He yanked my hair again, and his other hand pinched my nipple hard enough to make me cry out. "I'm not looking for excuses, Emily. I'm looking for acknowledgment that you understand what you did."

"I do. I get it. Now."

He twisted the taut bud, not painful this time, but as a reminder. "Then tell me, why shouldn't you have been with him?"

"Because anyone could get the wrong impression."

"Go on."

"We could have been seen." I was breathless and needy and desperate. My eyes closed, relishing his touch. "Anyone who saw might think that I'm with him or twist it to say that I'm with him. And I'm supposed to be with you."

Smack. His hand slapped my breast, making me jump. "*Supposed* to be?"

"I *am* with you. I'm with you and I wasn't acting like it." I reached out to stroke his chest with both my hands, determined to reassure him. "I'm with you. Only you."

"Precisely." He let go of me abruptly and backed away.

I followed after him, pleading. "I'm sorry, Reeve. I messed up. I won't do it again. I promise." I sounded pathetic. Like an abused woman begging for her lover to strike her once again, though I hadn't been abused. I'd been treated the way I loved to be treated and the possibility of losing that, of losing him, gnawed at me. Ripped at my insides. The things I'd said to Joe had been excuses, but I realized in that moment how much I'd meant them. My relationship, or whatever this was with Reeve, was more important than anything that could come between us.

He ignored me, standing with his back to me as he seemingly tried to make a decision of some sort. A decision about me, likely. Whether he was done with me or not. Whether he'd give me a chance or call it quits. Whether he'd end things by breakup or more permanently.

Whatever his choices were between, even as he might be considering the darkest of options, I still wanted him impossibly. I threw everything I had into my next entreaty. "Please, Reeve. You never said . . . and I didn't know that was what you expected of me."

He spun back to me, resolved. "Then since I 'never said,' I better make sure you hear it clearly when I say it now so that you can never say you didn't know what's expected of you in the future."

He undid his belt buckle, and I imagined he planned to use it. To hide me with, I hoped. Not to strangle. But he didn't pull it from his pants loops, undoing his zipper and pulling his cock out instead.

"On your knees," he ordered, and in the grit of his voice I could hear just how angry he was.

I didn't move.

Please, no. Not like this. I'd been okay when he said he'd do this on the phone, but I'd thought I'd have time to prepare, both physically and mentally. I'd been okay when he wasn't angry.

"On your knees, Emily, or I'll get you down there, and trust me you won't like it if I do."

I wouldn't say no to him. Not just because of Amber or because I was afraid of what he'd do if I did, but also because I didn't know how. Slowly, I got down on all fours, my head away from him, my behind displayed for him like a present. *Don't tense up,* I coached myself taking a deep breath in, letting it out. It would only make it worse if I wasn't relaxed.

"No, no. Not like that," Reeve said. "Face me."

Again, I didn't move, sure I misunderstood somehow. "You said this morning . . ."

His forehead wrinkled, then comprehension flushed his face. "That was this morning. I'm not doing that now. When I fuck your ass it'll be for pleasure not punishment."

I bit my tongue, hard, so that I wouldn't sigh in relief. But now with the unwanted element removed and the reassurance that I wasn't losing him, I remembered I was also mad. I circled toward him then sat back on my knees, a pout firmly planted on my lips.

Except then I saw his cock, nearly erect in his palm, and my mouth watered. My mouth watered, and I hated myself for wanting him like this. After he might have been responsible for Missy's death. After he'd had me followed. After he'd been an asshole with his jealousy and the hair pulling and the sniffing . . .

God, the sniffing.

Dammit. He was an asshole, and I was turned on.

He leered down at me as he stroked himself slowly. Once. Twice. "Take off your shirt."

I did as he commanded, tossing it to the floor before sitting back and peering up at him under my lashes. His cock got harder, turning to steel, and the anger in his eyes was diluted with desire.

He took a step toward me, and my lips parted automatically before he even said, "Suck me."

I wrapped my palm around him and took him in my

mouth, pressing my tongue flat along the bottom of his cock as I slid down his length and back. Again, taking even more of him. Once more, moaning as my lips pressed against his flesh.

That was as much as he let me do before he took over. He grasped my head with both hands and moved me up and down over him. Forcefully. So forcefully that I had to hold onto his thighs to keep steady. His fingers dug into my scalp as he pushed me to take more on every glide, until I was taking the whole of him, deep-throating his cock on each descent. Until my face met with his pelvis, my nose pressed against him tightly, and he held me there. Held me still. Held me firm.

Then he let me go. He returned to the aggressive pumping, maneuvering my head over him in long pulses. I was no longer giving a blowjob but had become his fuck doll. His toy to use and defile however he desired.

After several strokes, he held me still again. He bucked his hips up, sealing my face so entirely to his body that my nose was blocked off, his cock crammed so far inside me, I gagged. I pushed at his legs, trying to move him just enough to get a tiny bit of air. He didn't like that. He continued holding me with one hand, using his other to shove mine off of him. I squirmed, my knees burning as I rubbed against the carpet. I couldn't breathe. I couldn't swallow. Saliva gathered in my mouth, choking me, and my head started spinning. My eyes and chest burned with the effort. I was panicking now, desperate for him to release me, but the more I fought, the tighter he gripped.

It was a message, I realized. *Take it. You take what I give. I decide,* he was saying. *I decide who you see. I decide where you go. I decide if you move. I decide if you breathe.*

I got it. I stopped fighting.

He released me. He even let me take a break, catch my

breath. For barely a few seconds, though. Then he drove back in.

This time, he allowed himself to enjoy it, no longer proving a point. Holding my head in place, he fucked my mouth. "Like that," he told me, his voice rough and threadbare. "Just like that."

His strokes were deep and fast and demanding, but no longer a message. Now he spoke what he wanted me to hear in raspy clipped phrases. "It's hard to forget about me now. Isn't it? When I'm balls deep. In your mouth. When I'm throbbing. Against your tongue. When I'm using you. The way you're made to be used."

"Mm-hmm," I moaned against his rod. I was made for exactly this. To please men like him. To please him. I *wanted* this. Even as his thrusts became erratic and his tip knocked against the back of my throat, I wanted to give. Wanted him to take. Wanted him to use me. Wanted him to see that I did know my place. Wanted him to see that I liked my place.

It excited me even. I was desperate to have him finish. Have him explode in my mouth. I'd swallow it all, lick up every drop knowing it would be a gift. I was wet and aroused in anticipation of sucking him to the very end.

But, just when I was certain he was about to come, he pushed me off of him.

I tried to reclaim him, but he put one hand on top of my head to keep me still and used the other to jack himself to the finish. When he came, he aimed it at my breasts, covering me with his milky seed, bathing me in long spurts of cum. Marking me. Claiming me. Reminding me once more that I was his. Telling me loud and clear that he expected that I act like it first and foremost from now on.

He didn't let me clean him up. It was a punishment, after all, and he denied me even this gift, picking up my shirt to wipe the last beads off of his cock instead.

It only turned me on more.

"Maybe now you can remember who you belong to," he said, as he tucked himself back into his suit pants, in case I hadn't gotten the memo.

I pinned my eyes to the floor. "I remember."

"My dinner plans could take a short time or could take several hours. Regardless, you'll be waiting for me in my bed by ten. It would be preferable that you're naked."

My head jerked up. "I'm not going to dinner with you?"

He was standing at the mirror by the front door, straightening his hair and tie. "No. You're not."

I scrambled to my feet, ready to beg for him to change his mind. I needed to meet his ranch staff, but it was more than that. I needed him to claim me to others as completely as he'd claimed me in private. I needed to prove I could be his in the way he wanted me to be.

But before I could voice my plea, he turned back to me. "How would it look that you were at one man's house in the afternoon and then at dinner with me? It will look like I can't keep my woman in control. Until you can act accordingly, I can't claim you publicly as mine."

Everything inside me deflated. His declaration proved he knew me well. He knew what I wanted and he refused to give it. This was the true punishment of the afternoon. This was the thing meant to hurt me most, and it did.

He put his hand on the doorknob but paused to say, "And, Emily, clean up, but don't get yourself off. I know you want to, but it's for me to decide if you deserve it. Right now you don't."

He left, and I knew he was right. I didn't deserve it.

CHAPTER
20

I took a long shower to clean up and cry. Mixed with the hot burst of water that fell over me from the nozzle, my tears were easier to ignore. I kept my eyes closed and put my face in the stream so the salt-laced drops would wash away. If I tasted them, I'd have to acknowledge them. If I acknowledged them, I'd have to acknowledge their source.

The water was cold by the time I'd finished, but I still had a few hours before I went to Reeve's. I poured a glass of wine. I nibbled at a salad. When I couldn't take it anymore, I gathered myself and headed out. It wasn't yet seven, but he'd said to be in his bed *by* ten. Waiting in his room, surrounded by his smell and his things, was better than waiting at home alone.

I needed gas so I stopped at the Corner Mart and went inside for an iced coffee. After filling a cup, I stopped to peruse the magazine aisle, chewing on my straw as I picked out familiar faces on the covers. Someone came up behind me and without looking up, I stepped forward to let the person pass but instead he just moved in closer to me. *Too close.*

I went rigid.

Heavy breath came at my neck followed by a low whisper at my ear. "If you're being watched, don't turn around. Just nod."

I spun to face him. "Jesus, Joe. You scared the shit out of me." Paranoid that maybe I'd been followed by Reeve, and not wanting to be seen with Joe, I glanced out the window, looking for the black car from earlier. Over my shoulder, I asked, "What are you doing here, anyway?"

Joe picked up a *Hollywood Star* and began flipping through it. "I wanted to make sure you were all right after Sallis left you today."

Great, now I had two people following me. "I'm fine. I told you I was fine. Everything is fine." A person who was really fine probably wouldn't have to say it so many times.

"So you said. But I needed to verify that your 'fines' weren't coerced. It was the responsible thing to do."

My eyes found his reflection in the window. His head was buried in his magazine, seemingly engrossed in it, not me. He was protecting me this way. It was a nice gesture, so I tried to not be annoyed.

Certain there were no cars outside belonging to Reeve or his goonies, I turned to face Joe directly. "You've verified now. Thank you. I appreciate it."

"You're safe then?"

I didn't know about that.

But I didn't want him to be concerned. "Joe, I'm good. I promise. Thank you for looking out for me and especially for being discreet. I obviously don't want Reeve to know about this investigation. Or you, for that matter. He has somewhat of a jealous streak." Annoying as that was, at least it established that I had some modicum of meaning in his life.

Before Joe could say what it looked like he wanted to say, I added, "And not jealous like he's going to hurt me, so stop worrying." Well, Reeve *had* hurt me. I was just okay with it. The physical part anyway.

"All right," Joe said, his tone reluctant. "I'll let you be. But I also needed to show you something that came in today. After your phone call."

He had his cell out now and he was tapping at the screen. He probably had a picture of some newly discovered horrible person Reeve was connected to. Or a report of something he'd done. Whatever it was, I didn't want to see it. "I called the investigation off, Joe. I'm not interested in—"

He cut me short. "It's another Amber sighting."

"When?" Sighting meant alive, right? My heart was pounding in my throat, too scared to ask that question.

"Just before Thanksgiving. A woman went to an emergency room in Chicago with two broken ribs. She matched Amber's description and she used that date of birth. The doctor who treated her noted possible signs of abuse, which meant he also took a picture for the file." He stuck his phone in front of my face. "It's her, right?"

I stared at the screen. Familiar blue eyes looked back at me, darker than mine, darker than I remembered hers being. She was shirtless, wearing only a black bra and a necklace with a jeweled dove that she'd owned for as long as I'd known her. The picture was from an angle and I could make out the top of a red tattoo on her shoulder, two columns slanting away from each other. Faded bruises ran down her neck and chest above her breasts. More bruises, newer, stretched up one side of her torso. I could guess the causes of each set. Choking bruises at the top. Then hickeys. The marks on her ribs were most likely left from shoes. From being kicked.

I'd had all of those marks at one time or another. Some

of them invited, some—the ones that matched those on her torso—not. The Amber I knew wouldn't have invited any of them. I could feel her pain so vividly as I surveyed her injuries. I hated that it was her feeling them instead of me. It hurt to look so I forced myself to keep looking.

"She didn't press any charges," Joe said, after he'd given me a minute to take in what I saw. "She walked out when they discharged her later that night. No idea if she had anyone with her. The phone number and address she listed in the file are both fake."

I snapped my eyes up to meet Joe's. "It's not Reeve. He didn't do this."

"I didn't think for a minute that he did. Chicago is where Vilanakis is based and that tattoo is a V, according to the records."

A V like the one on Filip's neck.

Joe hesitated, as if trying to decide if he should say the next thing. Or how he should say it. "There's more. I'm sorry."

"What else? Why are you sorry?" When he didn't answer, I searched his face and found it more somber than usual. Traces of raw emotion peeking through his tough exterior.

My stomach clenched with fear—with horror—as I imagined the worst.

No. It couldn't be that. I'd have to hear it to believe it and he was staring at me dumbfounded, not saying anything. "What is it? Tell me, Joe. Just fucking tell me!"

"Yeah." He ran his hand across his face, sobering up after, as if the action helped him put his mask back in place. "A few days after that hospital visit, a Jane Doe was found."

"No. . . ." I didn't want him to go on. I needed him to go on.

"In a Dumpster a few miles outside of Chicago." His voice was even. An emotionless narrative.

"No." *Stop, please stop. It's not true.* My chest was aching, splitting open. For the second time that day, I felt like I was suffocating. Except this time there was plenty of air, just no room for it in my lungs as emotion squeezed against them, compressing them and rendering them useless.

"She was identified as the same woman in this picture." Joe gestured to his phone.

"No. No. No." Tears stung at my eyes and slipped down my face despite my refusal to believe they were necessary. They *weren't* necessary. They couldn't be. I latched onto the first alternate possibility I could think of. "*Who* identified? Maybe they got it wrong, Joe."

"Emily . . ." He rested a consolatory hand on my shoulder.

I knocked his arm away. "Show me," I demanded. "Let me see."

"That was four months ago now. She's been cremated. But I have a report."

Four months. Four goddamn months.

He flashed a new screen in front of me. An autopsy report that described the Jane Doe with blond hair and faded bruises, the tattoo on her shoulder, the jeweled dove at her throat. It was hard to refute. Plain as day, the dead woman was my friend.

But I still couldn't believe it. Refused to believe it.

"It wasn't her. It wasn't her, Joe." My voice was scratchy and too loud. People were staring at us, and I didn't care. Let them fill the tabloids with reports that I'd gone mad at the Corner Mart, I didn't fucking care.

The only thing I did care about at the moment was correcting this . . . this . . . misunderstanding. This *lie*. "Say it. Say it wasn't her, Joe." I clutched my fingers into his jacket, pleading. "Fucking say it!"

"It was her, Emily." He pulled me into him, wrapping his arms around me. "It was her."

"You don't know. You can't know."

"I do know. They know. It was her." He stroked my hair and I buried my face in his shoulder, not to sob, but to hide. Hide from the ridiculous nonsense this man was trying to feed me.

Yet, even as I closed my eyes and held my breath, the villainous veracity seeped into my thinking, forcing me to face its validity. She'd been gone before I'd started looking for her. She'd been gone before I even heard her message. As I'd wracked my mind for ways to find her she'd already lain in a cold morgue. When I'd told Joe that she was alive because she was a survivor, I'd been fighting for a corpse. The times I'd imagined her voice in my head and felt her presence and heard her memory speak vividly to me, it may not have been imagined at all but traces of her life imprinted on this world. Real remnants of her spirit in the form of a ghost.

I was dead, she said now. *I've been dead the whole time.*

Tears leaked silently onto his jacket, but I couldn't call it crying. This was shock. This was reality soaking past the truth I'd built up, drops of it spilling from my eyes. This wasn't the dam. This wasn't grief. Not yet.

But it was also anger. Anger at myself. Then, when I thought about it, anger at Joe.

I pushed back from his embrace. "How come you're only finding out about this now? You should have dug this up before. Shouldn't her name have come up in whatever search things you do? She wasn't a Jane Doe if they connected it to her hospital visit. Why didn't you find her before?"

It was misplaced rage, but it felt good to blame. Joe could have saved me the time and energy. Could have spared me the hope.

He seemed to expect my accusations, comfortable

enough with the natural path of mourning to not have to defend himself, but simply present the facts. "She didn't use her real last name at the hospital," he said.

I wiped at my eyes with the back of my hand. "What do you mean? What name did she use?"

"Yours." He cleared his throat. "Barnes."

My real last name. She was in trouble, on the verge of death, and thinking of me. While I . . . what? Rode the high of a breakout show. Complained about the inconvenience of an unwell mother and dealt with it by writing a check in an amount I didn't notice. Even as I searched for Amber, believing she was alive, how often had I forgotten about her? While I'd played a version of my younger self. Seduced her ex-lover. Lost myself in fascination with him.

This detail of the circumstances surrounding her death was only a small one. A tiny laceration amidst extensive injuries. But it stung and burrowed deep inside me, promising to resurface any time I looked closely at myself.

In the meantime, the wound that needed attention was the largest one, the one that gushed and bled from my spirit like a slice across the carotid artery: Amber. Was. Gone.

She was gone.

I was still trying to process. Trying to find reason. Trying to nail down the cause and effect.

My hand rubbed across my forehead—back and forth. Back and forth. "The slave ring, you think?" I had to see the whole picture, know what she'd suffered. Was that how she'd ended up beaten and bruised? Had she been abused by her "owner"? Was she too much trouble? Was she just not worth the inconvenience?

"Or Vilanakis himself." He stuck his hands in his pockets as if awkward now that he wasn't holding me. "Look, I don't know if this is any consolation, but I'm not convinced anymore that Sallis was involved."

"That's what I think." I said it too fast, before I thought

it through. It was a lie primed at the tip of my tongue, sliding off without any regard.

And yet, even as I acknowledged the lie in my head, I kept on with it. "We don't really know when she broke up with Reeve, do we? Maybe she was even with Michelis when she called me. Maybe she just met him through Reeve. Because they run in the same circles." *Or because they're related.* I didn't know why I felt the need to keep that secret still, but I did.

"I'm considering that." Joe's jaw worked as if chewing the information, preparing it for digestion. "I could look into it further, if you like. Try to get some closure."

I shook my head emphatically. "You can't risk it. It's too dangerous. They . . ." I swallowed, giving myself time to be sure of what I wanted to say. "I think Missy's death may have been related to Vilanakis's family, too."

Joe arched a brow. "Do you know something you haven't told me?"

"A friend of mine who knew her said that several members of the family hung around her. They were even at the island the day she died."

"And your friend thinks it was the mob, not Sallis, not an accident?"

"Maybe an accident. Not Reeve at all." I couldn't stop the lies regarding him. In truth, I suspected he was at least partially guilty in Missy's death and I didn't for one second believe the call Amber had made had anything to do with Vilanakis and all to do with Reeve. And I was convinced that, even if he hadn't been the executioner, Reeve still had culpability, still had some of the blame.

And yet, I kept defending him for a multitude of complicated reasons. Because I was afraid that Joe might try to keep me from Reeve. Because I didn't want his investigation to get Reeve in trouble. Because he'd reminded me I was his that afternoon, and I was determined to act like it.

Because now more than ever I needed to use Reeve to find some answers. Because I had to know what happened to Amber and he was the only sure lead I had.

And he hadn't actually killed her so my loyalty to him didn't conflict with my loyalty to her. At least, that's what my current story was and I wasn't about to challenge it.

"Why did you call off the investigation, Emily?" Joe asked, pulling me from my internal dialogue.

I blinked at him, trying to determine what he was looking for in my answer, suspecting it was another attempt to make sure I hadn't been pressured. But his expression gave nothing away, so I told him the truth. "I don't want to put you in that kind of danger. I don't want it to be my fault if anything happens to you."

"There could be others still in danger." He was quieter now. "Others that might be saved if we can figure out what happened with Amber."

He wants to keep investigating. It was a surprise flip of tables from when we'd first met and I was pleading and Joe was skeptical. "You said you didn't want to get in this deep," I reminded him.

He shrugged. "So I lied. I'm invested now. Let me find out what happened to her."

My voice was tight so I simply nodded. Once I swallowed down the ball in my throat, I said, "But no more looking into Reeve. I meant it when I said I didn't want this in the way of my relationship with him."

He let out a reluctant sigh. "Okay. Okay," he finally conceded. "I'll make up something when I bill you. I'll charge you for shooting lessons or something."

I forced a smile that I couldn't hold. "I'll see what I can find out through Reeve. I haven't dug nearly as deep as I can."

Joe's expression grew concerned yet again. "You can't

save her anymore, Emily. You don't need to do anything risky."

"I know."

"Okay. Because if you have any reason to think it's not safe, I can help you get away from him."

Was it fucked up that I didn't even consider it? "I told you, I'm—"

"I know, I know. You're fine." He ran a hand through his short hair. "I'll get you another burner phone. In the meantime, don't use your cell to call me."

"Be careful," we both said in unison. At least I was pretty sure that one of us would take the advice.

Numbly, I paid for my drink, which I tossed on the way out the door. I sat in the car in a daze, letting the engine idle as blame came in the form of "if only." If only I'd heard the message sooner. If only I'd visited my mother more often. If only I'd tried to contact her when I saw her picture in that magazine. If only I'd never left her. She'd saved me, and when I had the chance to return the favor, I'd let her down.

I beat my fist on the steering wheel, again, again, wanting it to hurt, wanting to feel better. Behind me, a car honked. All the pumps were in use and I was hogging the one I was parked in front of, but I leaned out my window and cursed at the other driver anyway. Then I took off, giving the bird as I pulled out into traffic.

I drove mindlessly, not paying attention to where I was or what time it was. Drove in complete silence. Even the thousand thoughts that wanted a spotlight in my head were respectfully reticent, as though granting a moratorium while I dealt with how to just *be* in a world without Amber. How to keep my heart beating and my lungs operational. How to keep my car on the road, in the correct lane, obeying the traffic signs.

After a while—minutes, hours, I didn't know—the reprieve tapered off and half-ideas slipped in with the conviction of plans. Promises. *Reeve's cousins. His guest room. Get to his ranch. His staff.* The common thread always him. He was my only chance for finding out what happened to Amber. He might not have all the answers, but he had some.

By the time I turned the Jag toward his house, he was pulling me in other ways. Distraction. Comfort. Reason. Preoccupation. He was the source of everything I needed now. The path to closure, an asylum for pain, a place to find truth, a place to hide.

For good or bad, all roads led back to him. Perhaps that's what it meant to really be his.

C H A P T E R

2 1

It was a quarter after ten when I arrived at Reeve's. If I got punished for being late, so be it. I welcomed it. I deserved it.

I took a minute to fix my makeup before going in, thankful I wore waterproof mascara. A staff member I didn't recognize let me in without any greeting or instruction. It was fine. I knew where I was supposed to be and I hurried toward my destination in case Reeve was already waiting for me.

As I crossed the living room, I heard men's voices and the distinct sound of a pool rack being broken. I might not have been compelled to look in if I hadn't also heard women's laughter.

Quietly, I went to the threshold of the game room and peeked in. Reeve was there, in loose jeans and a button-down open over a T-shirt, chalking a cue stick as he chatted with another man, indistinctive except for his cowboy boots. Two more men played darts on the other side of the space while two leggy girls that couldn't have been any older than twenty-two watched on.

A third girl—blond, busty, beautiful—was draped over the pool table, encouraging Reeve to take his turn.

With all the emotions already unfurled and waving in my stomach, it was surprising that such a petty, insignificant feeling as envy could still catch wind and flap with enough noise to notice. But there it was, boldly flown at full mast, drawing my attention. I leaned against the wall, watching them, watching *her,* as she teased and taunted, and the taste in my mouth grew sour. I was supposed to be in there with them. Three women, four men. I'd have made the teams equal. If I should have found comfort that I hadn't been replaced with some other bimbo, I didn't. Odd numbers didn't have to mean anyone got left out.

It didn't escape me that I'd once been one of them—a pretty young thing. A substitute for real emotion dressed in sex and sin.

Aren't you still one of them? It wasn't Amber's voice.

And maybe I was still one of them. But at least this was what I wanted. They were here for the attention and material gain. They were shells waiting to be filled with a man's desires, blank screens projecting someone else's wants. Even without reasons connected to Amber, I was here because this was who I was—a strong, independent woman with distinct wants and needs that were only met when I submitted to a man. When I submitted to Reeve.

I stared at him bent over the table, his eyes squinted on the stick and the ball, and found that despite my acceptance of my submission, I was pissed. I didn't deserve to be tossed aside, no matter how I'd wronged him. If I hadn't just recommitted myself to finding out the truth about Amber's death, then I would have walked out. Would have washed my hands of the asshole.

But I would stay, anger and all. For Amber. Which

meant I had to channel my anger and ignore the emotion underneath that—fear. It was a different kind of fear than the kind I usually associated with Reeve. Fear that I wasn't what he wanted. Fear that he didn't see how easily I could be. Wouldn't that be the icing on my life?

He took his shot, sending the ball precisely where he'd intended, sinking another into a corner pocket. His expression shifted ever so slightly from intense focus to smug satisfaction. Then his eyes widened in what seemed like surprise as they found mine.

I straightened, knowing I wasn't where I was supposed to be, but unable to break his gaze. *I'm here,* I said to him silently across the distance. And the way he continued to look at me, it almost felt like he was glad to see me. Probably because I was witnessing this—him, content in a world without me. It was yet another layer of despair, and I wouldn't have been surprised if he saw it in my face. Good for him. Congratulations.

Someone else caught his attention then, someone closer to where I was. He nodded once then turned back to his game.

I looked to where he'd nodded and found Anatolios headed my way.

"This is a private game," he said. "I'll have to ask you to leave."

"Yeah, yeah. I'm going." *Fucker.* And fuck Reeve for sending him after me. It wasn't like I was interrupting anything and I was positive I'd handed him a victory in my obvious misery. I brooded about it as I stomped up the stairs to Reeve's room.

Once upstairs, I went to his bathroom to scrub my face. I took the opportunity to give my reflection a stern lecture. "Look at you, occupied with sulking so that you don't have to feel the real emotions stewing underneath. You think that earns you compassion? You're pitiful."

I dried off and turned away, but another voice in my head challenged me. *What are you going to do about it?*

Grow some fucking balls, that was what.

Reeve was occupied downstairs, and the staff that was still working was attending to him and his friends. They'd turned on music now, the pulsing beat of the bass carrying easily up to me. If I used that to gauge whether the party was still going or not, I should be able to do some exploring. Some real exploring this time, no cowering when what I found got hard to look at.

There were many places in Reeve's room that I could rummage through, but I wanted to make the best use of this chance, not knowing when I'd get such an opportunity again. To get to the guest rooms, I'd have to cross the bridge where I could easily be seen from below. I could, however, slip up the stairs to his office without anyone the wiser. So I did.

The room was dark and it took a minute for my eyes to adjust. When I could see, I headed for his desk. There was a small lamp there, which I turned on, and his computer was my primary interest. It was already on, displaying the black screen of sleep mode. I jiggled the mouse and prayed there wasn't a password.

There wasn't.

Damn, I really should have tried to do this earlier. If only I hadn't been so absorbed with Reeve.

No, I wasn't doing the *if only's* right now. There were other more important things to do. Immediately, I opened a game of computer solitaire. If I did get caught, it could be my excuse for being up here. It wasn't like Reeve had named either the room or his computer off limits. If he was mad and wanted to give me another one of his "loud and clear" messages, that would be just fine. And be welcome, too.

After dealing cards and playing a few for appearances'

sake, I moved to snooping elsewhere. His document folders were numerous, but in a quick scroll through the list there were only a few that didn't seem to be related to Sallis Resorts. The first one, labeled R. OPTIONS, had pictures of modern kitchens and dining rooms. When I found one that looked an awful lot like his downstairs, I realized he used these for the remodel he'd done the summer before. A peek at the last opened date confirmed that it hadn't been looked at in almost a year. Until now.

Dammit. I'd forgotten that I'd leave an imprint. I decided to be ultra conservative when deciding what other docs to open. That ruled out most of the ones I'd earmarked. The last two, labeled KOSTAS and VALENTINE, were both password protected. In the Finder, I sorted all the files to put the most recently opened on top. Nothing stood out. I scrolled to the previous summer and found nothing had been opened at all between April and October, which made sense since that was when he'd evacuated the house for renovations.

His email, I decided, would be more helpful since it traveled with him. Plus, the messages wouldn't date stamp when they'd last been looked at. There were only a handful of unread messages, all business related. The rest were archived in folders. Dozens of folders. And in the folders were more folders. I didn't have enough time to sort through them like I wanted, so I searched for terms I was interested in first. *Vilanakis* brought up nothing. *Michelis* had the same result. *Missy* brought up several but nothing of value. Nothing that said, "I killed her."

Honestly, what was I expecting?

I hesitated before typing in the next term to take a deep breath and prepare. When I was ready, I put in *Amber*.

Four messages turned up.

I started with the oldest from October of the year that Amber and Reeve must have met. It was from a private investigator and included an attached file, basically a background report listing all her basic information. I assumed it was standard procedure for him to obtain one when seeking out a new girlfriend.

The next email was an application for a rush passport for Amber, from June of last year. Probably just before they'd gone to Wyoming. It was approved. So why had she needed a passport? And did she use it?

The message that followed was even more intriguing. It was dated November 1 and included a single attachment and only a simple line of text. *"I'm enjoying her immensely. Thank you much. M."* I opened the file and my heart nearly stopped. It was the picture of Michelis and Amber from the Colorado casino that Joe had shown me. The one that had been sent to him anonymously. Except, in this one, Michelis wasn't cut off, and I could see it was he who was taking the shot with his phone.

The email had come from noreply@mailmail.com, a third-party service, it seemed. But I guessed it was Michelis who sent it, that he was the "M" in the signature. Was it he who had sent the picture to Joe, then? If so, why? And the message—didn't that suggest that Reeve had given Amber to his relative as a gift?

Don't read into it, I told myself. It could mean something else. I didn't know what, but I was still defending Reeve, even to myself.

The last email was from the same address, dated the day before Thanksgiving, and was just as upsetting. It read, *"Thought you'd be interested. M."* Attached was the Jane Doe autopsy report that Joe had shown me.

I hadn't thought there was any more in me to deflate, but apparently there was. Because what further proof did I need that Reeve had been involved in Amber's death?

Except, I still didn't know that for sure. It didn't mean that Reeve had wanted her dead. He might have shared

Amber, as he'd told me he'd done with women before, and then maybe it had been Michelis alone who had decided to end her life. Maybe Reeve had thought that his relative would take care of her, love her even. Maybe Reeve had been just as upset about this turn of events as I was.

Though that was unlikely.

Either way, I knew I should send both of the last two emails to Joe. But I still wasn't ready to subject Reeve to further investigation. Not yet, anyway.

Instead I forwarded both the messages to myself, and then deleted the evidence.

I was exhausted now, too drained to handle any more revelations. I closed out of Reeve's email and clicked the icon for the solitaire game, but accidentally hit the system's photo displayer instead. A string of pictures popped up, filling the screen, all of them featuring the same two people—Reeve and Amber. They seemed to have been taken in the backyard by the pool, one after another, so that if I flipped through them quickly, they appeared animated. In them, Amber sat on Reeve's lap on a deck chair. Both were laughing in the first pictures, kissing in the last few. In stark contrast to the emails I'd read, they told a story of a couple that appeared very much in love.

Was it really also the tale of a man who would give her away to a murderer? It didn't seem possible, but how many times did pictures really tell the whole story? I'd seen only that afternoon how angry Reeve could get when provoked. If he could be like that with me, there was no telling what he could have been like with her.

Whether they were honest or not, I studied the images for long minutes, trying to find a clue that something was wrong, that something was off. They were hard to look at, for many reasons. Because I missed her. Because she was happy in them. Because she'd never be happy like that again. Because the man that was the cause of her happiness in these pictures was the same man who'd sent her to her death.

Because that man had never looked at me the way he was looking at her.

It was all I could take. I shut down the photos, turned off the light, and crept back to Reeve's bedroom. I undressed quickly, got under the sheets, and buried my face in the pillow where, finally, the dam broke and I grieved the loss of my best friend.

I awoke with a start, the room dark except for the nightlight. Reeve stood above me, wearing only his jeans, the corner of the bed sheet in his hand.

"Fuck," I said, rubbing an eye with the butt of my hand. "I fell asleep. I'm sorry. What time is it?"

"Almost three. And don't worry about it. Go back to sleep. I was just straightening the sheet for you." His voice was quiet so it was hard to be sure, but I didn't think I heard any spite in his tone.

"No, no. I'm not here to sleep. I'm here to be yours." I needed him right now. Needed him to take control like I knew he would so I could let go completely. So I could escape. So I could forget, if even for a moment.

He smiled but it was brief and didn't meet his eyes. Then, instead of initiating anything, he walked to the other side of the bed and started emptying his pockets on the nightstand.

I suddenly had a bad feeling about how his night had gone. "Unless you don't need me," I said, hinting at without saying my fear outright.

"Emily, the girls downstairs were here for my friends." God, he could read me so easily. "I'm sorry if you got the wrong impression, but I've explained my position on other women before."

"You have. I remember. You won't have sex with anyone else while you're with me. I was just making sure things hadn't changed after today." My throat felt thick, probably from the earlier breakdown, but also because I could sense something was wrong. Besides all the other things that were wrong.

He let out a sigh and circled back to my side. "About that," he said, perching on the edge of the bed. "There's something I need to say. I—" He stopped abruptly, bending closer to study me. "You've been crying."

I was on the verge of crying now, after the ominous speech he'd just begun and the heavy seriousness of his mood. But he was referring to the way I looked, which I imagined was like hell judging by how crusty and swollen my eyes felt. Though he hadn't asked a question, he was waiting for an explanation. I considered making something up. *I bumped into an old friend. He gave me bad news about someone we used to know.*

But even in a vague form I didn't want to share Amber's death with him. He'd already had so much of her, so much that I hadn't. This was mine alone and it was private.

So, at the expense of him thinking my tears had been because of him, I just nodded.

He reached his hand out to caress my face. "I didn't want this, Emily." And damn if my world didn't feel turned upside down for the millionth time that day.

He dropped his hand and cleared his throat, and I waited for more words I didn't want to hear.

"I overreacted earlier," he said, his voice thick with remorse. "I know that. I crossed lines. Like you said, I didn't tell you what I expected."

What he'd said wasn't what I thought I was going to hear. It took a beat before I figured out that he was referring to the way he'd "punished" me. It was so near to an apology from a man I was sure never gave them that I didn't know quite how to respond. Not to mention, I didn't want an apology for it.

I ran my tongue over my bottom lip and chose my words carefully. "No, you were right to do what you did. I should have known."

He smiled skeptically. "How could you? You can't read my mind, can you?" He grew serious again, avoiding eye contact. "I'll try to remember in the future to be clearer with you up front."

"Well, that would help, but really, I was the one who messed up, and I feel terrible for disappointing you."

"It wasn't disappointment that I was feeling, exactly. It was . . ." He looked up at me, and I thought for just a second that I *could* read his mind, thought that the sentence went, *It was fear.*

But that was silly. A man like Reeve, afraid? Of what?

He shook his head. "Anyway, sometimes I can get carried away. I don't expect you to tolerate me like that. I want you to know that I'm trying. Trying to be more in control of myself."

I was confused. On the one hand, he was being compassionate. It thrilled me, but it was also jarring. That wasn't what I wanted from him. And I was pretty sure it wasn't what he wanted either. So why was he offering it?

Whatever the reason, I had to nip it in the bud. "No. Don't do that."

"Don't do what?"

"Don't control yourself. I want you to be *you* with me. Whoever that is." As soon as I said it, I knew it was true. Despite what it opened myself up to accept from him.

He studied me. "You don't mean that. It's not fair to you to have to put up with my worst traits. My temper and impulsiveness."

I was still baffled about where this was coming from.

In my experience, men were only remorseful when they thought they might lose something. Might lose *me*.

It didn't make sense that Reeve feared that. Did it?

I sat up straighter, desperate to understand. "Do you think you hurt me today, Reeve? Did you think I'd leave?" The look he gave me said I'd got it right. So I assured him, "I wouldn't. And the only time I was hurt was when it seemed you might not want me anymore. Everything else you did, I let you do. I wanted you to. I liked it."

"Emily, you don't have to say—"

"I know I don't. I'm being honest here. I liked it. A lot." How did I not realize that he didn't get that about me? I thought I'd been so transparent. Apparently not transparent enough.

"I need that from you. I need you to be that way with me." God, I felt so exposed. But he had to know. "It turned me on, remember? Even just thinking about it now gets me hot." It wasn't a lie. I was wet.

He seemed surprised. And suspicious. He pulled the sheet off of me, leaving me naked before him. His attention fell first to my breasts, to the pointed nubs that confirmed my arousal. I spread my legs, inviting him to further verify my claims.

He accepted the invitation, dragging his fingers down the length of my slit, landing at my hole, which was drenched and swollen. His eyes flew back to mine. "You really do belong to me, don't you?"

I nodded. "Yes. I really do."

He stood and quickly dropped his pants before bending one of my legs up to my chest and settling in the apex of my thighs. "Tell me what you liked about it. Tell me which parts."

His cock hovered at my entrance, the tip throbbing, begging to come in. I bucked my hips, wanting what he held just out of reach.

But he wouldn't give it. Not yet. "Tell me, Emily."

I was needy and on fire, ready to say anything to get him where I wanted him, even the truth. "When you came on my tits."

He drove in with a single deep thrust. "Yes. What else?"

He held himself above me, inside me now, but not moving. I ground up. He remained still, waiting.

"When you smelled me," I said.

Finally, he withdrew. Slowly. Too slow. "Even when you found out why?"

"Especially then."

He plunged back in. "What else."

"When you shoved your cock in my mouth so far I couldn't breathe." I spoke quickly now, the words spilling out of my mouth, knowing they were the key to getting what I wanted.

"Yes." He pulled out then pushed back in. "Good. Good girl." He circled inside me, and I groaned. "What else?"

"When you said I belonged to you." It was almost a whisper, coated in lust and raw vulnerability.

"Aw, fuck, Emily." His tempo was steady now, each stroke hitting me in exactly the right spot. I was sighing, whimpering, greedy beneath him. "You like remembering it, too, don't you?"

"Yes."

He lowered his upper body on top of mine and braced himself with one elbow on the bed next to my head. With his other hand, he stroked my cheek. Sweetly. Tenderly. "I can tell. You're so tight around me. You're almost there, aren't you?"

"Yes," I gasped. I was so close already, and God did I need it. Needed to feel good for just a minute. Even if it wasn't going to be the mind-blowing sort of orgasm he usually gave me. Even if it was soft and gentle. Even if the aftermath was filled with a fresh surge of survivor guilt. "Yes," I said again. "I'm there."

"Good. Because I think you deserve this." Without warning, he clasped his palm over my mouth and nose. Hard. Letting no air through.

And I knew—I *knew*—that he was doing it for me, that this was his way of saying he was sorry. Men had done this to me before, usually by choking, but it was the same idea. Breath play. Denying oxygen to the brain, increasing the sense of pleasure.

But I only mostly knew that was what Reeve was doing to me now. Especially after his punishment that afternoon. And the little part of me that didn't know, it was small. Tiny. Barely even worth considering except that, tiny as it was, it was stark enough in contrast to the rest of me that it was noticeable. It was magnified. Like a single drop of blood on a large white sheet that can't help but stand out, can't help but scream for attention. And this tiny part of me that wasn't sure that Reeve was doing this for pleasure, this part that feared he was doing something malicious instead, it was a spot of red in my otherwise white composure.

I should have learned from earlier, but natural instinct was strong and I panicked. I shook my head back and forth, but he didn't let go. Didn't loosen his grip. I struggled and thrashed, wasting my oxygen but unable to stay calm. I brought my hands to his shoulders and dug into him, clawing with my fingernails.

Still, he held me, his eyes locked with mine, and I could see how turned on he was.

Now, I thought, as the fight began to leave me. *Now I should be scared.* This could be my end. There were certainly reasons that Reeve might want that. Because of what I knew. Because I'd snooped and told lies and had him investigated. Because of Amber. Because he could.

My vision glazed. Black crept in at the edges. My arms twitched and my hands fell from their perch.

All the while, Reeve pounded into me. And my body, not seeming to understand that it was dying, reacted. My core tightened with pressure and my skin tingled with electricity and my pussy clenched around his cock and then I was *there*. At the pinnacle. At the edge. Out of breath. Ready to burst.

Then Reeve removed his hand. And I did burst.

My orgasm broke from me with a tsunamic force as I frantically tried to draw in air, desperately tried to pull it inside. The needs conflicted—need for release, need for oxygen—my climax winning out, too powerful to be restrained any longer. It crashed over me, demolishing me with plunging waves of rapture, waves that broke every part of me then pulled me under again with a powerful backwash, only to gather me again on another crest of euphoria. My body convulsed with each surge. Spots formed in front of my vision. Tears spilled from my eyes. My head felt like it was falling down, through the bed, like I'd lost all sense of gravity and awareness.

Still I couldn't catch a breath. I chased it, gasping in between each swell, never quite getting anything in my lungs before the next rush.

And I wondered if I'd die like this. Die flying, soaring, rocketing to heights higher than I'd ever been. Would this be the eternity I'd be allowed to dwell in? In this overwhelming pleasure, so abundant, so consuming, so amplified that there wasn't room for anything else. No room for fear or doubt or worry or shame or grief. Just this.

If this was where Amber existed now, then it was home.

But then my vision cleared, and I saw Reeve above me, his eyes intense as he watched me, and he was riveted. Consumed as I was. Consumed with *me*.

And I no longer wanted to be anywhere but with him.

Even if there was worry and doubt and fear and grief. Even if it wasn't at all what he wanted. Even if it couldn't last, I would fight to be with him.

The epiphany settled over me and I realized I had air now. Realized I was breathing fine. Realized I was the sickest kind of fuck. Because I wanted to live, if for no other reason than to be with the person who possibly wanted me dead. Who probably sent my friend to her death.

The realization brought another orgasm, much quieter, but just as intense. It wracked through me, wrenching a guttural keening sound from my being. A sound that was both foreign and familiar. Both primal and complex. Both gratification and mourning.

Reeve followed with his own release, his body convulsing inside of me as he let out a low groan that strangely, beautifully harmonized with my own cry. He finished, collapsing beside me.

It took everything in me not to turn and slap the shit out of him.

Or punch him. Pound him with my fists until he told me why the fuck he'd done what he'd just done. Pummel him until he understood just how angry and jealous and confused and frightened he made me. Thrash and pelt until he promised never to do it again.

But I managed to hold myself. Because I didn't really want him to promise that. I'd asked for him to give me who he was. And I'd liked it, despite being scared, or maybe even because of it. For that, I was ashamed.

Emotion hit me then like a bowling ball scoring a strike, and I felt the threat of another crying jag. Not the sobs that had torn through me earlier when I was alone. Not even sadness, really. It was unidentifiable, something new, something that was pieces of a whole bunch of things all trying to get out of me at once. It was overwhelming.

And, a little bit, it was just that I hadn't ever been at peace with myself, and here, with this awful man, after I thought he was trying to kill me, on the day I'd lost my best friend, I felt the seeds of it burrowing inside of me. Maybe it was the product of a really good orgasm.

But it was probably more about where I was now with Reeve.

He jerked up, as if he'd sensed what I was thinking. He startled me with his sudden movement, then startled me again when, after he turned toward me, he reached out to stroke my face, as he sometimes did, with the back of his hand. My pulse, which had just begun to beat at a normal tempo, spiked again. He wasn't usually affectionate after sex and rarely touched me intimately like this. It made me wary and paranoid and I had to force myself not to cower.

But his eyes were warm when I met them, and I realized he was checking on me. Making sure I was okay. He kissed my forehead, and it was an apology, soft and genuine.

When he pulled back again, his expression was tinged with regret, and I felt a strange desire to comfort him. To tell him that things were fine and then scold him for showing any remorse about giving me exactly what I needed— fear of harm without actually hurting me.

But I was confused and fucked up, and all I could do was show him in my eyes that I was okay with what he'd done, even if I wasn't okay over all.

He seemed to understand something. His features relaxed and a smile teased on his lips. "Do you know what part I liked best?"

It took a minute to register what he was talking about. It hadn't been more than a few minutes since he'd been asking me what were my favorite parts of our earlier encounter yet it felt like a lifetime had passed.

"No, what?" I managed a steady voice, but tears were pricking at my eyes. I concentrated on not letting them fall.

Apparently, I didn't do a good job, because he wiped one away with the pad of his thumb. He leaned in to lick another as it trailed down my cheek.

A shiver rolled through me, and I honestly couldn't decide if I was moved or horrified. Probably a little of both.

He pulled back to look at me earnestly. "I liked the part where you still showed up tonight." He bent to brush a soft kiss on my mouth and then dropped again on the bed.

Like that, I was flying again, almost as high as I had been in my orgasmic bliss. He had that power over me, whether I wanted him to or not.

I squeezed my eyes shut, more emotional now than ever and on the verge of falling for a man I shouldn't fall for. Reeve was confusing and complicated at best. He could be tender as easily as he could be disparaging. He was definitely frightening. He'd done things that were very frightening. He may have even done things that, to know for sure, would destroy me.

But none of it had sent me running. That it didn't said an awful lot about me that I hadn't wanted to acknowledge. It said things I'd known for years and refused to accept. Since I'd torn myself away from Amber, I'd gone so far as to downplay my proclivity for depravity, said it didn't define me or own me. I couldn't get away with that anymore. I *was* owned by this, this type of relationship where a man, who did or did not have my best interests in mind, decided what I would do and be, what would be done to me. And that meant I was possibly even more confusing and complicated than he was.

It also meant I really did belong to him, in ways that were so much deeper than the way we implied when we said it to each other. I belonged to him the way that a good idea belonged to the person who thought it. Though I'd existed before Reeve in bits and pieces, he had put them together and named me, and now I'd never be what I was before him. In some way, no matter what happened with us in the future, I'd always be his.

But I'd also always be Amber's. She'd been the only person to recognize the woman in the scraps of nothing that I'd been. And because of that I'd keep looking for her truth. Searching threatened what I had with Reeve, but until I put her to rest, I could never wholly belong to him anyway.

He shifted next to me again, pulling the sheet up from where it was gathered at our feet. As he tucked the sheet around me he said, "I have to go on a trip. For a couple of weeks, at least. Maybe longer."

"Okay." His news pinched at my cloak of peace, causing my chest to tighten.

He turned on his side and dragged me into him so he could spoon. This was new too, and I loved it. I was sure it stemmed from our understanding. He felt as compelled to shelter me as I was to retreat into him.

He nuzzled at my neck, his breath warm and welcome on my skin. Lazily, he said, "You'll come with me."

"Okay." Anywhere he said, I'd go.

"Good." He kissed the back of my ear. "We'll leave for the ranch tomorrow."

The ranch. He was taking me to the ranch where Amber was last with him.

I'd never been very spiritual, but it was impossible not to see this as a sign. Even the gods wanted me to discover what happened to her. Even they were laying out the path to take me where I needed to go to do just that.

Or they desired that I find the same fate she did. I hadn't completely discounted that possibility either.

CHAPTER

22

Reeve woke me up early the next morning, sending me to my house to pack a bag. "Don't worry about bringing too much. We can get you anything you need in Jackson."

"Okay," I said, pulling on yesterday's jeans.

"I'll give you enough time to get a wax appointment. You've finally got enough hair to go in." He nodded in the direction of my crotch.

I blushed. "You noticed." Of course he would. He was down there more than I was.

"Yeah, and guess what." He beamed. "You're a natural blonde."

Just as I was about to head out, he called after me. "I meant to ask you, were you in my office last night?"

I swallowed the panic rising in my chest. How the hell had he known? "I was. I got bored waiting for you and played some solitaire. Was that okay?"

"Of course. You left your game open. I finished it for you before coming to bed last night."

My heart was still racing, but Reeve seemed genuinely

unbothered by it so I forced a bright smile. "Silly me. Did we win, at least?"

His face was hard to read when he said, "Oh, Blue Eyes, I always win."

Filip rang my doorbell at two that afternoon. I grabbed my sunglasses and carry-on and locked up while he put my suitcase in the trunk. He opened the back door for me and I slid in next to Reeve. He was dressed casually in loose jeans and a long-sleeve flannel button-down. A pair of Tom Ford Aviators hid the eyes that I was sure were brought out by the blue in his shirt.

"Where's the cowboy hat?" I teased. The western look was surprisingly good on him. Not really surprisingly— every look was good on him.

"I'll wear it later just for you." He laced his fingers through mine, which was a nice surprise despite the smirk on his face as he took in my tunic zip-front dress. "Wyoming is cold this time of year, Blue Eyes. Your legs are going to freeze."

"I have leggings in my carry-on. I'll put them on when we land." Reluctantly, I let go of his hand to buckle in.

"Good." He palmed my bare thigh, an acceptable substitute for hand-holding. "Though I'm glad right now that you aren't wearing them. Let's hope I have an opportunity to take advantage of that."

I might have purred. "What's wrong with now?"

"Now, we have things to discuss." He left his hand where it was, but his tone said that we weren't playing anymore. This was business.

Instantly, I tensed. "Like?"

"Expectations. I thought it might be a good idea to discuss them before we have any other misunderstandings."

"Great idea." I had to stop assuming every serious conversation we were going to have would be a bad one.

Anxiety was a natural side effect of lying, understandably. But I didn't have to be so paranoid. "Shoot. I'm ready."

"Kaya is not a resort like the other Sallis properties. It's a—"

"Kaya?" I interrupted, ignoring the irritated glare he shot me. That was supposedly the maiden name of his mother, the name that Joe hadn't been able to verify. "What's Kaya?"

"That's the name of the ranch. We breed and run cattle, but we do have twenty cabins that we rent along the western borders where the river runs. Mostly people interested in fly-fishing but other tourists too."

"Okay." I wanted to ask how a working ranch had become part of the Sallis portfolio, but he'd moved on before I had a chance.

"We'll be staying in the main house. Guests are not permitted there. The central office is by the front gates and is where all interactions with them take place. Even without the guests, though, the house sees lots of traffic. The key staff members come up for meals and various activities. Brent, the ranch manager, lives above the office but sometimes he stays at the house. Usually when he's drunk. He'll be on the plane today."

"Got it." These weren't exactly the kinds of expectations I thought we were going over, but they were helpful nonetheless. "In other words, I shouldn't walk around naked."

"No, you definitely shouldn't walk around naked. Under any circumstances." His tone was clipped and resolute. Annoyed, even, that I'd brought it up.

"You didn't need to snap. I was only joking."

"Well, I'm not." He glanced at me, then rubbed two fingers up the bridge of his nose. "I'm sorry to snap. Many of the men employed at the ranch are temporary or seasonal. I don't know most of them. I don't trust them. I can't be sure that they would respect you and that's not acceptable to me."

I took in his profile as I absorbed what he'd said. Around his home, he had me undressed around his staff so often that I'd assumed he enjoyed treating women—treating *me*—like property. Enjoyed flaunting me like he would a flashy car. And I liked it because, dirty girl that I was, it turned me on to be demeaned and ordered around as though I had no rights.

But sometimes it pinched at my self-confidence. As hot as it was, it would be nice to be wanted so entirely by a man that he didn't ever want anyone else to have the right to look at me like he got to. Because I was that important to him.

This, from Reeve, was probably the most perfect compromise. He liked to flaunt me. But only when he could protect me.

That was the kind of owned I'd always longed for and didn't realize it until now.

I wished there was an easy way to tell him exactly how I felt about his position. How much I appreciated it and how it made me feel safe with him. Safe. With a man like Reeve.

But there wasn't any way to explain something I didn't understand myself. So I just said, "Thank you."

"Now if I say that it is okay to be undressed in public, certainly that overrides the previous statement." He granted me a slight grin.

I returned it. "Certainly."

"Moving on." And the serious tone was back. "Breakfast is served every morning at six sharp. If you sleep through it, you'll need to fend for yourself. Lunch is at noon and dinner at six-thirty."

"And if I miss those?"

"Don't." It was authoritative with no room for argument, like pretty much everything he'd said so far. I liked the rules. The structure was comforting. I imagined there were women who would find that irritating. Amber would have. Had Reeve been different with her? Sometimes men treated us as individuals. Were the rules only for me?

I hoped they were. For her sake, but also for mine.

As much as I liked rules, it didn't mean I wasn't also headstrong. I crossed my legs and batted my lashes at him. "What else, *sir*?"

"Oh, no." Reeve scowled. "No sir's. I do not expect or want that."

"Master?"

He shook his head, trying not to smile. "Don't even think about it."

"Daddy?" *God, I hope not.*

"Fuck, no. Use my name and stop dicking around. I still have more to tell you."

"Of course you do. Mr. Sallis."

He narrowed his eyes, but went on with his list. "You'll have your own room at the main house. Use it however you like. It's your private space. But that doesn't mean you're free to do whatever you want. I'm your first priority. That's why you're here. I expect you to be available when I want you and I expect you to sleep in my bed whenever I'm there."

This last section of his speech made my stomach flutter and my thighs buzz. This was the basic principle that all his demands extended from—*I'm your first priority*. It was what turned me on most about Reeve. That he required me to service him. To think of him above everything else. To allow myself to be willingly used by him in any way he desired.

It was why I was a sick person. Because he could tell

me he expected me to jump off the plane without a parachute, and if I believed it was what he really wanted, I'd not only probably do it, but I'd get off on it.

I was so busy being aroused and chastising myself for it that I almost didn't notice what he'd said at the end. "Sleep with you when you're there? Are there times you won't be?"

"Yes. I have business with some of the other resorts in the state." He peered out the front window as he spoke, only half paying attention to what he was saying. "Sometimes that will require me to be gone for several days at a time."

You could always take me with you. But the reason I wanted to be in Wyoming was for finding out what happened to Amber, not Reeve. This was better, really.

So I don't know why I kept pushing. "Like, how many days?"

Now he was checking his watch. "Uh, I don't know."

"Will I know when you're leaving? And when you're coming back?"

Reeve leaned forward to tell Filip something in Greek. He mentioned the 405 so I guessed it was about traffic and arrival times. Whatever Filip said in response seemed to satisfy Reeve. He sat back in his seat and turned to me.

My mouth was open, ready to repeat my questions since I was sure he hadn't heard me, but he reached out and cupped my neck. "Yes, Emily. I'll let you know when I'm leaving and I'll make sure you know when I'll be back. Don't worry about it, okay? Just try to have a nice time."

"But—"

The pressure on my neck tightened. "Also, there will be no arguing in front of other people. What I say goes, no questions, no back talk."

My eyes flicked to Filip and back again. I guess he

counted as other people. I sighed. "Does that mean I can argue when we aren't in front of other people?"

Reeve's eyes lit up as he sneered. "How about try it and find out."

"Yeah, I'll have to see about that." Though, it sounded like it might be kind of fun. Except what did it matter if he wasn't around?

Admittedly, I was slightly pouty when I asked, "Is that all your rules and regulations, Mr. Sallis, or are there more?"

He put his arm on the back of the seat and angled his body toward me. He studied me with an expression that said he was trying to figure something out. Finally, he said, "I don't think you're as bothered by my rules and regulations as you pretend to be."

I clamped my mouth shut. That wasn't what was bothering me. But the things bothering me were inappropriate considering our relationship, or lack thereof, and ridiculous considering my personal reasons for being on this trip.

So I ignored his comment and concentrated on what I needed to know for my self-appointed mission. "Are there places that are off limits to me?"

He grinned, as if my lack of answer was an answer in itself. And of course it was. "No. You can go anywhere you want. My office is kept locked unless I'm there, but if you want computer access, there's one in the library in the main house. The ranch is very beautiful and I'm sure you'll want to explore, but it's twenty thousand acres of wilderness and prairie, and phone reception isn't always great. So if you do go out make sure you take a radio. You can get one from Brent. If you'd rather not go out alone, Brent can set you up with someone to show you around the property or take you into Jackson."

He hesitated, his expression suddenly hard to read.

Returning his focus back to the front window, he added, "If you'd like to borrow a car to go anywhere on your own, Brent can arrange that for you as well."

"Okay," I said quietly, wishing Reeve was offering to show me around himself. Then I was wishing that I wasn't wishing that. It was petty and unreasonable and, like the concern over his time away, a sign that I'd developed some romantic notion about us at some point. That had never been a problem with me and other men.

Or maybe I was just insecure and sensitive right now with all the emotions of the last couple of days. Yes, definitely that.

"What's wrong?"

I turned toward him, a bright smile pasted on my lips. "Nothing at all." In case he might press, I jumped to another topic. "Will there be any . . . social events . . . while I'm there?"

"What do you mean? Like parties?"

"I was thinking more like gatherings where the guests play pool." Yeah, I was still stewing about that. Might as well address it while I had the chance and hope it wasn't considered starting an argument.

He simpered. "There's no pool table at the ranch, Emily." He leaned in and continued in a low, rumbling voice. "But if there is any occasion where the staff might get together, you'd be invited—no, *expected*—to attend."

It was an improvement, but not everything I wanted. "Will there be other girls fawning over you on these occasions?"

He swept the back of his fingers across my cheek in a tender gesture. "Only girl fawning over me will be you."

It was the right thing to say, and made me feel all mushy and swoony inside. Naturally, I had to play it cool. "Oh, so you expect me to fawn?"

"No. I don't *expect* that," he said. "But you're certainly *invited*."

At the airport, we met up with Anatolios, a second body-guard I hadn't met, and the men who'd been Reeve's guests the night before. He presented me as his girlfriend, which was surprising and endearing. Brent, I learned, was the ranch manager and Reeve's right-hand man. He'd been the one wearing cowboy boots. The two dart players were Charlie, who oversaw the cattle, and Parker, who ran the stable.

After introductions were made, Reeve's attention went fully to his men and I became ornamental, hanging on his arm while we walked through the terminal and boarded his private jet. Anatolios and his assistant took a seat in the cabin nearest the pilots while Reeve and his men sat around the table in the next cabin. Ginger, the buxom blond stewardess—Reeve definitely had a "type"—greeted me and escorted me to a seat near the men.

Though I had no reason to be jealous of Ginger, I was pleased when Reeve gave his attention to her only long enough to order a drink. Then he went back to talking to his ranch hands. I did find myself wondering if he'd ever slept with her. Found myself studying her curiously, looking for any sign that she might know him on a more familiar level.

Then, when I'd found none and she'd continued to be nothing but gracious to me, I wondered how many women she'd attended to on these flights while Reeve was preoc-cupied with business. Had she known Amber? Had Amber befriended her or ignored her?

If I'd had the chance, I would have struck up a conver-sation with the stewardess. But as soon as she'd served everyone drinks, Reeve dismissed her to the front cabin with Anatolios.

The men stayed wrapped up in their discussion long after we'd left the ground. I listened for the first half-hour or so, but soon grew bored with talk of horseshoeing and feed crops and calf tagging. So I pulled out my Kindle and got swept away in a book.

We'd been in the air for an hour or so when I heard a word that made the hair stand up on the back of my neck—"Michelis." I'd missed what had brought his name up or who had said it, but the inflection had seemed to suggest it was a question. My ears perked up, and while I pretended to be lost in my e-reader, I eavesdropped instead.

"There were a bunch of chickens dead a couple of weeks ago," Brent said. "I thought it might be him, but I can't be sure."

"There's no footage?" Reeve asked.

"Nope. Camera was hit and angled wrong." This came from Charlie, though I had to glance up to be sure, not knowing his voice well enough to identify from just sound.

"Which means it wasn't foxes," said Parker.

"And it was someone who knows where the camera is in the barns." Brent again.

There was a brief silence. Then Reeve said, "Replace the system. Or, better yet, keep the system as a dummy and add another."

"Yep," Parker agreed. "That's it."

"Fucking asshole costs us a shit ton of money with these pranks of his," Brent said, frustration in his tone. "Could you maybe tell him it's not very nice to your employees?"

Reeve didn't answer. I peeked up and saw him rubbing his hand over his face. Tension rolled off of him in waves, but I couldn't be sure if he was angry, irritated, or just over the conversation. I tried to guess based on the conversation, but it was confusing. Was Michelis playing some sort of joke on the ranchers? Or was Brent's comment facetious?

After a long minute, Brent said somberly, "You got the yearly invitation from him again. Maybe you should go."

"I won't acknowledge that with a response," he snapped. *Angry it is.* "I'm done with this conversation. And stop giving him so much of your time. He already got something of mine that matters. That's all he gets." He stood and headed toward the back room. "Emily?" he called over his shoulder.

It took a second to realize that I didn't need to pretend to not be listening anymore. "Uh. Yeah?"

"Join me."

I tucked my Kindle in my bag, undid my seat belt, and followed him. His mood made me wary of what I was facing with him alone, but I also knew it could be an opportunity. If I could get him to talk, perhaps he'd tell me what was wrong. Tell me why he was mad at Michelis. Maybe it was even serious.

I hoped it was serious. I hoped Reeve and Michelis were not the close relatives that I'd assumed they were.

Wouldn't that change everything?

Reeve had left the door to the back cabin ajar. "Shut it," he said as I came in.

The minute I did, he was on me, pressing me against the cabin wall, sucking at my neck while his hands went up my dress to squeeze my ass.

"Mmm," I moaned involuntarily. *So much for talking.*

Trying to keep hold of my senses, I looked toward the door I'd closed a second ago, thinking of the people just on the other side and the conversation I wanted to have with him. "Reeve . . . ," I warned.

He stilled, his body stiff. "Are you telling me no?"

I was automatically angry that his subtext suggested it wasn't okay if I was. Also, angry that I liked that. But since I hadn't really been saying *no*—as if I ever could—I said, "I'm not."

"Good girl." He went back to nibbling my skin while his hands moved under my panties.

"But I'm sure you know they recommend twenty-four hours after waxing before sex." It was true, but I'd never heeded the advice before. I was just using the excuse until I could find a window to ask about the source of his tension.

Though, he didn't seem that tense right now. Or, if he was, his tension was focused on turning me on. He had his fingers now at my crack, the tips of them skidding along sensitive skin as he pulled my cheeks apart. "*Recommend* is the key word in that sentence," he said. "But if you'd prefer, there are other places I can explore." In case I didn't get what he was referring to, he stuck his thumb inside my tight hole and massaged the rim.

"Ah." It felt so good and I was so wet. But I needed more time to prepare for that. And, I hoped when that happened, I'd be in a bed, far from other people, with plenty of lube. "No, no. The usual hole is good."

"Yes, it is. Very good." With his thumb still in my ass, he slid a finger down to trace the entrance of my cunt.

I made one more attempt to divert him from his current plan of seduction. "Also. In case you've forgotten." I could barely talk with what he was doing to me. "Your friends are on the other side of the door."

"I haven't forgotten." He removed his hand from my underwear, and I immediately missed him. "And they aren't my friends. They're my staff." He bent to pull my panties down to my ankles then stood again and unzipped my dress. It fell open, and I knew that there was no chance of distracting him when his eyes lowered to my exposed pussy. A satisfied grin fell on his lips and his eyes clouded with lust. He ran his thumb across the fine hair that was left from my wax appointment. "This, I like," he said.

Then he put his hands under my hips, lifted me up and

carried me to the black leather couch that I hadn't realized was in the cabin until he'd dropped me on it.

"Prop yourself up on the arm," he commanded as he undid his pants to expose his already fully erect cock. "And spread your legs."

I scooted into the corner and, since my panties tied my ankles together, I let my knees drop open. Reeve knelt over me, and with no other foreplay, pushed inside of me.

"You're so wet, I just slide into you." His voice was gruff and the texture set my skin on fire. He glided in and out, making sure I felt every inch of him, waking my nerves. "Feel me?"

"Yes," I gasped.

"Good. Now let's see how fast I can make you come."

He tilted his hips up and began thrusting in earnest, his tip knocking against the most sensitive place inside of me. My breath hitched.

"That's right," he said, with pride. "I know your spot."

Damn, did he ever. The storm of pleasure began to gather, quickly. Too quickly. I felt off balance, my head spinning. I braced one hand on the couch and wrapped the other around his neck for support. Shooting to the edge this fast, I was going to go off like a bottle rocket, soaring high and screaming all the way.

I bit my lip so hard I tasted blood, attempting to keep my cries to a minimum.

"Don't be quiet," Reeve whispered, slowing his tempo ever so slightly.

"What?" Or that's the word I was going for. It came out more like a single syllable of unidentifiable sound.

He understood me. "Don't be quiet, or I'll stop."

I was in a daze from the way he was stroking me, my mental bandwidth taxed with the attempt to remain in control. My brow furrowed. "Don't be quiet?"

"Don't be quiet," he repeated, shifting his pelvis so that

he hit a new, equally tender spot. "I want them to hear you. I want them to know what I'm doing to you. Let them know that you're being fucked good and hard, just like you like it."

My throat was tight, my whimpers barely restrained. He had so much control over me, so much power to have me this close to destruction so quickly. I was exposed. Raw and vulnerable. Caught off guard by how easily he annihilated me each and every time.

It scared me. And, not in the way that I liked.

So instead of giving in to him like he wanted—like *I* wanted—I resisted. Trying to maintain some semblance of myself. Trying to hold on for just another moment. And anyway, wasn't it just as hot to try to be quiet? "Reeve, I—"

He pulled my head back with a yank of my hair. "You say my name again, Emily, you better scream it."

I almost came right then. Maybe resistance wasn't an option after all.

"Now." He yanked again, and I gasped from pain so wonderful that it shot sparks straight down to my pussy. His rhythm had slowed considerably, his cock barely pulsing in and out of me. "I told you what I wanted from you. If you're refusing, fine. I'll pull out and finish on my own. But you'll be wearing cum on your dress for the rest of the day. Either way those men are going to know you were in here being the dirty little slut that you are. Your choice. Do you understand?"

Okay, that was hot, too. Hotter than trying to be quiet.

"I understand," I said, kicking myself for thinking I could hold out against him. He was already so far under my skin that I barely recognized myself when I looked inside these days.

Letting out a slow breath, I locked my eyes on his, and cleared my mind of nothing but him. Nothing but the steady way he rocked into me. Nothing but the throbbing rod between my legs, filling me, invading me.

Lifting under my thighs, Reeve angled me so that my pussy was tighter around him and the first uninhibited cry fell from my lips.

"That's it," he said, increasing his drive. "Keep going. I'll help you." Slanting his mouth over my breast, he took my nipple between his teeth and pulled.

I cried out again, louder than before.

"Yes. Like that. Show them how naughty you are." He resumed his nipple play, pinching the other between his thumb and forefinger. It was all I needed. I was lost.

Whimpers turned to wails, gasps turned to screams. Every nerve in my body blazed as my climax shot through me, shattering me. Shredding me.

And as I was decimated, Reeve came alive, turned on by my utter destruction. He pounded into me with passionate fury, driving deeper than he'd ever been, coaxing my orgasm on and on with filthy words of alternating praise and castigation. Then he was there—I could tell by the moan that laced his ragged breaths—but instead of spurting inside of me, he pulled out. I tried to protest, but was still riding out my own orgasm when, with one tug of his hand, he climaxed, shooting onto my cunt, coating my newly waxed Brazilian with his cum.

He stood over me, one hand braced on the arm of the couch as we both struggled to find our breath. As soon as I could talk again, I half-heartedly complained, "You said you'd come inside me if I wasn't quiet."

"No. I said I wouldn't come on your dress. And I didn't." He shook one last drop onto the milky puddle he'd made then put himself away. "Don't move."

"I wasn't planning on it."

He crossed to the sink at the other side of the room,

grabbed a towel from the overhead cupboard, and got it wet. Then he came back, stopping when he was only a couple of feet away to scan the length of my body.

"What?"

"The way you look spread out like that, covered with my cum—" He finished with a groan.

"You branded me, cowboy." I was pretty sure I got that about him now. He marked me like this when he was feeling insecure about something. About me. When he thought he was going to lose me. So why did he feel that way now?

"It's almost a shame to remove it, but I suppose you'd rather I did." He didn't wait for me to respond, bending down to wipe the warm cloth over me, cleaning me with such thoroughness, such intimacy.

It made me feel close to him. Close enough to ask, "Reeve, out there—what were you so upset about?"

"You don't need to worry about it."

I reached my hand out and cupped his cheek. "But I do worry. I worry about you." The truth of it shuddered through me, and I trembled as I took my next breath.

He found the sides of my dress and pulled them together. "Now that is something I don't expect from you," he said as he zipped me up.

"It doesn't change that I do."

"It's my job to worry about you." He took my hand and tugged me up from the couch. "Not the other way around." He bent to pull my panties up.

"Why can't we worry about each other?"

He gave me a skeptical look as he drew my underwear up and over my hips. "We're about to land."

The change of subject pissed me off. His attitude pissed me off. His refusal to let me in pissed me off. "You are such a pain in the ass. It's not going to diminish your manhood if someone shows you a little bit of concern. And even if it did, you have more than enough to make up for it. So would you just tell me if you're okay?"

For the first time since I'd broached this topic, he looked at me. His expression was stony, but in the dark of his eyes, I saw him battling. Finally, he softened. He put his arm around my waist and drew me to him. His mouth inches from mine, he said, "I wasn't okay. But I am now."

He kissed me, molding my lips to the shape he desired, his tongue instructing mine as he stroked inside with affection and tender command. It was a kiss that backed up his words, a demonstration of just how I'd made him *okay*.

Something told me he wasn't just talking about the conversation he'd walked away from, which made it that much easier to lose myself in his kiss. Lose myself in him. If he asked me the same question, I could almost give him the same answer—*I wasn't okay, but I am now*. Since him.

Almost.

Just, there was Amber.

CHAPTER

23

Reeve's private driver from the ranch met us at the Jackson airport. It was too late for dinner at the main house so we and his staff went out to a restaurant in town. I'd never been in public with Reeve, and I was somewhat surprised to see both guards sit at the bar instead of with us, not that I minded. Actually, I wasn't sure how his security functioned at all. When I asked, Reeve told me Anatolios accompanied him everywhere and that was usually the extent of his detail.

"So why did the other one come too?" I wasn't the paranoid type, but if there was a reason for extra guards, I wanted to know.

"Tabor's here for you," Reeve answered. "When I leave, Anatolios will come with me and Tabor will stay to look after you."

To protect me? Or protect Reeve *from* me? I didn't have the balls to ask, but it would have been nice to know if I should be offended or flattered.

We lingered after our meal, drinking and enjoying some

friendly banter. Reeve, I learned, was happy with a beer but preferred bourbon if the bar had a good brand, which it did. I also discovered he had a real camaraderie with his men, jesting and poking fun at them with ease. He'd been like this occasionally with me, but I hadn't expected it with the staff members of one of his many properties. I made a note to ask about that later.

Parker was the youngest, just a little older than me, and was a regular comedian. Charlie, though quieter, had a laugh that made it impossible not to join in with. Brent had fifteen years on Reeve and was the storyteller of the group. He provided most of the entertainment, flirting with the waitresses, recalling how things were in the good old days. He'd worked the ranch since he was a teenager, I learned, when Reeve's father was still alive. A few times I'd tried to lead him to talk about the Sallis family or about more recent times—the months that Amber had stayed there, for example—but he never took the bait. He dodged so artfully, I almost didn't realize he'd been coached.

Until the end of the night when I asked if foxes often got in the henhouse, and I caught a look that passed from Reeve to Brent, a look that could only be taken as a warning.

If I hadn't seen it, I wouldn't have been able to tell from Brent. He scooted his chair closer to me and wrapped an arm around my shoulder, then leaned in close to say, "There's always foxes, darling. Whether they're in the henhouse scalping your chickens or the river eating all your fish, you can never be off your guard."

I laughed, hiding my disappointment as easily as he'd hid his cover. I'd hoped to learn things from him, but though he might be more likely to give me information when Reeve wasn't around, I had a feeling he'd be just as tight-lipped. He seemed pretty loyal. It didn't mean I wouldn't try.

Reeve took my hand as he added, "Sometimes they're even in your bed." His smile was amicable, but his tone felt off. He was moody after that, and I regretted trying to dig.

It was dark when we made it to Kaya. We stopped first at a security gate much like the one at Reeve's house, but this one was manned with two guards packing firearms.

After we drove through, the driver parked so that Reeve could run into the large building next to the gate.

"Security office," Brent said in explanation. "Cameras from the ranch feed in there. The guns are all housed there as well. Reeve also keeps his personal set of keys for the house in the safe there. He's getting those."

The keys made sense—I wouldn't expect Reeve to keep all his resort keys with him in LA. The security, on the other hand, seemed a little excessive. "Lots of security for a ranch. Is that typical?" Or were there additional measures because of the Sallis connections to mafia?

It was Anatolios who gave Brent a pointed glance this time and my question wasn't answered.

At the house, there was another man in slacks and a button-down at the doors, whom I presumed was another guard because of the gun on his hip. Though maybe that was a Wyoming thing. Our driver brought our luggage in, and though there was much to look at, it was too late and we were too tired to do anything but settle in and go to bed. Reeve showed me my private bedroom, which was down the hall from his master suite. I dropped my belongings there and unpacked a robe and some toiletries to bring with me to his room.

Once the door was shut in his quarters, I learned the true source of Reeve's moodiness. Turned out it wasn't about chickens or Vilanakis at all.

"You and Brent got along well," he said, loosening his

belt. "He's known around here for being a player. Is that going to be a problem?"

"For me? No. He's fun, but he's married and I don't enable cheating." *Anymore.* I realized too late my mistake. Blushing, I spun toward Reeve. "But none of that matters anyway. He won't be a problem for me because I'm with *you.*"

"Yeah, that should have been your first answer." His jaw was tight, but there was a conflicting gleam in his eye, as though he was debating whether he should be mad or not.

I decided to make the choice easier for him. With an exaggerated pout, I said, "That was very naughty of me. Maybe I need to be punished."

His jaw loosened, the gleam turned wicked, the belt came off, and I was thoroughly whipped, and fucked, before falling into a restless sleep.

Bad dreams and anxiousness woke me several times that night. I'd only just found deep sleep when I was woken again, this time with Reeve's cock rubbing at my pussy from behind. It was a blissful quickie that allowed me to stay half-asleep through it and still earned me a nice orgasm.

"That's got to last you a few days," Reeve said when we were done. "I'm leaving this morning for some business upstate."

"Yeah, that was for me," I said, referring to our fast fuck.

"Right." My grin faded. "How long will you be gone?"

"Three days. I'll be back the day after tomorrow." He leaned over and brushed the hair out of my face. He didn't smile or kiss me or touch my cheek, just looked into my eyes for a few precious seconds. It was sweet in a way I couldn't put into words. A much more tender goodbye than I'd expected from him.

When he stood back up, he beamed down at me. "And

that was totally for you. Your Kaya Ranch wake-up call. It's a quarter to six and I didn't want you to miss breakfast."

"Very kind of you. I'll get right on that." But I rolled over onto the pillow he'd used, burying my face in the traces of his scent. Then I fell back to sleep, partly because I was exhausted, but also because, without Reeve there, I didn't feel much like being awake.

When I woke up again, it was nearly ten. The sun streamed through the crack in the curtains, drawing me with its beams the way a spotlight in the city drew people to premiere events. I peeked out and was met with acres of rolling green grass flanked with wooded hills. Beyond, snow-capped mountains stretched up to a cloud-spotted sky. The scene was beautiful and dramatic, calling me to throw on some clothes and get outside so I could explore every inch of the landscape.

Except, I had other exploring that took priority.

Reeve would be gone for three days and I knew I needed to use that time wisely. The house was at the top of my research list. I planned to get into every nook and cranny of its ten thousand square feet. I also hoped to get some of the staff talking. Amber couldn't have been there as long as she had without making some sort of impact on someone. Hopefully I'd find that someone, and they'd be willing to talk.

I'd missed breakfast, but was able to dig up some cheese and apples from the fridge to tide me over until lunch. Then I went up to my room to shower and get decent. I unpacked my suitcase as well, then did a quick self-tour of the common areas in the house. I found a full-size gym in the basement as well as a theater room. The library was on the main floor along with the large dining hall that looked like it accommodated a hundred people. There was also a solarium, den, and sitting room. The rest of the space was divided among bedrooms, none of which seemed to be currently in use except for the one Tabor was staying in. Reeve's office was the only room that was locked, as he'd said.

I was glad to realize through my exploration that though Tabor was here for me, he wasn't here to watch my every move. He checked in on me a couple of times during the day and told me just to let him know if I wanted to leave the house. It was a huge relief to have space so I could do what I wanted.

It was also nice to know Reeve really had brought him for my protection and not to spy.

At noon, I went to the dining hall for lunch. It was served buffet style, an arrangement of cold sandwiches, soups, and salads. There was no triangle rung to announce the meal, but cowboys came rushing in on the hour exactly as if there were some sort of alarm that only they could hear. There were fifty or so all together. Parker and Charlie came in at the tail end and sat in the corner away from everyone else. I imagined as managers they got tired of their employees and wanted the break to be away from them.

I got my food and carefully surveyed the room, deciding to sit at a table with only a handful of ranchers. Here I made my move, talking up the lot of them, which mostly meant a lot of innocent flirting where I attempted to coax information about previous visits by Reeve and the women who'd accompanied him. All of the men I spoke with had been willing to talk, but none had worked there long enough to know anything that happened the previous summer. As Reeve had said, most were temporary employees who had just been hired recently for the busy season.

Dinner had the same lackluster results. I tried not to feel defeated when I went to bed that night, though it was hard not to be down. It was a lonely place to be without Reeve, and it had only been one day. I slept in his room, even though I had one of my own. In the large house, his room was the only space that felt comfortable.

I spent the next morning in the library, first examining the shelves and then poking around on the computer. It was possible, I'd decided, that Amber might have used it when she'd been there. If she did, she could have saved a document or maybe the browser history had something of interest.

But I found nothing useful.

At lunch, I got lucky.

This time, instead of sitting with the masses, I picked out the man sitting by himself wearing a security uniform. Tabor and the men I'd seen carrying around the house wore slacks and button-downs, but the guards at the front gate wore uniforms like this one. I was interested in the unanswered question about the high level of security, and certain I wouldn't get anything from the slacks.

"Mind if I sit, uh"—I bent to make out the name on his front pocket—"Cade?"

He appeared surprised to have anyone talk to him, looking around the room as if he didn't think I'd ask unless there was nowhere else to sit. "Um. Sure." Maybe there was a guideline about not talking to the uniforms, but since Reeve hadn't included it in his expectations, I wasn't too worried about breaking it.

"Great, thanks!" I sat and nibbled at my half-sandwich and salad while we made small talk about the weather and whether or not I'd ever been to Wyoming before.

Slowly I shifted the conversation to his job. "How long have you worked here, anyway, Cade?"

"Just hit ten years last month."

I almost flipped my tray from leaning forward too excitedly. "That's great. You must really like working here to have stayed this long. I bet you have great stories—like about the people who visit. The women that Reeve brings here."

He laughed. "Ah, I see what you're after. Sorry, sweetie, I'm not allowed to talk about Mr. Sallis's . . . *guests*." Dammit, Cade wasn't an idiot. "But it was a good effort on your part. And for the record"—he bent in and hushed his voice—"there have only been a couple he's brought here. So consider yourself special."

Special. I doubted that since Reeve had told me specifically that I wasn't. Yet, hadn't he shown me many times that maybe I actually was?

"Well, worth a try," I said with an authentic though exaggerated sigh. Still, the conversation didn't have to be a total loss. "Tell me then instead, is it normal to have this level of security at a ranch?"

He wagged his head back and forth as he contemplated his answer. "Ranch, yes. There are always people out to steal your livestock. Cattle are big business. Probably not usually this much security at a main house. But the Sallis family is . . . private."

Yeah, "private" was one way to put it. Or maybe in hiding, going so far as to bury Reeve's mother's real name from anyone who searched.

I deliberated what to ask next. "Does the ranch get many visitors? Not of the women variety. Just, you know, visitors." Like Michelis. Or other family members.

"I'm not allowed to talk about the people who stay in the house, as I said before. As for other visitors, I wouldn't really know. I've always worked the surveillance room here and never at the main gates."

"There's a surveillance room here as well? For just the house?" I expected a few cameras on the roof, but certainly not something that had to be manned.

"Yeah. There's three of us that work an eight-hour shift

each. I'm lucky because there are two guys on the house duty during the day so I grab one to cover while I'm at lunch. I should be getting back now, though." He wiped his mouth with a napkin then threw it on his tray.

As he stood up, I asked, "Would you mind showing it to me? The surveillance room, I mean." Reeve had said that nothing was off limits. "I get nervous out here in the wild when Reeve's gone. I'm sure you understand."

Cade shrugged. "I suppose there's no harm in that. Security here is tight, though, I'm telling you. You're safe here. But if seeing it will make you feel better, I get that. You finished with that?" He gestured to my food. When I nodded, he picked it up under his. "Follow me."

The surveillance room was behind a heavy door on the first floor just inside the house. I'd seen it when I'd explored the day before, but it was locked and I'd assumed it was to the electrical room or furnace since it was the only metal door I'd found.

Cade, of course, had keys. He let us in, and while he chatted with the guy who'd covered his break, I took in the room. It wasn't very large, about 150 square feet. A curved desk with three rolling chairs took up most of the space, wrapping around two entire walls. Above the desk were twenty-five or so monitors, several turned off. Another wall had two metal cabinets—both unlocked and opened so I could see they were filled with digital recorders, a key sticking out of each door. Finally, there was a gun rack with more than a dozen different types of artillery including assault weapons, rifles, handguns, and what I thought was a machine gun. Underneath this were drawers that I assumed were for ammunition.

"See?" Cade said, noticing my eyes on the guns. He'd dismissed his substitute and it was now just he and I in the room. "We're damn prepared here. This isn't even a third of what's down at the surveillance room by the main gates."

"Prepared is right." Question was, prepared for what?

I looked back at the monitors. Taking a seat in one of the chairs, I studied the screens. Each one flipped between two or three camera views, one screen for each room of the house, it appeared. I blushed suddenly remembering what Reeve and I had done the night we'd arrived. And the next morning. It was one thing to be watched during sex and quite another to be watched and not know it.

"Is there always someone in here?" I asked as casually as I could manage.

He sat in the chair next to me. "Yep. Twenty-four/seven."

"And every room in the house is under surveillance?" Silently I was thanking God that the only exploring I'd done so far was in trying to talk to people. I hadn't opened closets or rummaged through drawers. The last thing I wanted was someone watching me do something they'd report to Reeve. And if every room was watched—no wonder Reeve had cautioned me about walking around naked. Though, I'd never searched for a security room at his place in LA. He could very well have a similar setup there.

"Yes, every room is under surveillance," Cade said, looking me over suspiciously. Probably wondering what it was I was trying to steal.

I fluttered my lashes. "It's just that sometimes . . . well, Reeve and I often let our passion get away from us, if you know what I mean."

"Ah." His face reddened slightly. "No worries there. We only actively watch the main rooms. There are no cameras in the bathrooms, and we only watch a few of the bed-rooms."

Like mine, I noticed. He seemed to realize that after

he'd said it, his eyes darting nervously from the screens to his hands, anywhere but at me.

"I only keep my clothes in there," I said, reassuring him as well as me. "I sleep with Reeve." If I'd had any doubt about which room I'd stay in with him gone, I didn't now.

"Right, right, of course." Cade pointed to the blank screens. "These are to the other bedrooms. We don't usually have those on, to maintain guest privacy."

With all the guards at the ranch, it was hard to imagine why Amber would have called me with the safe word. Unless she'd been afraid of Reeve, in which case, did that mean his staff was okay with whatever he'd done? Had Amber called over something stupid? Like, had Reeve pulled out his belt with her like he had with me and she'd panicked?

I didn't like thinking that was the case and not because it was irritating to think of Amber being afraid of something naughty that I enjoyed, but because it made my stomach clench with jealousy.

No matter what had happened with Amber and Reeve, she'd had him first, and that was never going to change. I had to find a way to get used to that. But it didn't look like it would be today.

"Regardless if we're actively monitoring them," Cade added, "all rooms have cameras and they're all recorded on digital over there so we can go back and review if something happens."

"How long do you keep the recordings?" I was sure it wouldn't be very long, but it didn't hurt to ask.

Turned out I was wrong. "One full year," Cade said.

One year. Which meant there were still recordings of Amber. The realization sent a swarm of emotions buzzing in my chest like bees. The idea of seeing something that hurt her or scared her was not a comfortable one. And if the recordings showed her being intimate with Reeve I didn't know if I could take that either.

But to have the chance to see her again, even just on a black-and-white silent recording . . .

I had to see those recordings. It was a practically impossible task with the room always occupied. I had charmed Cade, but he didn't seem like the type who would break the rules, no matter how much I flirted. I made it a point to find out who the other guards were who worked the room. Maybe one of them would be easier to coerce. Or seduce, if I had to.

"So . . . who else works this job? And what time does his shift start?"

"Six. That's Mike. Donny works the graveyard. Neither of them is very friendly, though. They're straight by the book, don't talk to anyone, come in, do their job, and leave. You were lucky to get me today to show you this room. They'd probably both kick my ass for letting you in."

So much for that idea.

"Well, I appreciate it. You've alleviated my fears." I sighed, and looked back at the monitors. Reeve's room wasn't there I noticed now. "I'm guessing that Reeve's suite isn't actively watched?"

"Ah, Mr. Sallis's room is recorded, but the screen for his room is locked in his office in a cabinet like those." He pointed to the ones behind us. "The recorders to those are in there too. Only one who has access to that is the man himself."

Now this news was better. Because I had a better shot at getting into Reeve's office. All I needed was his key ring.

Cade leaned toward me and winked. "So no one's seeing anything inappropriate."

I pretended that was exactly the reason I'd asked. "Thank God. No one's selling our sex tapes."

He covered his ears with his hands and said, "Too much information, too much information."

I took that as my cue to leave.

The rest of the afternoon was spent inconspicuously searching through Reeve's suite. I knew no one was watching me over the cameras, but Reeve could watch the recording later and find out I'd done it. If he later came to me with accusations, I'd man up and tell him I was snooping, as many girlfriends do. I wouldn't have to tell him I was looking for something specific.

My search ended fruitlessly, but I wasn't that disheartened. I'd seen Reeve pocket his keys when he'd first gotten them from the security room, and I guessed he likely kept them on him at all times. Which just meant I had to wait until he got home to try to confiscate his office key. All I had to do was get his jeans off of him and wait for him to sleep, right?

Lucky for me, getting Reeve out of his pants hadn't ever been a problem.

CHAPTER

2 4

When I arrived at dinner that night, Charlie and Parker beckoned me to join them at their corner table. Brent was with them as well, and though I felt a pinch of guilt about eating with him, I figured it would be strange if I ignored their invitation, seeing how they were really the only three people I knew at the ranch.

Besides, this was my chance to see if they'd say anything useful now that Reeve wasn't here to give warning looks any time the conversation got interesting.

Unfortunately, they were just as tight-lipped, just as evading. Every leading question I asked got ignored. Every prompt turned into a story about something else.

And then Parker slipped.

All three of them had consumed a number of beers during the meal, and by the end, Parker, at least, was closer to drunk than not.

Without any elicitation from me, he put his elbow on the table, leaned on his hand, and, looking up at me with glazed eyes, said, "You know, Emily's the first woman our man's brought here who doesn't have a drug problem. That's kind of nice, isn't it?"

"Parker," Brent warned.

"I'm just saying it's nice to have a decent woman for a change." Parker gave me a sloppy smile. "You're a nice change, Emily."

Charlie had been quiet for most of the meal, but now he said, "You never liked the last one, but that doesn't mean she wasn't decent."

Parker sat up and thumped his fist on the table. "No, she wasn't. And you're right—I didn't like her. Because she was a high-maintenance pain in the ass. I'm glad she's off our hands, even ending the way it d—"

"Parker!" Brent thwacked the younger man across the head. "You've got a loose tongue. Shut it."

I hadn't realized how much I'd begun to believe that Reeve really didn't have anything to do with Amber's death until that moment. "What does he mean, 'ending the way it did'?"

"Forget it. He shouldn't have said anything," Brent said.

"But he did say it, and now I want to know." I *needed* to know. "What did you mean, Parker?"

Parker looked from Brent to Charlie and then at me. "I don't really know. I'm drunk."

Charlie stepped in. "He just meant it was a bad breakup. For lots of reasons that are too personal for an employee to get into about his boss. If you want to know more, you're going to have to ask Reeve."

At that moment, I thought I just might. I was frustrated from all the dead ends. Sick of feeling like a yo-yo, up and down with theories that changed with every new bit of information I gathered. It had been a while since the last time I'd asked Reeve about his past, anyway. Maybe it was time to try again.

And since he wasn't coming home until the next night, I had a day to think of what I'd say.

Or chicken out. Either was possible at this point.

The men left sometime around nine and the house suddenly grew quiet and still. It put me on edge, especially after Parker's remark. I was already wary of Reeve, knowing he might have participated in getting Amber killed. But if his staff was aware of it as well, then I was in much more danger than I'd thought. Anyone could be after me at any time. What the hell had I been thinking going on a trip with him?

Oh, shit. That reminded me I hadn't gotten a new burner phone from Joe before I'd left. I'd long ago deleted his real number from my cell. So not only did I have no way to contact him if I needed him, but also, no one knew where I was.

I tried to go to sleep, but all I could do was toss and turn and waffle between feeling panicked and feeling lonely. Either Reeve hadn't done anything horrible, I was reading things wrong and I missed him, or he had and I was reading things right and I still missed him. After an hour of it, I pulled my robe on over my night slip and headed down to the den to watch some TV and get my mind on something—anything—else.

I flipped through the channels for twenty minutes, finding nothing. Just as I was ready to give up and pick up my Kindle, a familiar face filled the screen—Chris Blakely's.

"It's not a theory. It's not a guess. It's a fact," Chris was saying. It was one of those late-night interview shows where the host sat behind a desk and the guest lounged in a modern deco chair. Not a popular show—he wouldn't be asked to one of those with his current career status—but one on some cable channel. I didn't even recognize the interviewer, a redheaded woman with big lips.

It was something to watch, at least. I tossed the remote aside and settled back into the couch.

"But you still haven't said why," Big Lips said next.

"I'm not going to get into all the reasons I have that I know he did it—let me say, though, that by reasons, I mean proof. Missy was completely robbed of her life. She knew things she shouldn't and Reeve Sallis took care of that."

My stomach dropped. *No. No, no, no. He did not just—*

"If this proof is as irrefutable as you say it is, how did Reeve Sallis get away with it?" Big Lips looked skeptical, which was admirable considering how quickly Hollywood liked to buy into scandals.

Chris sat back with a smug expression. "He's a rich, powerful man. Rich, powerful men get away with things all the time. It's the law of capitalism. It's especially an issue when those rich, powerful men have ties to men who are richer and more powerful."

And now he'd referenced the mob. I sat forward, tense, wishing I could stop listening, but needing to hear just exactly what the idiot was saying.

"What sort of connections are you implying?"

"I can't comment on that." *Good Chris. Stop there.* He didn't. "But people who live outside the law."

"Like government people?"

"No. Wrong type of outside the law. I'm talking about the type of organized people that deal specifically with crime-oriented situations."

I cringed. She was going to keep asking until she got something. That's the way those interviewers worked. Did he not know anything?

Sure enough, her next question was, "Like the mafia?"

I gasped. *Fuck. Just . . . fuck.*

Finally Chris's expression grew wary. "I've said too much already. Let's just say Reeve Sallis is not innocent. End of story."

Frustrated did not begin to describe how I felt at the moment. Angry was closer. Pissed off. Also, frightened. If Chris kept blabbing his big mouth, he was going to get himself in trouble. Hadn't he learned anything from Missy's death? And there was no telling how long it would be before his *reasons* led back to Joe. Back to me. Back to Reeve. I wasn't just standing on the sidelines—I was in the thick of it. His time in the spotlight could very well come at a price, and who'd have to pay it?

I doubted it would only be him.

It was too upsetting to watch further. I searched for the remote, but couldn't find where I'd flung it, so I crossed to the TV and switched it off manually before I heard more.

When I turned back, I was startled to see Reeve at the mouth of the room. He was wearing a dark blue suit, his tie loose, his jacket unbuttoned.

Without thinking, I smiled. I might have been anxious about Parker's words, but in this moment I realized it wasn't the emotion that weighed heaviest on my heart. I'd missed Reeve. Truly missed him. More than I wanted to admit to him or myself. I was two seconds from rushing into his arms, whether he *expected* it or not.

Except, then I noticed his narrowed eyes and hard expression. They told me he'd heard at least part of the interview. He wouldn't automatically assume I'd known about the whole thing, would he? I mean, I did, but there wasn't any reason for him to know that. And I certainly hadn't known Chris was going to take the information we'd figured out together and blast it all over national television.

Reeve had assumed things about Chris and me before, though. Would it be far-fetched to think he wouldn't now?

God, I wasn't sure. But tension flared from him like a heat storm, rolling through the room like flashes of lightning.

I crossed my arms, suddenly chilled. Hoping I was

being paranoid, I decided to play cool, pushing my lips into a smile. "You're back early. I didn't expect you until tomorrow."

His eyes pierced and pinched me. "Do *you* think I did it?"

"Did wh—?" It was halfway out before I realized what he was asking. I closed my mouth, unsure how to answer, not prepared to lie. Not prepared to tell the truth.

He repeated his question, his voice even and eerily controlled. "Do you think I did it?"

I didn't flinch. "Did you?"

He closed his eyes a second longer than a blink and his shoulders sank ever so slightly. When he opened them, he asked with disdain, "Does it matter?"

"What does that mean?" Of course it mattered. His answer mattered very much.

"It means that people seem to make up their mind without caring if it's the truth or not. I didn't take you for one of those people. I guess I was wrong." He turned and headed out of the room.

I flew after him, throwing words at his back. "Why the hell would you make that assumption? Because you walked in on me watching an interview? That wasn't me saying those things. It was Chris."

"Chris, who is your friend."

"That doesn't automatically mean I subscribe to his beliefs. I have my own thoughts and opinions too." It wasn't exactly an honest argument on my part. I did subscribe to the belief that in some way Reeve had contributed to Missy's death.

But only in my head. My heart held out.

"And when I asked you your opinion you answered with a question." Reeve climbed the stairs toward the bedrooms, taking them two at a time. "Hardly seems like you have your own opinion on this particular matter, does it? Or if you do, you're not willing to share it."

I followed him, trotting up the steps to keep up with him. "I don't know the answer. Which means I don't share Chris's opinion. And it's why I asked you. So that I don't just assume."

In his suite, he threw his jacket on an armchair and began undoing his cufflinks.

I stopped just inside the door. "Is this because it was Chris I was watching? Because you're jealous?"

"Chris has nothing to do with this." He tossed his cufflinks on the nightstand and then spun toward me, his eyes blazing with rage and hurt. "It was the wrong answer, Emily. You should have said *no.*"

"What?" I was as surprised by his sudden burst of rage as I was by his words.

"You heard me." He pulled at his tie to remove it and from his stance, from his tone, it wasn't crazy that it crossed my mind that he might use it on me.

But he balled it up and stuck it in his pocket. To put away later, maybe. Or to wrap around my throat when tired of the conversation. Wrap it tight and pull, watching my eyes as my life flickered away.

Except I didn't really believe he'd do that. Not to me. It was gut instinct with no basis in fact.

As for Missy, I didn't know what I believed. "I think I was pretty open-minded to say I didn't know, but you wanted me to automatically defend you?"

"Yes. I did. It doesn't seem like an unreasonable request to think the woman I'm sleeping with would be on my side. Excuse me for not thinking to include it on the list of expectations I gave you before we got here."

The comment stung so unexpectedly that I almost regretted the answer I'd given earlier.

Then I looked at the bigger picture, and no way. That wasn't happening. No regret. I would submit and demure to a lot, almost anything, but I would not give in on this.

And with that clarity, I was inflamed. "You can't be serious." He had his back to me, unbuttoning his shirt. "You can't possibly expect me to know whether you're innocent or not. When you've alluded to being dangerous. When you've perpetuated that image. You've wanted me to be afraid of you. Now you expect me to just assume you'd never really do something terrible? That's not what you led me to believe."

"I didn't lead you anywhere you didn't want to go."

"You think I want to believe that you killed someone?" I was as mad that he kept his back to me as I was with the things he was saying.

"At the very least you want to think that I could have."

He was right. That was my flaw, and I was seconds from readily admitting it. Then I thought better of it, because though I was willing to share that with him, this moment was about something else.

So I addressed that instead. "I do think you could have." I was calmer now, but my hands still shook with emotion. "Whether you actually did it or not, I don't know."

He turned to face me. His shirt draped open and his hands worked his belt. "Yes. I could have." He stepped toward me slowly. "I don't just mean that I have the money and the resources to kill a person, but I could do it. I could end a life without a second thought—if it was the right life." Another step. "A life that deserved it." Another step. "A life that had crossed me."

He had a tie in his pocket and his belt now in his hands. It wasn't the time to provoke him.

And yet I did. "Did Missy cross you? Was she *the right life*?" Was Amber the right life? Was I?

It was a split second that passed without an answer, but

it was a heavy second. One where I understood that these were the answers I'd been searching for since I met him and once he gave them, I'd have to make decisions that I didn't want to make. I'd have to decide if I believed him when he said no. Or decide if I cared when he said yes. I'd have to decide if I'd stay.

And if I had to decide, I'd rather decide when I didn't know. I'd rather decide to leave when it was only possible that he was a killer than stay when I knew he was one. Because I was afraid that would be how it would happen, and I wasn't sure I was ready to live with myself when I did.

So I decided to run.

"Never mind," I said already out the door. "Don't tell me. I don't want to know." I whisked toward my bedroom, my mind set.

Reeve was on my heels. "Why? Because if you find out that I didn't, you might no longer find me interesting?"

He was so close to understanding me and yet so far. It felt like being thirsty and being offered a glass of sand. He was trying to understand, in his alpha, tyrannical way, and that touched me. But he missed.

I flicked the light on in my room and went straight for the bed. "There's no reason for me to answer, is there?" I pulled my suitcase from underneath and laid it open on top of the covers. "Since that's what you've decided. Talk about people who make up their mind without caring." My back was to the door, so I glanced back to see he'd stopped at the threshold.

"Don't do that, Emily. Don't try to egg me on." The edge in his words said he was past warning. Said he was ready to act.

"I'm not egging you on. And that's exactly my point." I crossed to the dresser and gathered my T-shirts, not bothering with keeping them folded. "You've decided what my motives are. What I think. What I feel. You care as little to know what's real about me as you do to share anything real about you."

I *was* egging him on. Taunting him. Because as much as I didn't want to know who he really was, I was compelled to ask. One last-ditch effort to find out the truth about Amber. About me.

"That was always the arrangement between us. Don't act like—" He stopped short. "What are you doing?"

I threw my shirts in the suitcase. "I'm packing."

"Oh, for fuck's sake. Why?"

"I've suddenly realized that there isn't any point to all of this." I gathered all my underwear.

"Stop packing."

"No point to our 'arrangement.'" I headed back to the bed.

"Stop packing. You're not leaving." He'd stepped into the room, but hadn't come in far enough to be an obstacle.

I paused, facing him. "Are you going to make me?"

When he didn't make any indication that he was, I continued to the suitcase.

"I said, stop packing." He grabbed me by my upper arm forcefully.

The underwear spilled onto the floor instead of in my bag as I turned toward him, clutching him at the forearms. "Make me stay, Reeve. You can do it. You have the resources. You have the capability of doing whatever you want."

He could make me stay very easily. Really, all it would take was for him to ask.

"I'm not going to do this. You stay if you want. I'm not making you." He let go of me—pushed me away, actually—and every secret hope I had for Reeve and me together fell away, as if I had hid them high on a shelf where I could pretend they didn't exist. Until now when they came crashing down around me.

"That's what I thought." I turned my back and stooped to gather the panties off the floor, away from him so he couldn't see that my eyes had filled.

"It has to be your decision to stay, Emily." He hadn't moved. He was still standing behind me. "I kept someone before. I'm not doing it again."

I twisted to look up at him. "What do you mean you kept someone?"

He opened his mouth, but then he shook his head. "I'm not doing this. I said what I'm going to say. You do what you want." He spun and left the room.

Oh, hell no. He'd slipped and there was a chance that he was talking about Amber. But that wasn't why I was eager to hear more. It was because it had been the first real thing he'd ever shared with me, and it was like heroin, and I, a junkie, craving more. That, I would fight for.

I flew into the hall. "You're a goddamn chicken."

He stopped in front of his door, turned back to me slowly. "What was that?"

"You heard me." I took one step toward him. Just one. I was brave but not *that* brave. "You leave it as my decision because you don't want to take any responsibility for what happens between us. That's not the sign of someone with power. That's the sign of a coward."

I realized that this was what this whole argument was actually about. Not his guilt or his innocence but this— about us. About what we were. About what was happening between us. And as difficult as it was to bring this to a head, it was somewhat inspiring that he was battling just as hard as I was. As if it was just as important to him as it was to me.

He narrowed his eyes and took half a step in my direction. "Are you taunting me?"

Or, maybe he just didn't like to be goaded.

No. I didn't believe that was the whole truth. I balled

my fists at my sides, hoping any courage I had would flow through my fingertips and fill back inside me, a closed circuit. "I'm calling it as it is. But you are responsible, Reeve. Whether you want to be or not. You're the reason I'm confused about who you really are. You're responsible for the things you've made me believe about you. About us."

His eyes widened with incense. "About *us*? I've never—"

My finger flew out to point at him, shaking with rage. "Don't you dare finish that sentence. Because you have. You say one thing but then you show me something else. You make sure I know that I'm not special and then you do everything to make me feel like I am. Well, I'm not settling for that anymore. I can take either reality as long as I know what it is. So you want me to choose if I stay or go? How about this instead—decide what I am to you or I leave."

We stood there at a stalemate, staring hard at each other, as my words settled and the ultimatum sank in for both of us. It hadn't been anything I'd ever intended to say, but now that the words were out, I would stand behind them. I was his—we both knew that. But either I was his plaything or I was his prize. All I was asking for was a definition.

He didn't give one.

He held his stance and I held mine, neither of us willing to back down. And the longer I let him go without an answer, the weaker I became. I had to follow through.

So I turned away and went back to my room to finish packing.

Tears pressed at the corners of my eyes as I gathered a handful of clothes from the closet and brought them back to the bed. One by one, I pulled the items off their hangers and tossed them in my suitcase. I didn't really want to leave. But I couldn't stay. Not like this. Leaving was better, anyway. I'd set out in the beginning to save Amber, and having failed that, at least I could save myself.

But then, in between my sniffles, I heard him. Heard him behind me. He was so quiet in his approach, so stealthy, that my pulse shot up, my heart thundering in my chest.

He came closer. Came right behind me and I wondered, is it the tie? Or the belt? I was paralyzed, waiting for it. I wouldn't fight it, I decided. It wouldn't matter. He'd win anyway, and so I'd let him. After, he'd toss my body in a landfill. No one would come looking for me. I would be forgotten.

His body was hot at my back. I could hear him exhale. Then he said quietly, "I wasn't there."

I didn't move, didn't breathe.

"I had nothing to do with it. There was a party. I was fucking some other woman on the beach. Some other *women*. We recorded it on my phone, for kicks. I didn't know Missy was looking for me. I didn't know she had gone out to the cliffs. I'd texted the recording to one of the girls. It was time stamped. I was completely cleared. I can show you if you want to see it."

I shook my head, barely perceptibly. If I needed a time stamp to come to a conclusion about his innocence, then we were already over. I hadn't asked for proof. I'd asked for his story and he'd given it. Either I believed him now or I didn't.

And I did believe him. For no other reason than that he wanted me to. He didn't need to tell me anything—he hadn't told anything to anyone before. But he'd told me this story now. Whether it was true or not, it meant he wanted me to stay. So I believed it.

I also believed it could actually be true.

I didn't face him yet, though, because there was more I had demanded from him in exchange for staying. "Is she the woman you didn't let leave?"

"No, that was someone else. Missy wasn't even anything to me. I fucked her. She was around for that."

Swiveling my head, I met his eyes. "Like me?"

He scoffed. "No. Not like you."

I turned my entire body toward him, opening myself up to him. "How are we different?"

"For one, she was a tweaked-out cokehead. For another, I would care if you were gone." He regarded me with anticipation, seeming to want me to acknowledge that, though he hadn't given me what I demanded, hadn't given me his decision about what I meant to him, he'd still given me *something*.

And the something he'd given me *did* have meaning. It burrowed quickly into my chest, a new hope for me to hold on to.

But I refused to let that show. Because, while it was *something*, it wasn't *enough*.

I hugged my arms around myself. "What do you want me to be, Reeve?"

He scrubbed his hands over his face. "Emily. I didn't want to want anything from you. It was you who pursued me."

I reacted quickly. "Have to make sure I remember that, don't you?"

He cocked his head and looked at me with narrowed eyes. "Are you going to let me talk?"

"Are you actually going to say something useful?"

That glint flashed in his eyes—the one that said he'd like to take a paddle to my ass. I ignored the tingle that sent to my lower regions and held my stance.

His eyes fell to my mouth, to the frown pulling at the corners. He reached his hand out and brushed his thumb across the downturned point. "I do want a deeper relationship with you."

My lips parted in surprise.

Then his hand dropped. "But I fucked up my last relationship so much that it was barely recognizable in the end.

And I'm not sure any future relationship would be any different."

"Tell me what happened then." I dropped my arms, desperate to touch him but afraid of losing ground. "Tell me and I can help make sure it doesn't happen again." My motive, for once, wasn't Amber. It was genuinely a plea for us.

He lowered his eyes. "No. It's the worst of me."

Here, I did think of Amber. Because it was impossible to hear that he'd done the worst things with her and not think they were actually the worst things a person could do. Not when I knew what had happened to her in the end.

But even though I'd thought about her, I wasn't sure she mattered anymore.

He glanced up at me again. "I don't want you to know that."

"Ever?" When he didn't respond, I coaxed him. "You can tell me. It's not going to change anything."

"Then it doesn't matter if you know or not."

We were going in circles. One step forward then one step back. I closed my eyes for a beat and gripped the bedspread behind my back so that I wouldn't be tempted to touch him.

Then I opened my eyes and asked with finality, "What do you want this to be with me, Reeve? Decide."

His gaze lingered. He let the flame between us flicker and flare before his attention skidded down, down past my throat, down to where my chest rose and fell with each anxious breath. Again, he reached his hand out to touch me, this time cupping my breast.

Reflexively, I leaned into his palm.

His thumb circled my nipple until it stood erect. Then he trailed his hand down my ribcage. He stepped closer, raising his face toward mine as his hand grazed over my hip. "What do *you* want?"

There was no need to think before I answered. "Whatever you let me have of you."

"What if it's everything?"

"Then I'll take everything." Our voices were whispers, as if these kinds of words were easier to say quietly, in hushed tones so that we had to really listen to hear them. And I had heard him. Had heard him and was clinging to his implication. Clinging to the almost promise of *everything*.

He continued his hand down my satin slip, down to the hem and underneath where he lazily traced up my thigh toward my cunt. In a moment he'd reach my core and then all talking would be over.

But in this moment, I was still thinking of *everything*. "Is that what you want to offer?"

His focus was already gone. "Right now I want to make you come."

He fell to his knees and wrapped his hands around my panties. "I came back early because of you." He pulled the lacy material down my limbs. "I needed to be inside you. I wanted you beneath me and next to me and with me." He lifted one foot out of a leg hole, then the other. He pushed my nightie up to my waist and leered appreciatively at me exposed.

"And now I need to make you come." Placing a hand on my belly, he nudged me back against the bed where there was just enough space between the edge of the mattress and the suitcase for me to perch. He lifted one of my legs over his shoulder.

Then he lowered to my pussy, sucking my clit into his mouth.

I gasped, my hands flinging out to hold on to the bedframe with one and the mattress with the other. In all the weeks we'd been together, in all the ways he'd given me pleasure, he'd never put his head between my legs.

Because he was selfish, maybe. Because it wasn't his thing. Because it had never been a priority. I'd never known the reason, and it hadn't been a big deal.

But as he licked along my seam, as he dipped his tongue into my entrance, as he went lower and circled the rim of my asshole, I understood why he hadn't done it until now. Because before, he hadn't meant it. The way he washed me with his mouth, lavishing me, adoring me, taking his time, this kind of attention sent a message. *You're important to me,* it said. *I want to give you what I can, starting with this.*

I knew it was also a stall tactic. I knew that giving in would mean I accepted his lack of answer. I knew that Mike or Donny was watching this private, intimate act in the surveillance room.

And I didn't care. This moment was organic and needed and beautiful because of what it was, despite what it lacked.

I knew that I could still let this be our goodbye.

His tongue swept over me and inside me, his fingers stroked all my most sensitive spots, his lips sucked and nibbled. He was dominating me but in the subtlest way he ever had. There was nothing demeaning about what he was doing. Nothing to be embarrassed about submitting to. It was selfish because it was for him but it was selfless as well. It was sincere and affectionate and progress and I thought, *vanilla is good, too.*

He brought me to climax three times, each one taking me higher than the one before. And each time, he stole my breath and my balance and I'd think, *I can't anymore,* but he'd show me I was wrong and send me there again.

After the last, when I was torn apart and boneless, too spent to fight anymore for what I needed from him, he lowered my leg off his shoulder and reached up to brush the hair out of my face and said, "Stay, Emily."

A tear leaked down my cheek that might have been left over from the final time he'd made me come. He wiped it away. "I want you to stay," he said again. "We can figure out what this is together. Say yes."

The place those words sent me was more gratifying, more pleasurable than any of the orgasms he'd given me. "Yes," I said, with as much emotion as if I were accepting a proposal. "Yes."

He pulled me down to my knees in front of him and he kissed me. His tongue was gentle against mine. His lips were firm but yielding. He tasted like me, like my desire and my submission. Tasted the way that pleading must taste, soft and imploring, vulnerable and exposed. It wasn't a kiss that took; it was a kiss that *asked*. For the first time, he didn't demand from me.

So what I gave back was honest and unforced and open. When before he'd been a blustering wind that I'd chased and sometimes was lucky enough to catch—or be caught up in—now we were both still, coming together on our own accord. We originated in this. Everything now was new. A start. A beginning. The brush of his hand across my cheek, though he'd done it many times before, it was as if this time was the first. His whispers were unheard whispers. The gasps at the back of my throat were sounds I'd never made. The way my knees buckled, how he pulled me tighter against him, the sighs between us—all new.

This was our first surrender.

First embrace.

First kiss.

First touch.

CHAPTER

25

A sudden change in room temperature woke me the next morning. I came to enough to realize I was missing my covers, and, with my eyes still shut, I searched blindly for the blankets.

"I pulled them off of you," Reeve said.

I squinted up toward his voice and found him standing above me. "Why would you do that?"

"Because it's time to get up."

This wasn't the wakeup from Reeve I was used to. Usually he used his cock to rouse me. This time he was fully dressed, wearing what I called the ranch uniform—jeans and a long-sleeve flannel button-down shirt.

I hoped his attire meant he wasn't leaving again already. It had already been late when he'd come home the night before and we'd stayed up much later, moving from my room to his where we'd moved together under the sheets for long hours.

It had been wonderful and magical and all the adjectives that people use to describe "making love." We hadn't done any talking after he'd knelt before me, however, and there was still so much to be said. Hopefully today we'd have time to remedy that—if his business didn't pull him away.

Even if it did, I had his attention now.

I rubbed at my eyes with my fist. "I prefer your usual wakeup method."

He laughed. "I do too, Blue Eyes. But we don't have time for that. We have plans."

I stifled a yawn as I sat up against the headboard. "What are we doing?" Swear to God, if he'd forced me up just so I could make the six a.m. breakfast, I was going to be very unhappy about it.

"We're spending time together in a location that isn't a bed." He sat on the bench against the wall and pulled on a boot.

I curled my knees up to my chest and wrapped my arms around them for warmth. "A bed has never been required for your dick to find its way inside me."

"No, it hasn't," he said, grinning and pulling on his other boot. "But today I'm putting something else between your legs. Get up."

"Fine, fine." More than fine, actually. He was spending the day with me. Or, at least part of it. Like I'd said the night before, I'd take whatever he gave.

I pushed myself out of the bed and padded into his bathroom for a much needed shower.

After, I dried off and put on my robe, planning to head to my bedroom to get dressed. But when I opened the door, Reeve was waiting with a tray of eggs, toast, and fruit.

"You know breakfast in bed works best when I'm still in bed," I teased.

He swatted my ass hard enough to make me yelp. "I let you sleep in. I didn't have to make you anything."

"Sorry, sorry." I bowed my head in dramatic fashion.

"It was very kind of you, Mr. Sallis. I don't know what I was thinking."

"Keep it up, Blue Eyes." His tone suggested he'd very much like for me to keep it up. But he switched gears quickly. "I had riding clothes and boots sent up from the general store." He nodded to a shopping bag on the bed.

"Ah, that's what we're doing." I'd been horseback riding before but it had only been a few times and many years ago now. It had been something I'd always wanted to try again. The ranch was the perfect place.

"Yes. And I took the liberty of picking out some underwear from your room."

I peeked inside and found a pair of white lace panties and a matching bra lying on top of tissue-wrapped bundles, which I assumed were the riding clothes. "The virginal look. How very naughty of you."

He smirked. "You mean, how very naughty of *you*. I'm not the one who will be wearing them."

He crossed to me and kissed my forehead. Which was different and made my stomach swim with a rush of excitement.

"If I stay here with you," he said, reluctantly, "you'll never get dressed. And I have a few things I need to do anyway. Meet me downstairs when you're ready?"

"Okay," I said around a mouthful of toast.

"You know where my office is?"

I nodded, my gut tightening at the mention of the locked room.

"Don't take all day." He eyed me a moment, as if enjoying the sight of me, then he left.

The minute the door shut, I let out a heavy sigh. The morning so far had been perfect. Beyond perfect. The day ahead seemed to be promising more of the same. Reeve was going beyond my expectations to prove his commitment to the change in our relationship. It was a relief, for one, as I knew how easily promises made in the dark disintegrated in the daylight. It also produced a whole host of emotions I couldn't even identify, most of them pleasant. I was thrilled. I was excited. I was flustered. I was flattered.

But I was also overwhelmed.

Things were happening suddenly, and I still had baggage that I hadn't had time to figure out what to do with. Amber-shaped baggage. While part of me wanted to let it all go and follow this new path with Reeve, I couldn't give up on the promises I'd made to *her* in the dark. Whether that meant I still wanted to swipe his office keys to check out the recordings, I hadn't decided.

And it didn't have to be decided now. Today would be for Reeve, to find out what we could be to each other. I'd given enough days to Amber to let at least one be my own.

Two hours later, I was sitting on the back of a chestnut quarter horse named Milo winding through the most beautiful mountain countryside I'd ever seen. Reeve rode beside me on a black stallion named Playboy, which I'd remarked was fitting. My boyfriend—I'd started calling him that more in my mind, testing it out, getting used to it—was a skilled rider. Though he'd stayed with me for the most part, he'd also made sure that I saw him show off his form, galloping ahead at times then circling back to me a few minutes later.

We'd chatted for some of the ride, about nothing important, the scenery mainly. But we'd also been silent, letting the landscape speak for itself. Letting the things between us stretch and yawn without manipulation or force. We'd been out for an hour now, and, while we weren't technically anywhere closer to figuring us out, it felt like we'd settled a great deal. It was well worth the ache to my tailbone, though I was about ready for a break.

As if he could read my mind, Reeve said, "We're almost

to the river. We'll stop there and let the horses drink before heading back. I brought some sandwiches we can snack on there."

"You packed us a picnic? Whoa there, cowboy. You'd better be careful or someone's going to call you romantic."

He laughed. "Don't get ahead of yourself. It's not substantial enough to be called a picnic. But I am glad that my attempts to impress you haven't gone unnoticed."

As if he had to impress me. Yet, it was impressive all the same. And strange, since I'd never really been wooed before. It gave me a feeling of unbalance that had nothing to do with how high I was up from the ground. Sweet and sappy wasn't exactly in my realm of understanding, nor was it what I truly wanted. It was good in small doses—necessary, even, to repair the parts of me that ached and mourned. But I hoped it wasn't a replacement for the elements of our earlier relationship.

"Thank you for the clothes, by the way." The outfit he'd bought me had included stretchy form-fitting breeches, a white button-down, and a riding jacket. Along with the boots, I looked like a western wet dream, which was why I added, "I think they may be as much of a gift for you as they are for me."

His eyes seared over me. "You do look pretty fucking hot; I'm not going to lie."

That's all he had to say and I was fantasizing about him pulling me off my horse to ravage me amongst the scores of yellow wildflowers.

I squeezed my thighs against Milo and tried to distract myself. "Why did your father buy a cattle ranch? I mean, it's breathtaking, but odd considering that most of your properties are focused on luxury."

He was silent for a beat. Long enough for me to worry that the changes I'd perceived in him were only superficial. That he still wasn't willing to open up to me.

But then he said, "My mother." He glanced at me before going on. "She'd always wanted to live in the country. She was a city girl who wanted a . . . different life. A quieter life than the one she'd been born into. My father showed up and swept her off her feet, but he was already successful and the life he offered didn't feel much varied from her own. Still business and greed and all the things that come with being a person of power. She almost didn't marry him because of it.

"But she loved him. And he loved her. So he promised her the country. He bought this ranch for her as a wedding gift and called it Kaya. That was his nickname for her."

"He called your mother Kaya?" It explained where her alleged surname had originated.

"Yes. It means 'rock' in Greek. My mother broke her family ties when she left the country to marry my father. It was what she wanted, but it was a hard decision for her to follow through with. He said she was strong like a rock." He grinned over at me. "Though sometimes he said he called her that because she was stubborn and immovable like a boulder. Both fit who she was."

The tone he used to speak about his parents was even and unsentimental, but there was still something—in his body language, in the undercurrents of his words—something that portrayed the deep fondness he had for them. They'd been people I'd researched and studied, names on paper with no context. Reeve breathed life into them for me. Made them real. Made them important.

He trotted ahead of me to take the lead as the trail narrowed momentarily. When it widened again, he fell back into step with Milo and me. "Anyway, we traveled a lot when I was growing up, visiting all the resorts as they were built, but this place was always the place we came back to. This place was always home. Even though they aren't here anymore, I try to come back for at least part of each year."

I tried to fit this story into the one that already existed in my head. Elena Vilanakis, aka Elena Kaya, had been unhappy in her life. Because of the mob ties? Had that been what Daniel Sallis had rescued her from? Then had it been Reeve who had reclaimed them when his parents died and he had nowhere to go but to them?

But those questions were for Amber and today was for Reeve.

"Thank you for bringing me with you to Wyoming," I said. "It means a lot to me."

"It means a lot for me to have you here." Our gazes got caught in each other, and we held them. Maybe sweet was good in larger doses too.

A minute later we were at the creek. It snuck up seemingly out of nowhere. I'd heard it rippling in the distance with no sign of it until we were upon it. We dismounted and Reeve tied our horses to a tree. Then we perched on a large rock that jutted out of the water and ate our sandwiches.

"I love that sound," I said when I'd finished eating. "The river babbling as it winds along. It's so peaceful."

"You can hear it from the house when it's really quiet," Reeve said, stretching out beside me and propping himself up on his elbows. "It's peaceful and yet it's a sound that has the potential to carry."

I nodded. "I know what you're talking about. I woke in the early morning the first night we were here. Couldn't sleep. So I went out on the balcony and I could hear it."

He frowned. "Why didn't you wake me? I would have fucked you back to sleep."

I gawked at him. "I can't wake you up for sex."

"Why not?"

"Because every time I've initiated something with you, it hasn't gone well for me." He'd been very clear about our roles in this arrangement: He was the director. I was merely a player.

"Well, that's true." He sat up so we were in line with each other. "Except you're still here. Maybe you weren't initiating the right things."

I considered that, playing back our time together in my head, searching for any missed cues. There were probably many, but I couldn't identify them.

I twisted toward him. "Then tell me, what would happen if I jumped you sometime instead of waiting for the other way around?"

He shrugged. "Try it and find out."

He stood and held his hand out to me to help me up as well. He jumped down from the rock ahead of me then turned to lift me easily to the ground. The wind blew the loose strands of my hair into my face, and he reached to brush it away. Our eyes met in another mushy moment that had my chest tightening. The kind of moment that ended in a soft brush of lips, and all I could do was wish he'd push me against the tree and rip my clothes in his eagerness to get inside my pants.

I broke away before he even leaned in.

We started toward the horses, a light tension between us that I was sure had to do with the abrupt way I'd blown him off. Hesitantly he said, "I need to ask you a question."

"Yes?" I braced myself, preparing to answer what was going on in my head, the question I was sure he'd ask.

"When we first got together, you asked me if you needed a safe word and I told you no."

That was not at all the question I'd been expecting. It also wasn't quite accurate. He'd said if I needed a safe word that I shouldn't be there. "That's not exactly how you said it, but anyway."

"I might have been wrong."

I stopped walking. "You think I need a safe word?"

He'd taken a few steps past me before noticing I'd halted. He pivoted to face me, his hands thrust in his pockets. "I'm not sure. I've never used one, but I've never been with a woman who didn't make her limits absolutely clear."

My throat tightened. I'd let him do humiliating things to me and yet, somehow, admitting this was more embarrassing than anything else.

My eyes fell to study my boots. "It doesn't matter if I had one. I wouldn't use it."

"Even if I went too far?"

I wrapped my arms around myself. "I don't know what that is, Reeve."

He was silent but I knew it wouldn't last. He was going to ask me to explain—I could feel it. And it was arguably a conversation we should have had long ago, though it had only been recently that I'd come to accept it myself. Now that he'd brought it out to the open, I couldn't avoid it.

So I plunged in, walking past him as I spoke so I wouldn't have to look at him. "It's a problem of mine. I'm, I don't know, sick or something. I like it when men do things to me, things that some women would consider horrible. Abuse, even. I mean, I more than like it. I need it."

"You're a natural submissive," Reeve said, his voice close behind me. "That doesn't make you sick. Modern psychologists don't even call it an illness unless it interferes with your life."

I'd come to Milo now, and I reached out to stroke his neck, using him as a focus point. "That's just it. It does interfere with my life at times. Because I don't know when to say stop. I don't know when to say no. I've let myself be hurt, Reeve. Really hurt." Amber had always blamed the men I'd been with, but while they'd had culpability, so did I.

I turned back to him, my vision glistening with unshed tears. "What kind of a person doesn't know how to stand up for herself when she's being broken? What does it make me that I crave parts of it so much that I keep coming back to it? I understand parts of it. Like, if someone else is in control, then I won't have to admit that I'm part of it. That I like it. It helps me feel less ashamed. But the part where I let myself be shred to pieces—" My voice caught, and I couldn't finish the sentence. I wasn't sure where it went next anyway.

I shook my head, trying to free the lump in my throat. "I can't stay away from it though. When I try, I'm dead inside. So all I can do is hope that I'm lucky. Hope that whoever I'm with will care about protecting me more than I do."

While I'd talked, Reeve had stood patiently, watching me, listening to me. Now I waited for him to say something trite and comforting. Something that would attempt to dismiss my shame by belittling its source. I wouldn't blame him. Because how else was he supposed to react to someone so obviously crazy?

But he didn't say anything. Instead, he stepped in to me, brought his mouth to mine, and kissed me. It wasn't a tentative or soft kiss, just as it wasn't aggressive or forceful. It was a kiss with no answers, only acceptance.

We stayed there for long minutes while he let me pour out my anguish and self-hate in subtle strokes of my tongue and the varied pressure of my lips. He let me cry like this. Let me shed my skin. Let me be raw without taking advantage of my vulnerability like so many others had done.

We kissed and kissed and would have probably kept kissing if it hadn't been for Milo nudging at us with his head.

We broke apart, chuckling. "He's jealous," Reeve said. "He wants you all to himself." He pulled the horse's head to burrow in his neck, stroking his face. "Sorry, Milo. She's mine, and I'm not giving her up. You're not the only one she likes to ride."

My laugh sounded embarrassingly like a giggle.

"Can you believe her? Acting as if that kind of talk flusters her. I know for a fact that it doesn't."

I wasn't ready to lose our honest moment. "That wasn't the part of what you said that flustered me."

Reeve abandoned the horse and pulled me to press his forehead to mine. He stroked my cheek with the back of his hand. I'd never felt so connected to him. So unified. I was sure our hearts were beating in tandem. So connected that I swore I could hear the unspoken words in his head: *I'm trying. I'm going to keep trying with you.*

Silently I promised him the same even though I wasn't sure yet if it was a promise I could keep.

By the time we'd returned to the stable, I was more than recovered from my emotional episode, but I was anxious and antsy. We'd spent too many hours playing nice and romantic, and no time at all playing lusty and sex-driven. I was becoming desperate for the release that only he could give me, more and more afraid that it had been lost in our transition from *arrangement* to *deeper.*

We'd stalled Milo first and now Reeve was putting Playboy away. I waited for him to lock the door so we could start walking toward the stable entrance. But as soon as the lock had clicked, he grabbed me unexpectedly, drawing me firmly to him so I could feel the hard form of his cock at my pelvis.

"I hope you aren't too saddle sore, because I can't have you in those tight pants a second longer. I need you naked. I need your cunt out. I need to be inside you."

"Then let me go so we can get back to the house."

He surrendered me, but it was to undo his buckle. "I can't wait that long. I'm so hard I'm in pain."

My heart tripped a beat. "Here?" *God, yes.*

"Here." Abruptly, he pushed me up against the next stall

and pinned my hands over my head. His breathing was heavy, like mine, the cold air causing twin puffs of condensation to drift and mingle between us. Despite the temperature, I radiated with warmth.

This was what I needed. This was what was missing. The anticipation was hammering inside my chest, making my panties damp, causing me to shiver and sweat all at once.

His mouth was only an inch away from mine, his eyes glued to my lips and the effort of restraint etched clearly on his features. "How do you want me?"

His words swirled around us. It was another form of the question he'd asked over and over. The question he kept coming back to. *What do you want? How do you want it?*

I never felt like I had a good answer. For the first time, I realized why. Because what I wanted was to not be asked the question.

And, if I knew Reeve like I thought I was beginning to, I didn't believe that he really wanted to be asking, either. He'd rather just decide.

"No," I told him. "*You* tell me what I want. *That's* what I want."

His eyes darkened, confirming my suspicion. He liked this answer. It was the right answer. For both of us.

He changed his grip so that only one of his hands held mine in place. With the other, he undid one of the buttons on my jacket. "You've wanted to fuck me all day." His voice was low, raw. "You kept thinking about the ways I could take you. By the river." Another button undone. "In the fields." Another button. "On the horse." The last button now.

Yes. "Why didn't you?" It came out barely more than a whisper.

He released me and I turned automatically to let him take off the outer garment, which he flung to the ground. "Because out there we were being sweet. And you wanted to be dirty."

Yes, so much yes.

He pulled the hem of my shirt from my pants. "So now it's going to be especially dirty because you made me wait for it."

With one quick movement, he ripped my shirt completely open, sending buttons flying. Goose bumps scampered down every inch of my exposed skin, caused as much from his words and the primal act as from the sudden cold air. I shuddered. My nipples were taut beads poking through the lace of my bra.

He pulled the ruined material of my shirt from my shoulders, then reached behind to unhook my bra. As the straps fell down my arms, his eyes grazed over my breasts, heating me with his gaze.

No matter how many times he'd seen me undressed, he never failed to look at me like that—like a starving man. Like he wanted to eat me up. Like he couldn't get enough.

I understood how he felt. I couldn't imagine ever getting enough of that look.

The sound of whistling drew my attention down the aisle toward the entrance. Reeve pinched his fingers on my chin and jerked my face back to him. "Eyes on me," he said sharply. "You don't care about who's around. You want me to worry about that. You want me to decide who sees you. Isn't that right?"

I nodded.

He yanked my chin up higher. "Say it."

"I want you to decide who sees me." Dammit, if I wasn't wet before, I was now.

"Good girl." He released my face. Grabbing my arm, he dragged me forcibly to the feed storage a couple of feet away where hay was bundled in varying heights. "Turn around," he ordered. I did and he shoved me down on a double-high stack of bales.

He curled his fingers around the waistband of my pants.

"You want your cunt on display for me." He pulled them down as far as they'd go with my boots on. "I can't see you like that, Blue Eyes. You need to spread."

Shuffling my feet outward, I started spreading my legs, but I was too slow or didn't move far enough because Reeve put a hand on my lower back and kicked one of my boots then the other until I was spread wide.

He trailed his fingers at the crotch of my underwear. "You're soaked, Emily. Good thing these are coming off." He gripped my panties with one hand on each side of the seam on my right hip. In the same way he'd torn my shirt, he tugged and ripped the flimsy lace material apart. He repeated the action on the other side then removed the remnants.

"Beautiful, Em." His tone was thick with appreciation. "You wanted me to see your cunt, and I can see it perfectly now."

I glanced over my shoulder and found him standing several feet away, admiring the view. My pussy pulsed, enjoying the spotlight.

"Eyes front," he snapped when he saw me looking. I heard his steps as he crossed to me. "You don't want to see what I'm going to do to you. You want it to be a surprise."

Yes. I do. "Do I want it rough?"

"So rough." His hand slapped against an ass cheek, and I squeaked. "And fast." He slapped the other. Then he rubbed the sting away in a circular pattern, spreading the burn throughout my skin.

"Do I want you to hurt me?" My voice was gritted.

"Yes." He smacked me again, each cheek in quick succession before he massaged. "And you want to think that I might hurt you a lot."

He knew me. Knew me so well. Knew what I wanted. Knew how to give it to me.

Maybe he even knew when to stop.

He came around to where my head was now. "Give me your hands."

I lifted my wrists to him and he bound them with my bra, knotting it as tight as he could manage with the make-shift rope.

He leaned down to meet me at eye level. "Don't talk. Don't move. Do you understand?"

I nodded.

"Parker," he called out. "I need one of the crops."

"Which one?"

"The Weaver. Twenty-four inch. And a lead. A short one will do."

My skin tingled from my scalp to my toes. I wanted to look behind me, see where Parker was, wanted to sit up in a less disgraceful position. It was one thing to be naked in front of strangers. Another to be naked in front of people I'd met that I wasn't sleeping with. And quite another, still, to be scandalized in their presence.

But as the anxiety about it itched through my chest, arousal sang through my veins in equal proportion.

Reeve ignored me while he waited for Parker. Didn't talk to me, didn't touch me, and as the seconds ticked by feeling like hours, my breathing grew heavier, my heart pounded in my chest, my cunt throbbed.

Finally, *finally,* footsteps sounded in the distance. They slowed as they got closer. "Well, this is new," Parker said from behind me, his tone edged with lewdness. "Great addition to the stable."

"Prettiest filly I've ever owned." Reeve's palm—at least, I guessed it was his—stroked down my flank. "Gorgeous, round hindquarters."

Parker whistled. "Yeah, they are."

Feet shuffled closer then halted when Reeve said, "Touch her, I'll break your neck."

"Gotcha." A pause. "Here's your stuff. Have fun."

I could hear the *clank, clank* of Parker's retreat, the spurs of his boots jostling with each step. His retreat was still echoing through the barn when something tapped me on my cunt. Not hard, just a whisper of a tap. "We'll have lots of fun, won't we, Blue Eyes?"

He dragged the object through my folds then, swirling around my clit before going lower, so the only answer I had was, "Mmmm."

"You're even wetter than you were. I knew you were looking forward to this. Want to see?"

"Yes."

Reeve came around to my face and stuck the end of a crop in front of me. The tongue glistened with fluid. "That's from you." He brought the tip to his mouth and sucked. "You taste good, Em." It was so base. So depraved.

It made me so hot, I was almost sure I could come right there.

"You want to taste what I taste. You're so dirty like that, how you love the taste of yourself almost as much as I do. Guess what, Em. I'm going to give you what you want."

The crop was thrust back toward me, but instead of rising to my lips like I'd expected, it tapped underneath my chin. "Open," Reeve commanded.

I let my jaw fall open and he stuffed familiar white lace material inside—the remnants of my panties. He'd made sure the lining of the crotch was what hit my tongue, and as I tasted myself I was at once repulsed and turned on. Or, rather, turned on more. I couldn't begin to understand the opposing reactions. They pulled at each other, feeding into each other, fueling my desire to limits above and beyond the lust I'd felt before.

He wasn't done though. "Bite around this." He stuck a green braided rope, less than an inch thick, in my mouth.

I bit around the rope, securing the panties behind it. "Don't drop it. Understand?"

I couldn't talk anymore now that I'd been gagged, so I simply nodded.

"Good girl," he said as he walked back to my rear, dragging the crop along my ribcage.

There was no warning before the first thwack hit my skin. No warm-up. Just *thwack*, a sharp, concentrated sting across my cheek, causing me to grunt and my leg to lift reflexively.

He didn't massage the bite away, didn't touch me before the next hit. The other cheek now, but higher up than the last one. He continued like this, one swat after another in no identifiable pattern so that I had no idea where the next one would land. On and on until my grunts turned to cries, until my ass was on fire, until my eyes were watering and my jaw ached from clenching.

By the time he was done, my pussy was trembling with need and I imagined my backside was streaked with red. He pressed his body against the burning flesh of my ass and I felt the tip of his cock at my wet entrance.

He entered me then. Plunged into me with a sharp, hard thrust that reached so far inside of me, so deep that I gasped, nearly dropping the rope from my mouth. The climax that had been building little by little while he'd spanked and whipped and played shot through me, exploding like carbonated soda out of a shaken-up can.

While I was still twitching and groaning, I felt the tug of the rope in my mouth from both ends, and I realized Reeve was gripping them, pulling my neck back as though they were reins, and I was his pretty pony to ride.

And he did ride me. He pulsed into me with his cock, one hand pulling at the lead, keeping my head erect, the other digging into my hip. All the while he talked to me.

Spoke sinful, licentious words that made me buck and flail underneath him. Said things like, "You want this because you're a slut." And, "You're dirty." And, "Such a filthy girl who wants to be fucked like she's a nasty whore."

My second climax came on even faster. The third was on its heels, shuddering through me with aching leisure. Squeezing the breath from my lungs, causing my legs to give out even with the support of the hay bales underneath me.

Reeve dropped the rope, pulled out of me, and flipped me over to my back. He shoved inside me, pushing through the clenching of my pussy to continue his assault. The bra had loosened during the shift and my hands were free now. He leaned over me, pinning me down as he fucked me with more fury and fervor than he ever had.

His eyes bore into mine from above. "I'm the perverted sick asshole who likes to say this shit to you," he said, his voice raw and rough. "Who likes to fuck you like this. What does that mean about me?" His tone tightened and his inflection drifted upward as his orgasm came rumbling through him with brutal force. He ground his pelvis against mine, the fabric of his jeans prickling at the sensitive skin of my behind. He groaned and growled, his fingers clawing into my wrists, his eyes clamped shut.

As soon as he'd released enough to let go of my hands, I sat up, spit the panties out of my mouth, and pulled his face toward me. "Maybe that just means you're made for me."

I kissed him, hard, my mouth claiming his, my lips shaping his with vicious, unyielding devotion. Soon, he was kissing me in return. His hands came up to wrap around my face. When our mouths broke, we clutched onto each other, our heads huddled together as we gasped for breath.

Eventually, he began mumbling. Incoherent words that turned into my name. "Emily, Emily, Emily." He stroked his palms up and down my back. "You're freezing cold. We need to get you warm."

I hadn't noticed until he'd mentioned it. It was only fifty degrees out and about the same temperature in the barn. "Well, I don't think my shirt's of use anymore."

"I suppose not. Here." He took off his jacket and wrapped it around my shoulders. "Get dressed as best as you can. I'll put this stuff away and then we'll go give you a hot bath. Then, later, if you're up to it, maybe we'll get a bonfire going."

"I'm in."

He took a step away, but came immediately back. "One more," he said as he slanted his mouth over mine.

One more and one more and one more, I thought. *Always another one more.* I'd take them all. I'd take even more.

Reeve headed down the aisle. I pulled up my pants and zipped his jacket over my breasts. I found my bra and shirt and wrapped them in my jacket. Cradling the bundle under one arm, I stuck my ice-cold hands in my pockets. Reeve's pockets. My right hand closed around something metal. Keys. I pulled them out to study them, my heart pounding.

There were nine keys in total on the ring, a mix of gold and silver. I had no idea what they all opened, but I was sure one of them went to his office.

Before I could think too hard, before I could doubt or second-guess or talk myself out of it, I tucked the keys inside the bundle of my clothes. *No guilt,* I said silently. *It's done.* I could decide what I did with them later.

"Ready?" he asked from down the aisle.

"More than." I tightened my grip on the bundle and hurried up to meet him, already rationalizing my actions in my head. He'd left me no choice really. He still hadn't told me about Amber. If I had to find out my own way, I felt justified.

Never mind that I hadn't told him about Amber either. Things were changing between us, but we both still had secrets.

CHAPTER
26

Back at the house, Reeve set me up in a hot bath with Epsom salt to soothe the lashes from the crop and the sore muscles from the day's ride—both of them. Later, after dinner, we went out back to the fire pit with a group of men from the ranch. It was Friday and warm for April, according to Charlie, the kind of night for "boozing and blazing," as he put it.

Brent and Parker joined as well and though the latter grinned knowingly every time he happened to glance my way, it wasn't as uncomfortable of a gathering as I might have imagined. This was the closest thing Reeve had to family, I realized now, and explained his relationship with Kaya's staff. He relaxed with them, joking and laughing unlike he did with anyone else I'd seen him with. Not that I'd seen him with many people. Through the stories shared among them, I learned Reeve had been quite wild in his youth and long past. He'd dabbled in recreational drugs and gambling and women.

"Lots and lots and lots of women," Brent said and Reeve

kicked his boot. "Hey, I'm speaking with admiration. You were a God."

"Shut the fuck up." Reeve took a swig of his beer. "I still am a God."

When the laughter from that settled down, I asked, "What made you clean up your act?"

The guys looked to my boyfriend who, once again, looked as though he might let the question go ignored. But I was learning he liked to take his time with personal answers and, sure enough, eventually he said, "Missy." He worked his jaw. "Her death was a big slap in the face that my life was out of control. So, I stopped with the drugs, cut out some key people, quit throwing over-the-top parties, and—"

"And you've been a control freak ever since," I finished for him.

Again everyone laughed. "You know our boy well," Charlie said and I thought, *I'm beginning to.*

Around ten, the group dispersed—some going into town to drink at the bars, others, who had to work on Saturday, going home to sleep off the alcohol. "There's no Monday through Friday when you're working with livestock," Charlie said in parting. "And five a.m. comes sooner than you think."

Then it was just Reeve and me. I shifted my weight on the rock I was sitting on, partly to angle myself toward him, partly because my sore behind had kept me shifting all night.

He noticed and patted his thigh. "Come here."

Eagerly, I accepted the invitation into his lap. It wasn't really that much more comfortable than the rock, but sitting with my back pressed to him, his arms wrapped around me, made everything feel better.

"So . . . a party boy, huh?" I asked, though I'd really known that already. The media had portrayed him as such and I'd seen evidence from his birthday party pictures at his Palm Springs resort and from Chris's description of Sallis gatherings.

Reeve nodded, but didn't elaborate. When he did speak again, he had to repeat his question, I was so certain I'd heard him wrong the first time. "Have you ever been in love?"

I craned to look up at him to see if he was serious. He was. I settled my head back into him and said, "That's pretty unexpected coming from you."

"Why? Because a 'party boy' can't ever be interested in mushy things like love? Maybe I just want to find out if I have a reason to be jealous. So I can kill him."

I rolled my eyes but my chest warmed, as if the fire was also heating me from the inside.

He nuzzled into my neck. "I'm serious. About some of it, anyway. Tell me. I want to know."

"No. I haven't." There was a time I'd thought it was another of my flaws. Thought that I was incapable of falling in love with a person or of having another person love me.

But there was someone I had loved. Someone who loved me. Someone who proved contrary to the illustration I'd drawn of myself. "I did love someone once though," I said, wanting to answer his question honestly. "A girlfriend."

Reeve moved my hips so that he could face me. "Emily. Are you saying you go both ways? Because I think I just got hard."

I chuckled. "No. I don't. Definitely all man for me. I mean, I've had threesomes. With her."

He adjusted himself underneath me. "Yep. Definitely got hard."

I could feel his bulge—he wasn't hard. Semi maybe. I ignored it, more interested in explaining my relationship with Amber at the moment. "It wasn't like that. It wasn't sexual even when there was sex involved. We were just really good friends. We went through a lot together and she always understood me like no one else ever has."

Or, like no one else ever *had*. Because Reeve seemed really good at getting me.

"Plus you had threesomes. We should call her up." He tipped his beer to his lips.

From his wink, I knew he was kidding, but I said anyway, "No, we shouldn't. First of all, I can't call her. We parted ways and then I lost track of her."

I took the bottle from him and finished the end of it in a long swallow before adding, "Besides, I don't think I could share you with her. With anyone."

Reeve put the empty bottle on the ground and cupped my cheek. "Then I'd never expect you to."

"Thank you."

He kissed me, or I kissed him, lips molding by the firelight. Heat spreading from the inside and the outside.

He broke away first. With his mouth still inches from mine, he asked, "How is it that you've never fallen in love besides with her? You can't say there hasn't been opportunity."

I turned away, leaning my head back on his shoulder. "There have been lovers, yes. But I never found anyone I trusted."

"Why did you split up with her, then? With your girlfriend. If you were so close."

It was weird to talk about Amber with him yet wasn't all at once. But the answer to his question was hard to talk about with anyone. Was hard for me to even think about.

So I just shrugged. "People move apart sometimes, I guess." I sat forward and looked back at him. "What about you? Ever been in love?"

He surprised me when he didn't hesitate. "Twice. The last one—you remind me of her sometimes."

Amber. He had loved Amber.

A ball formed in the back of my throat, and I felt truly conflicted. I was jealous, of course. But also, it was just another thing that connected him and me. Another thing that brought us together.

And I reminded him of her. "How?"

"I'm not sure. It's hard to put a finger on because you're really quite different. Like, she didn't care for, well, for a lot of the things that happened in the bedroom. And elsewhere. She didn't always like my approach. She was kinky, but not . . . submissive. Eventually that came between us."

"How?" I asked again.

"It doesn't matter."

I needed these answers. For me. For us. "Is she the person you didn't let leave?"

"Are you saying that trust is a factor for love?"

I glared, letting him know that I hadn't missed that he'd dodged me entirely.

But then I answered him, because this topic was important to me, too. "It's *the* factor. What else is it? Fondness? What about when he gets mad and beats you senseless? Or fucks your friend? Trust. All that matters."

I pulled away from him, standing to stretch my legs or to try to relieve the sudden constriction in my chest or to escape the one thing it felt like I was endlessly trying to escape.

But it followed me, as it always did, wanting to come out, wanting to be exposed.

For once, I gave into it. "And that's why she and I split ways. Because I lost her trust."

"How did you lose her trust?"

"It's complicated." I already regretted saying what I had, yet I also feared I'd opened up a floodgate and was now being drenched in words that needed to be said, words that were going to leak out one way or another.

"Try me." Reeve was like the riverbed, coaxing the deluge to flow in a natural direction. "You obviously want to talk about it."

So, because I was drowning and tipsy, because I *did* want to talk about her, because I'd wanted to tell someone this story for a long time, because I'd been wanting to tell Reeve everything that I'd been hiding, I took a deep breath and said, "Okay."

I sat down on the rock next to Reeve, uncertain where to begin. "Like I said, she and I had shared men before, but we hadn't for some time at this point." We'd been back from Mexico for almost two years and had resumed our long-term live-in relationships with men, just separately now. "She had a boyfriend. Bridge was his name."

Reeve sneered. "Bridge?"

"Yeah." For half a second I worried Amber had told him this story—it was a name he'd certainly not forget.

Except the Amber I knew never looked back. Never talked of the past. And Reeve was likely just making fun of the awful name. "Terrible, wasn't it? Anyway, he was an okay enough guy. Much older than her. Fifty or so. Wealthy. She was really into him, but I don't know. Let's just say, she'd done better. But she said she loved him. Really loved him. And he was good to her, so I was happy for her."

Bridge had been a drinker, but Amber was a complete coke addict by then. Together they made sense somehow.

"I, on the other hand, had just left asshole number too-high-to-count, because when I'd told him I was pregnant, he thought he could give me an abortion by kicking the shit out of me." Richard had been his name. He was married, running for a seat on the senate, which he'd lost. Karma sometimes works out.

"You were pregnant?"

I nodded. Admitting an unplanned pregnancy always

seemed to open the door to judgment, more than admitting a drug addiction or an interest in sexual perversity. Not that I'd told anyone about my baby.

Perhaps it was my own judgment that I'd been avoiding.

As if to back that theory up, Reeve's expression was absent of condemnation and full of something else—compassion, maybe? "Did he—?"

"He didn't succeed," I interjected, "but he left me in bad shape. And, as she always did when I got in trouble with a guy, Amber came to my rescue."

Now Reeve's brow furrowed and I realized too late what I'd said. "Amber?"

Fuck.

I'd been so careful the whole time I'd been with him to never mention her name, and now I'd let it slip in the worst story ever.

Fuck, fuck, fuck!

My heart pounded so hard it felt like it was coming from my stomach as much as my chest. My hands felt sweaty, and my throat dry and chalky. I coughed, pretending I'd gotten something caught in my throat while I talked myself through recovery.

There could be lots of people with the same name, right? My Amber didn't have to be his Amber. There wasn't any way to recognize her from this story was there? That I could never know since I had no idea what she'd told Reeve and what she hadn't. All I could do was hope.

When I felt confident enough about it, I said, "Yeah, that was her name. Amber." Innocently, I smiled up at him. "Why?"

He shook his head, incredulous, perhaps. "It's just odd. Amber is the name of the woman who reminded me of you."

"Ah. Strange coincidence. I hadn't realized it was that common of a name." I picked up a stick from the ground and poked at the fire, hoping the act would distract or calm my panic attack.

"Funny that we both have an Amber that had an impact on our lives." Reeve's eyes narrowed as he considered me. "Anyway. I didn't mean to interrupt. Go on."

I cleared my throat and dove in as if the name situation was no big deal. "I didn't have any money. Didn't have anywhere to go. I'd been instructed to take it easy until my body fully healed." Specifically—no sex. "Which meant I couldn't depend on, um, my usual methods of survival. Besides, I'd decided with a baby I didn't want to do that anymore. I had to find a better life."

"You were going to keep it?" Again, there wasn't judgment in his tone. There may have even been awe.

"Yeah. Dumb, I know."

"Not dumb. It was yours."

My throat tightened. Even Amber hadn't understood my reasons for not terminating the pregnancy. But Reeve had hit it square between the eyes—I'd never had anything that had been mine. Earned and created by myself rather than given to me by someone else. That tiny multiplication of cells, though its makeup was half dependent on a man, was still half dependent on me. On my existence.

It was the first time I'd felt there was a reason to my life. The only time—until I'd gotten the call from Amber.

"So she invited me to stay with her and Bridge until I got on my feet." I tossed the stick to the ground and waved at the smoke, pretending that was why I was choked up and teary.

But Reeve wasn't stupid. He knew. He didn't say anything, though. Just waited for me to go on.

I still coughed to keep up the act. Cleared my throat again. Plunged ahead. "It was great for the first couple of weeks. Bridge seemed generous. He gave me whatever I needed. I had my own room in his mansion. I got to be with her. And I was growing a child. It was maybe the best time in my life.

"But it was all a mirage. The more time I spent with them the more I realized it. Underneath Bridge's nice-guy exterior, there were dark undertones that she never noticed because she was out of her mind addicted to cocaine."

"Dark undertones?"

"Well, one time when they were both high, I watched him fingerbang a stray cat while she looked on and giggled. When he moved to reach for the fire poker, I left the room."

Bile gathered in the back of my throat. God, if I couldn't get through this part of it, how the hell was I going to get through the rest?

It didn't matter how. The words were surging now and wouldn't be stopped. "I tried to talk to my friend—to Amber—about it. But Bridge had never done anything to hurt her, and that's all she really cared about. And I get it. I do. He wasn't married and he treated her like more than a mistress. Like a wife. Let her run his house and play Rich Girl of Beverly Hills, and that was really all she'd ever wanted in her life. To feel safe and get to be in charge of things."

Reeve lowered his eyes, as though he felt guilty, and I wanted to assure him that Amber and I had been very different in our wants. Wanted him to not worry that those were the things I was after, in case he was feeling bad about not offering it.

But it wasn't the time. This wasn't *that* story and I'd already hinted at those things earlier in the day, the kinds of things *I* wanted from a man. "Anyway, when I mentioned concern over Bridge she denied it. Said that I was the one who was into 'the really sadistic things' and so I saw things out of context."

"Ouch."

"She had her reasons for saying that." After everything

she'd seen from me, she was justified. "She also told me that if I was looking for an invitation into their bedroom that it wasn't happening because she and Bridge were completely monogamous."

"Double ouch."

"No. It was fine. And something that warranted being said after our past live-in relationships." I caught Reeve's skeptical expression. "What's that look for?"

"Nothing. Go on." Except, he went on instead of letting me. "I just wonder if you were selling yourself short."

Maybe this would be a little of *that* story after all. "I didn't have a pretty past before this Reeve. I told you that earlier. I'd earned every assumption she made about me."

"People change."

"I didn't."

"But you said you were trying. She should have at least given you credit for that." He was oddly defensive, as if he was taking Amber's accusations personally.

"I *was* trying. She knew better than I that it wouldn't get me anywhere because it was in my nature. I've accepted that now, but I hadn't then. No matter what you do, you can't deny who you are, Reeve. I can't deny who I am."

His expression hardened, and I had the distinct feeling he didn't like hearing that. "Go on," he said.

Now I was the one who felt defensive. Did he expect me to try to change those things again? I wouldn't. I couldn't, and I'd made that clear. And he hadn't seemed like it had bothered him earlier. "Is that a problem?" I asked cautiously. "That I can't change?"

He softened just slightly. "No. No. Of course not. Go on."

His reaction still had me befuddled, but I pushed it off and ventured back to my tale. "So, what's next? . . ." The worst parts, that's what. The blood and pain and bruises that went so deep they could be felt for months. Longer. I felt a rush of panic just thinking about it, let alone saying it.

So, maybe I wouldn't say it. "Jesus, this story is really a damper. I shouldn't be telling—"

"Finish it, Emily." It was his commanding tone. The one I couldn't argue with.

"Okay." I ran my tongue over my bottom lip, my mouth dry. Best to just blurt the rest out. Cold. Clinically. I focused on the fire. "One night, after everyone had gone to bed, I had a knock on my door. I thought it was her, but it was Bridge."

If I looked in the darkness, anywhere other than at the flame flickering in front of me, I could see him again, his face etched with cruelty, alcohol fuming on his breath, his eyes gleaming with wicked intent, the weapon in his hand.

"I didn't invite him in, but he came in anyway. I told him I wasn't interested. I told him no. But he didn't listen. Said that he'd heard all the stories about what a bad girl I was and how I liked it naughty. And after all his generosity, I owed him."

"He raped you." It wasn't a question and I knew Reeve had said it so that I wouldn't have to. I nodded, barely perceptibly. An inch of forward motion with my head. It was such a hard word to come to terms with because of all I'd allowed men to do to me in the past. Hard to defend myself, as women always had to do when they used the R word. And hadn't Bridge been right about me? I was a bad girl. I did like it naughty. It wasn't that I thought I'd deserved what he did. I just didn't know that I didn't either.

I wrapped my arms around myself wondering if Reeve felt the same. Wondering if he thought that Bridge had every right. I wouldn't blame him if he did.

Forcing myself not to care, I went on. "I tried to fight him." The one time in my life I'd fought. It did no good. "But he was a big guy. And he had a pair of scissors."

Reeve cursed under his breath.

I shut my eyes, closed my lids tight, tight. Blocking out the images, the memories. Putting up the wall.

When it was back in place, I opened my eyes, cleared my throat once again, and jumped to the conclusion. "After it was over—"

"No." Reeve was so forceful, so commanding, he left no room for me to do anything but halt. I lifted my eyes to his. "Don't skip to the end," he said. "Tell me what he did. Tell me the details."

My stomach lurched, my worry from earlier confirmed. "I'm not telling you this so you can get off on the fucked-up—"

He lurched forward to the edge of his seat. "You think I'm getting off on this? I want to have him killed, Emily. I want to know his name so I can track him down and have him destroyed. But first I want to know everything he made you suffer so that I can make sure he suffers equally."

His rage stirred and stunned me. It moved me that he would say he'd kill for me, except that he might actually mean it and then I was still moved, but then I felt guilty about it.

And regardless of what he meant, I wasn't worth that kind of trouble. "Reeve—"

"Tell me." It was an order. It was law.

Again, I concentrated on the fire. Pretended the details were about someone else. "He, um, forced me on my stomach. He cut the curtain cords with the scissors and used them to tie my hands and feet to the bedframe. Then he put his fingers in me. Uh, like, all his fingers at once. It wasn't gentle. Then he put his cock inside and put the scissors at my throat and told me if I made a sound that he'd . . ."

I covered my eyes with my hand. No matter how much Reeve pressed, I couldn't say the things that Bridge had threatened to do to me. They ended in death and that was the best part of it.

"So I was quiet," I said finally, summarizing. "And I was really good at obeying." Once again, my sick perverted proclivities failed to protect me. I obeyed my rapist. I hadn't struggled. Maybe deep inside I really had wanted it.

I lifted my eyes to Reeve who was now pacing in front of the fire. He was probably already thinking it. I might as well say it for him. "I should have fought more."

He stopped abruptly and spun toward me. "Do not do that, Emily. Do not blame yourself."

"Yeah, right." Just because he said it in that forceful way of his didn't mean I could do it.

Maybe I wasn't as good at obeying as I thought I was.

"I mean it, Emily."

I glared at him.

But I wasn't in the mood to argue about it so I continued instead. "He got bored with that after a while and he moved to . . ." I had to stop to take a breath and it shuddered on the intake. "To my ass." In my head, I was still in cold, clinical mode, but my words were shaky, full of lumps and cracks that hadn't been there before. "He didn't use lube and I couldn't help it, I screamed. He said for that, I needed to be punished. He used the scissors. In me."

"In your ass?" His tone said he knew the answer already.

I shook my head no.

Reeve let out a string of obscenities that ended in his foot meeting one of the empty beer bottles and sending it flying.

The reaction was foreign to me. It hadn't been one that I'd experienced after Bridge hurt me. I'd been angry, but never full of rage. And honestly, the only person I'd been angry with was myself.

Watching Reeve's outburst, seeing him feel the fury that

had eluded me, was fascinating. It seemed so freeing to have an emotion that could be so easily concentrated into outward action. My pain had always turned inward. My anger only destroyed me.

Reeve, though, had the power to hurt others. I'd known that. In this moment, I saw it.

In some twisted, fucked-up way, it was inspiring.

He began pacing again. He gestured with his hand for me to keep going as he said, "What next? Tell me what happened next."

I pinched at the bridge of my nose. It should have been downhill from here, but the worst parts were yet to come. Hoping they'd hurt less, I hurried through them, letting each syllable tumble out nearly on top of each other. "When he was done, I was bleeding. Bruised. Every time I moved, my uterus spasmed with intense cramps. Bridge was passed out, and I knew I needed to get to a doctor, but I was still tied up. That's when she walked in."

God. The look on her face. It had mirrored Reeve's in many ways, but it wasn't Bridge she'd been angry with.

"You fucking bitch," she said. *"You knew I loved him, you fucking bitch."*

It should have felt like a betrayal, because she'd automatically assumed the worst of me and the best of him, but the real bitch of it was I got her point. I got her point and I could even stand up for it if need be.

"She blamed me," I told Reeve now.

Once again he halted his movement. "She blamed *you*? How the fuck could she—could anyone—have blamed you for that?"

"She thought I'd wanted it, but"—I put a hand up to silence whatever it was he was about to say—"before you get mad at her, remember she'd seen me put myself in those kinds of situations on more than one occasion. She'd never pointed a finger before. And she'd always helped me out of them. Then this was how I'd paid her back? In her eyes, I'd stolen her man when she'd been nothing but compassionate to me."

Reeve shook his head incredulously, scoffing to himself.

I continued to defend her. "She got me to the hospital. Even when she thought I'd asked for it, she still helped me."

"She's a goddamn saint," he said, drenched in sarcasm.

"Well, not a saint. But she cared about me. Despite everything." I glanced at Reeve. He looked appalled but he stayed tight-lipped, his hands working at his sides, fists clenching and unclenching.

Whatever. I knew what I knew about Amber. He couldn't change my mind.

"That's pretty much the whole story," I said. "I miscarried by the end of the next day. I pressed charges, but Bridge didn't even get arrested. I had too much history or he had too much money. I don't know. When I was released from the hospital, I tried again to explain to Amber, but Bridge had a story that she thought was equally believable."

She didn't realize that the ten grand that Bridge had allowed her to give me had been retribution instead of charity. I didn't blame her for taking his side. And she said she didn't blame me either, but that maybe it was time for us to rethink our situation. I agreed. I wanted out, wanted to live a life where I depended on myself and my own money. A life where I felt safe, for once.

I'd begged her to come with me. I'd begged her to leave Bridge and start again, without drugs, without abuse. *"We always said we'd find our own life someday,"* I'd reminded her.

"We did," she'd said. *"And I'm sure someday's gotta happen for us all one day. But it doesn't mean mine's happening at the same time as yours."*

I'd clung to her when we said goodbye. She'd cried—

she was always a crier. It was shitty to have that be my last memory of her, sad and bleary-eyed. Whenever I thought of her, it was hard not to think of her as crying.

I wondered if she'd always thought of me as clinging. And was it really inaccurate if she did?

The summarized version was what I told Reeve. "We decided it was time to part ways. I moved to LA and tried as best as I could to get my life together. Got some modeling gigs. Then some acting. And here I am."

"And that was it? You never heard from her again?"

Until she called for help from here. But I twisted the answer so it wasn't a blatant lie. "I haven't seen her since. That was almost seven years ago."

"Why the hell do you sound like you did something wrong?"

I flew to my feet and faced him. "Because I did! I let her go with him. I let her stay with a sadistic fucked-up rapist. I didn't get her away from Bridge or away from the drugs. She rescued me every time I needed it, and I didn't rescue her." The whole time I'd been talking, this was the most worked up I'd been.

He stepped toward me. "You're carrying a whole lot of regret over something that was not your fault."

"It's my fault she made those assumptions." It sounded stupid when I said it out loud. I couldn't explain what I meant. I huffed. "You don't know, Reeve."

He threw his hands up. "Fine, I don't know."

We stood silently, each of us facing a different direction, both of us brooding. I chewed my lip trying to figure out what to say or do next. I felt horrible. And I did have regrets—I regretted telling Reeve anything because now he was upset and I was upset.

Though, I wasn't quite sure what it was he was upset with. Bridge, yes. I knew that. But then, it seemed he was also ticked off at me.

I kicked my toe in the dirt and mumbled, "Are you mad at me now?"

"What?" Before I knew it, he'd pulled me into him. "No, no, no way." He kissed my hair, wrapping me tighter in his arms. "I'm mad at what that piece of shit did to you, and I'm mad at . . . at Amber, for letting that happen to you. I'm mad that you're blaming yourself, but I'm not mad at you." He pushed me away, his hands on my shoulders, so he could look at my eyes. "You got that?"

I nodded, unable to speak, and he drew me back into his chest. He rocked me like that, both of us not saying anything, rocked me and hushed me even though I wasn't crying. It was soothing though. For both of us, I think.

So I hugged him closer to me and enjoyed the sweetness of being comforted.

Eventually he spoke. "God. I can't stop thinking about what he did. . . ."

"I didn't want to tell you."

"I wanted you to tell me. You lived it. The least I can do is know." He took a big breath that lifted me with it.

When he exhaled, he stepped away.

"It's cold," he said, rubbing his hands over the sleeves of my shirt. "I should get you inside. I'll run you a hot shower and you can . . ." He paused. "You can get the smell of campfire off of you."

"Only if you're planning on joining me." When he looked at me uncertainly, I began to panic. "Goddamn it, you're going to be fragile with me now, aren't you?"

He laughed, caressing my cheek with the back of his hand. "No. I'm really not. I'm still going to fuck you as hard as ever because I'm not a good man." Then he grew serious again, meeting my eyes. "If you want me to, I'll join you. I just wanted to make sure you had space if you needed it."

My chest felt tighter and looser all at once. Like something that had been stuck inside had been released but now there was something new filling up its place, expanding and swelling.

"I think you're a better man than you think you are." But what I meant was, *maybe you're a better man than I think you are.*

C H A P T E R

2 7

Reeve showered with me, but despite his reassurance from earlier, he didn't manhandle me the way he usually did. Instead, he soaped me up and washed me off, only touching me with the purpose to clean me, never to pleasure.

In stark contrast to his gentle treatment, tension sat taut in his shoulders and back. As he wrapped a large white towel around me, his jaw set and his lips turned down, I considered suggesting that a hard fuck might do us both some good, but I held my tongue. I'd had over six years to learn to live with the reality of what Bridge did to me. I could give Reeve at least one night.

Or, that's what I told myself I should do, anyway. But then when he placed a soft kiss on my nose instead of crushing his mouth to mine like I wished he would, I couldn't help myself from saying, "Is this one of those times that we're being sweet, then?"

He pursed his lips. "We're getting clean," he said, as if that was an explanation that would make sense. Then he headed into the bedroom.

"As long as we're eventually going to get dirty again."
But the door had shut behind him and I was alone in the
bathroom.

I wiped the condensation off the mirror above the sink
and studied my reflection. It was the same face I'd always
seen and yet I felt like I was only just beginning to get a
sense of who I was looking at. Someone damaged and broken. Someone who'd lost. A lot. Also, though, someone
who'd rebuilt. She was still a work in progress, but she
wasn't the catastrophe that she'd thought she was.

I'd come a long way since Bridge. Since Amber. I hadn't
realized that until now. I'd thought I'd just run away, that
I'd been hiding. Not ever looking back, it was impossible
to see the distance I'd traveled. Revisiting the past with
Reeve, I could see it. I could see that I'd survived.

*And now you're worried about a man who's treating
you too kindly.*

I had to laugh.

Then, leaving a towel wrapped around me, I took off
the one from my head, brushed my teeth, and joined Reeve
in the bedroom.

The fire was going, and it hadn't been before, which was
a nice touch on a cold spring night after a hot shower.
"Thanks for that." I nodded to the hearth.

"Hmm? Oh. You're welcome." He'd put on boxer briefs
and was sitting on the bed, his hands laced behind his
head, looking distracted and as delicious as one of those
underwear models—not the too skinny, boyish waifs, but
the ones built like warriors. The kind of man who looked
like he could fight for a woman and win. He'd protect her
from harm and then brutalize her himself but only *just
enough*. Complete trust.

Was that what love looked like? Was *Reeve* what love
looked like?

I had a confiscated set of keys that said I didn't trust him like that yet, so not likely. And obviously he couldn't trust me either.

The thought scratched at my insides, uncomfortable and itchy. Adding to it was the fact that Reeve wasn't naked. We'd never gone to bed with any strip of clothing between us. We'd never gone to sleep without sex.

I bit back my frown and settled in on the bench with a bottle of lotion. If I wasn't in bed yet, then the status quo hadn't changed. And I had dry legs. That ought to buy me some time.

Though Reeve watched me as I rubbed the lotion into my skin, I'd almost completely finished with my legs when he finally said something.

"Have you . . ." He hesitated until I looked up. Or maybe he'd hesitated until he'd found his words. "Have you had anyone take you in the ass since what happened with that fuckface?"

I smiled, because of his term for Bridge and also because he'd finally revealed what was going on in his head. This was what he was worried about, then. This I could deal with.

Pouring lotion in my hand for my arms, I answered truthfully. "I have not. Before, yes. Not after."

"Yet, you were going to let me . . . ?"

"I told you I'm not very good at saying no." I stroked the cream up and down my left arm, hoping if I acted like the topic wasn't that big of a deal then Reeve would adopt the same attitude.

Even if it was a partial lie. It was a big deal. Potentially.

He shifted on the bed, sitting forward. "You mean you'll never tell me no?"

"As far as sex goes? I doubt it."

"Now I'm mad about that too." He swung his legs off the bed, got up, and moved around the room aimlessly.

I'd known he was agitated, but had believed him when

he said it wasn't directed at me. "Then you are mad at me." I hated the emotion in my voice. "Because I didn't tell you? Or because I don't say no?"

He ran a hand through his hair that was now nearly dry. "Not mad at you. Mad at me." With hands on his hips, he faced me. "If you're not going to have a safe word, we need to set some limits between us."

"I wouldn't say *no anal*. I wouldn't say *no objects*. I'd never think I'd need to say *no scissors*." Frustrated, I popped the lid closed on the bottle of lotion and began working my right arm. It was a good conversation to have, actually. I just didn't know how to participate in it. "I told you I don't know what my limits are."

"You have to know some things," he insisted. "You don't want to be shared. That's a limit."

"We established that together."

"You mean if I hadn't said it first, you would have let me give you to whoever I wanted and you wouldn't say anything? Even if you didn't want that?" He must have sensed my answer without me giving it because he asked, "Why would you do that?"

I stood and snatched up the lotion bottle to take it to the bathroom. "I don't know why." But I did, sort of, and after I grabbed my robe from the hook, I came back into the room and tried to explain. "I'd do it because you wanted me to. That's more . . ." What was the word? "Satisfying, I guess. I like that better. Sometimes that's what makes something really good, even. Because I don't want to do it but I'm pleasing you."

He conceded a tight smile. "And that's what works so well between us. Because I like that too." Then the concession was gone. "But men have gone past that. Have hurt you. Was that worth pleasing them?" When I shook my head, he said, "So you do know some things that you absolutely don't want to explore again."

"Okay, my limits are *don't damage me. Don't destroy me*." I sounded exasperated because it was an exasperating subject. On the one hand, I should have boundaries, shouldn't I? It was embarrassing to harp on the fact that I didn't.

On the other, it seemed like *do not harm* should be a no-brainer. Where was the confusion in that?

"Emily, I don't just want to do things with you because you let me."

Dropping my towel, I slipped an arm into my robe and gave him an incredulous look.

"Okay, sometimes, yes I do." He crossed to me and took the belt out of my hands to tie it for me. "But I . . . I don't want to do something to you that you don't at least at some level want me to do."

I placed my hands on his chest, assuring him. "And so far you haven't."

His hands stayed at my hips when I wanted him to draw me closer, wanted him to wrap me up in him. "How am I supposed to know when that changes?" he asked, his brow pinched.

I inspected my nails, ragged from horseback riding and the campfire and rough sex. "I don't know, Reeve. I'm sick. I told you."

He pushed away from me. Gently, but pushed away all the same.

My lip quivered. "You *are* mad at me."

He spun back toward me. "Yes! I am."

"What can I do to change that?" I'd do anything. Not just because I was a pleaser, but because if we had any chance at a relationship, this would have to be resolved. "Tell me what to do."

"Stop blaming yourself for your rape. Stop blaming yourself for your friend. Stop calling yourself sick. Stop letting men—"

I cut him off, choosing this point to defend. "I'm not 'letting men' anymore. I'm letting *you*."

He let a beat go by and his expression transformed, easing. With the slightest hesitation he asked, "Because you trust me?"

Hope flickered in his eyes, and I understood the basis of his question. I'd said that trust was equivalent to love. He was asking if I loved him.

I twisted away from him and placed my hands on the dresser for support. "I didn't say that." I wanted to say that. More than anything. But it was complicated, and I was confused.

"Then you don't trust me." He'd come up behind me. I could feel his body heat rolling off of him, tugging at me like gravity pulling at the moon.

He deserved honesty. As much as I could give him.

I met his eyes in the mirror above the drawers. "I'm not sure you've opened up enough for me to know that I can for sure."

His hands settled on my hips and he pressed in closer. "You've seen what I am. How I've been with you—that's how I'll always be. I won't ever hurt you more than you like. I won't ever do any real damage. I won't fuck around on you. I'll allow people to watch you and hear you, but they won't ever get to have you."

"Those could just be words, though."

"If you trusted me, they wouldn't be." He nuzzled his chin against the top of my head. "Is it odd that I want you to so badly?"

My throat ached and my stomach knotted. "Only if it's odd that I want to as well."

"Then what's stopping you? Give me your trust, Emily." His hands circled my waist and he laid kisses on my neck.

I let my head fall, giving him access to my skin. He

could have my body. He could have my pleasure. He could have my desire.

But I couldn't give him my trust. Not yet. Not only because of the lingering questions about Amber but also because I couldn't be sure he wasn't asking just to satisfy some selfish need to be important. Wanting my love when he hadn't given me his. While reciprocity wasn't a requirement of the emotion, I already felt unequal in my relationship to him. This was the only card I had left.

Reeve moved to nip at the shell of my ear. "What do I have to do to earn it from you?"

Steeling myself, I answered him. "Tell me what came between you and the woman you loved."

He stilled.

After a few seconds, he stroked his hands down and back up over the curve of my hips. "What does it matter, Emily? That's another relationship. It isn't relative to you."

My hands balled into fists against the wood of the dresser. "It matters because it's a piece of you. Trust isn't just about sex, you know. It's about opening up. You want my trust and you won't give me yours? It doesn't work that way."

He dropped his hands and I saw his expression tighten in our reflection.

His withdrawal stung. "Hey, you asked," I snipped.

He backed away. Turned away completely. "I told you before, I don't want you to know the worst of me."

I spun around, keeping my hands behind me, still needing to lean on the furniture for strength. "But it's okay that you know the worst of me?"

He perched on the edge of the bed, still strong, but with just the barest hint of defeat. "Your story was the worst people had done to you. Not the worst *you'd* done."

Yet it had still had an impact on him. Still created a trench between us. "And why do you think that's different?

Because you think I might run? In case you haven't noticed, I've never been good at running. Even when I should be."

I took a shaky breath in as I realized what I'd said. Realized I meant it. No matter what I found out about Amber, I wouldn't run.

As if to prove it, I went to him.

He opened his arms to me as I stepped between his legs. "Maybe I'm afraid that you should run from me."

"If I should, would you let me?" God, I was pathetic. I was begging for a sign of his affection as blatantly as he was begging for mine.

"I said I wasn't going to keep anyone again." He placed a kiss at my cleavage. "But honestly, Emily"—he lifted his eyes toward mine—"I'm not sure I'd be able to stop myself if you really tried."

I cupped his face with my hands. "I'm not going to run, Reeve. And I *hope* that doesn't get me hurt in the end. So my trust isn't really even a big deal, is it? It's still win/win for you." Maybe it was manipulative, because I still wanted him to confess his secret. Because I really did want to trust him.

I really did want to love him.

He really wanted me to love him too. He confirmed it again when he pulled my hands from his face, kissed each of the palms, and said, "It is a big deal. To me."

His expression, his posture, his tone—something told me he wasn't trying to bully me into giving him what he wanted anymore. That he was ready to earn it.

Tentatively, I tested him. "How did sex come between you, Reeve?"

"It wasn't sex. Exactly." His jaw ticked.

I barely dared breathe let alone speak, but I asked anyway, "Then what was it exactly?"

"Well." He ran his thumbs over the backs of my hands.

"The thing that bothered her in that area was actually a part of my personality, not just limited to the bedroom. She thought I was, uh, controlling."

I scoffed. "You *are* controlling."

"But you like it."

"Sometimes."

He flinched, so I squeezed his hands reassuringly. "A lot of the time, Reeve. The times I don't aren't a problem for us because I like pleasing you. But, was that not the same with her?" It would fit the Amber that I'd remembered. The Amber who liked men to please her more than the other way around.

"No, that wasn't her style," Reeve confirmed. "She put up with it in the beginning. Then, when it became an issue, I reined it in. I behaved. For her. I kept it out of our sex life, which is where it showed up most of the time anyway."

I pulled away from him and sat on the bed next to him. It was hard to listen to him talk about Amber without being jealous, and while I wanted to prove that his openness was good for us, it bothered me enough to require a little bit of distance.

If he noticed my withdrawal, he didn't show it. He angled himself toward me. "The more I refrained from that in the bedroom, though, the more it came out in other places of my life. It was a constant argument between us. Both of us always trying to figure out how much we were willing to compromise for the other."

"That's what healthy relationships are. You find a balance, or, if you find that you're compromising too much, you call it quits." Not that I knew much about how to have a healthy relationship. Amber had called it quits with me, though, and I found myself wondering if she'd felt like she was compromising too much for me.

"I wanted to marry her." Reeve's statement drew my attention back full force.

"You proposed?" The question came out a bit choked. I hoped he assumed I was surprised rather than hurt. Truthfully, it was a bit of both. A lot of both.

He averted his eyes. "Not exactly proposed."

"Let me guess. You arranged a minister and a dress and set it all up and then told her." My words were bitter with envy, meant to stab at him. I hadn't expected that they were also accurate until I saw the guilt in his eyes. "Are you kidding me? You didn't."

"It was meant to be a surprise. It was romantic."

"You can't surprise a woman with a wedding." Especially not Amber. "Any woman. Even if she likes your dominant side." Well, maybe if she liked his dominant side. I did recognize the romance in it.

He scooted back to lean against the headboard. "I'll remember you feel that way." There was no time for me to properly digest that before he'd moved on. "She felt that way too, it turns out. She refused the marriage. In front of the minister and the guys. It was here that this happened, if you haven't figured that out. And instead of giving me another chance, she told me she was leaving."

I tensed, all of a sudden remembering that this wasn't going to be a pretty story. It wasn't that I'd forgotten, really. He'd warned me it was bad, but it took a lot to shock me, and I'd forgotten that whatever he'd done had made Amber call me. Had scared her enough to use the safe word.

Hugging my legs up to my chest, I urged him on. "And then . . . ?"

"I couldn't lose her. So I didn't let her go."

" 'Didn't let her go'? That's what you meant by you *kept someone*."

He nodded.

I tried to imagine the worst. "Chained up? Caged? Locked in her bedroom?"

"No." He gave me a look that said he was appalled I'd even asked. "I just didn't allow her to leave the ranch. I made it impossible for her to even think about going."

I'd been at the ranch without him, and not only had I had free rein, I couldn't imagine how he could pull off keeping me captive. "How? Was your staff in on it?"

"Only Brent and a man I hired to be her bodyguard. It's easier to control someone than you think, Emily." When I rolled my eyes, he clarified. "Even someone who isn't you."

A chill ran down my spine and I couldn't exactly say what it was that had caused it. He was so direct with his admission here. So up front about his ability to keep someone under his thumb. It was frightening. Especially considering how he wouldn't have to try very hard with me. Especially considering that he knew it.

I sat very still as he explained. "I threatened her. Told her what would happen if she tried to leave. Even when I wasn't here, she was constantly being watched. I had cameras already set up on most of the ranch. I set up more. I bugged all the phones."

My heart started to pound when he mentioned the phones. Had he heard Amber's call to me? But I calmed myself down by remembering she hadn't said anything. She'd made the entire message sound benign. I'd been the only one who recognized that "blue raincoat" was a cry for help.

But my pulse stayed rapid because of something else he'd said. "She had a bodyguard to prevent her from leaving? Like Tabor is for me?"

"No. Tabor is one of my men. He's here to protect you. I swear. You can and always have been able to leave whenever you want." His body language said he was sincere. And before we'd come on the trip, he'd seemed reluctant when he'd offered me access to a vehicle and encouraged me to go into Jackson if I wanted. Was his reluctance rooted in the memory of what he hadn't given Amber?

"The man who watched her wasn't even hired for that in the beginning. He was one of my uncle's guys, and he got her coke now and then. I didn't find out until later that it was a lot more than now and then, but that's not the point."

One of his uncle's guys. Was Michelis his uncle, then? He was older than Reeve by nearly twenty years. Was that how Vilanakis had gotten involved?

"What had you hired him for originally?"

He exhaled before answering. "Let's just say that Amber *did* like to be shared."

"Oh." Then Vilanakis's guy had been hired as a sex toy. Having her lover watch her with another man had always been a favorite of Amber's. And Reeve had been okay with that. With sharing her, but he wasn't okay with sharing me.

Huh.

Christ, Emily, this is not the time to be finding comfort in anything he says. But it wasn't just comfort. It was pride. And I'd needed something to bolster me after he'd said he tried to marry her.

I pressed two fingers to my forehead and forced myself to focus on Amber. "You said you threatened her. What with?"

Reeve surveyed his lap. "By this time, by the end of our relationship, she was an addict with no money. It was easy enough to threaten to cut her off from both." He leveled my stare. "But I considered telling her I'd kill her."

I gasped, my surprise throwing me backward, and I would have fallen off the bed if Reeve hadn't reached out to catch me.

When I was balanced again, he continued to hold on to me. "Emily," he said, but I couldn't meet his eyes. "Emily. Look at me." Always the pleaser, I did. "I told you it was the worst thing. The absolute worst. But I only considered it. I never would have told her that. I never would have done that. I loved her. I was desperate and irrational, and honestly, cutting her off from drugs was a much worse threat to her than death would have been."

I nodded, wishing he'd let go of me so I could think.

"Emily, I'm telling you the truth. I'm not leaving anything out even though it's ugly. I'm the same man I've always been. You know me."

I nodded again but said, "Let me go, Reeve." Because I didn't know him. Not really. And there was still the end of the story to tell.

He held on a second longer. Then he dropped my hands.

I scurried off the bed and paced the room in long, slow figure eights. Almost the way Reeve had paced the ground when I'd told him my story earlier. He was right—it was ugly. It was hard to hear. But men had done much worse to me. And he didn't actually say it to her. If I believed him, he didn't.

It was enough rationalization for me to stay in the room. "What happened next?"

"Nothing," he said. "After six weeks or so, I came to my senses and realized that taking away her freedom was not the way to win her back."

"Yeah, no shit." I crossed my arms over my chest, tracing the same path on the carpet. "So then what?"

"I gave her the keys to my car. Could you stop pacing now?"

I ignored him. "Go on."

"She took it and her bodyguard and left. Emily, come sit with me."

"No." I needed the end. Needed to hear the worst part. The part where he changed his mind and asked his uncle, or his uncle's guy, to end her life. "She took your car and left and then what?"

"And I haven't seen her since." He flew up from the bed and stepped in front of me, halting me by gently placing his hands on my elbows.

I balled my fists and looked up at him sharply. He immediately took a step back, raising his hands in the air in a surrender position.

"I let her go," he said again, "and I haven't seen her since."

We considered each other. I didn't see someone who wanted to hurt me. Well, not someone who wanted to damage me, anyway. I also didn't see someone who would lie about a horrible thing he'd done. If he'd ordered her death, though, would he have told me that?

As if he'd tell me the truth—as if I'd believe it—I asked, "You didn't have her killed afterward?"

"No. I did not. I would never have killed her, Emily. Never."

But Amber was still dead. There had to be a reason. "Weren't you afraid she'd go to the police after?"

He let out a short laugh. "Amber's a drug addict. And not a big rule follower. She's not fond of the police."

"You weren't afraid that she'd go anyway?"

"No, Emily. I wasn't. This is a shitty, shitty thing to say, but even if she ever did, nothing would come of it. You said it yourself—she has a history, and I have money. It's fucked up, I know. But it's how things work."

His expression turned grave. "If you're wanting me to be punished for my crime, let me tell you that I have been. First when she left me. It destroyed me. Though, to be honest, we destroyed each other long before she drove away. When I met her, she was a casual drug user. In the end, she was a high-strung junkie. When I met her, I was a man who liked being in control. In the end, I was an abuser of power."

He took a step toward me. "We were bad for each other,

but it was hell when she left. I'm being punished again now seeing you look at me like that."

My defenses slid ever so slightly.

"What are you thinking, Emily? Please tell me."

I shook my head, at a loss. I wasn't even sure he'd told the whole story. Though, wasn't it possible he was telling the truth? Probable, even? I'd already known it hadn't been Reeve who'd actually killed her. Was there reason to still believe he'd had anything at all to do with her death?

"Emily?"

"I don't know. It's a lot to process." The suspicious part had been that she'd gone with Vilanakis, someone who was connected to Reeve. But if Amber had left Reeve on her own, where would she have gone? To someone else who could take care of her. And if her bodyguard worked for Reeve's uncle, then it made complete sense that she'd go to him.

Reeve took another step toward me, but didn't try to touch me again. "Talk through it with me. We can process it together."

"There's nothing to talk through." Then why would Vilanakis have emailed Reeve about her afterward?

"Emily—"

"Reeve, I just need some time to let it settle. Please."

His jaw set. "Fine. Let it process on your own. Or settle. There's a lot of things I need to process myself, but I'm going to sleep." He flipped off the overhead, leaving the blaze of the fire as the only light in the room.

"You can join me when you're done." His voice was hard. Hurt. "Or not. I'm not going to tell you what you want to do this time." He climbed into the bed, pulled the covers over himself, and turned his back to me.

I stood where I was for at least a full minute before I left his room and headed down the hall for mine.

CHAPTER
28

My room was still in disarray with my suitcase on the bed and my clothes half-packed. It looked like what was going on in my head—chaos, confusion, indecision. My mind was half-set like my bag was half-packed, torn between staying and leaving.

I sat on the chair at the vanity and tried to *process*. And settle. Tried not to cry, too. Which was silly because I'd been the one who had pushed Reeve away. He had every right to get huffy and go to sleep without me.

I wasn't even sure if that was the source of my tearfulness. It was more likely a combination of things. What Reeve had done to Amber was horrible. Thinking about it too hard—thinking of Amber bullied into staying with a man she didn't want to be with—made my stomach ache.

But if I was honest with myself, it really wasn't the worst thing. Not compared to the things I'd put up with from men. Not even compared to some of the things *she'd* put up with from men. There was even a little part of me—a small part, but a part nonetheless—that thought maybe she deserved a little bit of discomfort. Because she could get uppity and pretentious and full of herself and it wasn't hard to picture her driving someone to want to throttle her.

When I looked at her from Reeve's point of view, she seemed almost obnoxious, or at the very least, a bad match. I wasn't thinking of just the things he'd said, but also the things I knew about her and pairing it with the things I'd learned about him. Of course their sexual preferences differed, but also their tastes in other things. Reeve was comfortable in jeans on the back of a horse. Amber barely tolerated animals. Reeve swam for exercise. Amber swam to cool off before lying out again in the sun. Reeve liked to plan and dictate. And so did Amber.

None of that condones imprisonment.

No, it didn't. But if she hadn't been so addicted to drugs and money, she could have left at any time. And Reeve had admitted it was a mistake. Didn't he deserve then to be forgiven? If not by her, then by me? Didn't everyone deserve a chance to change?

He'd said that in reference to me earlier. When I'd said that Amber hadn't believed me about Bridge, he'd defended me. I got why now. Because he understood what it was like to do something horrible and have to live with it. And he hated himself enough for it that he wanted desperately to believe that he could change. That people could change.

I didn't think people could change. Not that much. But I also didn't think Reeve would have gotten to the point that he had if he hadn't been trying so impossibly to be the man that Amber had wanted.

It really was impossible for people like us—people like us—to be the kind of people Amber wanted. Comparing my situation to Reeve's, I could see my life with more perspective, and I was more than a little irritated that she'd tried so hard to change me. Yes, she'd rescued me. But instead of helping me figure out how to protect myself, she'd forced me to hide.

In fact, I wasn't just irritated. I was mad. Mad that she'd wanted me to be someone that I wasn't. Mad that she hadn't believed me when her boyfriend had raped me and ended my pregnancy. Mad that she'd kicked me to the curb. Mad that she'd been hooked on drugs for much of our friendship. Mad that she'd dragged me into her petty domestic dispute with Reeve. Mad that she'd tried to make him into a princess-pleaser. Mad that she'd gone and died.

Mad, now, that she was coming between me and a man who might actually be good for me. A man I might actually be able to love.

I was so mad, in fact, that I didn't feel guilty about it like I would have expected to.

But even through my rage, I could see it for what it was and what it wasn't. It wasn't the kind of anger that made me love her any less. It was the kind of anger that made me wish more than ever that she were still around to work things out. The kind of anger that pinched with regret. The kind of anger that made it just a little easier to let go of some of the blame I'd been carrying around.

Wouldn't Reeve be happy to hear that?

God, Reeve . . .

He was a much more complicated puzzle piece to deal with. Because he was alive, and things between us could still alter and change. He swore that he wouldn't have tried to have Amber killed. He swore it ended at keeping her captive and then letting her go. Either I believed him, or I didn't. He'd answered the questions that had sent me looking for her without knowing I was even asking them. If there was any other version of the story, she was the only one who knew it. But she was gone and couldn't tell it to me.

Except, I still had Reeve's keys. And he was asleep. And the surveillance room couldn't see what happened in his office. This was my chance to sneak in and watch his recordings from the previous summer.

I jumped up and went to the closet where I'd dumped my clothes after the stables. I rummaged through the bundle until I found the key ring. Cloaking them in my hand, I slipped out of my room, and headed for answers.

I made it down four stairs then stopped short.

If you need to see what's on those recordings to believe him, then you shouldn't stay with him anyway.

It was that voice in my head, the one that sounded a lot like Amber, the one I half-believed *was* Amber. And halfbelieved was me going crazy.

Crazy or not, the voice had a point. It was one thing when I wanted to see the surveillance data so that I could find out what had driven Amber to call me. But in the course of the evening, my motives had changed. Now I'd been told what had happened. Watching the recordings wouldn't give me any more insight into her death. Possibly it could verify Reeve's versions of events, but from the way he'd told it, I probably wouldn't even be able to tell she was being held against her wishes. The only way they would clear things up for me at this point was if they showed something terrible happening to her that Reeve hadn't told me about. And wasn't that a long shot?

So it came down to the same thing it had before—either I believed him, or I didn't. If I didn't, if I had to watch to be put at ease, then I didn't belong with him any more than Amber did.

When I thought about it in those terms my choice was simple. I didn't even have to decide that I trusted him. I just had to know that I belonged to him. And I did know that.

Without any further thought, I headed back upstairs and

into Reeve's room. In the closet, I found the jacket he'd worn on our ride. I tucked the keys in the pocket and went out to join him in bed.

He was asleep already, but I wanted to wake him up. I needed to tell him—

Actually, I wasn't sure what I needed to tell him. I'd just made a big decision, though, and I needed to let him know I'd chosen him. Chosen *us*. Eventually I'd have to come clean about everything. Come clean about how I'd come into his life and what I'd thought he'd done and it would be hard and maybe he wouldn't forgive me. But whether he did or didn't, I'd meant it when I said I wouldn't run.

Maybe he meant it when he said he wanted to keep me.

I slipped out of my robe and climbed in under the covers next to him. My trust would come later, but I did have something I could give him now. He shifted, turning toward me, as if even in his sleep he sensed me.

I cupped my hand on his cheek. "Reeve."

He opened his eyes. Looked straight into mine.

"I don't want to take things from you anymore," I said. "I don't want value for value. I don't want to be with you because you give me cars or take me on trips. I just want you. I just want to belong to you."

It only took him a second to react. His mouth seized mine, his hands threaded in my hair, and he kissed the hell out of me. Kissed me hard and soft and everything in between. He was still kissing me when I climbed on top of him. I broke away to move down his body, down to where his crown peeked out over the waistband of his boxer briefs. I pulled them down just far enough to free his cock. He was throbbing steel. Thick and bulging.

My cunt was wet and wanting, but so was my mouth. I fisted him with one hand and licked up his shaft. Then I swirled my tongue across the tip, and I swear he got harder. When I parted my lips and sucked him inside, he moaned, and damn, that turned me on. Turned me on that I could please him. Made my chest swell that he kept his hands tucked under the pillow and let me play with him the way I wanted instead of taking over as director.

It wasn't always what I wanted with him, but he seemed to understand this was conversation. This was me telling him things I couldn't begin to say.

I licked him and sucked him until his breathing started to become ragged. When it seemed he was about to come, I straddled him and lined my entrance with his cock. With a groan, I slid down onto him, sheathing him with my pussy. He fit so well inside me, fit just right. Had I noticed that before? I wasn't sure. It felt like a new discovery and yet it felt like something I'd always known. Felt like home. I would have been happy just sitting with him inside me, just enjoying the tightness of my cunt as he stretched me and pulsed against my walls.

But Reeve liked it hard and fast. So I worked my hips, grinding on him, riding him like he'd ridden me so many times before. It didn't take long before the tightening began deep inside and my nerves began to sing.

"Does it feel good?" I asked, my voice thin and breathy.

"You do. You feel good." He sat up suddenly and yanked a handful of my hair, grinning at my yelp. He bit my lower lip then said, "It's cute, too, that you think your seduction tactics alone will give either of us what we need."

"I don't know. It seems my seduction tactics got us here, didn't they?"

"Yes. I suppose they did." The look in his eyes told me he knew that *here* meant more than just where we were at that moment, me on top of him, his cock between my thighs.

He kissed me, placing his hand between us to massage my clit. Making me dizzy from two angles at once. It wasn't even a minute before I was coming apart in his arms, milking his cock, tumbling with my orgasm. When it finished, I collapsed onto his shoulder.

Reeve's chest shook as he chuckled. "Oh, no, you don't. No passing out on me. You had your fun. Now it's time for mine."

He pulled out of me and flipped us around with ease, pushing me to my stomach. I turned my face toward the fire that was now barely smoldering. Reeve placed a hand on my lower back, then, from the shift of weight on the bed, it felt like he was reaching for something behind us.

Before I heard the drawer open and close, before I heard the snap of the bottle lid, I knew. I knew without a doubt. The familiar conflicting feelings of excitement and terror gripped me. My throat tightened like my body was preparing to cry, but also I wanted to laugh. This man—*this fucking asshole*—everything always had to be on his terms. No matter what the circumstances. Even when it looked like he was giving me the director's chair, it would always be temporary. It would always be him who called the shots.

It was just the way I liked him. The way we both needed him.

But it didn't mean I didn't also want to kick him in the nuts a little.

His finger entered my tight rim first. It was cold with lube, which he'd applied liberally and was now spreading over the walls of my asshole. I was already moaning, my heart already pounding like a stampede inside my chest. It felt so good, and I wanted more, yet was unsure at the same time.

It didn't really matter what I wanted anyway, because Reeve would tell me like he told me everything.

Damn him for deciding I wanted this.

But then, he surprised me. He removed his finger then stretched his body lengthwise over mine. His mouth at my ear, he said, "Tell me to stop, Emily."

I cursed silently. So much for him deciding.

"Tell me to stop," he said again, "or you're choosing this."

Seriously, he was brilliant. I'd told him that he couldn't trap me like this, and yet here he had trapped me in all sorts of ways. He was forcing me to tell him yes or no. Whichever answer I gave him, I would either be asking him to stop or asking him to fuck me in the ass. He was forcing me to set this limit. He was forcing me to either move on from Bridge or not.

"Tell me to stop," he repeated.

The trickiest part of it all was that even while he was telling me what to say, I knew what he really wanted me to choose. And while that would normally be what I automatically chose—to let him do this, to not stop him—our earlier conversation had put a different frame on anything I *chose* for him to do versus something I *let* him do. If I chose this, then it meant I trusted him. Then it meant I loved him.

Fucking trapped.

He was waiting for me to respond.

Well, I didn't have to answer. "I'm not saying anything."

"Then you're choosing this." He crawled back down my body. I heard the bottle open and shut again. Then it was his cock pressing at my rim, his crown alone feeling impossibly big against my hole. "You're choosing this, Em. If you don't stop me, this is your choice."

It had been years, but I knew the drill. I closed my eyes and took a deep breath in and out. Concentrated on relaxing. Readied myself to push out as he entered me.

And as I prepared, I asked myself what I really wanted.

If it weren't a trap, if I didn't know what would make Reeve happy—what would I choose?

He pressed into me, slower than when he usually drove inside my pussy, but by no means gently. His crown hit the point of resistance, and, without pausing to let me adjust, he pushed past it.

I gasped from the pain, tears leaking down my cheeks.

"It hurts, doesn't it?" Reeve taunted me. "I know it hurts. Tell me to stop."

He thrust in farther. Pain seared through me, waking every nerve in my body. It hurt—so much—but it was nothing like the nightmare that Bridge had put me through. This hurt, but it hurt good. It hurt, and I knew what I'd choose.

It hurt, and I would still choose this.

"Tell me—"

"Don't stop!" I cried.

As soon as I said it, as soon as I chose, he was different. He stilled, letting me get used to him as he lay over me.

"I won't stop, Blue Eyes," he said, stroking my cheek. "I'm not going to stop. And I'm not going to be considerate because that's what I want, and I know that pleasing me makes you happy. But I'm also going to make sure you find pleasure in it too."

More tears spilled, less from pain now and more from emotion. He scooted back to his knees and urged me up to all fours. By the time he had me in the position he wanted, I'd adjusted to him. Which was good, because, as he'd said, he wasn't considerate. He dug his fingers into my hips and pulled back slowly, pulled back like the car of a roller coaster trekking to the summit. And then he was over the crest, plunging back in with speed, his hips thrusting with wild abandon.

I screamed through gritted teeth, balling my hands in

the sheets below me as the pain tore through my ass, lighting the nerves on the opposite wall. It was agony, but as it stretched and yawned, it reshaped, transforming into overwhelming ecstasy. It grew like a ball of fire in my lower regions, the source no longer identifiable. It was almost impossible to tell what parts of me were even being touched. Because everything felt touched, every part of my sex organs shouting with the sensation of having been rubbed.

Then he reached around to press a finger against my clit, and I exploded, bucking underneath him as every single neuron in my body shot off like dynamite. It was too much. Too much, everywhere, all at once. Rainbow-colored stars flashed across my vision, goose bumps rippled over every inch of my skin, and cum poured from me like water from a fountain.

Reeve said words as he chased his own orgasm, dirty words, words of praise, curse words, words I didn't understand or remember. I was still coming, or coming again, I wasn't sure, when he stilled, grinding hard against my backside, still tender from being whipped in the barn.

He pulled out of me, and I collapsed on the bed, completely spent. Completely transformed.

Reeve fell on his back next to me. His eyes danced as he let out a content sight. "Next time we do this, you'll be on top so I can finger fuck you at the same time."

If I weren't so exhausted, I would have laughed. Already planning for next time, was he? So typical.

He exhaled once more then turned on his side to face me. He drew me to him, tilting my chin up to study my face. "How are you?"

I answered truthfully, "Perfect."

"Yes," he smiled. "You are perfect." He kissed my forehead then my eyes. Then my nose. Then his mouth found mine. My lips molded to his as if they'd been made to fit each other. The way every part of my body was made to fit his. He was perfect like that, too. Perfect for me. And I told him that as perfectly as I could in the form of the most perfect kiss.

I'd just begun to doze, my cheek pressed to Reeve's shoulder, when something occurred to me.

I lifted my head and rested my chin on the back of my hand, which was on his arm, so I could look at him better. His opposite arm was draped over his eyes so I couldn't see if he was already sleeping, but I said anyway, "You didn't tell me who the other woman was you loved, the second one."

"Mm," he said, then was silent. His breathing was steady underneath me, and after a few seconds, I laid my head back down, deciding he was too out of it to talk now.

I'd ask him later, I decided. Or not at all. If it was important, he'd tell me. I let my lids close.

But then he said, "The problem with her is she's the first one's best friend."

My eyes flew open. "What?"

The phone by the bed started ringing, sounding through the dark room with an unusual tone. The kind of tone that signaled the call was from someone specific. The front gate, maybe. Or Brent. In the middle of the night, it had to be one of the ranchers.

But even with the blaring of the phone, all I could hear was the siren in my head shrieking its own alarm.

"Wait," I said, as he reached for the phone. "What did you just say?"

He seemed to consider my question for a fraction of a second. Then he picked up the phone. "This better be important."

The distinct voice of a man buzzed through the line, but I couldn't make out anything of what he was saying.

Whatever it was, it alarmed Reeve. He bolted up to a sitting position. "When?" A slight pause. "How bad?"

He jumped out of bed and cradled the phone on his shoulder while he put the jeans on he'd worn earlier. "Yes. Let him in. And get Jeb." He tossed the phone on the bed and slipped a sweatshirt over his head.

He was pulling on a boot now, obviously on his way out.

I sat up. "Reeve, wait." He glanced at me but didn't say anything, putting on his other boot. "Where are you going?"

"Stay here," he commanded then rushed from the room, shutting the door behind him.

I fell back onto the bed with a groan. He'd mentioned Jeb, the ranch vet. Likely an animal was sick or one of the pregnant cows was having trouble with her birth. Reeve had mentioned it was calving season when we were on our horse ride, saying it was the most stressful time of the year because of all the complications that could occur.

It was just my luck that one would occur right when I was in the middle of one of my own.

The panic that had begun gathering from Reeve's declaration was swirling inside me, waiting to be calmed or stirred up further. Calmed was most appropriate. Surely I hadn't heard him right. Maybe I'd been dreaming.

But I'd been awake when he'd said it. And I didn't think I'd heard him wrong.

Which still didn't mean he'd been talking about me. It was possible Amber had found a new best friend. In fact, it was likely, wasn't it? It had been six years. More than enough time for her to have bonded with someone new.

Except what were the chances that she'd had another friend that had hooked up with Reeve?

So if he did mean me, if he was in love with me . . .

Well, first of all, I was flabbergasted. And overwhelmed. And overjoyed too. I hadn't even known how much I'd hoped that he felt that way until there was a possibility that he did.

And I couldn't think about that because if it *was* me he was talking about—then he knew about Amber and me and probably knew why I'd sought to get close to him in the first place and if he was still declaring that he loved me, did that mean he didn't care?

Dammit. I had to talk to him now.

I flung the covers off of me and sat on the edge of the bed, thinking. I could go to my room, get dressed, and try to find him in the stables. One of the security guards would be awake and could tell me how to get there in the dark.

Though, now that I thought about it, if there was a ranch emergency that involved the vet, wouldn't he have been called before Reeve? And if I paid attention, I was pretty sure I could hear voices downstairs. An injured animal wouldn't have been brought to the main house.

The panic in my chest grew to a rattle. Something was wrong.

Ignoring Reeve's command to stay in the bedroom, I put on my robe and slipped quietly downstairs.

The voices were coming from the front of the house. Staying in the shadows, I followed them to the foyer. There were several people to my right in the living room, but my eyes caught the familiar figure standing just inside the door.

The panic washed through me now in torrents. It was Joe, his expression somber, his brow knit in worry.

Joe had come looking for me. He'd said he would.

Fuck.

I should have gotten that burner phone from him so I could get a message to him. When I'd disappeared without a trace, he'd probably assumed I'd gotten into the same trouble as Amber.

I probably should have been flattered, but I was too concerned with how I was going to explain him to Reeve.

Joe must have caught sight of me in his peripheral vision because he turned toward me and made eye contact. He didn't seem relieved to see me, however. Now, in fact, he looked even more concerned. He frowned then looked back toward the living room.

My eyes followed his to the others now. Reeve was there and Brent and Jeb and three of the security men. Reeve was crouched down on the floor, the others huddled around him as they spoke in concerned voices over something. Over *someone*. A soft keening underscored their conversation, like the sound of a wounded animal.

I took another cautious step into the room so I could see better and stopped cold in my tracks. There, in Reeve's arms, was the injured creature. No, human. Her blond hair was matted and her face bruised, the V of her tattoo exposed on her shoulder, her sobs quiet, but clear now that I recognized what they were.

And then I was sobbing along, my breathing in tempo with the shuddering of her body, my fists clenching and unclenching as she gripped onto Reeve's shirt. There were no words for the overwhelming elation that swelled through my body. No words for the jolting dread as my entire world collapsed under me in the resurrection of the woman he and I both loved and hated. Amber.

PROLOGUE

Amber took her sweet time saying goodbye to Rob that Sunday afternoon after my seventeenth birthday. She'd kissed and cooed over him at the door of his convertible while I stood at the curb, knee bouncing, worried we'd miss our bus if we didn't run for it soon. Worried that my mother would find out that we spent my birthday shacked up with Amber's rich "uncle." Mom's wrath would have been tolerable, but the fear that she might keep me from spending time with Amber made me fiercely anxious. That week-end was the first time I'd explored my sexuality. The first time I'd felt sensual. The first time I'd experienced real desire. Now my life had possibilities; I didn't want to go back to before.

"Amber." I'd meant to nudge her gently, but I couldn't mask my anxiety. Her name was both a prayer and a curse.

She'd twisted her head sharply in my direction, the arch of her eyebrow letting me know she hadn't appreciated being rushed. She'd worn that expression only a few seconds before her features had relaxed and her lips slid into a playful grin.

"Emily," she'd called to me, sugar dripping from her voice. "Don't you think Rob deserves a decent kiss for all he's done for us?"

"Of course he does." I'd matched her sweetness, though I'd been pretty sure that most of what had been "done" had been done for Rob, not that I'd objected. It had been fun and he'd bought us pretty things and given us pretty drugs and that had been well worth the blowjobs and the aching thigh muscles. "Just, the bus . . ."

She either hadn't heard me or hadn't been as concerned about the time because she beckoned me closer with a nod. "Come say goodbye to him, Em. Come kiss him."

At her request my pulse had begun to race, my cheeks flushed, and heat barreled between my thighs, and not simply because I'd wanted one last kiss. My concern about the bus had faded into the distance, so I'd taken the three steps over to them, then tilted my chin up and met his mouth with mine, letting my tongue dot against the tip of his before sliding it along the curve of his upper lip.

"Jesus, Em. The bus is about to leave. We have to run." Amber's inflection had been teasing, proving she'd been aware of my distress all along. Grabbing my hand, she'd tugged me away from our "Uncle." She'd waved to him once more before we broke into a run, making our ride just as the doors had been about to close.

We'd taken a seat in the back, and, once we'd caught our breath, lost it again in a fit of giggles. "He's great, isn't he?" she'd asked after we'd settled down, but before I could respond, she'd bounded on. "I knew you'd like him. You didn't mind when I got bossy back there, did you? When I told you to kiss Rob goodbye?"

"Not at all. I liked kissing him." It had felt like a lie, or at least, not the whole truth. I had liked everything we'd done that weekend together, the three of us. Every new experience. But half the reason I'd enjoyed that last kiss so much hadn't been because of what it was—the feel of lips on lips, the twining of the wet, thick muscles of tongues—but because Amber had told me to do it . . . ordered me out of equal parts playfulness and love.

It wasn't the first time I had recognized my desire to submit. When we'd met several months before, Amber had uncovered my longing to yield. To please. To surrender.

But this time her command had also awoken my sexual tastes. She had summoned a creature to life inside me—a deeply-seated beast with an appetite for carnality and a desperate need to be stroked as she knelt at the foot of the one who would feed her.

It was then I caught the first glimpse of the person I would become, and the role Amber would play in my life as the first master I wanted to please.

CHAPTER

1

My feet moved automatically, pulled by a force that couldn't be simplified with a label of compassion or curiosity or obligation. I crouched in front of Reeve and took Amber's limp wrist into my hands. My body was present, going through the motions of a concerned friend, but my head was in a fog. The smell of sex still lingered in my nose, the orgasms Reeve had given me still rang through me, low and wide, like the faintest waves sounding off a tuning fork.

Then there had been Reeve's declaration. He'd hinted both that he loved me and that he knew who I was, knew that I'd been Amber's friend. That had sent me into shock long before I'd been confronted with her ghost in the flesh.

She was supposed to be dead.

I was confused. I was relieved. I was more than a little scared.

Around me there was a buzz of voices, discussing Amber, but nothing they said made sense. All I heard was a steady drone and her whimpers softer than when I'd first seen her and barely audible. She didn't seem to be conscious, whatever pain she carried so great that it slipped out in her sleep.

Reeve tried to get her eyes to open, slapping gently at her face with the same hand that had caressed me earlier in the evening, had been inside my mouth and cunt. The concern etched on his face and the tight emotion in his tone as he coaxed her were mirrors of the way he'd spoken to me in our most intimate moments.

"Emily. It's you," Amber whispered.

My focus snapped to her. I was aware now—of her, of her injured state, of the frenzy occurring on her behalf. Aware that Reeve now knew conclusively that *his* Amber was also *my* Amber.

"Yes, it's me." I stroked the length of her arm, forcing my gaze not to zoom in on her black eyes, her bruised nose, the sallow color of her skin. She'd been beaten badly. Her body was stick thin, her wrist fragile under my hands. I wrapped my fingers around it and registered a pulse, stronger than I'd expected from the near skeletal figure before me. This couldn't be the confident, vibrant woman that I'd known, and yet it couldn't be anyone else. My shoulders threatened to sag with guilt and grief and my throat felt coarse like I'd swallowed sand.

But she needed strength, and I was a good actress. So I held my head high and made my voice a balm. "I'm here."

Her lip was too fat and bloodied to smile, but the corners of her mouth turned up slightly. "It *is* you." Her words were labored, her breath short. "Joe said you'd sent him. To save me. I—"

I glanced back at Joe as she broke into a coughing fit that tried to curl her torso in, but she couldn't manage to lift her head, the exertion too much for her.

"Save your energy. We're going to get you to a bed, Angel." Reeve nodded at his men.

Angel. Was that what he called her or simply an endearment he was using now? Either way it felt private. Like I'd walked into the middle of another couple's love scene.

"I need a few things from my office," Jeb said to one of the security guards. "An IV kit, my bag. There are pain killers in the safe." He continued to issue orders, and I stood to get out of the way as Reeve gathered Amber in his arms. I turned to Brent, the ranch manager. "Shouldn't we call a doctor?" I was sure Jeb was good at what he did, but he was a veterinarian.

Brent shook his head. "Jeb's got all the training we need and we don't want to raise any unwanted attention."

I started to protest, but Amber called out, drawing my attention back to her.

Reeve was standing now, Amber in his arms, headed for the stairs, but he paused and spun so that she could see me easily.

"I'll be right there, Amber," I promised. "I'm just going to talk to Joe for one minute while they're making you comfortable."

She nodded, her lids closing as though they were too heavy to keep open.

I turned to the man who held her. Who moments ago was *my* man—now I wasn't so sure. His expression was hard and unreadable. But when his gaze caught mine, the room tilted. His eyes held a dark brew of emotion, so murky and filled that I couldn't determine *what* he was feeling, only that he *was* feeling. And that he wanted to share it with me. Even though it was obvious now just how much I hadn't shared with him.

My chest tightened, and I looked away breaking the intense connection. It was all too much. I pivoted toward Joe, aware of Reeve behind me as he held his position a second longer before taking Amber upstairs.

I forced my full attention on Joe. I'd seen him as I'd come into the room, before I'd noticed the battered girl in

Reeve's arms, but I hadn't gotten a chance to study him. Now I scanned him for similar injuries, for any sign that his rescue had caused him harm. When I saw nothing, I asked, "Are you okay?"

"Besides being exhausted, yeah. I'm fine."

I let out a shaky breath of relief. "I told you she was alive." Joe chuckled. "You did."

In the beginning, I did, I'd insisted on it until he'd shown me the autopsy report of a Jane Doe that had matched Amber's description, a woman who bore the same V tattoo that Amber had on her shoulder. I'd found the same report in an e-mail to Reeve when I'd been snooping on his computer, which had further ended any hope that she was still alive.

"How did this—?" I wasn't sure how to ask the question. "How is she not dead?"

He ran a hand through his hair. "I don't know. I think we were deliberately thrown off ." His expression told me exactly who he'd thought had done the throwing—Reeve Sallis. Joe had never trusted him, and with good reason. Reeve's reputation was shady at best. Five years before, his girlfriend, Missy, had mysteriously died while with him on his island in the Pacific. He'd been cleared from any blame in the crime, but my friend Chris Blakely, who had been close to Missy, had painted her relationship with Reeve as volatile. Chris was convinced that Reeve had killed her and had even gone so far as to hint as much on a recent talk show.

I wasn't sure which side of the fence I sat on. Reeve had assured me he'd had nothing to do with her death, and while I didn't know if I believed him, I'd decided the answer didn't matter. Now that Amber had returned, I had less reason to doubt him.

Joe, it seemed, was still skeptical. After months of investigating, he'd only found more incriminating evidence.

Evidence that tied Reeve to the Greek mafia and a sex slave ring that Joe had been certain Amber had wandered into.

I thought of her bruises and shuddered. Joe was probably right.

"What happened?" I asked him, not wanting to know but needing to all the same. "Where did you find her?"

"With Vilanakis."

Michelis Vilanakis, the mob boss who I had pinned as a low life villain. It was the name I'd expected. Amber was last seen with him. Reeve was also connected to him—I'd seen pictures of the two at various events, as well as a few e-mails to Reeve from him.

"You just swooped in and rescued her from his house in Chicago? Or—" I left the question open-ended, not able to imagine what the scenario had been.

"I got lucky actually." He shook his head, demonstrating his incredulity. "Really lucky. I'd been tailing Michelis for three days before I saw her. I didn't even realize who she was at first. But while I was in my car watching, she ran out of his house, upset about something. He followed after her, Emily. He grabbed her by the hair and yanked her back so hard I swore he was going to break her neck. Then he went off on her. Fucking pounded her face in while she struggled and cried. I don't know how her screams didn't draw a crowd."

I felt sick. "Maybe his neighbors are scared shitless of him. They ignore what goes on." Where I grew up everyone turned a blind eye. No one mentioned the drug dealer that lived next door. No one bothered looking in on me when my mother was passed out drunk in the front yard. No one intervened when Amber and I would arrive home with newly purchased designer clothes and unexplainable cash in our pockets.

"Probably so. He left her like that in his driveway. Whether he was leaving her for dead or planned to come back and get her later, I don't know. I grabbed her and took off."

"Why didn't you go to a hospital? Or the police?" I understood why Reeve's men would be wary, but Joe had more faith in the legal system.

"She refused to go anywhere but here. She was insistent and scared. She'd been to the doctor before, remember? With other bruises, and somehow she ended up back with her abuser. I didn't know who to trust. So I brought her here."

He tilted his head and studied me. "Didn't figure I'd see you here when I arrived."

"Yeah, well." I'd hired Joe to investigate Amber's disappearance, but I hadn't always been forthcoming with him about my own snooping. At the moment, I didn't want to think about the circumstances of my presence at Reeve's Wyoming ranch let alone talk about it. "How did you know to look for her there? How did you realize she was still alive?"

"I didn't. She's not why I was following him." I wrinkled my forehead. "Then why—?"

He gave me an incredulous glance, one that said he couldn't believe I had to ask. But I did have to. I needed him to say it.

And he did. "I was looking for you."

There was affection in the way he held my gaze, his expression so much easier to read than Reeve's had been, but equally hard for me to bear, for such different reasons.

I lowered my eyes to the floor. "Thank you, Joe. For finding her. For bringing her here." I couldn't manage to thank him for what he'd done for me. He'd gone willingly into danger, after I'd eluded him and been uncooperative. When I'd put myself in the damn situation after his countless warnings. I didn't deserve his concern. I couldn't condone it with gratitude.

He took a step toward me. "Emily, there's something else you should know." He waited until I looked up before he went on. "The tattoos. I found out what they mean."

"The V tattoos?" Besides Amber and the Jane Doe from the autopsy, I'd also seen one on an employee of Reeve's in Los Angeles. "Doesn't it just stand for Vilanakis? I figured it was some show of mob support. Like a gang tattoo."

"It does stand for Vilanakis. But the tattoos aren't inked voluntarily. They're like a brand. Anyone wearing the mark belongs to Michelis." In case I didn't get the picture, he clarified. "As in indentured servant."

"That's not even legal." Which was a ridiculous thing to say since I knew the mob didn't care much about the law. My throat grew thick. "What does that mean anyway? She got away. She's safe now. Right?"

"My impression is that Michelis brands people when their debt to him is too great to pay back in a lifetime. Which, if that's true, if Amber owes him that big, then he's—" He broke off at the sound of footsteps.

I wanted to know more, but when I turned I found Reeve approaching. I forgot about branding and servitude, and got swept up in the confusing mix of emotions that rose at the sight of him. There was so much unsettled between us—and that was without anyone else involved. Amber and Joe only complicated things that much more.

"She's asking for you, Emily," Reeve said, his eyes pinned on Joe. "She's in the suite next to yours." It was a dismissal that left little room for refute.

Besides, I really did want to be with Amber, so I nodded and headed upstairs, despite knowing that Joe could very well reveal all my secrets. Maybe it was time for those secrets to come out anyway.

If she really had been asking for me, she wasn't by the time I arrived upstairs. Now the only thing on her mind was getting something for the pain. Her shirt was off, and there were several bruises down her chest and arms, some yellowed and fading, others were much newer. Several near-black angry splotches lined one side of her torso. Jeb was pressing on them when I walked in, and though his touch seemed tender, the examination had her in tears.

I ran to hold her hand and stroke her hair, but she was in such agony, I wasn't sure how much my presence helped. Jeb finished tracing the lines of her ribs before looking up at me. "Emily, would you mind going down to the kitchen and making some ice packs? If there's some frozen peas or something, that would work just as well."

"Sure. Broken?" I'd had broken ribs before. I knew that pain. "Just fractured, I think. But her breathing's not great. I'd like to get her on some oxygen so that she doesn't develop pneumonia." "We have some for emergencies in the main office," Brent piped in. "I'll call down and have it brought up. And, Emily, there's ice compresses in the small freezer in the pantry."

I bent to kiss Amber's forehead. "Hang in there. We'll get you feeling better soon." She squeezed my hand so I knew she'd heard me, although I'm sure it was hard to believe in her current state of discomfort.

The men Jeb had sent for supplies were coming in as I left the room and by the time I returned with ice packs, Amber had been hooked up to an IV and fluid was dripping down the line into the vein at her wrist. Her eyes were closed. She was either asleep or almost there so I didn't disturb her. Instead I handed Jeb the compresses, then sat on the loveseat near the bed and watched, helpless.

I was actually grateful for that helplessness. Of the myriad complex emotions that were weighing on me at the moment, helplessness was the easiest to carry. It was the one I knew.

Brent returned with the oxygen tank as well as a heart rate monitor. Reeve came along with him, taking a perch on the opposite arm. Together we watched as Jeb and Brent hooked Amber up to the machines. We didn't speak or look at each other. Tension buzzed between us like a fly caught in a closed room. I was desperate to know what he was thinking and feeling. Was he as focused on her as he appeared to be? Or was his mind as caught up in us as mine was?

The longer I sat without his acknowledgment, the more my anxiety grew.

It was just after three when Jeb gestured for us to follow him out to the hallway for a powwow.

"Well?" Reeve asked, impatience in his voice.

Although he'd shut the door behind him, Jeb kept his voice low. "She's bruised up mostly. Her ribs are tender, but they seem to be just fractures. Her wrist is sprained and she has a concussion, all of which can be healed with time."

Reeve rubbed at the back of his neck, nodding, taking it in.

"When she wakes up," Brent said, "she might be wanting some kind of upper, if you know what I mean. She was pretty fond of the white stuff when she was here last."

Reeve shook his head. "Joe—the guy who brought her here—said he thinks she's not into that right now. He's pretty sure she's moved onto opiates."

So that's what he'd talked to Joe about. He was looking out for Amber, and I was grateful. And I was also selfish because it was disappointing to realize he hadn't been asking about me.

Jeb considered, raising a brow. "Heroin?"

Reeve shook his head again. "Codeine. Oxy maybe. She got beat up pretty bad, but he said she's been begging for a pill every two hours."

"Do you know if he gave her anything?" Jeb asked.

"Some Vicodin. He said he gave it as directed to help with her pain. The last was about four hours ago."

Jeb seemed to do a mental calculation. Satisfied with his result, he said, "I just put some morphine in her IV as well as something to help her sleep. We'll have to watch the clock carefully and only give her what she needs rather than what she asks for. In the morning I'll see if I can get my hands on some methadone."

Brent clapped a hand on Reeve's back. "I'm going to go check on security, make sure we're covered in case—"

Reeve cut him off . "He won't come here looking for her." "With all the other activity lately, are you sure?"

Reeve hesitated, then said again, "He won't come here. But extra security is a good idea."

A chill ran through me as I thought about what Joe had said about Amber's tattoo. But I trusted Reeve's perception of danger. If he said he didn't think Vilanakis would come around, I believed him. The additional security was likely just a measure of precaution.

As soon as Brent left, Reeve addressed Jeb again. "What do we need to do for her tonight?"

I nodded, wishing I'd asked first.

"There's nothing you can do at this point." Jeb looked at his watch. "She's probably going to be out for a while. I'd take this opportunity to get some sleep. I'll stay with her until the morning in case she wakes up."

"I could take the first shift." Again Reeve spoke before I could. His offer rubbed me in places that I didn't know were raw. I told myself it was simply because I wanted to be the one by her side.

Well, if he was going to stay, so was I.

But then Jeb said, "I'd rather it be me. I want to be there in case she has any strange reaction to the medicines or in case she takes a turn."

Reeve hesitated before conceding. "Come and find me
if there's any change."

"Will do, boss."

"Then I'll see you in a few hours." Without even a
glance at me, he turned on his heels and headed for his
bedroom.

Jeb gave me a tight smile then opened the door to
Amber's room, leaving me in the hallway, alone.